About the author

During his 30 years service with the Sussex Police Jonathan S. Harvey spent some 25 years as a detective; both the investigatve and intelligence disciplines when much of his work involved operations and covert techniques. His first novel *His Life was a Lie*, has received good reviews from readers in the UK, Spain and America. *His Life was Revenge* is Jonathan's second novel, all characters and the storyline are completley seperate from *His Life was a Lie*.

His Life Was Revenge

First published in Great Britain in 2016 by
The Book Guild Ltd
9 Priory Business Park
Wistow Road, Kibworth
Leicestershire, LE8 0RX
Freephone: 0800 999 2982
www.bookguild.co.uk
Email: info@bookguild.co.uk
Twitter: @bookguild

Typeset in Sabon

Printed and bound in Great Britain by
CPI Group (UK) Ltd, Croydon, CR0 4YY

ISBN 978 1 9108781 4 9

British Library Cataloguing in Publication Data.
A catalogue record for this book is available from the British Library.

His Life Was Revenge

Jonathan S. Harvey

Book Guild Publishing

6476494.

In writing these stories, I want to put on record huge thanks to my wife and family for their support and patience. Without which I think at times I may have allowed 'writers block' to become permanent rather than temporary! I would also like to place on record that although in my writing of fiction stories, I include a corrupt police officer character, I did not during my service ever come across such an individual while I could name hundreds of officers who gave much more effort and dedication to their work than they were ever paid or rewarded for.

1

Raymond Black shuffled on his old and worn slippers from the lounge into the kitchen, still tying the cord to his dressing gown. His attention was drawn towards the window above the kitchen sink where water cascaded down from the broken guttering above and fell on to the windowsill outside. He didn't care, though he noticed the steady drum noise it made as he filled the kettle to make his cup of tea. He didn't care either that it was raining for the fourth consecutive morning – he wouldn't be going outside the bungalow except to fill the old metal coal scuttle around lunchtime, in four hours' time. Once he had switched the kettle on, he walked slowly back to the lounge, turned on the television set and drew back the curtains. He had time to visit the toilet before returning to the kitchen, washing the mug that he had used yesterday and putting a teabag in it before the kettle boiled. He poured the water and fetched the milk from the fridge that still had a broken bulb in it. He noticed it but he didn't care, just as he didn't care about most things.

Today was Tuesday when, as every Tuesday, his fifty-three-year-old daughter would visit with some prepared meals that she would buy during her lunch break, and which he would force himself to eat over the next seven days. She would also bring other provisions that were necessary, items of food such as a loaf of bread and tins of ready-made soup, and monthly the large shop that would include a box of teabags, toilet rolls and the like. She would arrive precisely seventy-three minutes after she finished work as an assistant in a shop in the departures lounge at Gatwick Airport, eleven miles to the north of Raymond's bungalow. As it

1

was Tuesday, he would make the effort – today he would shave and run a brush through his thinning hair and today he wouldn't have a slug of whisky until after his daughter had left.

This was a routine that she had started with the best of intentions nearly four years ago but which was now more of a chore both for her and him. Initially she had been greeted warmly and he had looked forward to her visits, her breezing in with news of friends and family, an injection of energy as she quickly moved from room to room tidying and putting things in order. The vitality she had always had since she was a young girl – excelling at sport at school, cycling everywhere and her general zest for life – had helped and comforted him. There wasn't an event that had changed the relationship; it was more of a gradual process of him not wanting the fuss and her feeling resentful at not receiving any thanks for her efforts. Recently her visits had become shorter.

Of course, nothing in their lives could ever again be normal after the events of nearly four years ago. Physically and mentally their lives were forever damaged and though each tried to cope with their trauma in their own way neither had been successful. It was true that Sandra had the comfort and support of her husband, their friends and the routine of work. She had thrown herself with a new zeal into her life to show that she wasn't going to be beaten by the people who had been variously described on the television news as 'thugs', 'scum' and 'murderers', though the words didn't truly reflect what she felt about each of the five – four men and a woman.

The newspapers from the day were still on the table in the bay of the front window of his lounge, yellowed and crispened by the sun that managed to filter through the net curtains on a summer's afternoon. 'Old Couple Left for Dead after Torture by Thugs' the headline on the top newspaper screamed – a reminder every time Raymond sat down in his armchair next to the fireplace directly in front of the television.

Raymond took his mug into the lounge, sipped the tea and gently put the mug on to the small table by his right hand. In the same movement he picked up his pouch of rolling tobacco and the cheap throwaway lighter. He didn't know it but the smoke from the newly lit cigarette actually improved the stale smell in the room where the ceiling and walls had yellowed in the four years that Raymond had taken up smoking again, after a twenty-plus-year period during which he had stopped. The sudden noise from the hallway took Raymond's eyes away from the television screen temporarily but he knew it was just the postman delivering advertising mail that he had no interest in. His routine would see him sit in front of the television while he smoked two cigarettes and finished his tea before going to the bathroom for a shave and shower and finally getting dressed.

As today was Tuesday he would run the vacuum cleaner around the lounge and flick a duster on some of the surfaces and put the dirty crockery and cutlery into the dishwasher. He would empty the kitchen rubbish bin no matter how full it was and throw out any other rubbish that had accumulated in the past seven days. The front and back doors would be left open for half an hour to rid the bungalow of his cigarette smoke. The combination of tasks would at least mean that Sandra wouldn't be too critical of him this week. Not that he really cared.

It was close to lunchtime and Raymond was standing at the open front door watching the rainfall from the solid dark-grey sky. The back door was held open by a bucket that he had placed there for that reason. A gentle breeze entered through the back door into the kitchen then through the hallway and out of the front door. The lounge, the two bedrooms and the bathroom each had their windows open to assist in the freshening-up process. Raymond looked at the grass in the front garden, a patch roughly ten yards square where yellow dandelions, white clover and white daisies fought to show their heads above the six-inch grass. The driveway that ran by the side of the house to the prefab garage in the back garden had been tarred over by some men only two years ago but weeds were growing through, not just at the crumbling edges, but also in the central area and where the drive met the pavement. The hedge at the front of the property had grown untended for the past four years and now was as tall as a man.

Raymond drew again on his cigarette and was about to throw the butt into the grass when a man walked into the driveway from the road. Raymond stood still. He didn't recognise the man, nor did he want to buy anything and he didn't want any visitors either. The man was over six feet tall and of stocky build, wearing a green cap and camouflaged jacket with blue jeans and polished but sodden black boots. His jacket and jeans looked soaked through, his shoulders hunched and his hands were in his jacket pockets. He looked up and saw Raymond.

He broke into a large smile. 'Good morning,' he said brightly before looking up at the sky and adding, 'not entirely true, is it? But it's only water after all.'

He walked closer to Raymond and stopped some six feet away, the smile still on his face as he brought his hands out of the pockets. In his right hand he held a single piece of paper. He handed it to Raymond.

Still smiling, he said, 'Hi, Sir. I'm Adam and willing to do anything.' He looked up again into the rain. 'In any weather – and, as they say, no job is too small but some could be too big.' He laughed.

Raymond took the sheet of paper but didn't look at it. Instead, he looked at the man. He was in his early thirties, clean-shaven and, though his clothes looked old and very wet, he appeared to be clean. His hair didn't show beneath the cap.

'Don't need anything doing, thanks,' Raymond said.

'Sir, I'm not asking you to give me a job to do straight away, though that would be great, but can I ask that you hold on to my details for a week please? Just keep that piece of paper, in case you think of something. Any job I do I won't ask paying for unless and until you are happy with what I've done and only for the price that we agree before I start. That paper has my home address and home telephone number on it. I'm not a fly-by-night or …' – he glanced meaningfully at the driveway – 'a cowboy.'

Raymond saw that Adam was still smiling, he looked at the paper, shrugged his shoulders and mumbled. 'Don't need anything doing.'

Adam smiled. 'Don't worry, Sir. Just please hold on to my details for a week. You never know you might think of something and I would be very grateful. Thanks.' He turned and walked up the driveway and then right on to the pavement where the very top of his cap could be seen bobbing up and down above the hedge as he made his way towards the next address.

At five thirty-three that evening Raymond was sitting in his chair with his eyes closed as he tried to doze when he heard a key in the front door. He waited for the doorbell to ring at the same time to indicate Sandra's arrival. The bell sounded followed by Sandra calling out as she did every time she arrived.

'It's only me.'

Sandra was wearing the same red anorak over her work uniform that she seemed to wear throughout the year except for the height of summer, and was carrying two laden carrier bags. She looked into the lounge.

'Hi, Dad, I'll just unpack these. Is the kettle boiled?'

Raymond forced a slight smile and slowly raised himself from the chair and followed Sandra into the kitchen where she set the bags on the small kitchen table. She gave him a peck on his cheek then turned her attention to the packets and tins she had bought for him.

'Twenty-one pounds for cash,' she said, putting the supermarket till receipt on the work surface next to the mug that Raymond was pouring boiling water into. Raymond went to a drawer and from the back he found a twenty-pound note and a one-pound coin that he put on top of the receipt.

'Thanks,' he said quietly.

For the next twenty or so minutes Sandra sat in the armchair the other side of the table next to Raymond's chair and tried to coax her father into contributing to a conversation, but with little success. She told Raymond about her week at home and at work, knowing that really he didn't care very much, if at all.

A little while later Raymond watched as, with exaggerated care, Sandra reversed her shining new blue BMW out of the driveway and into the road. There was a short toot of the horn and she drove out of his view. Almost with relief he went to the cupboard of the sideboard in the lounge, took out the one-and-a-half-litre bottle of supermarket own-brand whisky and poured a good half-inch measure into the glass he used every night. It was early October and the evenings were drawing in, so he prepared himself for the evening. The fire was struggling to get a hold. He drew the curtains, checked that both the front and back doors were locked, and sat down in his chair. He picked up his glass and took a large sip. Life would be back to his routine for the next six days.

The television programmes changed as the evening wore on but with the sound lowered Raymond was barely aware of what was on. He did what he always did: he drank whisky and got lost in his thoughts, his memories, sometimes good, sometimes with fondness but always with the same ending – grave unhappiness. This led to tears, the final drink and a stumbling around the lounge to put the fireguard in place, to turn out the lights and then to the bathroom and bed where sleep would eventually come.

Adam had spent all the afternoon walking up driveways, knocking on doors or ringing bells, offering his cheerful words as he sought work, any work from anyone. He wasn't upset that, as yesterday and the day before, he hadn't been offered any work – it would happen, he told himself. He switched on his small radio and sat in the same hard-backed wooden chair that he used all the time.

The other chair on the opposite side of the table was tucked in between the edge of the table and the wall. Also in the room were his single bed, which was fully and properly made, and a plastic airer on which he hung his washed clothes every night. The single wardrobe contained his other clothes including a suit, some shirts and two ties all hanging from plastic clothes hangers, along with his well-polished shoes and boots lined along the bottom. The small kitchenette was old and worn but scrubbed clean with every item spotless and in its allotted place. A small shower area, called a wet room with a plastic curtain dividing it from the rest of his room was next to the kitchenette. It, too, was perfectly clean with every item in place.

Adam had few personal possessions. Those ornaments he did have were either on the windowsill or stored in his suitcase that he kept tucked under the bed. A wallet that he always had with him contained everything that he could say was of value: a photograph of himself with a group of lads all in their twenties, all unshaven in various scraps of clothing, a bankcard to an account in which he had saved over twenty thousand pounds, and also several banknotes. The other item was a photograph of a woman in her early twenties, blonde hair, pretty and smiling at the photographer, with a large manicured lawn in the background. The head-and-shoulder view just captured the thin gold necklace with a locket that hung about her neck. Adam was not going to think of her this evening. He was going to listen to the football commentary on the radio, he would prepare himself a meal, he would finish reading his book. He would, he knew, at some stage think of her, and then the tears and anger would return.

2

The rain that had started as the month began had stopped by the beginning of the second week. That Tuesday Adam was walking the route he had taken the previous week, hoping that, with the dry weather maybe, just someone would trust him enough to give him some work. He arrived at Raymond's driveway and saw the same man from previous week smoking a cigarette on the doorstep. Although Adam was wearing the same jacket, it was unbuttoned and now, without a cap, his short fair hair could be seen.

'Hi again,' said Adam, smiling.

Raymond saw him and recognised Adam from the previous week, though he hadn't thought of him.

'Don't need anything,' he said taking a last draw on the cigarette.

'No problem,' replied Adam, still walking towards Raymond. 'Did you keep my details?' he added brightly. 'Bet you didn't.'

Raymond thought for a second while he blew out the smoke and threw the butt on to the grass. He remembered putting it in the drawer where he kept his money. Before he could reply, Adam continued. 'If you kept it, I'll do half an hour's work for nothing.'

Raymond looked at Adam, not sure what to make of him, his brightness and almost innocent openness, but he'd learned that looks cannot be relied upon to judge a character of a man – or a woman, he corrected himself.

'I'm on the straight. I just really want to do something to break up the routine. All I do is go from house to house – don't care what job it is.' Adam turned and waved his arm over the grass. 'I'll cut that for you, for free.'

'Nah, it's OK,' said Raymond, turning and going indoors, closing the door behind him. Adam shrugged his shoulders and, after watching the door close, he turned and walked away towards the road.

Raymond walked into the lounge and through the window he just caught the sight of Adam's back as he reached the pavement.

Something about the lad, he thought before he sat back in his armchair glancing at the clock, which told him that he had four hours until Sandra would arrive.

Sandra arrived as punctual as always and went about her task of putting her shopping away while Raymond made her a mug of tea. It was when he went to fetch the money for her shopping that he saw Adam's piece of paper, which he picked up and looked at for the first time. It was handwritten, neatly laid out in clear printed words and numbers. He saw that in size it was a third of an A4-sized sheet and that the paper was torn slightly at the top and bottom.

'What's that?' asked Sandra, looking over Raymond's shoulder.

'Oh someone looking for work. Told him I've got none for him,' Raymond said.

'Dad, for goodness' sake, haven't got any jobs!' exclaimed Sandra. 'You've got enough to keep an army of workers busy for a week. Come on, Dad, why not get him to just do a job and see what he's like? Any good, give him more. If not, just have the one job done.'

Raymond folded the paper and dropped it on to the work surface. 'Said he'd do half an hour free if I still had his paper, his details,' Raymond said, turning around to return to the lounge.

Sandra let her breath out. 'Dad, if it's free, why not let him do half an hour? It's not the money, is it? It's just that you don't want to have anything done – that's it, isn't it?'

Raymond sat in the chair. 'Funny he should come back and ask if I still had the paper. Didn't ask for it back.'

'Maybe he's desperate for work. At least he's got off his backside and trying to do something about it, not just waiting for the dole. Come on, Dad, give him some respect like you would have done before ...' She stopped. 'Come on, he's trying. Give him a ring. If you're worried, get him to come around when I'm here next week and I'll see what he's like as well.'

'Maybe,' Raymond said.

Adam had called at all the houses and bungalows as he had the previous week, making the same offer to anyone who would speak to him but only one person asked him to do a small job, and that was only after Adam had made the free half-hour offer. He wasn't too disheartened, though, as the sun was warm on his face as he retraced his steps looking forward to the evening when he would meet with an old friend of his, a friend who had plenty of reasons to be unhappy and resentful, but wasn't.

As Sandra reversed on to the pavement she saw a man walking towards her, smiling and slowing to allow her more time to make her manoeuvre.

She recognised the piece of paper in his hand and for some reason she pressed the button to lower the passenger-side window. The man bent down to her level.

'Are you the man who's trying to find work, odd jobs, and spoken to my dad?'

Adam noticed that the voice wasn't accusatorial. 'Yes, anything at all, no job too small, but some may be too big,' Adam said, breaking into a large open smile and laughing a little.

In that instant Sandra made a decision. 'Right, come on,' she said as she pulled back into the driveway.

Raymond had been watching Sandra reverse on to the pavement then saw her stop and lean over towards the passenger side and appear to talk to someone. Inwardly he groaned. He wanted her gone so he could pour himself a drink and settle down for the evening. It was his routine. Now he watched as she drove back into the driveway and Raymond could see the man come into view. Instantly he didn't know what he felt: some anger that his routine was being disturbed but also a slight lifting of his spirit in that something was being done. In truth, he knew a lot was needed to restore the property into the immaculate condition he and Ann had kept it in. But he really wanted to have the drink, to keep to his routine, to go back to happy days in his thoughts.

He watched as Sandra got out of the car, smiling at the man as he offered his hand. They talked together for less than a minute during which time Sandra had pointed to the grass and the man had laughed. Raymond had watched until they went to the side of the bungalow out of his view, towards the garage where all his gardening equipment and tools were kept. He hadn't been in the garage for at least a year but assumed that all the tools and equipment would be just as he had left them, everything cleaned and in their place, either freestanding or on nails hanging from the walls. The centre of the garage was vacant and though large enough for a car he didn't now own one – not after that night. He went and sat in his favourite armchair.

He could hear voices and heard them both laugh before he saw Sandra walk in front of the lounge window towards the front door, which opened shortly after. The sound of the petrol mower spluttering several times told Raymond what the man was about to do. He inwardly shrugged. The mower hadn't been used for years and probably wouldn't start, he thought, and anyway it wouldn't have any fuel in it. He didn't really care whether the grass was cut or not. Sandra didn't appear in Raymond's view but he saw her walking back towards where the man was obviously still trying to start the mower. Raymond listened to the silence, which lasted for several minutes and had just started to concern him, when he heard another attempt at the mower being started. This time there was a roar as the engine burst into life followed

11

by a rhythmic sound as it was walked the length of the grass then turned round again. He sighed knowing that there was no point in arguing about this man cutting the grass – it was a fait accompli.

Sandra walked through the front door and looked into the lounge with a big smile. 'You wait – I bet he does a good job – he seems nice.'

Before Raymond could reply Sandra had headed towards the kitchen, reappearing a minute later with the man's piece of paper. Raymond stood and walked to the window where he watched Sandra go up to the man and show him the paper. The man had stopped and adjusted the machine to just the engine idling, glanced at the paper and threw his head back with laughter. They said something, then they both laughed and Sandra returned to the house. When she came into the lounge she was still smiling.

'Adam is going to cut the front grass and then the back one for nothing. He said he'd do half an hour for nothing and he's keeping his word,' she said.

'How did he get the mower working?' asked Raymond.

'Ha!' she said, laughing. 'No fuel but Adam said that as my car was petrol he could syphon some from my car and try the mower. See!' she said, pointing towards the window, 'you'd have been proud of someone using their brains and initiative a few years ago, wouldn't you?'

For what seemed the first time that Sandra could remember, in months or even a year, she saw her father give a smile, not a broad open smile, but at least the start of one.

It was just over a half hour later when Adam had finished cutting the back lawn that Raymond saw him and Sandra talking in the driveway before she offered him some money. Adam laughed, refused to accept the cash and walked away to the pavement where Raymond lost sight of him. Sandra went into the lounge and persuaded Raymond to inspect the lawns. He agreed that they were well cut with neat stripes down their length.

'What state's the mower in?' he asked in a voice more sullen than he had intended.

'Come and see for yourself,' replied Sandra, taking his hand and pulling him towards the garage that was still open. Raymond looked at the garage floor, newly swept he thought. He walked to the mower and tilted it to look at the blade area, as clean as he would have left it.

'Good job, grant you. He did well.'

Sandra beamed at her father and gave him a hug, the first for over a year and, after a few seconds, he responded by putting his arms around her. They stayed like that for over a minute before Sandra broke away and, trying to hide her tears, walked to her car. Raymond turned to close the garage door and felt tears forming in his eyes and by the time he turned and saw Sandra reversing into the road the tears had slowly rolled down his cheeks. He didn't wipe them away, using the back of his sleeve, until she had driven from his view, He looked at the cut grass again then went indoors for his delayed whisky.

That evening was a little different for Raymond. It was as if something had stirred his feelings. Perhaps for the first time he had seen a person besides Sandra with some good in them. Of course, his thoughts were still focused on Ann and the terrible fright, humiliation and pain that she had suffered, about which he hadn't done one thing to lessen or prevent. It was his fault and nothing would take the feeling that hurt him so much and so deep inside – *nothing*.

Adam returned to his room and after showering changed into clean clothes, washing the dirty ones in the shower water. By doing this he avoided the launderette that was down the road, where he had previously sat watching the clothes spinning around while listening to the inane conversations around him. He wasn't interested in the activities of the halfwits who performed in various contestant games and then went on to become some sort of 'celebrity'; for him, they were nobodies, not worth a light. They couldn't hold a candle to the men he had worked with, or to the pretty blonde woman he had a photograph of. He didn't look at her photograph every day but knew that, as and when he wanted, there she was, for him.

He sat down with a cup of tea and thought of what he was doing with his life. He knew he wasn't doing very much but he didn't really care. He enjoyed being outside, so the walking round the houses trying to find work was quite pleasant, no matter what the weather. He didn't need the money, but he felt disappointed that he hadn't been asked to do more work. He thought back to the morning. He had clipped a hedge for an old lady, and he smiled at the recollection. He doubted that she could see what he had done, her eyesight was so poor, peering through the window at him. Far too trusting, he had thought, but that was because she was lonely. She really wanted company, not a job doing. She had insisted on making him a cup of tea, which he had refused to drink inside, choosing instead to sit on her doorstep. She was a vulnerable old lady – how old? Yes, ninety-two, she had said, with no one from her family caring for her. If it wasn't for the Council she had said, 'Wouldn't be able to live.'

He had refused to take any money from her, though he wouldn't be surprised if she could have afforded his time many times over, but it just wouldn't have been right. Then his thoughts went to meeting Sandra and the cutting of the old man's grass. Adam smiled as he recalled the obstinate man, moody and ungrateful, but she was so bubbly and lovely towards him that he had been pleased to do the work for her. There was more to her wanting the grass cut, he was sure – not any sort of attraction towards him but rather making a point or something like that towards her father. Adam had been surprised by the tidiness of the garage, the quality of the equipment and tools, and the way they had been cared for – all that was so at odds with what he could see of the old man and his home. He looked at his watch and decided that after a meal he would have an early night before retracing his steps in the morning and trying a new area in the afternoon. The forecast was for heavy rain and strong winds, so he in all likelihood wouldn't be doing any work but he enjoyed being out in that weather anyway.

The following Tuesday he had been out again delivering his leaflets. A whole week had passed and he had only six jobs to show for his efforts that barely covered the cost of photocopying his hand-outs. It was getting dark as the nights closed in earlier and there were lights on in many of the houses he visited. The day had been clear and crisp with the promise of another frost that night. For some reason that he couldn't really explain to himself he was drawn back to the bungalow where he had met Sandra the previous week. Every Tuesday, she had said, she visited her father, after work, and so he made a point of walking past the bungalow at the same time as the previous week. Her car was in the driveway and lights were on in the front room so he rang the bell, which was answered shortly by Sandra. He smiled at her.

'Thought I'd pop in to see if my favourite, almost my *only* customer come to that, wanted any job doing, nothing is too small ...' He paused and laughed. 'You know the rest.'

Sandra returned the laugh. 'Yes there is. Come on, I'll show you.'

She passed by him and headed round the side of the bungalow to the rear garden and pointed to the sagging gutter that was above the kitchen window. 'That drives me up the wall every time it rains and look, it's making the windowsill all green and the earth is becoming a pond where the water is settling.'

Adam took a few seconds looking at the guttering that ran along the whole of the back of the bungalow.

'Right, no problem, need a ladder of some sort, a hammer and nails or screws and a screwdriver.'

Sandra directed Adam to the garage for anything he needed

then returned into the warm lounge beaming at her father. 'Adam is fixing that bloody guttering. You may not care about it but every time it rains I feel so frustrated, as you'd have done that yourself in a jot.'

Raymond responded with a faint smile and a heavy sigh.

'And I'm going to give him other jobs to do outside that really need doing – the gardens, the hedges – all that need sorting and then we can think about painting the windows, and I don't know,' she said, 'maybe some jobs inside as well.'

Raymond was initially taken aback by Sandra's suggestions, as a part of him didn't want all the fuss and disruption to his routine, but there was a part of him that was happy at the news, though he didn't say so.

It took Adam less than fifteen minutes to fix and clean the leaves from the guttering and replace what he had borrowed from the garage which he was closing as Sandra prepared to leave. Raymond watched from the lounge window as Sandra handed Adam a note of jobs that he could do in the garden and some cash for fixing the guttering, all the while both were smiling and laughing. He saw Adam look his way and give a wave before walking towards the road. Sandra blew Raymond a kiss and was laughing as she got into her car and drove off. Raymond went to the kitchen then into the back garden and looked at the work Adam had done. It was as good as he would have done, the guttering was straight, the leaves buried under the newly filled in hole where the water had cascaded and the window sill where the green mould was starting had been washed clean.

It was mid-November and Adam was at Raymond's house, as he had been once a week, every Tuesday, arriving at five o'clock and working for one hour doing various jobs in the garden that Sandra had listed for him. He waved at Raymond and called out to let him know he was there but otherwise didn't want to intrude.

Adam looked forward to Sandra's arrival as she was always cheery and thankful for his efforts and it was with some reluctance he accepted the payment, which she insisted he take. Sandra approached him as he was preparing to leave. Raymond saw them talking, with Adam nodding his head in agreement with whatever Sandra was saying. Raymond knew that she was telling Adam that the outside work had been completed and that it was the list of indoor jobs she was presenting to him, which she had shown to Raymond a few minutes earlier. In the intervening weeks since Adam had first been to the bungalow Raymond hadn't made the effort to speak with him, although he had at least greeted the younger man through the window by means of a vague wave. He had thought it a little strange that Adam hadn't tried to talk to him, to force the issue, but was glad that he hadn't.

Adam waved towards Raymond before walking off while Sandra returned to the house.

'Dad, Adam hasn't got any other work at the moment so I've asked him to come in tomorrow morning, after ten so you don't have to get up early. The job is to empty out the kitchen pantry, paint the walls and put everything back again. After that to move the washing machine and dryer, and clean behind them. I don't know how long he'll take, but I've suggested we pay him ten pounds an hour. He thinks that is far too much but I've insisted.'

She hugged Raymond and said quietly in his ear, 'You'll like him, Dad. He's done every job really well, you know he has. Do you know, he hasn't said a single word about you not talking to him? He just accepts and respects your wishes. That makes him a little special in my mind ... and Dad, he doesn't talk about himself – I've had to ask him questions to learn anything about him. Please, Dad, give him a break. I think he is hurting over something as well.'

Raymond listened to Sandra and thought the words she was saying could have been spoken by her mother – sensible and caring. He had watched Adam, both as he worked and with

Sandra. In truth, he had quite liked the way any job was greeted with a smile and completed well and with enthusiasm. Raymond had realised as well that he appreciated Sandra's efforts – having positive activities happening around him had helped to lift his gloom a little.

Raymond was dressed and ready when Adam arrived the following morning, wearing his usual clothes and, as always, smiling. Raymond had decided that he would make an effort. He opened the door just as Adam had been reaching towards the bell, introduced himself and shook Adam's hand. He made Adam a coffee then, after showing him the pantry, sat at the kitchen table and made small talk while watching him methodically empty the pantry of all the items and carefully stacked them around the kitchen. Both men avoided asking any personal questions of the other, keeping the conversation general and light. Raymond was growing to like Adam and also the way Adam talked while never breaking his concentration from what he was doing.

It was with total innocence, then, that Raymond asked Adam why he was working doing odd jobs when he clearly had the ability to do more challenging work. Raymond recognised instantly the effect his question had had on Adam, who for a fraction stopped replacing plates into the completed pantry. His ever-present smile dropped and he turned his head towards the pantry's inside.

'I apologise for the personal question,' Raymond quickly added. 'I shouldn't have asked it – it's no business of mine.'

Adam straightened up and checked the kitchen for any item he might have missed before looking at Raymond. 'No, the question is fair. It's just that I don't like talking about myself ... you know, dwelling on the past ... got to look forward.'

He gave a short smile then turned his attention to the washing machine. Raymond continued for a few minutes to watch Adam work but found it hard to restart their conversation and made an excuse that he needed to watch the television news. In ten minutes Adam had finished his job and was about to gently knock on the lounge door to tell Raymond that he was ready to leave. He half expected to find the elderly man asleep but instead he found Raymond sitting on the edge of his chair, his body leaning towards the television, his mouth wide open and his right arm raised, fist clenched so hard that his knuckles were white. Veins stood out at the side of his head.

Adam was shocked but before he could react he heard a car door slam outside, followed by the quick click of heels along the path towards the front door. The front door flew open and Sandra rushed in without closing it. Crossing the hallway in two strides she pushed past Adam and made towards her father. She saw his posture and looked at the television screen, then moved to him.

'Dad, I heard it on the radio and came to stop you watching it.'

She reached for the television controls and in an instant the screen went blank. Adam watched Sandra kneel before her father and put her arms around his shoulders before closing in for a strong embrace. Adam saw her back moving in jerks then heard her sobbing that in seconds turned into uncontrolled crying. Raymond hadn't moved a muscle. It was if his whole body had turned to stone, as his daughter held him tightly and cried into his chest.

Adam looked at the blank television screen and tried to remember what had been on when Sandra had suddenly arrived. He thought back and saw a group of young men in their twenties, together with an older couple, perhaps one of the men's parents, with a bottle of champagne or something. They were in a street, just stepping on to the pavement, stone steps behind. The building appeared to be old, built of stone, light-coloured large blocks of stone. A set of large wooden doors was at the top of the steps. Adam was trying to develop the sound to accompany his recollection when he was brought back to the lounge.

'Bastards!' screamed Raymond at the top of his voice. 'Bloody bastards!' he screamed again, still facing the television. Sandra withdrew slightly from Raymond and gently stroked his face with her hand.

'I'm sorry, Dad!' she managed to say between her cries.

'Bastards, bastards, bastards!' screamed Raymond.

Adam watched Raymond and Sandra for a few more seconds before slowly moving back to the kitchen and filling the kettle. He put out three mugs, a teabag in each, as he heard Raymond continue shouting out, 'Bastards!' Sandra's crying could be heard in between Raymond's shouting and screaming. When the teas were made he slowly and quietly carried them into the lounge where he saw Raymond had slumped back into his chair, his breathing laboured after his exertions, and Sandra sitting on the carpet at his feet with her hands covering her face. Adam gently placed the mugs on the table next to Raymond and caught Raymond's eye.

'Is there anything I can do?' he asked quietly.

Raymond shook his head slowly from side to side. 'Unless you want to kill the bastards there's nothing you can do.'

Sandra took her hands from her face and appeared to notice Adam for the first time. She shook her head and slowly stood. She stroked Raymond's face and looked at Adam. Her mouth opened as if she was about to say something but she decided against that and turned her gaze towards her father.

Adam fetched his mug of tea and stood in the lounge doorway sipping it when Raymond turned towards him.

'Thanks for what you've done this morning … Good job!'

Adam nodded. 'It was a pleasure but seeing you and Sandra upset is not. I don't want to intrude. Tell me to mind my own business and I'll go but …' – he paused before continuing in a quiet voice – 'seeing you both so upset …' He left the sentence unfinished.

Raymond looked at Sandra then back at Adam. Then he said in a voice that Adam had to strain to hear: 'They're the bastards that ruined our lives. Now look at them – they're laughing. My wife is dead and I may just as well be … and Sandra, too.' He looked towards his daughter. 'Oh God. No, that isn't right …. there isn't a God …. If there were, those bastards would be dead … the bastards!'

Adam shifted his stance and quietly asked Raymond: 'Can I get you something?'

Raymond smiled. 'A gun … otherwise a whisky. Bottle's in the cupboard, glasses in the kitchen.'

Three minutes later Sandra and Raymond were sipping their drinks that Adam had prepared, sitting in the armchairs next to each other. Nothing had been said and Adam, feeling uncomfortable, was wondering how he could leave. Suddenly Raymond spoke.

'Adam, there's nothing you can do for us except fetch another bottle. What's left in that one won't last us very long.'

Adam left the house, pulling the front door to but not closing it before making his way to the parade of shops. He bought the same brand of whisky that Raymond drank and returned to the house. Peering into the lounge he saw Sandra sitting on the floor with yellowing sheets of newspaper spread out in front of her. Adam gently placed the bottle on the table, noticing that the bottle he had used previously was now on the table and its contents lower than he had left it in the kitchen. He looked over Sandra's shoulders and read the headlines: 'A civilised country?' read one; 'Tortured and murdered' read another; 'Pensioners tortured in their own home' raged another. Others were only partly visible to him but he could see that they contained the same or similar words.

Raymond looked up at Adam, waved an arm towards the chair. 'Have a drink.'

Adam fetched a glass from the kitchen and poured himself a little whisky then sat in the armchair vacated by Sandra.

Adam pointed to the newspapers but was unable to ask the question. Raymond answered anyway.

'Four years ago, here, those bastards' – he pointed towards the blank television screen and composed himself with a deep breath – 'those bastards murdered my wife and nearly me. Got away with it. Now some other poor sod has been half beaten to death and they've got away with it again.'

Adam hesitated. 'I don't know what to say, I'm sorry. So how did they get away with it?'

'Police made a cock-up in their evidence, didn't go through the correct procedures, didn't get the authority they needed, so the evidence couldn't be used. CPS said there wasn't enough to charge the bastards without that evidence so they got away with it. We buried Ann, that's Sandra's mother, two days after we were told that there was nothing else they could do. I was still in a wheelchair. He broke my legs and ankles … I mean Kieran and his dad.' He took a deep gulp of whisky before continuing. 'They enjoyed it, laughing they were.'

'Dad, don't,' said Sandra.

Raymond waved an arm towards her. 'Why not? Why shouldn't the world know? Why should they get away with it?' He turned towards Adam. 'They tortured Ann for three hours … did things that I didn't know a human could do to another … made me watch.'

Adam was horrified. 'Jesus Christ, Ray, I don't know what to say.'

'Nothing can be said, we've heard it all, the police, victim support, council care people, you know, Social Services, reporters, even the MP, all said what everyone thinks but they still got away with it. Not even a day in prison between the five of them. They should have all been hanged, slowly. I'd do it to them, believe me.'

Adam was still absorbing what Raymond was saying. He hadn't heard or read anything about the attack, but then four years ago, he remembered, he would have been somewhere where a television or even a radio wouldn't work.

Sandra turned to face Adam. 'Dad worked really hard to walk

again, brilliant doctors, and the scars have healed around his body, as well as they could, but it's all in here' – she indicated her head – 'nothing can cure that. Every day Dad has to think of that night, every day he relives it. I do and I wasn't here, just what I was told afterwards, but for him' – she looked at the blank television set – 'and now the same people have got away with nearly murdering another person.'

Adam spoke to Sandra. 'Can I read the papers, please? Would you mind?'

Sandra shuffled them together and handed them to Adam. 'Will you bring them all back in the morning?'

Adam agreed and, taking the gentle hint, finished his drink before leaving the bungalow.

Adam carefully put the newspaper on top of those he had already read – it was the last one. He had read them all, in date order, every word that related to the attack on Mr and Mrs Black, two pensioners who were attacked, tortured and robbed in their own home. Every word described the abject terror that these two decent honest people had been subjected to, their pain and their agony, the cruelty inflicted on them. The injuries were only briefly mentioned but Adam knew from experience that how they had been caused would have been unbearable even to most younger and fitter people. Ann had died but Raymond had just about lived when purely by chance he had been found. A dog walker had seen the front door open at close to midnight and investigated – he had found Ann and Raymond lying covered in blood in their bedroom. The paramedics who attended must have done a good job, thought Adam, to save Raymond's life. Wouldn't have been nice for them either, probably traumatised them, too, he thought.

The following morning after a poor night's sleep Adam arrived at Raymond's house just before midday, fearing that Raymond would have spent the evening drinking heavily. He was surprised to see Sandra's car still in the driveway and pleased to see her when she opened the door to him. She was wearing the same clothes and she quickly explained that she had stayed the night to be with her father. Raymond himself was in his chair and looked better than Adam had expected. He placed the newspapers on the table in the bay window.

'I read them all … Just about managed to read them without being sick. I can't imagine what it was like for you, Ray. You called them by the right name, sure enough. In fact, bastards doesn't get anywhere near it. I've also read today's papers about them. It was the son who attacked a lad, nearly killed him, kicked him up to fifty times all over his body when he was down on the ground. Mum and Dad gave him an alibi. There wasn't any forensic evidence and the jury believed him, not the two people who identified him, who saw it, who told the police and went to court to swear on oath that they saw it. That was at the crown court, at Lewes. I can understand why you joked about wanting a gun.'

'I wasn't joking, believe me,' said Raymond.

Sandra looked very serious, so different from the woman who laughed and joked with him a month earlier. 'He's not joking. Only, of course he can't get one and even if he did he wouldn't be able to use it, would you, Dad?'

'You can be sure that the police would catch me. There'd be no mistakes with their evidence, and even with an alibi and no witnesses I'd be found guilty!' Raymond said.

Adam looked him in the face. 'I couldn't sleep last night after reading all that. I just felt a rage towards them. They were on the television news last night as well, gloating about how the police couldn't investigate them. They're animals, no lower than animals. You know, Ray, Sandra, they deserve to die, they deserve to suffer the fear and pain before they actually die, to realise what it is like to know that there isn't any hope of them living. To feel the pain and be told that it is revenge for what they did to you and Ann.' Adam spoke with all the passion that he felt inside.

'Funny thing really, everyone says that, *we've* said that! We want that to happen but of course it won't,' said Sandra.

'When I first met you I offered to do any job that you wanted …' Adam started to say.

'No job too small but some maybe too big,' continued Sandra, adding a smile.

'It wouldn't be too big for me to do it.'

'To kill them?' asked Sandra in a quiet and frightened voice.

'To kill them.'

'You can't be serious. I mean you wouldn't actually do it?'

Adam looked straight at Sandra and said deliberately: 'I am serious. I have personal reasons for evening the score against the scum that walk our streets.'

There was silence as each looked at the other trying to come to terms with how the conversation had developed, the enormity of what they had just said.

'I've got fifty thousand pounds that I'll give you, every penny that we saved … That's ten thousand for each of them!' said Raymond, his voice hardening.

'Dad! You can't, come on, it's how we feel but we can't actually do it. Let's all just get real,' said Sandra whose voice now sounded panicky, scared.

'Sandra, my darling, thanks for being here but I think it's time that you went home. You have your family to think of and your job. I'll be fine now the shock has worn off a little. I'll be all right. I'll give you a ring this evening to let you know that I've eaten and not been drinking all day.' He smiled.

Sandra looked from man to man, 'No, Dad, this is harebrained for goodness' sake. You're not hiring a killer and, Adam, you're not a killer.'

Adam looked directly at Sandra. 'I am. I am a killer. I *have* killed. Not in the crime world but I was in the Army for over ten years, until last year in fact. Believe me, I can and would be happy to do it. I would like to rid the world of them. I've lost mates, brave honest men, seen others suffer terrible injuries, then I see these scum, these gutless useless apologies for human beings … believe me, I will do it.' He turned towards Raymond. 'And, Ray, I won't take a penny from you.'

Sandra stood and looked down at both the men seated in the armchairs. 'We've had a shock, we're angry, we've every reason to take the law into our own hands … and, Dad' – she looked at her father – 'that's *we*.' Sandra pointed to herself and then her father. 'Not *you*, but *we*, so I have a say.'

Raymond nodded in agreement. 'Sure, you're right, you do have a say, but if what you say is something I don't want to hear, then I won't take any notice of it.'

Sandra was about to say speak but Raymond held up his hand to interrupt her. 'And Peter, when he was twelve, what happened? I'll remind you: he was beaten up at school because he refused to hand over his bus fare. He was punched in the face and kicked in his groin. Other kids saw it but they were all too afraid to say anything, so what happened? You took Peter out of that school where he was doing well and moved him to another school. And you had to take him to school and collect him. Ann and I did as well because we were frightened that it could happen again. We both know that the lout who beat Peter up is now nothing but rubbish, he's in the papers, been at court for burglary, for assault, for stealing cars, all manner of crimes. What's to say he won't join a gang and do something like what happened to your mum and me? The country is full of these, these …' – he struggled to find the word – 'these bastards.'

Sandra stood looking at her father. She heard everything and understood exactly what he was saying. It was all true.

'Dad, Adam, let's all think about what we really want to do. I really do want to do something, but killing someone? What if we were caught, we'd go to prison forever. I have to think about Dennis. I love him and he's going to retire in four years. And Peter, he may be coming up to thirty but if we were caught it could ruin his life, Kate's life, and what about your great-grandchildren? There's a lot to think about and I suggest we all leave it. We can each gather our thoughts. How about meeting up tomorrow evening to air our views then? *Without* having a drink first.' She pointed at the nearly empty bottle and smiled at her father, who lowered his head and smiled back, acknowledging her point.

'Agreed,' Adam said.

Five minutes later the ex-soldier waved at Sandra as she drove away from the house and he started to walk in the opposite direction towards his digs. He didn't feel any concern about what he had offered to do; it was rather a relief. He had mentally crossed a threshold. He didn't feel elated but if asked he would have said that he had a spring in his step.

3

Sandra had arrived home and thrown herself into finishing off the housework she had been neglecting all week. She had just finished preparing dinner when Dennis arrived from work, just after six, as was his routine. As always, he placed his briefcase by the hallstand, hung his rain mac on the peg in the under-stairs cupboard before calling out to Sandra announcing that he was home. Sandra smiled. It was always the same but there was nothing wrong in that – they had just settled into their routine since Peter and Kerry, their twenty-six-year-old daughter, had left home. The only time when Dennis's arrival home was different was during the school holidays when Sandra collected Peter and Kate's four-year-old twin boys and they would be in the front garden waiting for their grandfather to return home, hiding behind a small tree and jumping out at him.

Through dinner Sandra pretended to listen as Dennis explained how the new rules on taxation had meant that he and some of his team would have to devise a new computer system in time for the annual returns starting the following autumn. Her mind was elsewhere though, thinking of the mad idea that had somehow entered the conversation at her father's house. The fact that Adam had been in the Army didn't really surprise her; she had frequently wondered about his past but because of his unwillingness to raise the subject she had respected his privacy. He had spoken with some feeling about having his own reasons and she wondered what they were. He had spoken of his colleagues being injured and killed, so perhaps the motivation lay there. Her evening followed the usual routine except her mind wasn't focused on any of the television programmes she watched, or on her husband's small talk.

Adam had showered, dressed and heated some pre-cooked pasta, which he struggled to eat at the table. After washing the dishes he was going to start to think about the practicalities of how he could kill the five people. The whole operation had to be planned. He would have to cover his tracks and not leave clues for the police to find. Although he wasn't making a lot of his life at present, being arrested and imprisoned for the rest of his life wasn't part of his plan. An hour later he put his pencil down and examined the sheet of paper he had been writing on. He had used pencil so that he could erase any words or passages and had written smaller than usual so that he used only a single sheet. He had even used the table to lean on to prevent indented words being found during any forensic search. After all, that piece of paper held enough detail to ensure his arrest and possible charge of conspiracy to murder. Unpicking a few threads of plastic at the top of the shower curtain, he rolled the piece of paper up tightly then slid it into the hem of the curtain. He cut the threads then pulled the curtain several times to ensure that the paper remained in place and couldn't be seen.

The following evening Adam arrived to find the curtains drawn at the bungalow with lights clearly on inside. Sandra's car was parked on the driveway but it was Raymond who opened the door. Adam couldn't hide his surprise at how well Raymond looked: there were no sign of tiredness or effect of alcohol around his eyes, and he gave a large open smile to greet him; even his posture was more upright. If Adam had felt a spring in his step, then Raymond must have been jumping – he looked years younger. Sandra was drying her hands as she also welcomed Adam and shortly after they all sat in the lounge sipping mugs of tea.

Sandra told Adam that after he had left yesterday her father had poured all the whisky away and gone for a walk to the woods some half a mile away, then climbed a stile and walked over several fields before returning home. His whole attitude to living had changed, she added. Raymond sat there nodding in agreement.

Raymond took a deep breath and then spoke slowly: 'Right, that's out of the way, let's cut the chatter and concentrate on what is going to happen. Firstly, I want to go ahead, I want to see all five dead. Sandra, are you in or out?'

Sandra had made her decision. 'In with reservations,' she said, her voice barely audible.

'Adam?' asked Raymond.

'In, no reservations.'

'Sandra, love, you have more to lose than me if we're found out, so I think it best that you know nothing,' said Raymond.

Adam held up his hand and looked at Raymond. 'Ray, Sandra, I don't want *either* of you involved. I said no reservations but that is only if I act alone. I will need a couple of facts from you and then I will leave, do what I have to do and won't contact either of you. You may read or hear something about what I am doing but you won't be able to contact me and I won't contact you. This is for your, *our*, protection – no contact because you can be sure that sooner or later the police will look at you, probably use surveillance, listening, all manner of things and, if we are in contact, that could lead them to me. So, after some initial help, we go our separate ways. This isn't up for negotiation.' He looked at Raymond, expecting an argument, but saw him just nod slowly in agreement. Sandra also gave a short nod.

'Money,' said Raymond. 'Sandra has withdrawn two thousand pounds this morning from my account and given notice for a further ten thousand next week. You'll have that.'

Adam replied quickly: 'And say the police look at your bank statement and see the withdrawals. They'll ask "Mr Black, what did you do with the cash. Please show us the receipts." You'll be stumped and you, Sandra, will be also. So no thank you. I'll use my own money. And that's not up for negotiation either. A couple of questions though: firstly, why assault you and Ann? And secondly how did the police get on to them. They live a long way away – in Brighton, wasn't it?'

Raymond sat back in his chair and looked towards the ceiling as if trying to recall something. 'Why us? The police couldn't find a motive. How did they catch them? Because of a snitch in Brighton.'

Sandra was looking at her father as Adam picked up one of the newspapers and appeared to be looking for something in an article. 'Says here that you have a son, Ray, but you've never spoken of him.'

Sandra was looking at Adam's back and shot a glance towards her father, who suddenly looked towards her.

'My brother works abroad. He lives away, on the move,' Sandra said. She became aware that her father was about to say something so she continued. 'He's a freelance photographer working in Africa most of the time covering wars mostly, poor people, that sort of thing.'

Adam replaced the newspaper on the pile and turned back to see Sandra smiling at him and getting up from her seat. She crossed to a photograph album on a shelf among some books. She opened the album and walked towards Adam. 'That's one of his, in *Newsweek*.' She turned a page. 'This one appeared in *Time* magazine.'

Adam took the album and turned various pages noting that the subjects appeared to be young teen soldiers: underfed, wearing badly fitting green uniforms, some of which bore an old camouflage design, each holding an automatic rifle, Chinese AK-47s, he noted.

'Good photographs. Brave to be among these types,' he said as he read a paragraph printed from a German magazine in which the name David Black appeared in bold print.

'He's been doing that for so long now that he is well known, so gets access,' Raymond said, exchanging a glance with Sandra.

Adam put the album down. He embraced Sandra then, before Raymond could fully stand, placed his hand on Raymond's shoulder.

'It's OK, Ray, stay there.' He looked at both of them, gave each a smile then turned on his heels and walked out of the lounge. Sandra and Raymond heard the front door close then watched as Adam walked across the cut lawn then turned on to the pavement, out of their view.

Adam returned to his room where he retrieved the piece of paper and made further notes.

4

In the morning Adam was outside the Crawley library as the doors were unlocked at nine thirty and made for one of the free computer consoles that were available for the public's use. He spent the next three hours researching all he could find on the attack of Raymond and Ann, before moving on to the coverage of the arrests in Brighton. Four men and a woman were named, all local to the area. He researched the names and found they had appeared in the local paper previously, all in connection with their arrests for other crimes spanning some years. The father was likened in one article as being akin to an Italian Godfather in that he appeared to head a crime family. His wife was mentioned as being a 'Godmother' but of the crime variety, not the family-friendly type. Their son was the subject of an article in which it was reported that he had been sentenced to three years' imprisonment. Adam noted the name of the reporter and saw that his name appeared on every article written about the Townsend family. Adam was satisfied with his morning's research. He had learned a lot about the people he wanted to kill, where they lived and their lifestyles, but he still wanted to cover all the bases and speak to the reporter.

Adam left the library and used a telephone kiosk to call the newspaper, asking to speak to Keith Mendip. He was told that Mr Mendip no longer worked there; he had retired and no address was known for him. Adam replaced the receiver, cursing his luck, 'Retired?' he said to himself. Thinking back to one article, he recalled a photograph of the reporter: he was in his forties, not even in his fifties!

He returned to the kiosk and this time when the switchboard answered his call he asked for the Crime Desk. He spoke with a young-sounding female named Julie to whom Adam introduced himself as Charlie Wright, an author writing a book about the 'crime families' of England. He was, he said, aware of the family called Townsend who lived in Brighton and wanted to include them as representing an area away from the big cities such as London, Manchester and Newcastle. He wanted to show that such families existed all over the country. He wondered whether someone could help him in an unofficial capacity. He would, of course, reimburse any expenses.

'I don't know,' Julie said. 'What you're suggesting is irregular.'

Adam recognised the hesitation. 'I appreciate that, but it's just an informal chat – over dinner perhaps? Your choice of restaurant. I'll happily cover any expenses and I'm sure my publisher will be happy to compensate you for your time.'

There was silence on the line for over ten seconds. 'OK, but not in Brighton, though.'

'Great,' said Adam. They fixed the place and time for that evening and how they would recognise each other.

Adam returned to the library to look up the restaurant and its location before taking a train to Gatwick Airport, where he hired a car for a week.

He looked again in the mirror and, though he felt strange in his suit, he was pleased that it fitted him well. He left in plenty of time to drive to the restaurant, arriving half an hour before the eight o'clock time arranged with Julie. He was sipping a tonic water, inwardly laughing to himself as he realised he felt a little nervous.

He instantly recognised Julie the moment the swing door opened. As she walked into the bar, he jumped to his feet, at the same time smiling and extending his hand. They made their introductions, with Adam using the name of Charlie Wright.

At the table they each ordered their food and after Julie agreed with his choice of wine Adam ordered a bottle of claret. He took the initiative, asking questions about Julie's career. He found out that Julie had always been interested in crime and criminal stories and so, when she had decided to be a journalist, there wasn't much doubt about her preferred specialist role. She was now a crime reporter and had built up a good knowledge of local criminals. She had contacts in both the police and defending solicitors from whom she could gather titbits that she could never use directly but which nevertheless helped her learn more about the crime scene in the city.

Adam tried to talk generally about where he had been and what he had found out, knowing that there was a good chance Julie would have contacts in other papers that she could use to check up on his truthfulness. When he first broached the name of Townsend they had finished their main course and were waiting for their pudding. Julie had enjoyed the evening and liked 'Charlie', as she knew him. He was younger than she had expected but appeared to have a good experience of life and, though he talked about subjects in a serious manner, he used humour to lighten the mood. She knew that the dinner would involve her talking about the Townsends but at the mention of the name she felt her stomach tighten. She was hesitant talking about the family but gave an account of what she knew.

As he listened Adam realised that he was being told only what he had read in the library that morning. Nothing new was revealed and nothing said that could help him. He asked some questions that he hoped Julie would be able to answer but she insisted that her knowledge was basic. She apologised for not being able to give detailed information but said that as a junior reporter she didn't have dealings with the family. Adam pursued his questioning and gradually implanted a seed into Julie's mind that there might be another reporter who could help him, or a police officer or solicitor perhaps. Julie laughed at the suggestion.

'I don't know of anyone who would talk to you about the family. I've tried to find someone myself. Rumours are that the family has been looked after by a policeman over the years. You know, a warrant executed in the morning and nothing found. An arrest for something and the witness can't be located for a while. Evidence going missing from a secure storage area in the police station. These are rumours – I'm not saying that they're true or anything … A solicitor? No way, absolutely not. They use the same solicitor every time and there is no way that he'd talk to you. For heaven's sake, you've got to appreciate that there are a lot of very frightened people where this family is concerned.'

Adam sat quietly for a minute. 'What about someone who isn't involved anymore with the family in any way, perhaps moved on, away to pastures new?'

Julie's eyes narrowed a fraction as her guard went up. 'In what way?'

'Well, someone who did know about the family but for one reason or another doesn't now – for whatever reason.'

'Look, Charlie, I don't know you. For all I know you could be working for them trying to see if I would say something out of turn, to find out who else might say something about them.'

Adam looked at Julie and nodded to acknowledge the point she had made. He had been concerned that she would raise this all evening. He knew that he didn't have any fall-back in place such as a business card, or address, or even the name of a person he could pass as his publisher. Inwardly, he swore to himself: while she had been professional in her approach, he had been the opposite. Slapdash didn't nearly cover it. Poor planning equals poor performance and that was exactly what he had done, piss poor.

'I know,' he said, wondering if it was worth continuing with his lies, 'that's a good point and I can't prove anything about myself. I deliberately don't carry any identification. I've no wallet, just cash. The car's hired by a friend. I'm very close to stepping on to a landmine every time I try and find out about a family. Every one presents their own problems but there is always the fear. I appreciate what you've done just by meeting me, I really do. That took guts and I admire you for that. I do need though to speak with someone who can tell me more "off the record" things, chitchat, speculation, rumours, like you mentioned. I haven't said anything about the people I have already worked on – I can't – it's as simple as that.'

'Have you got a mobile?' Julie asked.

'Not with me,' lied Adam, knowing that it lay on the floor under his driving seat in the car. He gave her the number and she repeated it back to him.

They separated in the car park and Adam waited until Julie had driven away before returning to his car, which was parked among others. He drove in the opposite direction and was soon lost in his thoughts about Julie and how the evening had gone. He was still cursing himself for his lack of preparation. He really was unfit, both physically and mentally. Tomorrow would be the first day of the rest of his life: running and cycling, press-ups and small weights, for the physical side; more detailed planning and contacting an old friend for the mental side.

Julie drove steadily towards her parents' home where she was going to stay for the weekend, having worked the past three and been on call for the previous three before that. She had cleared her desk and her diary, a long quiet weekend: Saturday morning to catch up on some sleep, the afternoon with her mother shopping for clothes and, in the evening, a visit to the local pub for a drink and dinner. Sunday morning she hoped would allow another long sleep followed by a large home-cooked roast lunch and a gentle walk along the seafront in the afternoon, whatever the weather. She would return to her flat in the new development close to the Brighton railway station later in the evening ready for work on Monday morning.

As she drove she was thinking about Charlie – if that was his real name … somehow she doubted it. She also doubted that he was an author given that he had no journalistic background – so what was it all about? Certainly, he had been charming company with good manners, was educated and spoke well. He appeared to be worldly and streetwise, though he didn't seem keen to talk about his background. 'Interesting man Charlie,' she said to herself. Undoubtedly, he wasn't telling the truth, or certainly not the whole truth, so who was he and what was his game? It could be dangerous, that was certain. Dangerous for her if he was working for the Townsend family and dangerous for him if he wasn't.

'Right, Charlie or whoever, you can wait for Monday,' she said out loud and concentrated on her driving.

5

Adam finished his run through Tilgate Forest outside the town of Crawley near the M23 and checked his watch. He had planned the route from a map and knew the seven miles would be testing for him, especially with the diversions he had incorporated, running straight uphill rather than following the path that ran diagonally along the hill. He was out of breath and sweat poured off his chin while his legs and back ached. It had been good and he was pleased with the effort he had been able to sustain.

He drove back to his room and completed a hundred press-ups and sit-ups in alternate blocks of twenty then lay on his back, allowing his breathing and aching body time to recover. That afternoon he walked to the town centre and bought a hybrid bicycle, riding home then carrying it upstairs into his room. Every time he thought of the meeting with Julie he cursed himself, but then in more positive moments he looked on it as a wakeup call.

It was teatime when he made the call to his best friend whom he had met when he first entered the Army as a raw seventeen-year-old recruit. Like Brian Chopra, Adam had been intimidated by some other recruits who had grown up in cities and who seemed physically and mentally stronger. The two had formed a bond from that first day. They spent nearly all their time together, encouraging and motivating each other, wanting to be the best at every activity and prepared to accept the ridicule that was directed at them by some of the underachievers. Both Adam and Brian were liked by the training staff, who saw the effort they put into everything and their willingness to learn. Both were reluctant to be selected as leaders on exercises but when told to do so showed confidence and leadership beyond the capabilities of the rest of their intake.

Over the ten years that each served in the Army they had continued their relationship, even when each had selected a different arm of the Special Forces to serve in. Adam had developed into a soldier, a fighter who liked to be in the thick of all the action, thriving on the hardships that being in the SAS demanded. Brian, however, had found an ability that had never surfaced in all his years at school: his memory was exceptional, for facts and faces. It was only as part of the Recce Platoon when he was tasked with drawing up plans for the Company that his skill came to the fore. He was able to reproduce on paper what he had learned from a Close Target Recce to the smallest degree. His attention to detail was such that whatever he wrote was accepted by his senior officers, who had no hesitation in entrusting their men in an action based entirely on his Operation Order. It was from there that he had been selected for Intelligence work in the Special Forces.

Adam's call was answered on the third ring. They hadn't spoken for over a week and spent a minute catching up on some gossip. Brian had heard from a mutual friend of theirs.

'Bri, something has come up, unpaid but rewarding work that I am going to do and I really need your skills. I don't know how you'll feel about it but what if I run you through everything and then you can decide, in or out?'

The last phrase, 'in or out', was one they laughed at and which they had first used when under enemy fire and trapped in a small alley in Baghdad. Rounds were thundering into a wall, shattering the bricks and mud that covered their exact location: 'What do you think, Bri?' Adam had asked as he crouched by the dust-covered bricks. Brian had looked around him, shrugged his shoulders. 'It's a two-second run to the wall,' he had indicated with his arm, 'another two seconds to jump and fall over. At least six feet high that wall, the ragheads won't make it. It leads to another alley, then gardens, through a house and into the street, meet up with the rest of the lads. Next time a magazine is changed by them we do it ... In or out?' They had nodded in agreement. Then, hearing the click of the empty magazine, they had leapt to their feet from a crouch and covered the distance and wall before the enemy could react. Ever since, when an important decision had to be made the question had been asked.

Brian heard the question and immediately he felt the excitement, a quick rush, an extra heartbeat.

'Meet in the boozer, seven tonight?'

'Fine, see you,' replied Adam, closing the connection.

As usual, Brian was the first to arrive and had already grabbed the corner table away from the main door and bar area. He had his back against the wall and had moved the other chair to the side next to him. Adam wouldn't want to sit with his back to the door either. The pub itself was in the town centre but had never in their experience been busy. From the outside it had a neglected appearance and that was confirmed in the bar where a spot of modernization had been due years ago, but it was their pub – its beer was good and they could sit and talk freely without any fear of being overheard.

As Adam walked in he smiled at Brian sitting in his favourite chair and at the pint on the table in front of Adam's chair.

For the next twenty minutes Adam explained the situation faced by Raymond and Sandra and of his own research into the Townsend family, including his meeting with Julie. Brian winced when Adam explained how he had failed to prepare properly but before Adam had said what he intended Brian had anticipated where the conversation was heading.

Brian looked at Adam for over ten seconds before he spoke. 'This means a lot to you, no everything, everything your life's worth, your reputation, your legacy. You are prepared for history to show you as a murderer?'

'I don't see it as murder any more than we were when in the service of our country. We killed then because it was right to do so, to protect innocent people from the murdering bullies, but after all we've done what has been happening right on our doorstep? Look, mate, as I've shown with meeting Julie, I'm crap without your support but I will give it a go anyway.'

'Yeah, you're right,' said Brian with a smile, 'you are crap without me.'

Adam returned the smile. 'Your brains are what I need, but are you OK with …' He looked at Brian's hand that rested by his glass on the table. Even from only two feet away it was difficult to see it was a prosthetic.

'Yeah, I'm fine but one condition though,' – he paused – 'it has to be done properly, no short cuts, no winging it and certainly no more meetings with Julie. God, Adam, you didn't have a clue about her. She could be involved with them or people close to them, whatever.'

Adam held up his hands in surrender. 'All agreed.' He finished his beer, grabbed both glasses and refilled them at the bar.

For the remainder of the evening they sat close together discussing their plans and the logistics of carrying them out. They agreed actions for each to undertake and that Brian's home would be their operating centre. Adam hadn't wanted that at first but had agreed after Brian had shared a secret with him, that he had built a false wall in his loft behind which he kept various pieces of equipment that he had retained when he had left the Army. The equipment didn't include any firearms – those were too dangerous to have retained and would have possibly drawn attention to other missing equipment which was more valuable. In response, Adam had disclosed that he knew of three soldiers from their original platoon who had stolen a gun each some years ago and then sold to people they knew in their home towns. Brian was amazed that Adam hadn't told him before.

Julie decided she had to make a decision and she made it. She checked her watch. Eleven o'clock on a Sunday morning. It was very unlikely that Keith would be at church so she rang his mobile. It went through to voicemail so Julie left a message just asking him to call her. Within a minute her mobile rang and she saw that it was from Keith.

'Hi, Keith.'

'Julie, how's it going?' Julie heard the voice and for a second wondered if she had called the right number. The voice had aged but it also sounded strange, tired … Maybe it was a hung-over voice.

'Yes fine, things are good with me. How about you?'

'Ha ha, well, it could be worse. Betty's gone, taken the kids and the magazine decided they didn't want any more work from me. So all alone and no job. Betty wants the house sold so she can buy back in Brighton or Worthing, somewhere in that area anyway. So, what's the reason for your call?'

Julie told him about her dinner date with Charlie and her concerns.

'Why don't you ask your editor? He knows the bloody family, doesn't he?' Keith said in response to Julie's 'What should I do?' question.

'Thanks, Keith,' she said angrily. 'Thanks a bunch. I rang you because I know you have integrity. You're honest. I daren't say anything at work. You know what it's like – a word and the Townsends could know about it within minutes. I've rung you for advice, because I have respect for you but maybe I was just wrong about you. What is it, Keith? Everything gone wrong with the world or are you on the booze? No, don't bother to answer that, your voice tells me the answer.'

She closed her mobile and immediately swore to herself. That was unkind. Keith had never recovered from the run-in with the Townsends; his work was suddenly marked as not being up to scratch by the then subeditor and he was 'allowed' to leave. He'd always been a drinker, she acknowledged, most crime reporters were. He hadn't been able to find any peace in Sussex and had moved to Wales with Betty and their three children. Now she had gone with the kids and the magazine job had come to an end. Julie suspected that Keith was more often drunk than sober these days.

Her mobile rang and a contrite-sounding Keith said: 'Sorry, Julie, I was out of order. I'm bitter, that's for sure. Sometimes I just wallow and hit the bottle for a day or two, then of course regret it. I'm OK now. So, your question what to do? Julie, the Townsends are really bad news. You are not to get involved with anything to do with them, nothing at all. Give me Charlie's number and I'll ring him. You forget everything, make an alibi for Friday evening, wipe your mobile, computer and memory clean of Charlie. Deny everything even in a year's time.'

Julie have him Charlie's number and thanked Keith before wishing him well. She reflected on the call. She had done something at least and Keith was probably right to say that she should forget everything.

Adam had spent the whole of the morning exercising. He ran the same route over thirty seconds quicker then returned to his room on his cycle by a twenty-mile route that encompassed both road and bridleways before completing his press and sit-ups. He showered and dressed, feeling some aches in his body but overall he was enjoying the exercise. He checked his mobile and wasn't expecting to see any calls, so was surprised to see that he had a missed call from an unknown number. There was no voicemail. He returned the call and it was answered by a male voice.

'Hi,' said Adam brightly. 'I'm sorry I missed your call earlier. How can I help you?' He was secretly hoping it wasn't a call from someone he had called on wanting a small job doing.

'Is that Charlie?'

Adam's brain quickly adjusted to his persona. 'Yes, hello. I'm sorry, I don't recognise the voice.'

'I was given your number by an old friend who I think you met on Friday.'

Cagey, thought Adam, no mention of Julie's name.

'It was thought that I could perhaps be of some help to you, though I doubt it.'

'You have me at a disadvantage, I'm afraid. I don't know who you are.'

'You're asking questions about a family that I knew. My name's Keith, not necessary to mention my last. Now who are you and what's your game?'

'Keith, yes. I hoped that maybe my interest was explained to you.' Adam replied, thinking that they were close to a stalemate. 'Look, can we meet? It's easier to talk face to face.'

Keith gave a chuckle. 'And why should I want to meet with you, given the subject you are apparently interested in? What's in it for me, I wonder? Nothing good, maybe a lot of trouble. Maybe you want to find me for some reason. Maybe there is still a score to settle, maybe anything. All I know is that I get a call out of the blue.'

'Listen,' Adam interrupted, deciding that the stalemate had to be broken now. 'Last week I read a lot of papers that are kept by an old man, name of Ray from outside of Crawley, an old man and his wife who suffered terribly four years ago. I met his daughter who loves and cares for him. You will remember them, I'm sure. You wrote several articles about the assault and murder. You were the driving force against the bastards at the time, but the police cocked up, and shortly afterwards you left Brighton.'

Adam heard the laugh at the other end of the phone. 'Police cocked up! police cocked up,' he repeated. 'The police didn't cock it up – don't believe that! It was done exactly as they wanted. Enough to satisfy the public, an apology for an unfortunate mistake, then in the classic phrase, "move on". It wasn't a cock-up, Charlie, or whoever you are.' Keith was about to shut the call when Adam replied.

'That's just it, the injustice of it all, to everyone. Last week the son was found not guilty of a bad assault on a lad. Ray saw it and it brought it all back to him. The son found not guilty because his parents lied in court. People are still being affected by this family. What happened to you? You didn't leave of your own accord, did you?'

There was silence as Keith thought about what Adam had said. He identified anger in the voice, genuine rather than put on. He thought about what Julie had told him and made his decision. He agreed to meet with Adam and they made arrangements for the next day at the eating area of the westbound Membury service station on the M4. They each gave a description of what they would be wearing for the other to recognise.

Adam decided to use the rental car for the whole week, during which time he would buy one of his own, though he wouldn't use his correct identity. He arrived at the services twenty minutes before the agreed time of eleven o'clock. He was wearing his worn brown leather jacket over a red V-neck jumper and blue jeans. He was also wearing an old plain-black baseball-style cap with a long peak and carried a rolled-up newspaper. After walking through the eating area where he had arranged to meet with Keith he visited the toilets and retraced his steps back to his car. As he arrived at the car he fiddled with the keys and appeared to inspect the bodywork on the driver's door, slowly wiping his hand across the paint. In fact, he was using the glass and the side mirror to see if anybody was taking any interest in him. He opened the door and leant in towards the back seat. He moved his hands as if adjusting or moving something then turned back to give himself a direct view towards the entrance of the building. He instantly recognised Keith Mendip as he made his way into the building. He scanned the people standing nearby: only a very obese man was still in the same place as when Adam had exited the building. The man stubbed out his cigarette on a metal wall ashtray then slowly walked away towards where a coach was parked. Adam locked the car and moved into the building where he saw Keith Mendip sitting in the eating area.

Adam walked up to him and the men shook hands before Adam sat down opposite Keith. He looked around the area, noting the people who had been there previously and whether they were still eating and drinking or just sitting there.

Mendip said, 'I have an issue of trust with you, Charlie, if indeed that is your name. I don't know you and from my searching the Internet I can't find you as an author or a journalist. You have never been registered with any association or union, nor is there any work published under that name. You're not Charlie Wright, are you?'

'No, that's just a name. My name isn't important really, but I can understand your concern. I need to speak with you and was blocked by the newspaper. Someone said that you had retired, with no forwarding address or other information available. I used Julie to try and learn what I want to know but, and I think she did well: she gave nothing away except for what I can read on the Internet and old newspapers. I can understand why nobody would want to talk about the Townsends – they radiate fear – but I'm not scared of them and I mean them harm. That's why I don't want to use my real name. I am not interested in learning anything about you, Keith. I just want this meeting for me to learn what I need, then we need never speak or see each other again.'

'Harm?' Mendip asked, quietly looking around him.

'Harm,' repeated Adam as from the corner of his eye he saw a single man finish a cup of drink and leave his table. 'I don't want to go into details, for obvious reasons.'

'Well, if you are genuine, there's nothing to stop you doing them harm, is there? Say to the son, he's always at the night clubs in Brighton.' Mendip stared directly into Adam's eyes.

'It's the dad I really want. I want to remove him and his influence from the scene before I look to the others.'

'I'll tell you what I am prepared to do, Charlie, or whoever you are. You do what you have to to the son and then I'll contact you and tell you about the rest of them. I'll be interested to hear how serious a person you are. Until then I'm saying nothing.'

Keith Mendip immediately stood up and walked away without a backward glance, taking Adam by surprise. Adam stood and watched as Mendip walked around the back of the building. Ten seconds later a battered blue car drove away with high revs and blue smoke showing from the exhaust.

6

Adam returned to his room and over the next two days devoted his mornings to exercise, followed by a train journey to Brighton where he shopped in the afternoons and walked around the streets identifying the various nightclubs and their locations. The third day he arrived in Brighton just after lunchtime and after studying the free paper he took a taxi to an address on an estate where he bought an old Saab car with over a hundred thousand miles recorded on the odometer from a middle-aged woman. He was careful when he bought the car to remember the parts he touched during the inspection and immediately when he was out of sight of the house he put on a pair of thin black leather gloves. The cash he had obtained from the bank and when he gave it to the woman to count there had been two notes too many. He retrieved the top and bottom notes. Those would have had his fingerprints on.

He returned the hire car earlier than planned and took a taxi to a street three away from Brian's house. He was surprised at how many anti-surveillance and chain breaking methods he remembered and how quickly he was falling back into thinking along his military experience lines.

Brian answered the door wearing his usual tan-coloured cord trousers with a thick brush-cotton tartan-patterned shirt buttoned to the top. They shook hands before Brian led the way upstairs to the landing, where he retrieved a metal pole from inside a cupboard. He used the end of the pole to undo the hatch cover to the loft then used the same pole to pull down the metal steps, which glided without any sound to the ground. Brian led the way into the loft, reaching for a string that he pulled to switch a light on. The single bulb was bright and there was only one area that was in some shade. Brian carefully made his way there and moved his hand into a small hole. There was a slight click before a portion of the wall opened towards him. Adam had seen a similar hide before when he had worked with Brian's Intelligence team but was still surprised at how Brian had constructed it. He looked around for signs of brick dust, pieces of mortar or a dropped nail, but there was nothing. He smiled and followed Brian into a small area that ran from the front to the back of the house and was about six feet deep. Given the size of the loft, even a detailed search would have failed to detect the hide, unless they knew what they were looking for. At either end of the hide were shelves made from netting attached to the beams, strong as wood but silent when items were placed on them. Adam scuffed his foot on the floor and looked down.

'Polystyrene chips between the beams packed solid, then rubber one-inch matting on top,' Brian said, smiling.

Adam looked at Brian's right hand. 'And with a prosthetic hand?' he said in amazement.

Brian laughed. 'Yep, you haven't noticed this is a new one. I've got really good movement for the index finger, thumb isn't bad and the other fingers can grip quite well.' He held it up and moved it so that they could both examine the hand.

'And the arm is OK? No problems with that?'

'No, the arm's just fine. The muscle is never going to be the same again obviously but it works with the hand just fine for lighter work,' said Brian cheerfully.

'You know, I forget about your injury. It's just on some occasions that I remember but you've just adapted so well it honestly isn't noticeable'

Adam looked at the long table that ran the length of the space. It too was covered with the same type of rubber sheeting as was on the floor. On it stood a computer, some paper, a printer, clips and other paraphernalia.

Adam walked to a netting shelf and examined some of the items: various night viewing pieces of equipment, rifle sights, infrared lights and markers, small tracking devices attachable by magnet, sticky tape or clip on, listening devices of different types and sizes, relaying signal beacons, door lock opening sets and cameras of both covert and overt ability. All were in their original packaging and Adam recognised them as being first-class pieces that he had used before. He knew that each piece was selected for its reliability.

'Fully equipped operational centre at your service,' said Brian.

Adam laughed. 'No wonder the bloody MOD overspend when this lot has been pilfered.'

'Just a few bits and pieces that I thought I could lend out to mates. You remember Geoff? Well, he's got one of my cameras at the moment, doing some private work for a husband to catch the wife with her toy boy. He's doing well, operating out of Reigate, just up the road.'

Adam remembered Geoff. He and Brian had both been injured in the same incident and while Brian had lost a hand outright and suffered horrendous burns to his chest and neck Geoff had probably suffered more, losing a leg as well as an arm. Adam liked Geoff, whom he had met frequently while Brian and he had worked their way together through hospital then rehab.

'OK,' said Adam, 'let's bring you right up to date.'

For the next two days Adam spent the time walking around the countryside that surrounded the Townsend house. This was situated on the northern outskirts of Brighton and was of mock tudor style. He kept at least a quarter of a mile away and at times had lain flat on the grass using scarce bushes for cover as he examined the ground surrounding the house. He took photographs in the morning from the east and then in the afternoon from the west to give a fuller perspective to what he was seeing. The main two-storey house was set back from the road by a hundred yards, with the front facing the road. At the front of the house was grass that was cut, bisected by a sweeping driveway that led to two large wrought-iron gates that appeared to be electronically operated. The perimeter was marked by a mixture of four-feet-high brick walls topped with three-feet metal railings at the front and both sides, while at the back – which faced open countryside – was six-feet chain-link fencing with four-feet-high *leylandii* trees planted inside to form a hedge. Outside the front gates was an area of scrub grass from the wall to the road. There was a double garage to the right side of the house as viewed from the front and a barn structure to the left and slightly behind the house. From the rear Adam could make out a patio area close to the centre of the house with a covered gazebo next to a swimming pool, which was covered with a blue plastic cover. There was a small brick built building near the pool that had a glass frontage. Adam guessed that it was a summerhouse and changing area, with the pool filtration system at the back. He wondered if the pool was heated, or just for show. There were no large trees on the land but some smaller specimens had obviously been planted to act as a screen to the left side of the house. He and Brian pored over the photographs that Adam had taken, working out where they might best position the cameras that they intended to install so that they could watch the happenings at the house from a safe distance. From the outset Brian had said that they would have to expect that, firstly, the police would probably have installed similar watching devices and, secondly, the Townsend family would be aware of such surveillance. This made Adam's job more difficult trying to second-guess the actions of the family as well as the police. By the third evening they had their plan and Adam spent the night confirming their selected positions while Brian acted as support from his car a mile away, ready to pick up Adam if he got into trouble.

On the fourth night, exactly as forecasted, the rain was heavy with the moon hidden behind heavy clouds. This was perfect. Moving in a circle clockwise from the front of the building, and never closer than a quarter of a mile away, Adam carefully positioned a camera to give a view towards each of the four corners of the house. He set up a fifth camera that gave a closer view of people at the back of the house. This was the higher-risk position that entailed him crawling forward to the edge of the wire fence and digging the camera into the ground so that only the lens could be seen. A wire to remotely transmit the picture was disguised as a thin piece of wood then attached to a trunk of a *leylandii* tree. From the car Brian was able to see each picture appear on his small receiver and confirm with Adam that the camera gave them the picture they had decided on. The pictures needed to be relayed to Brian's attic, which was over twenty-two miles away, but they were delighted when they viewed the results: the picture quality was even better than they had hoped.

During the following evenings they used the handheld monitor as they sat in their cars a half-mile away, watching the coming and goings from the house. They were able to follow the son Kieran, who had a routine of leaving his house around nine o'clock, a quarter of an hour after two other men arrived at the house. The route taken by Kieran Townsend when he left the house was down Dyke Road, to the city and the seafront. The first night they followed Kieran to the area known as Seven Dials, where seven roads meet at a small roundabout. It was while they were held in traffic that they decided to pull out of their surveillance of Kieran, as they knew that there was a strong chance of their being discovered if they continued. The following night Adam spotted Kieran leaving the house and used his mobile to tell Brian, who was waiting at the junction, that Kieran was heading towards him. Prior to the junction Adam took a side road and made his way down to the London Road that ran parallel, allowing Brian to make the surveillance at the roundabout. Brian saw Kieran take an exit and was able to keep four vehicles between him and Kieran for over two minutes until a junction where his covering cars took a turn towards the London Road. Brian told Adam of Kieran's last location and they divided the streets into a grid for a street-by-street search.

An hour later Brian radioed that he had found Kieran's car parked among others in a small side street.

The following night Adam and Brian were already in position when Kieran's car arrived and the three occupants got out and walked towards the bar and club area, hogging the pavement as they swaggered along, forcing other pedestrians into the road. Several times they physically shoved a person from their path and laughed as the victim was sent into the road. Adam and Brian discussed their options and arrived at a decision, after which Adam returned to his car while Brian returned to his house.

Kieran Townsend was drunk as usual at one in the morning in the nightclub, shouting to his friends above the incessant beat of the music and trying to invite a particular girl to his table. She had been flirting with him but, knowing his reputation, had resisted his advances on the dance floor and invitations to join him at the table, instead preferring the attention of another man who wasn't associated with Kieran. She and the other man danced together for the next hour during which time neither paid any attention to Kieran or any of the others at his table. Kieran was drinking yet another bottle of champagne all the while fixing his eyes on the girl.

'Slag!' he shouted towards her, though his words wouldn't have carried even halfway in the noise created by the music.

Two of his friends laughed. 'Yeah, slag!' shouted one of them.

Kieran got to his feet and unsteadily wound his way towards her. This was spotted by her dancing companion, who leant in towards her and shouted something in her ear. She swung her head round to see Kieran staring at her and raising his arm. His fist was balled and before she could move Kieran punched her in the middle of her face. Blood shot from her nose and mouth area as she stumbled and fell backwards. Her companion managed to grab her under her shoulders and was holding her when he received a similar punch to his face. He crumpled to the floor and fell over the body of the girl.

'Slag!' shouted Kieran at the girl as he walked around the two bodies towards the foyer, where he was joined by the two friends who rushed to congratulate him with pats on his back.

Kieran saw the dinner-jacketed door supervisor in the foyer, who was looking past Kieran at the commotion at the other side of the dance area.

'Sorry about that, Pete,' Kieran slurred. 'I'll see you right if you square it, OK?'

Pete had known Kieran for over three years through his work at clubs in Brighton and had previously cleaned up and sorted out problems Kieran had created. He didn't like Kieran but was aware that not only would he be in trouble with Kieran's father if he didn't manage to brush the incident under the carpet, but he would be losing out on his reward for helping Kieran.

'Sure, Kieran, no problem,' he said. 'Compo for them?'

'Yeah, she can have a grand, but nothing for him,' Kieran said as he negotiated the steps to the street with a friend on either side. They walked unsteadily along several streets and seeing a CCTV camera pointing towards them Kieran raised his hand and extended his centre finger.

'Swivel, you prats,' he shouted at the camera, while his friends joined in with similar signals and words. They turned the street corner laughing, failing to notice a shadow in a doorway and a hand crashing down on the neck of one of Kieran's friends. A split second later the other friend fell to the ground, having also been struck on the back of his neck. Kieran looked towards the first friend who was just hitting the pavement and was about to turn to look at the second friend when he was grabbed around the neck, pulled nearly off his feet and thrown to the back of the doorway. He landed on the floor dazed, his mind trying to react through the haze of alcohol and the confusion of what was happening to him. Any train of thought he had tried to start was interrupted by the bodies of his two friends being thrown in next to him. He could make out a man wearing dark clothes who looked very big in every way. He saw the man lean down to him and felt the hands around his neck, thumbs poised to push in his wind wipe. The man sat on Kieran's chest pinning his arms against his side and restricting any movement. He leant forward.

'You are going to die in about a minute. I'm going to press my thumbs into your windpipe and cut off your breathing. You will be gasping for breath and your head will hurt. You will hear a ringing sound and then you will fall into unconsciousness and die. Now, Kieran, I want you to think of the old man and lady you and the other four tortured before you killed her. You do remember them, Kieran, don't you?'

Kieran's eyes opened slightly as he remembered the night.

'You were laughing. What were you, nineteen or twenty, laughing as the old lady was dying? Well, Kieran, I'm laughing now, so is the old man. He's been thinking of you and your dad. Now, Kieran, think hard about the old lady, think of her!'

The thumbs pressed together and Kieran tried to shut his eyes to focus his efforts on breathing but was unable to. His eyes showed the fear that he felt. There was a sound and Kieran's bowels emptied. The thumbs were held in place for a full minute before releasing the neck. There wasn't any pulse.

The man stood and looked slowly out of the doorway, noting that a CCTV camera fifty yards away was still pointing in the opposite direction. He knew the route he was to walk and he started along the pavement. He hunched his back slightly and held his hands into the pockets of the oversized overcoat pulling the sides out to make the width appear greater. He walked with a pronounced limp and at a slower pace than normal. His hat was pulled low down on to his face as he used the edge of the pavement to guide him along the route.

7

'Anything happening?'

'Fairly quiet, Sarge. A couple of minor scuffles on the seafront, a robbery outside the pier and a couple of domestics. Nothing very much, in fact quite boring,' replied the controller as she moved her joystick, adjusting one of the many CCTV cameras in Brighton city centre.

'Sarge, I think I've got it,' said a voice from another position.

'Come on, Geordie, another of your brilliant ideas?'

'Good one this time, Sarge. We should attach a gun to the cameras, then, when we get shits like Kieran Townsend giving us the finger and shouting at us, we shoot him straight between his eyes. Then – and this is the best bit, Sarge – we show it on television, a special programme put out twice a year: his last minute on God's planet – a winner.'

'Jesus, Geordie, you just get worse,' the Sergeant said with a chuckle.

'If any political party include the idea in their manifesto, they'd be winners without any doubt at the next election,' said Geordie with another laugh. 'You could do a voiceover: "Happy Christmas, Kieran."'

'OK, that's enough, Geordie. Let's concentrate on what we're doing. It's still two weeks before Christmas. Let's keep on top of things and try to prevent someone's Christmas being ruined,' said the Sergeant, bringing an end to the chat.

Geordie made another sweep with his cameras over the area he had last seen Townsend in without finding him or his friends. There was just a fat old man in a large overcoat and hat limping painfully away towards the side streets north of the town centre.

Adam reached his car fifteen minutes after leaving the doorway. He opened the car boot and put his overcoat, gloves and hat into a black rubbish sack and placed it in the boot. His drive towards his home was uneventful while he replayed the evening in his mind, trying to find a mistake that he could still rectify. He checked his watch and saw that it was past three o'clock. He pulled off the main road and parked his car. He got out and pushed the door to without closing it properly. Although the nearest house was over fifty yards away he didn't want to be seen. He stood still for five minutes, allowing his eyes to adjust to the darkness and his hearing to the silence. He walked on the sides of his soles checking the ground as he passed some houses and bungalows. He knew exactly where he was and turned down the driveway to the bungalow, crossing the grass to get to the front door. He knew he hadn't made a sound but he still looked around before gently pushing the plastic letter flap sufficiently for a small piece of paper he retrieved from his other pocket to be slipped through the gap. He retraced his steps to the car then drove home by using side roads avoiding the cameras that he had mentally marked into a plan in his head. He knew he had just been reckless and unprofessional, acting against all the rules he himself had laid down, but now it was done.

Geordie was puzzled as he again used the cameras to tour the neighbourhood without seeing Kieran or the other two men. He had been working in the CCTV room for over nine years and knew every street and alley in the city, as he widened his search. Such was his experience that he could recognise people from their posture and gait as being regulars in a particular street on their way home and he had seen several people who he regarded as regulars making their way after the clubs had closed. He was particularly concerned about Kieran Townsend, such was his reputation for indiscriminate violence as well as about the two lads with him who also had previous convictions for assaults.

What, he wondered, were they up to now? An innocent person could have become their latest victim.

'Well, twenty minutes to change over, lads and lassies, so let's start to get ready for the early-birds,' called the Sergeant. 'Well done, everyone. It's been a good night and I think our sharp eyes prevented several incidents from escalating, so a good job.'

There were a few comments as the early shift made their way to their respective bank of consoles and the night shift were happily vacating their seats. Geordie was ready to leave as soon as his replacement arrived, his desk now cleared of his sandwich wrappings, his notebook and pen in the desk drawer. It was then that he saw something moving on one of the screens. It wasn't an animal – the movement was different. He moved the camera and began to examine the street again more slowly. He saw it, movement in a doorway, just the back of someone. He zoomed in and saw the person appeared to be a man, younger than thirty – was he drunk? If so, he might have vomited in the doorway. Disgusting article, Geordie thought. 'Right, mister,' he said under his breath, at the same time opening the link to the Operations Room where he relayed to the controller what he was seeing. A police officer was diverted to investigate.

PC Thomas was looking forward to finishing the night shift when he received the call. It had been a long cold night walking the streets of that area of Brighton. He would be there in under a minute, he confirmed, and hoped that it wouldn't be something that would detain him from leaving on time at six o'clock. When he arrived in the street Geordie was watching the doorway and had zoomed in sufficiently to recognise the man.

'Sarge,' he called.

The Sergeant arrived and stood near Geordie as he watched the monitor.

'He was with Kieran Townsend and that idiot Shane earlier, when they fingered at us around the corner. Why's he been there? No wonder I couldn't find them.'

He updated the controller to let PC Thomas know the identity of the man, and to exercise caution.

PC Thomas approached the doorway quietly with one finger on the transmit button of his radio. Although he knew he was being watched by the CCTV camera operator were he to be attacked, he wanted to put a shout for assistance that would be instantly heard. He saw two pairs of legs lying in the doorway with a figure crouched over obscuring the view of whom they belonged to.

'What's going on?' said PC Thomas in a loud voice.

The hunched figure slowly turned towards PC Thomas, who recognised him as being a youth named Ryan, only his eyes appeared dazed, his movements slow.

'It's Kieran and Shane.'

PC Thomas got a view of the two prone men. Both appeared to be unconscious. The constable relayed exactly what he was seeing and being told, and was informed that paramedics would be with him in less than five minutes. Ryan slumped back against the door of the shop, his head hitting the glass and instantly set off the burglar alarm, taking both him and PC Thomas by surprise. Ryan covered his ears and lay down crying while PC Thomas retreated around the corner of the street to lessen the impact of the noise as he used his radio again. The sound of the bell ringing was incessant as he waited for the paramedics to arrive. He was alerted to their arrival, which came sooner than expected, by the blue strobe reflecting from buildings and he showed himself at the doorway where Ryan and his friends were. The two paramedics walked to the doorway where they were unable to communicate except by hand signals to each other but they managed to move Ryan from the doorway and lay him on the ground where PC Thomas had been standing. One paramedic stayed with him while the other returned to the doorway. PC Thomas was watching the paramedic attending to Ryan when the other returned to him.

'One of them is dead,' he shouted. 'The other is unconscious and needs to be got to the hospital.'

PC Thomas relayed the message, hoping for guidance. The cardinal rule when a dead body is found is to preserve the scene as much as possible and to keep the witnesses where they can be interviewed. The two paramedics were lifting Ryan on to a stretcher and strapping him in as PC Thomas waited for instructions. Once Ryan was in the ambulance, they lifted Shane into a chair and strapped him in.

'Got to go,' said the paramedic. 'They are both in quite a bad way. Are you coming?'

PC Thomas was anxious to get away from the noise and knew that someone would need to be with the two injured people as they were taken to hospital. Just then more blue lights appeared and effectively closed the road, though no traffic had passed along it for the past hours.

PC Thomas received instructions that he was to remain at the scene with the dead man while another officer was deputed to travel in the ambulance. No names were to be used over the radios, as nobody wanted Mr Townsend senior throwing his weight around. The CID would be attending, the street would be cordoned off and the key holder would turn off the alarm. PC Thomas crossed his arms, took a look at Kieran Townsend and muttered 'Happy Christmas' before turning his back on him.

Raymond Black was up and passing through the hallway towards the kitchen when he noticed the piece of paper by the front door. He continued to the kitchen where he put the kettle on, while making his way to the toilet he picked up the paper. It was typewritten on one side: 'Watch the news for Brighton. Happy Christmas.' He read the words again, then turned the paper over to check that there wasn't something else that he had missed. Ten minutes later he was sitting in his armchair sipping his tea and smoking a freshly rolled cigarette watching the local news. There wasn't anything that interested him. He threw the piece of paper into the fire ashes in preparation for his lighting the fire an hour later when he was dressed.

It was just after ten o'clock in the morning when Adam, sweating in his T-shirt and running bottoms, knocked on Brian's door. On seeing Adam struggling to recover his breath, Brian laughed and walked back towards his kitchen at the end of the hallway, at the back of the house.

'Hope you ran hard,' he said over his shoulder, 'or are you just really out of shape?'

Adam didn't answer but followed Brian into the kitchen and helped himself to a slice of toast covered with strawberry jam that Brian had just finished preparing prior to opening the front door.

'Help yourself, won't you?' said Brian with a grin.

Adam bit into the toast and managed to give a thumbs-up at the same time.

Ten minutes later they were settled into the canvas chairs in their operation centre as Adam told Brian exactly what had happened, down to the smallest detail.

'So you were right, in every respect,' Adam concluded. 'Kieran did use that route, though I have no idea why.'

Brian shrugged. 'No, but we saw him use it. He liked to park his car in a side street. Maybe he feared he'd be targeted by the police if they saw him driving in the city. Safer to drive away from all the cameras and police patrols, but in any event the hornet's nest has been rattled.'

Adam wondered how Ray and Sandra would greet the news. He regretted posting the note now: gloating wasn't clever and nor was playing the 'big I am'.

They decided that it would be better if Adam left his room and moved into Brian's house, which was only about two miles away across the town of Crawley. The packing took Adam less than an hour and after thoroughly cleaning his room he drove away without a second glance. He had left a note on the table saying he had gone travelling, which he knew the landlord would find the day after the next month's rent was due.

Once Kieran's body had been formally identified by his parents, news of his death was made public by the police, who had launched a murder investigation. People greeted the news in different ways. There were those who telephoned the family house with their condolences and others who sent notes and flowers. Some, though, were pleased with the news and many who were frightened and predicted correctly that Mr Townsend would be blazing mad and people would suffer. By late afternoon Townsend had called in his two most loyal and longstanding friends, whom he took into the garden for a talk. He knew, or was fairly certain, that his house was under surveillance by the police and so it was highly possible that they had managed somehow to place listening devices inside. He and Pat ensured that all their conversations were neutral in their content while in the house; any conversation they regarded as serious always took place in the garden. The preferred spot was close to the summerhouse where the pool pump could be switched on to create a background noise. It was inconvenient, especially in winter or inclement weather, and although Townsend knew he could be viewed there at least he felt he was safe from being listened to.

Townsend and his two friends were huddled together very closely, their arms around each other's shoulders as if offering sympathy, but in fact they were each setting out their plans to find the culprit for Kieran's death and ensure that their summary justice would precede any that the police would take. Townsend and Pat had spent the day with police officers at Brighton police Station giving scant information regarding their son's activities and refusing to cooperate with the investigation if it involved any police going into their house. They had insisted that, if the police wanted to search their son's room for any evidence, then the officer would have to be accompanied at all times by one of them. The police would not be given the opportunity to plant a listening device, a camera or false evidence in their house, he told the officers several times.

Brian and Adam were in the operations room looking at the images being shown on the quarter-divided screen at the side of his desk. All the images were sharp and they were able to watch Townsend and the two men in their huddle.

'Very clever,' said Brian. 'Switching on the pool pump provides background noise and makes it impossible to identify who is saying what, even if they are being recorded. Still, we have time on our side so we can leave them and concentrate on another of the four. I have done some research on the Internet ...' Brian stopped talking as Adam's mobile phone rang.

'Yes,' said Adam, before adding, 'fine,' as he ended the call.

'That was Keith. He's heard about Kieran and is ready to meet. Same location and time as before – so eleven tomorrow.'

The following morning Adam was already seated with a coffee and Danish pastry when Keith Mendip entered the area and fetched himself a coffee. He joined Adam at the table and leant forward to speak, though his voice was quiet.

'Is that what you meant by harm?' he said with a serious expression.

Adam pointed to Keith Mendip's shirtfront and indicated it should be opened. Mendip looked about him before undoing several buttons knowing the reason was to ensure no listening device was being worn. Pockets were emptied without drawing attention from other customers.

Satisfied, Adam said, 'Harm comes in many ways .... Apart from his parents, I doubt Kieran will be missed. Will you give me the background information now?'

Keith studied Adam before letting out a sigh. 'That's why I'm here. No notes, and I'd prefer it if we spoke in my car rather than here. I don't want to be seen, even if the chances are minimal. I gather Dad isn't in the best of moods at the moment.'

Adam followed Keith Mendip out to his old blue Mondeo. Adam made a search of the interior of the car, though he knew the chances of his finding a professionally installed device were just about zero. For the following two hours Adam listened as Mendip gave a detailed account of the Townsend family, their friends and criminal associates. He also told Adam to not ask questions regarding the family in Brighton as they had their tentacles in many areas. He finished by telling Adam the name of the still-serving but shortly-to-retire police officer whom Keith suspected of having helped the Townsends for many years. 'He's a Detective Chief Inspector now and from all accounts he has been a bloody good detective over the years, but I was once told that he used to receive information from an unknown source, always reliable, and by coincidence, always against another established criminal who Townsend had had some conflict with. Coincidence stretches only so far … This DCI may be involved with the investigation into Kieran's death so don't be surprised if Dad gets ahead in trying to find whoever' – he raised his fingers and made quotation signs – 'harmed little Kieran. And of course you will have read from the paper article I wrote that he was leading the enquiry into Mrs Black's murder when it folded.'

Adam thanked Keith for all the information, which he said would be useful. As Adam left the car, they agreed not to contact each other again unless it was important or they needed to warn the other.

Adam arrived at Brian's house mid-afternoon to find a piece of paper on the floor next to the coffee table in the lounge. The paper on the floor was their code for saying that the other was in the operations room; on the table meant that they weren't in the house. Adam joined Brian in the operations room and saw twelve new mobile phones all still in their boxes on the table beside the computer keyboard that Brian was typing furiously on.

'The police have had six beatings in the past twenty-four hours reported to them,' Brian said without looking up. 'All show signs of having been tortured in some way but all six have refused to say anything. They're all in hospital under armed guard, though why I'm not sure. If they've been tortured and released by Townsend's men, they couldn't have known anything, could they? I'm bloody sure if they said something that implicated themselves or someone else, they wouldn't have been released.'

Adam sat down and tried to read over Brian's shoulder but Brian was scrolling down too quickly. Adam leant back in his chair, closed his eyes and recounted to Brian what Keith Mendip had told him. Brian made notes on the computer. When Adam had finished Brian looked at the screen and told Adam that he needed an hour to get everything into order during which time Adam could prepare their dinner.

When Adam called Brian to the table and served the spaghetti and meatballs in tomato sauce, Brian spread four sheets of paper between them.

'Let's forget about Target 1 for the moment – Mr Townsend – and concentrate on the others. What we know from Keith and what I've found on the Internet is that Target 2 is Lenny Townsend, forty-six years of age, older brother of Geoff Townsend. Lenny is a nasty piece of work, though not as bad as his younger brother. He now lives in Spain, outside Málaga, living the quiet life. He has a bar or restaurant in the town called Nerja up the coast an hour or so from Málaga and I think he may be divorced. I've got to check up on that. Target 3 has to be Jackie Smith, thirty-four years old, single with a child of four, a girl. Father is Mr Townsend,' – Brian gave a large smile knowing that Adam would be surprised – 'Again, I've only had a quick look but I think Keith is right when he said that she controls girls, prostitution and shoplifting. She looks a nasty piece of work in her own right, especially from the account of what she did to Mrs Black. Target 4 is Gregory Williams, fifty-three years old and an old friend of

Lenny Townsend's, as Keith said. They are like brothers, involved in crime from their teenage years – along with Geoff, of course. Williams was living with his wife but the latest electoral register shows just her at the address and he hasn't died, so I will have to find him. Shouldn't be difficult.'

Adam thought while he finished his meal. 'So what's our next step? Do we concentrate on one or try and find out and plan against them all?'

'There's a lot of work to be done. What we don't want to do is alert either the police or the others as to why one of them has been killed. It would also be worth considering if we couldn't manage for at least the next one to die in more "natural" circumstances. I don't know how, just thinking out loud,' said Brian.

Adam asked Brian as to what was happening at Townsend's house and was told that it was very quiet. There had been few visitors, though one of the two men they had seen previously in the huddle by the summerhouse was a constant visitor. They always followed the routine as before, going outdoors and walking around or standing close to each other and talking.

Adam smiled. 'Wouldn't it be great to bring down his empire piece by piece, so he knows he's doomed.'

Brian nodded. 'We could do that I think; we can give it some thought. Adam, fancy a trip to Spain, take a look at Lenny's place and his setup?'

'Yeah, sure,' replied Adam. 'You've got enough to do here. If I go alone, we can make progress more quickly.'

Pat looked at Geoff Townsend and indicated with her head that she wanted to talk outside. They were both in a bad mood and, for the same reason, they had been told by 'Dutch', their regular visitor, that, although six people had been abducted and 'spoken to harshly', as Dutch had put it, no one seemed to have any idea of who was behind the murder. Dutch had also been in contact with their 'plod', as they all called their friendly Detective Chief

Inspector, who luckily for them was working as deputy Senior Investigating Officer on Kieran's murder investigation. He had told Dutch that all the police efforts had been to trace the large man captured on CCTV leaving the area, but unfortunately all their work had so far produced nothing: the man had walked away from any CCTV coverage. Checks were being made of all the vehicles seen on the road that night after Kieran and his friends had been captured on Geordie's CCTV camera. Every owner was to be traced and interviewed. All CCTV footage from the railway station and bus station had been seized and, together with shop CCTV footage, were being held for examination as and when manpower allowed.

Pat held a hand over her mouth when she spoke in a whisper. 'What is going on? Who is the fat old man, Geoff?'

'Plod hasn't a clue, and Dutch says that by now something should have been picked up by one of his men. He's spoken to Jackie. Her girls are on board asking around as well but nothing – which makes me think.'

'What?' asked Pat

'Who did it and why? Whoever it was knew what they were doing. Shane and Ryan can be a handful but Plod says a single blow to each of them put them out. They think that a similar but softer blow was then given to Kieran. Then all three were dragged into the doorway and Kieran was murdered … expertly. They say that it could have taken a minute or so. It was coldblooded. Because of the pressure on his windpipe he couldn't have spoken. So he was singled out. Shane and Ryan could have been murdered as well but they were spared. Pat, he was targeted. Dutch says that the fight in the club isn't connected and I think that he's right about that. There wouldn't have been the time, so we haven't a clue who did it or why Kieran was murdered.'

Pat said slowly and quietly. 'When you find out I want to be there to see him. I want to watch what happens to him.'

Geoff wasn't surprised in the least to hear what Pat said. She had always been aware of what he did, the methods he used, and when he was in prison she continued to keep up the family's reputation. She had carried messages to and from Geoff to Dutch and others, and all those she spoke to knew that she would report back to Geoff if any instruction from her were not obeyed. Kieran might be dead and vengeance would be sweet, but she knew also that the business had to continue and their reputation must be upheld. Any pretender to Geoff's throne had to be ruthlessly crushed. To many she appeared as a pleasant woman, smiling and always generous with her time and energy, but to the police she was a spiteful and vicious woman whose loyalty to Geoff was supreme, no matter what. Even when a police officer had found out about Geoff and Jackie and had made sneering phone calls to her about it, she, in public at least, stood squarely behind her husband. She brazened it out, ignored all the snide comments and letters, and knew that she and Geoff would get through it. They would now.

'Sure, no problem there, my love,' Geoff said, knowing that Pat would not blink an eye when seeing the man slowly and painfully killed. He briefly wondered if she would want to actually kill the man herself.

8

For the six days that Adam had been in Spain the weather had been warm during the day and cool during the nights. It was three days before Christmas when he returned to Brian's house during the evening and the temperature had dropped to several degrees below freezing. Setting down his holdall which was all he had taken to Spain he relaxed in front of the log burning stove, which with the door open generated enough heat for the whole house. He sipped on his whisky and told Brian what he had found out about Lenny in his absence and how things had changed when he returned for Adam's last three days. Brian had produced satellite pictures of Lenny's house obtained from Google Earth and Adam referred to them as he detailed the security arrangements of the villa.

'Bri, it's quite extraordinary. The house as you see is on the side of a hill near the top but not overlooked by anywhere other than the sky unless you managed to abseil down from the actual village. There is an overhang just below the top. Access to the house is by a single track, one hundred yards long, with sides cleared of any plants for thirty yards each side going uphill from the main road. There are cameras at the junction with the road and along the track. More cameras on each corner of the house and two back and front under the guttering moving automatically unless overridden by a person in the house. There's a camera by the entrance gate.' Adam indicated the places on the pictures. 'Around the house, there are walls nine or ten feet high. That entrance gate is the only way in and out. It's wooden, looks strong and is electronically controlled. There's a peephole for physical verification of any visitor and two very narrow slits in the walls to the side. My guess is that's where the security guard will be. The slits are wide enough to shoot from but too narrow for shots to enter. There's no obvious electricity source.'

Brian moved to another photograph and pointed to a row of solar panels within the grounds.

'Yep, guessed as much,' said Adam. 'Callers: none when he wasn't there, a female who stayed the night, the night before last … Staff?' Adam let out a long sigh. 'An older woman who must live in. She came out the day Lenny got back. She was driven in a black Audi four-by-four by a large bald heavy-looking guy. Their car was followed by a Porsche four-by-four with two more heavy-looking guys in the front. The rear windows are tinted so couldn't see anyone there. The woman and bald guy returned a couple of hours later. I got a better look at her then. She must be fifty to fifty-five. She's got white hair and she's maybe overweight, but she was wearing black clothes so we can only judge from her face. She looked miserable, though. Keith said Lenny was the quiet one and thought he was out of crime, relaxing in the sun. The bar is actually a small place but it has a nightclub above that was busy on the Friday and Saturday nights I looked. It's down a side street from the Balcòn de Europa plaza where the Salvador church is. It's quite famous but you wouldn't know that,' he grinned. 'Anyway, in the square there are lots of cafés and bars and the whole area is nice, pedestrianised and busy with tourists during the day. At night after eleven or thereabouts the whole area, the plaza, the streets, was busy with youngsters. Quite a few were Brits; some looked like holidaymakers but some looked as if they lived in Spain. I suppose Lenny makes a few bob from the bar and club, but the house – and the security that goes with it – is just over the top, way more than a bona fide bar owner could afford.' Adam looked at Brian for his opinion.

'As you say,' Brian agreed, 'the security is far more than a bar or nightclub owner would normally have. I've had a peep into the Spanish system and through a contact asked for further searches to be made. Nothing current really is known of him. It's more or a less as Keith said. Lenny has been seen with a couple of known Brit players out there, socializing at their homes, but he isn't in regular contact with them as far as anybody knows, he just appears to be living the quiet life and keeping low. He doesn't seem to have a lot of contact with Geoff either – just a phone call every couple of weeks –but as far as the police here are concerned Lenny is right off their radar. A case perhaps of out of sight and out of mind.'

'How the hell do you know all that?' asked a genuinely surprised Adam.

'Let's say, I still have some old contacts kicking around.'

Adam shook his head and smiled. It was typical of Brian to find a way around any problem.

'OK,' continued Brian, 'a plan. I haven't found Mr Williams yet so let's put him on the back burner for the time being. It's proving to be harder than I would have expected. This leaves us with Jackie and Lenny as options. Jackie is the obvious one in so far that her murder would be connected to Kieran's. I'm pretty certain, which would make it close to home for Geoff and bring on his paranoia. The police would connect the two murders and maybe they would tighten the enquiry around Geoff and his activities. That could hurt his business interests as well.'

'Right, I see where you're coming from, but if we want to really scare Geoff, how about Lenny? If we get to him, Geoff will know that he is vulnerable, so what will he do? He could tighten his security but with whom? New people? He wouldn't dare – too many new faces, any one of which could be a police informer.'

Brian thought for a minute. 'There's lots of merit in your argument. My feeling is I think we should monitor the Spanish investigation better. I know I suggested we make the next one look accidental, but what if it looked like an out-and-out murder. The newshounds from England and Spain would track down all they could; they'd find the dirt and publish it all. There could be a lot of adverse publicity for Geoff, with first his son then his brother being murdered someone will ask if he's next. Or maybe someone with a cynical mind would ask if Geoff killed them or arranged for them to be killed.' He chuckled. 'Your decision, Adam. You know the practicalities of working in Spain better than I do.'

Adam sat there thinking and weighing up the possible outcomes of their next step. His head was upright but his eyes were closed: a position he had used over the years to calm himself and think clearly. As when he was in his previous job there were many options for him to consider, each having repercussions, and it was these that he was weighing up in his mind and trying to put into some sort of logical order. Brian understood what Adam was doing and quietly left him to it, knowing that the answer when it arrived would have been thought through and there would be no going back on it. He knew that, once a course had been set, Adam would move heaven and earth to ensure it was completed.

When he opened his eyes, Adam found Brian had cleared away all the dinner plates and pans. The room was dark with just the light from the hallway casting a sharp line of light across the carpet. Adam saw the piece of paper on the carpet and made his way to the attic operations room. Brian was making notes on a sheet of paper referring to and from the computer screen then looked up at Adam.

'OK, decision time.'

'I think Bri we have time on our side, Lenny and Geoff are there, we can finalise the details of how, when and where to kill them but at least we have some ideas of their movements. Jackie is the tricky one, plus Williams and I think I would like to get them both in the frame next. This could all go wrong and I'd like to have plans in place for them all before we do the next one, it could be that we have to move very quickly. I'm not discounting the police investigation but I'm satisfied that they don't present a threat to us at the moment, nor does Geoff but if we mess up the next one perhaps it will unravel. What if for instance, someone puts two and two together and the answer is Ray Black? OK, we could get him out of the way, a long holiday somewhere, but that would draw attention to him and don't forget he has children and grandchildren.'

'And great-grandchildren, you said Sandra had mentioned. She's a grandmother.' Brian smiled.

'True,' agreed Adam, 'so I would really like to concentrate on finding Williams and taking a look at Jackie. If we can get them lined up, we could perhaps just do them all very quickly, who knows maybe they'll all be together at a party.' Adam laughed.

'Also,' Adam continued, 'we need to think about equipment. I'm sure you have, or can get, everything we need for surveillance but I'm thinking of a weapon. I'd feel happier if I had a Sig with me, and thinking ahead something for a longer shot in case it is needed. I'm not too worried about what I have, but a Sig for preference as we've got to think about possibilities. I can't imagine it will be so easy to get my hands around their necks like Kieran, although that would be my personal preference.'

'I'll make some calls in the morning,' Brian said. 'Now, Williams is off the radar, he's proving elusive. I found an old picture of him in the local newspaper but it's ten years old so no doubt he'll have changed a lot, but other than that there is just no decent trace of him. He does have a bank account, over twenty-three thousand pounds in it, makes a withdrawal of £200 every month, nearly always on the first of the month.' Brian, sensing Adam's growing excitement, raised a hand. 'But the withdrawals are at different banks and at different times of the day, though – the good news – always in Brighton or Hove.'

Adam thought. 'So a thousand possible places spread over twenty-four hours – not too hopeful. Unless, Brian, you can tap in in real time so, supposing I was out and about, you could tell me the minute he withdraws the cash. I just may get lucky.'

Brian shook his head, 'Twelve to twenty-four hours after the withdrawal is the best I can do. Now, Jackie …' Brian pushed a photograph towards Adam. 'Good-looking girl and got a good figure. I see what Geoff saw in her, but she's foul-mouthed and, as we know, a really vicious cow. Lives here in this square.' He put a photograph on the table between them. Adam leaned in then smiled. 'A wine bottle?'

Brian looked at it. 'Yes, the top half anyway. The shape is just like one, isn't it? What we have here at the foreground is the seafront road, the A259, Portslade to the west and Brighton to the east, with parking on both sides of the road, then immediately north of that and running parallel is a type of feeder road that, to use your analogy, takes us to the sides of the wine bottle. There's a large green and gardens in the centre, with roads running north and south both sides of the green.' Brian moved his finger above the photograph. 'Then, as it were the shoulders of the bottle coming together towards the neck, where the roads go north again until they meet the main road at the top – that's Western Road.'

Adam looked at other photographs and identified the 'neck of the bottle' as Palmeira Square with the shoulders and sides as 'Adelaide Crescent'. 'Looks nice,' Adam said.

'Not just "nice", Adam, beautiful, elegant and very expensive. Not to bore you with the details, but built in the 1840 to 1860s in what they call the Regency Victorian/Italianate style. Some of the buildings are Grade II listed and most have been subdivided into flats, but the house we are interested in is here, on the east side and near halfway along this stretch.' Brian indicated a house about halfway up the right side of the 'wine bottle', then produced another photograph of the front of the house. 'This is Smith's house – all of it belongs to her.' He paused and looked at Adam's response, which was as he expected, a look of amazement. 'It has a basement flat with its own entrance directly from the street, then the house itself has a ground floor with the lounge at the front with the two large windows facing on to the street, and the kitchen and dining room at the back. The black front door has an intercom with video facility at the side, all very discreet. Anyway, on the first floor are the bedrooms, three I think, then an upper floor with three smaller rooms and an attic area that I think has been converted into a self-contained two-bedroom flat.'

'How can she afford this? It must be worth millions,' said Adam.

'She paid over two for it with a small mortgage, then had work done, so I guess it is worth a pile. Goes to show what profits there are in drugs, prostitution and shoplifting – not a CV to be proud of, but a lot of money in it.'

Adam looked at all the photographs, noting that every house was painted the same shade of cream or white – it was difficult to tell in the light from the photographs the exact colour. He noted that there were no cars parked alongside the pavements on either the east or west sides but instead in marked spaces around the central grassed area where signs warned that the parking was for permit holders only. In the main, many of the houses had multiple bells by the front door indicating that the house was divided into flats, perhaps four to a house, Adam surmised.

He returned to look at the house. 'Rear exits?'

'None except into neighbouring gardens, though that is just from looking at plans and photographs. I haven't done a foot survey to see for myself yet.'

Adam thought Brian was probably correct but it was something that he would determine for himself when he visited the area. It could be an important piece of information. It could make a difference and therefore the question would have to be resolved at some stage.

Adam looked at the photographs again and saw that the neck part of the square was shorter, perhaps forty or so yards long, and had bollards in the road preventing traffic from entering or leaving the square from the busy Western Road.

Brian leaned forward, pointing to the seafront area.

'That's the main seafront road and immediately north of it another road than runs parallel for a few hundred yards either side giving access to Adelaide Crescent itself. The roads each side of the crescent are two-way so, although vehicle access and exit is only by the seafront road, a vehicle can travel either clockwise or anticlockwise around the crescent.'

Adam continued to study the photograph. 'Keith said Jackie lives on the ground floor and first floor, which leaves the basement flat and two top floors. He thinks one or two girls could be working as prostitutes from the basement and even from the top flat, but of course that information is more guesswork than knowledge.'

Brian agreed. Planning permission was granted for the top two floors to be divided into separate flats, and also for the basement but there isn't any trace on the electoral register of anybody ever living there, so maybe they are rooms for her girls ...'

'Is there anywhere we can look at her place from?'

Brian produced further plans of the area and explained what his research had found, including a flat available for rent at the north-west end of the crescent directly facing south-east towards the seafront and with a good view of the front of Jackie Smith's home on the east side and halfway down the square, approximately one hundred yards away. Brian explained the flat had been available for rent for three months, but there had been only four viewings during that time, so there was a good chance that they could use it without anyone having knowledge. The flat was on the top floor, which was both good and bad from their point of view: good in that it gave a commanding view over the top of cars and vans that might use the crescent, but bad because the escape route, should it be required, was limited. The house didn't have a lift and a single staircase ran from the ground floor to the top of the house.

Brian showed Adam the plan of the house: the entrance to the loft area that contained the water tank was accessed by a further flight of steps next to the vacant flat on the fourth floor. There were no windows in the landing or small loft area and in other circumstances it would have been in this area that they would have put their camera equipment, the lens poking from underneath a roof tile, or focused through an air brick or similar. In the present circumstances, they decided that they would have a camera mounted on a tripod in the lounge window, trained closely on the front door of Smith's house to gain quality close-up pictures of people as they entered and left, as well as another camera – again on a tripod – to cover that side of the crescent in general. Both of the cameras and tripods would be covered with a white cloth, which against the white background of the flat's walls and ceilings would conceal their existence from outside. In addition, Adam would take a handheld camera to identify any vehicles that visitors might use that were not in either cameras' view. He also selected a small camera that he fitted in a small day rucksack that he could use if following someone. They agreed that the objective would be to try to identify visitors and occupants of the house and establish any of their routines, especially Jackie Smith.

They discussed what equipment they would need and agreed that a reconnaissance the next day would be the first step.

Christmas day was a sombre affair at the Townsend house, with Pat and Geoff refusing either to invite friends to them or to accept invitations from others. They sat barely talking to each other watching television programmes, many of which were repeats from other Christmases when their house had been filled by parties, drink and laughter. Geoff Townsend was brooding, wishing the whole Christmas thing was over, so he could concentrate on finding out who had murdered his Kieran, and exact his revenge. Pat Townsend was thinking the same and when they did speak it was mostly in the garden to discuss any ideas either of them had that they had not put into action already.

At the other end of the county of Sussex, Raymond Black sat at the head of the dinner table wearing a red paper hat and joking with his great-grandchildren while Sandra busied herself in the kitchen, assisted by Kate. Peter ensured everyone's glasses were replenished while Dennis fussed about everyone, stoking the fire, clearing away discarded wrapping paper and moving the toys where the boys had abandoned them on the floor. Music played and occasionally Raymond or Dennis would join in the singing, much to the amusement of everyone else. Kate, Peter and Dennis were all pleased to see Raymond at the festivities and they had noticed his zest for life had returned a few weeks previously – for no reason that they knew of. Sandra had spoken with her father about the death of Kieran and their hope that Adam had been responsible for it. They hoped that they would have further celebrations the next year.

9

Adam and Brian spent Christmas evening examining photographs on Brian's computer from Adam's past two days' surveillance on Jackie Smith's home. They quickly identified one man as being a frequent visitor, who stayed for less than a quarter of an hour each time, though it was four times the first day and six times the second day, Christmas Day.

'Strange,' Adam said, 'he parks his car at the end of the crescent near my position and walks across the grass to Jackie's house even when there is parking outside her house. Also, given the rain we've had, the grass is very wet. From my spot I can see water laying on the surface but he walks directly to Smith's side barely touching the paths that are dryer. He then retraces his steps to the car, drives past her place and back on to the seafront road, always turning left back towards Brighton.'

'Ruud van Brubeck the car is registered to, lives in another area of Brighton, Roedean, to the east of the city near the Marina. His house is large, worth probably a couple of million. Lives with a Mrs Ruth van Brubeck, no children. No trace of income for either, so private means, though Mrs Brubeck is a partner in a café in the city centre. It's been running for two years and she's not taken a penny from the business, according to the returns. No trace on her with the police but Mr Van Brubeck has two previous convictions in the Netherlands: for importation of cannabis in 1998 he got three years in prison and 2004 for importation of cocaine, six years in prison.'

Adam was amazed at how Brian could so quickly carry out searches that provided so much information and said so.

'Internet, Adam, but mostly ways and means. There is always a pathway and usually they are not too difficult to find. It's what I did when I was working Intel.'

'Jackie Smith doesn't seem to go out much. I've got a woman who took a small girl, I assume Jackie's child, out a couple of times yesterday, to the shops. Both times Mr Van Brubeck was in the house,' said Adam.

'Maybe rehabilitation didn't work for Mr Van Brubeck and he hasn't changed his chosen career path, because,' – Brian switched to another screen and after touching a couple of keys a face appeared – 'Mr Van Brubeck himself visiting the bereaved Mr and Mrs Townsend no doubt offering his condolences. He's been to the house several times, into the house then a minute later out the back and a conversation in the garden.'

'What do they do when it rains?' asked Adam

'They stay in the garden, just go closer to the pool house to escape the worst of the rain but they still meet there. They're dedicated to fresh air, it appears.'

Adam was thinking about the lengths that Townsend was prepared to go to ensure that his conversations weren't overheard. If he and Pat Townsend seriously thought that their house was bugged by the police, why didn't they move or put the radio and television on loud or have the house debugged?

The fact that the Dutchman was visiting both addresses suddenly struck him.

'Bri, do Van Brubeck's visits to Jackie Smith and Townsend have any relationship?'

Brian examined a page on his computer. 'I would say yes, but we haven't very much to go on. Perhaps he visits Townsend then Jackie. Looking at the times it would seem that is a possibility. Are you thinking about him being a courier or message man?'

'Don't know but he may hold the key and have answers that we could spend months finding out,' said Adam.

'Ask him then,' said Brian lightly.

'Just thinking, but that is a possibility – only, having spoken to him, he would report back … unless …' Adam left the sentence unfinished.

Brian understood exactly what Adam was thinking.

'Adam, if you want to do that, and I think it is a sound idea, I'll have to find somewhere we could talk to him, and I mean *we*. You're too full on with your questioning style. A little bit of subtlety could be useful, and I can have a laptop with me to check on anything he says.'

'Do you know of anywhere?'

'At this time of year there are possibilities. Lots of factories are closed until the New Year so we could have a week or more. A couple of days and I'll see what there is. In the meantime, let's keep on with Jackie Smith.

10

Boxing Day morning was the start of what was forecasted to be a crisp cold day with a blue sky and the temperature at freezing point. After Adam reached his observation spot in the flat, he set all the cameras into position and opened the first of his three Thermos flasks to have a hot coffee. It was still dark outside as he checked his watch. It was just before six o'clock, which, he judged, was early enough to start the day given that, unlike he and Brian, most of the population would be nursing hangovers from the Christmas Day festivities.

The first light appeared at Jackie Smith's front ground-floor room just after seven o'clock and ten minutes later Adam saw headlights as a car drove northwards up the western side of the crescent towards his position. Adam strained to look and saw the car pull in to a parking space facing the green and instantly knew by the position it would be Van Brubeck. He was pleased to see Van Brubeck get out of the car and stand in the road looking about him.

'Interesting,' muttered Adam, 'normally he just walks straight to Jackie's place.'

Another set of headlights appeared from the same direction as Van Brubeck had done and a Blue Jaguar parked next to Van Brubeck's car. Van Brubeck walked to the passenger side of the Jaguar. Adam was ready with his camera already trained on the driver's position, though he couldn't see anyone through the reflection on the windscreen. As Van Brubeck opened the car door, the interior light shone and Adam pushed his finger, creating a slight clicking and motor sound as images were recorded. He changed the focal point a fraction until the light went out as Van Brubeck closed the car door. Adam moved to the other room, from which he could gain a slightly different angle and waited, using concentration to hold the camera still. He could have held that position, barely moving a fraction and with controlled breathing, for an hour if he had needed to but within a minute the interior light came back on as Van Brubeck opened his door and stood beside the car. Van Brubeck slammed the door closed and within a couple of seconds the car drove off. All the while Adam kept on taking photographs, using one eye through the camera sight while using the other to follow Van Brubeck.

As the Jaguar car drove beneath his position Adam saw Van Brubeck open the rear door of his car and bring out a square-shaped package that he estimated to be less than a foot square in size and which didn't appear to be heavy from the way it was carried. Adam noticed that it wasn't wrapped in Christmas paper as most boxes or packages were at that time of the year. Van Brubeck closed the car door then followed his usual route to Jackie Smith's house and rang the bell. Smith answered the door and allowed Van Brubeck in, then Adam saw her turn and appear to shout at someone inside the house. The child appeared at the doorway illuminated by the hallway light from inside the house and a second later a woman appeared who like the little girl was wearing a warm winter coat. Adam took photographs and checked his watch: seven ten.

'Too early for the shops, my little one,' he said as he quickly made his way to the landing outside the flat. All was silent in the house as he expected but he quietly and quickly removed the boiler suit, latex gloves and flat cap he had been wearing and stuffed them into the small rucksack he had. He skipped down the stairs as fast as he could while remaining as silent as possible. As he opened the front door, he silently swore as the woman and child walked on the pavement past him. The woman looked directly at Adam who caught off guard gave her a smile. The woman didn't return the smile but carried on walking, holding on to the child's hand. Adam delayed descending the steps on to the pavement, counting up to five as he pretended to check his pockets for something. The woman looked behind her towards Adam, a slow and deliberate look.

Bloody hell, thought Adam as he descended the steps and still fumbling in his pockets began to walk slowly after the woman. He continued on the same pavement as the woman and child, still checking his pockets as the woman walked steadily towards the north end of the 'neck' where it joined the main road. The woman and girl turned left and walked past a church in the general direction of the shops further along the main road. Adam held back a few seconds before turning the corner to follow. He saw the woman and girl cross the main road to the north side and head towards a shop that had a light on. Adam knew that this was in fact a small café that had opened early every morning he had been in the area and which he hadn't as yet been into. He watched the woman and child enter the café at which time Adam knew that he had either to be brazen or return to the flat and wait their return. His decision was instant and he followed them into the café where he saw they had taken a seat towards the rear of the small area of eight tables. He chose a table in front of them and on the other side of the room and took a chair with a view out of the front window to the street.

As he slipped the rucksack from his shoulders he looked at the woman behind him and smiled at her. The woman gave a half-smile then spoke with the child in reassuring terms. He noted the woman spoke with an accent as she told the little girl that they wouldn't be long and then they could go home again. In the meantime they could have a lovely breakfast and talk about all the presents the girl had received from Father Christmas. The girl wasn't happy and though not crying was answering with short curt words that the woman was trying to ignore. Adam heard the woman order a full breakfast for each of them and he did the same. Adam ran the slight accent in the woman's voice through his mind, but realized that he hadn't heard her loud or long enough to identify it accurately. From time to time he appeared to again search his pockets and gave a sigh as he finally gave up his search. He hoped his acting was good enough for the woman to perceive him as not being a threat to her or the girl and that they weren't the focus of his attention.

The café was now silent except for the clinking of cutlery against the china plates and the occasional sounds from the café owner as she prepared the café for business. When Adam had finished eating, he collected his rucksack and headed past the woman and girl's table towards the toilets at the rear of the café where he waited two minutes before drying his hands under the noisy hand-dryer and re-entering the eating area. He walked past the woman then stopped and turned to face her.

'Can't believe it! Locked myself out of the house. How stupid is that?' He gave a smile, which, this time, the woman returned. The girl giggled a little.

'Am I daft or very daft?' he laughed at the girl, who giggled some more.

'Not only have I locked myself out but I have to wait for an hour before my friend wakes up for me to get a spare key from.' He shot his eyes to the ceiling, 'I suppose I will have to stay here and just have another breakfast, won't I?'

The girl laughed. 'Don't be silly! You can't eat another breakfast – they're too big.'

Adam looked at her and said, laughing, 'You're right and so early in the morning as well – I should still be asleep in my nice warm bed, not here.' He looked around the café and heard the girl quickly say, 'So should I but Mummy told me to get dressed and get out with Monica.'

The woman interjected quickly. 'Sshh!'

'Why?' asked the girl in a loud voice.

'Because I tell you,' the woman named Monica said.

Adam recognised the accent better and while she spoke in near-perfect English there was definitely a Spanish accent there.

He looked at the woman and breaking into a small laugh he said, 'Kids, aren't they lovely? Being told to go out by Mummy on a cold winter's morning – where do they pick that sort of thing up from?'

The woman smiled but her eyes looked worried.

The girl looked at Adam sincerely. 'But it's true: we were told to get lost for an hour.'

Adam stopped laughing and, looking concerned, said to the woman: 'Is that true?'

The woman started to stand and pull her coat from the back of her chair.

'It's true,' the girl almost shouted as the woman gave a louder 'shush'.

The woman slipped her coat on and reached for the girl's coat that was on the back of her chair. 'We have to go,' she said quickly as she tried to push the coat on to the girl.

'I don't want to go!' shouted the girl, folding her arms to frustrate Monica's attempt to put the coat on.

'Hold on a minute,' said Adam quietly to the woman, 'if this is true, perhaps I should contact the social services or the police.'

The woman stopped, her mouth dropped but no sound came out. Her eyes stared at Adam and he could see panic and tears there.

'Sit down,' he said quietly in what he hoped was a comforting and soothing tone. His mind was racing: should he just leave or trust his gut feeling. The woman he was speaking to was the same one he'd seen taking the little girl to the shops. Today they had been ordered out for an hour – what if they were always ordered out when that Van Brubeck arrived?

He decided to press on. 'Look, I could contact social services or the police but that would cause a lot of problems for you, wouldn't it?' he asked, again in a reasonable and soft voice.

The woman sat down and unbuttoned her coat while still holding on to the girl's coat. She gave him a frightened look. 'Please don't,' she said quietly.

'Going to the toilet,' announced the girl as she stood up. Adam watched her march to the back of the area and head straight towards the ladies' toilet.

'You don't know what trouble you will cause if you do,' the woman said.

Adam knew he had little time before the girl would return. 'Tell me what is going on then? What's your name? Monica, did the little girl say?'

The woman looked at him. 'Yes but please just go away and don't ask questions. It has nothing to do with you.'

'Your choice,' said Adam as he reached for his mobile phone.

'Don't,' Monica said, 'don't do that. It's just … that her mother has things to do that she doesn't want her little girl around to see.'

'At seven in the morning?' asked Adam quickly.

'Yes.'

'What could her mother be doing at seven in the morning?'

'I can't tell you. You don't know what will happen if I tell you,' Monica answered quietly.

'Tell me or I'll make the call,' countered Adam holding the mobile phone.

'I can't … oh God,' said Monica, fear openly displayed in her eyes. Tears started to form as she and Adam both heard the hand-dryer start.

'I can't tell you,' said Monica, standing up, 'her mother is not a good woman and if I tell you I will be very badly hurt, so will other people, so please do not ask questions and leave us alone.'

Just then the girl returned to the table and Monica forced the coat on to the reluctant girl.

But Adam, still holding the mobile phone, pressed on. 'Last chance!'

Monica looked at the little girl, who now wore a petulant

face. 'Not here, not now!' she hissed. 'Here two hours.'

Adam felt his heart skip a beat but he showed her nothing.

'The owner,' he said in a whisper, indicating the woman now looking at them, 'she's seen us and I'll call her as a witness if you don't turn up. I promise you I don't mean you any harm, nor her,' Adam pointed slightly at the girl, 'but I can't say the same for her mother.'

Monica looked at him and gave a firm nod of her head to show that she had heard and understood what he had said.

Monica went and paid at the counter while Adam returned to his table looking up to give the little girl a smile as she reached the door.

'Adam, it's risky,' said Brian after listening to Adam's account of his morning. 'How do you intend to play it?'

Adam had thought before calling Brian about how he was going to handle the meeting with Monica and trying as best as he could to imagine the questions he should ask and the answers that Monica would give him.

'I've got a view of Jackie Smith's house and there haven't been any callers. All is quiet. I accept Monica could have just returned and told Jackie about me and the arrangement to meet, in which case I expect a visit from some heavies, but somehow I'm not convinced that she'll tell Jackie. If we do meet, then I'll try to find out what she means by Jackie Smith being a bad woman and see if I can get any Intel about her and her activities.'

Brian and Adam agreed that Adam wouldn't have any equipment or ID on him and that his mobile phone would be on an open line to Brian so he could hear any conversation or confrontation.

Monica had returned to Jackie Smith's house and, not finding her, had gone to the basement where Greta, a friend of hers, lived and worked. Greta told Monica that Jackie had been to see her and said something important was happening and she passed on Smith's instructions that Monica, Katja and she were not to have any customers that day and nor were they to answer any telephone calls or the front door. They were to look after Jackie's daughter and she expected to be back either that night or the following morning. Monica and the others had greeted the news with some relief as they hated Jackie and a day without her shouting, bullying or attacking them was good news, made even better by the fact that they wouldn't be working. It would mean no money for any of them, true, but they received only a small fraction of what they earned for her anyway. Greta agreed to look after Jackie's daughter while Monica went to the shops to buy some food that Jackie had asked her to get – or so she said.

Monica left the house just after nine and was watched by Adam as she walked past on the same route she'd taken earlier that morning. He made sure that she wasn't being followed from the crescent before letting himself out of his house and walking in the same direction as her but on the eastern pavement to the main road. Here he stopped and lingered by a bus stop while he looked about him before crossing the road to the central area of the main road then over the other side of the road on to the north pavement where he turned to his right and away from the café.

He kept his hands tucked into his jacket pockets and didn't make any backward glances until he reached a small road junction. As he shaped to cross the junction he had a look at the few people who were on the pavements and didn't see any person suddenly darting off or looking in another direction. He didn't see any cars parked that contained any men and after crossing the road he continued to walk away from the café. After a hundred yards he suddenly turned into a small newsagent's and bought a newspaper looking out the window to see if any person walked past while he waited for his change. He left the newsagents then retraced his steps towards the café, peering into some shop windows and doorways before he was satisfied that he wasn't being followed.

He didn't hesitate as he entered the café where only two tables at the window end were occupied. He waved to the owner and went to the back of the café and chose a table where the counter was behind him and from where he could see the whole area including the front door. He was halfway through his coffee when Monica entered carrying a shopping bag. She instantly saw Adam at his table and sat opposite him with her back to the door.

'If anyone comes in and sees me I'll say that you are a customer of mine who I haven't seen for a month. You've been away,' she said quietly.

'A customer?' asked Adam with as much innocence that he could manage.

'A customer,' she replied with an embarrassed look.

'Where's the little girl now – being looked after by Mum?'

'By another girl. Her mother has gone out,' Monica replied as the owner came for her order. Monica ordered a coffee and wondered if the owner recognised her from earlier and if so whether her now being with the man from that morning would raise any questions in her mind. If they did, the owner didn't show any signs.

Adam knew he had to start the conversation and be in charge of the questioning but at the same time as being slightly threatening he had to put some compassion in his voice. 'I'll be honest with you: she did something that I want to pay her back for and I want your help. I will do anything to hurt her: reporting her to social services for throwing her child out on Boxing Day morning just after seven may be a start but maybe you know something else?'

Monica looked directly at Adam sensing his strength. She didn't hold him in the same contempt that she did for other men, or Jackie, come to that.

'Why should I talk to you? If you reported her to the social services, she will have everyone call you a liar. Even the café owner would not speak against her, nobody would, so why should I?

Why should I trust you? I've never seen you before.' She spoke quickly, never taking her eyes from Adams'.

Adam sighed. This was how he feared she would react to a stranger. It was now that he had to make the decision.

'I will show I trust you, then perhaps you will trust me,' he said. He took a breath then leant forward with the coffee cup raised close to his mouth. 'Jackie Smith is a grade-one bitch who controls the girls who shoplift for her and girls who prostitute for her. The little girl's father is Geoff Townsend and this morning you were told to leave the house because a certain Mr Van Brubeck had arrived.'

Monica couldn't control her reaction. Her eyes opened wide and her mouth opened in surprise. The owner appeared suddenly at the table and gently placed the mug of coffee in front of Monica.

Adam sipped some coffee from his mug but kept the mug close to his lips while he watched her response. Monica looked down at the table, which allowed Adam to glance up at the door and the other customers, but nobody was taking any interest in either him or Monica so he pressed her some more.

'Tell me about Mr Van Brubeck. As you can imagine, I know quite a lot but I want to see if you are telling me the truth,' he said.

Adam knew that this was the decisive moment: a refusal now and she wouldn't tell him anything. He had showed his hand and now he waited, allowing the silence to put pressure on Monica. She looked at him then half-opened her mouth as if to say something before looking around the café.

Returning her gaze to him she said, 'I don't know who you are but you won't report her to social services. You will hurt us. At least at the moment we can work and nobody gets hurt. Are you police?'

Adam felt let down by her response and tried to harden his eyes towards her to show his strength. 'No, I'm not in the police.

I don't have a rule book to follow. I don't have to be nice to people and I'm not frightened by her or Van Brubeck, or Geoff Townsend for that matter.'

'Not frightened by Jackie or Dutch – you are mad. Not frightened of Mr Townsend – you are very mad.' She suddenly stood up and in one movement had picked up her shopping bag and started towards the door. Adam sat and watched her leave and immediately turn left towards the crescent. He felt the same way that he had after meeting Julie – poor preparation, again. He knew that, now the meeting was over, if it had been a set-up, now was the moment he would be attacked as he left the café.

He waited five minutes before leaving the café and examining the street but saw no obvious threat. All the people were walking at various speeds, nobody was loitering in a doorway, no two people were walking together towards him and no cars were parked against the pavement within fifty yards of him. He put his hands loosely into his pockets and sauntered slowly towards his car as if he didn't have a care in the world or was wasting time. Several times he stopped altogether and openly looked about him. There wasn't any point in being subtle at this stage: if he was going to be attacked, they would be pumped up and he wanted the earliest possible warning of the imminent danger.

Nothing.

He returned to his car where he pulled the mobile phone out of his jacket pocket. Brian was waiting for him and they discussed how the meeting with Monica had failed to achieve anything. Brian had heard most of what had been said and was more upbeat than Adam.

'Well, it was worth a try,' Brian said. 'Question is where does this leave us now?'

Adam felt dejected and knew that Brian was concerned, as was he, that the observation position had been compromised. He told Brian that he would remain in the area for the day until it was dark when he would recover the equipment and return to

Crawley in the early evening. After switching the mobile off he banged his fists on the steering wheel.

Van Brubeck left Geoff Townsend's house after a ten-minute meeting in the garden and drove straight to the town of Newhaven on the south coast. Newhaven is a small town some twelve miles or so east of Brighton and notable only as being a port from which the cross-Channel boat service to Dieppe in northern France sails. He drove to a small industrial estate on the edge of the town that had either one- or two-storey buildings out of which one- or two-man businesses operated. Many had small signs attached to the walls at the front and the majority showed that in one way or another their main business concerned the repair of cars, whether it was accident damage repair, exhaust and tyre replacement, re-sprays or everyday maintenance. The other similarity was that all the premises were closed for the holidays.

Van Brubeck drove past the locked and deserted units and on to the end of the road, where there was a unit that didn't display any name or advertising but which also appeared to be closed. He parked at the far side of the unit, the front of which comprised of a metal roll-up shutter that covered the whole of the ground floor. Over this roll-up shutter was the first-floor brick-built office. He banged his fist against the metal shutter causing it to shake through its entire length and height and seconds later the small door inset to the edge of the shutter opened inwards. Nobody appeared but he walked to the door, then stepped into the warehouse where he saw three men seated on deckchairs around a small table covered in playing cards. The fourth deckchair had been occupied by Jack who was the man who had opened the door to Van Brubeck. Jack checked the street area before closing the door.

'Not taking your eyes off the camera are you, boys?' Van Brubeck asked them.

'No, boss,' said Jack as he bolted the door closed. 'Saw you coming and was ready at the door for you.'

Van Brubeck looked at another table near the card table and saw that the monitor into which camera pictures were being streamed was facing the men who could all casually watch it in between their hands of cards. Apart from the two tables and deckchairs, there was only one other item on the floor, a portable gas heater that was only sufficient to warm those within a few feet of it while the rest of the area was bitingly cold. Van Brubeck strode to one side of the open space where there was a flight of stairs. These he took up to the first-floor open-plan office space. It was completely empty except in one corner where there was a single stainless-steel sink and draining board unit under which was a cupboard. On the draining area was a kettle plugged into the wall with some mugs and packets of tea and coffee strewn about. On the floor was a plastic shopping bag that contained the empty wrappings from sandwiches that the men had purchased that morning from a petrol station and eaten. Satisfied with what he saw, Van Brubeck returned downstairs where Jack had retaken his seat and held a handful of cards.

'Listen up, boys,' Van Brubeck said. 'This afternoon a lady will arrive, early thirties, good-looking – you haven't seen her before. Don't any of you get any ideas on that front – she'll eat you alive or just as happily put a bullet in you depending on her mood.' He saw Jack and another man smile but he remained serious as he continued. 'I'm not joking, believe me. She'll have two men with her, one of whom you will recognise. Neither of them will have any hesitation in killing any of you if you step out of line. Remember, they are all acting on behalf of the boss – upset him and you know what will happen. They will bring in a box …' He indicated a size of two feet long by one foot high and wide. 'They will put the box down and they will leave. You will stop playing cards and one of you at all times will be watching the camera. That will be you, Chas, as before.' He looked at a bearded man of about thirty-five years of age. 'Jack will be outside in the hide in the wood where you have a view of the area behind here.

Derek and Pete, stay here with the box. Any movement from anywhere you know what to do. You've all got silencers and you know the score. Shoot *anybody*, I don't care if they are coppers, shoot them then get out and go through the woods to the river, same as always. The boats are ready in case they are needed. The engines are fuelled and will take you upriver to Lewes or, if the weather and water is OK, the sea, but that is a last resort. You know where to stop. Two cars are there, one to go east, Derek and Pete west to that place in Lewes as before. Jack and Chas create chaos as you go. I want the cops to be after you two, to take the heat from Derek and Pete. It is the same as before but I want you to understand that the operational order hasn't changed. Check mobiles are on silent. Leave nothing to chance.'

'Boss, this is the twenty-second time we've done this for real and the hundred and fifth time we've done it including practices, we know the score. A couple of points have changed but basically it is the same,' said Jack.

Van Brubeck rounded on Jack, pointing at him with his hand. 'Don't be complacent – that's when things go wrong. Twenty-one times we've been successful, two hundred and ten thousand pounds each you've made, but the first time it goes to rats is the time when you are looking at twenty years apiece. Think two hundred and ten grand is worth twenty years inside, because I don't, that's ten grand a year, Jack.'

Jack knew he had stepped out of line. 'Sorry, boss, you're right. We're on to it.'

Geoff Townsend was in the back garden with a mobile phone and was trying to control his anger.

'Half an hour.'

He shut down his mobile and walked back into the house where Pat was waiting car keys in hand. They walked through the house and out the front door to her white Mercedes, which she unlocked with the key remote. Geoff got into the back seat and lay down while Pat got into the driver's seat and started the engine. Neither spoke as she gunned the car forward to the electric gates that opened as she reached them, closing as soon as she had passed through. She sped quickly on to the country road that ran north from their house to the village of Saddlescombe, where she turned right to drive parallel to the Downs. She constantly checked her mirror but was happy that no one was following her. She knew the roads well and, though twice frustrated by drivers who were in no hurry, she kept a good speed that would have meant any vehicles following would have to be driven hard to keep up with her.

She crossed over the M23 motorway towards the village of Hurstpierpoint and after rounding a long bend suddenly pulled over. Geoff Townsend had the door already open and jumped out, slamming it behind him as he ran towards a side gate of a house set back from the road. He was through the gate and had moved another two steps before he glanced behind him and saw Pat's white Mercedes turning the bend, continuing on her journey, her speed already fast for the narrow lane.

He stood still behind a tree and waited. Any following car would be in view within a minute even if they were tracking Pat's car electronically, and they would be travelling quickly. He waited for a full two minutes without seeing a car in either direction before looking about him and making his way to the back of the house. The house was set in half an acre of land surrounded on three sides by trees and thick hedgerows. The front had stones as a driveway, double gates leading to the lane and the small side gate through which Geoff Townsend had entered. The rear garden was mostly grass, with fruit trees providing interest. A small old wooden shed stood in one corner, which he looked at several times as he walked towards the kitchen door at the back of the house.

As he arrived at the door, the Detective Chief Inspector dressed in casual clothes and jeans came out. Looking nervous he pointed towards the shed and walked quickly towards it, with Geoff Townsend a stride behind. Both men entered the shed and closed the door.

'What's so urgent?' said Townsend.

'Geoff, thanks for coming. I couldn't say on the phone even if it isn't mine. It could still be tracked. I was having a lunchtime drink in the local, and met up with a couple of lads from Surveillance.'

'Bloody all right for some. Hope it was nice,' Townsend replied sarcastically.

'Actually it wasn't very nice but I think you'll be pleased that I spent an hour making sure they were enjoying their drink. They started talking about work and I got them around to you. The long and the short of it is that they aren't working on you full time at the moment, after Kieran.' The Detective Chief Inspector looked at the floor in embarrassment before continuing. 'They know you'll be after who did it and they are letting you have some freedom, not following you, etcetera. But, Geoff, they are monitoring cameras that they've got around your place, you know, to identify callers and monitor when you go out, that sort of thing. I asked if they had anything inside the house and they said no.'

Townsend stood there absorbing what had been said. The news about the cameras around the outside of the house was to be expected really, but the claim that there was nothing inside the house – true or bluff? He had always thought the sneaky bastards could have put some listening device in the house, which was why he talked outside no matter the weather. Trust no one, he reminded himself. Was this just too convenient, a bluff by the police? Perhaps the DCI's position with him had been compromised and he was being sent as the messenger, two-timing him. If he did, he'd be finished and with that he made up his mind.

'Thanks, I understand. Anything new happening?'

The DCI shook his head. 'The investigation is still on going. We've over a hundred cars still to trace. The man on camera who we think killed Kieran just disappeared. Could be he lives nearby but no suspects have come up. We've spoken to known people. I think you may have as well.' He looked at Townsend and smiled. 'Nobody is saying a dickie bird, nothing at all, and I've got to say, Geoff, that surprises me. You'd expect someone would come forward even if it's crap, just to drop you in it or whatever, but no one has. I'll let you or Dutch know if anything comes up that I think you ought to know.'

Geoff Townsend was listening but he knew already what the DCI was saying was the truth about the investigation, Dutch had already said as much and he had heard it from another friendly police officer only that morning.

The men talked another minute before Geoff pulled his mobile phone from his pocket and used quick dial. It was answered on the first ring.

'Ready,' he said, 'right.'

He shut the phone. 'Throw-away. Got a friendly who supplies them.' He laughed, seeing the relief on the DCI's face as fear of a call from his address by Geoff Townsend went away.

The pick-up by Pat was exactly as planned as she slowed and without stopping the car allowed Townsend to clamber in before she picked up speed again. Fifteen minutes later Townsend was in his back garden using another mobile phone.

He was speaking to Lenny for over a minute after which he finished the call and took out the SIM card. He carried that inside and threw it on to the log fire, watching the metal and cardboard burn and melt.

Jackie Smith arrived at her house and threw her coat on to a peg in the hallway before walking past Monica into her lounge where she poured herself a large measure of vodka, to which she added an equal amount of tonic water and downed the whole drink in three large gulps. Monica stood in the doorway waiting for Jackie to address her. It was a bad sign when she came back to the house and drank straight away.

'Anything happen while I was away?' Jackie asked.

Monica knew that she would be asked the question. It was routine and she knew that her future and that of others could depend on her reply. All afternoon she had played with Jackie's daughter Charlene, first card and board games, then painting, trying to be pleasant to the child while all the while agonising over what had happened that morning. She knew that her boss didn't give a halfpenny about her. She was just another tool that she controlled and which she could break at any time it suited her. She had at one point decided to say nothing about the man in the café but then changed her mind when she realised that a word from the child would compromise her. Any approach from any stranger should be reported. She knew the rules. Anything, however trivial, had to be reported to Jackie. Any disobedience and a girl would be punished – a beating given by Jackie with the other girls made to stand and watch as a lesson.

For all that she suddenly heard herself saying the word 'No'. She shocked herself by saying it but all of a sudden she knew she couldn't retract the word – it was done. Jackie wasn't looking at Monica but refilling her glass, so missed Monica's sudden change of expression.

'Right, Dutch will be bringing a package in the morning. It's top-grade stuff so I want you and Katja to be ready to run it around, the same as before. Nine deliveries, four for you and five for Katja, so early nights for both of you. I want you out at six thirty. Where's Charlene?'

Sort out the drugs delivery before asking about the welfare of your child, thought Monica. Her loathing for Jackie intensified.

'In the bath playing. Katja's with her.'

'I'll see her in the morning then,' Jackie said, gulping down her second glass of vodka and tonic.

Monica turned and went upstairs to the bathroom, intending to put Charlene to bed and read her the bedtime story. Her thoughts returned to the man she'd met that morning: who was he? He was mad surely – not scared of Jackie or Dutch? In Monica's experience, Dutch was much worse than Jackie. He enjoyed hurting people, especially a girl when Jackie offered him one for free as a reward. She shuddered as she remembered a new young girl who had arrived one evening when Dutch was talking to Jackie, drinking and laughing. Jackie had instructed the girl to strip naked in front of Dutch. Monica had tried to say that the girl was only fourteen years old but had been silenced by a slap from Jackie. Dutch had pawed the girl, horribly touching her, making her cry. The young girl had tried to resist but Jackie had slapped her also and made Monica translate the threat. Dutch had raped her that night, more than once, and he and Jackie had laughed about it afterwards. And now, this man was saying he wasn't scared of Dutch, a madman for sure.

But what had she done by not telling Jackie about him? Even as she tucked Charlene into bed that night, she shuddered.

Adam arrived at Brian's house feeling down. He and Brian sat in the living room churning over their thoughts, trying to find something positive about the day.

Adam had been able to spend some time looking at the house owned by Van Brubeck and had toured the area to acquaint himself with the roads. Van Brubeck's house was on a small road set back and separated by grass from the main coast road that ran east from Brighton towards Newhaven. His house was only a few away from the exclusive fee-paying girl's school Roedean and from the front of his house he had a commanding view down to the sea. The back of the property backed on to a field where the farmer was growing a cereal crop, though as yet the green shoots were barely showing. The neighbouring houses were of a similar size with probably five bedrooms or more each, Adam had guessed. Brian had been able to obtain a plan of the house and as well as one of the neighbouring streets. Brian tried to lift Adam's spirits by pointing out that at least they knew a lot more about Van Brubeck. He also offered the news about Geoff Townsend jumping into the back of the Mercedes driven by Pat Townsend. Where they had gone he didn't know but this rather curious departure meant that something was happening. They speculated over what the possible reasons for Townsend leaving his house and fortress might be.

'Right,' Adam said, getting to his feet. 'Nearly ten, I'm off to get some sleep, then back to Jackie's first thing. If I see Monica again, I'll let her see me and judge her reaction.'

'OK, but I think that tomorrow you may need this. It arrived by courier this afternoon.' Brian was smiling as he gestured for Adam to follow him.

A minute later they were standing in the loft while Adam unwrapped the oiled paper. He knew what it contained: the weight, size and overall feel were just right. Before he had finished unwrapping the paper he was smiling. 'Where did you get this?'

Brian gave a chuckle and tapped the side of his nose with a finger. 'The long will be with us in a couple of days. So will another short like that.'

Adam looked up surprised.

'Don't argue, Adam. It's insurance for when you need help and I'm riding in to save you.' He smiled.

Adam was smiling at seeing an old friend once again in his hands: a Sig Sauer P226 that he'd used for years and knew to be reliable and totally trustworthy. He examined it from every angle and held it in his hand before starting to break the pistol down, something that over the years he had done so often that he could strip and clean the weapon before reassembling it in darkness or blindfolded. It was new, brand new, and felt beautiful in his hand. The manufacturer's oil still clung to its surfaces. Brian pointed to the cleaning kit and the three magazines that were also in the box. Brian went to another box and showed Adam the 9mm parabellum rounds that the weapon would fire.

'For reasons I won't go into, the piece doesn't have the magazines with it, but these three,' – he held the magazines – 'will all fit OK. I got different sizes as I don't know what the future holds or the circumstances in which you'll be carrying it. One holds ten, the other two fifteen, which should be more than enough.'

Adam was still examining the weapon and smiling at being reunited with what he considered the finest weapon he had used.

11

It was the day after Boxing Day. Adam took more care than previously as he entered the house and walked cautiously upstairs. He had listened to all of Brian's advice carefully, Brian, after all, was the undisputed font of knowledge with regards to observation. What if the girl had told Jackie about his approach and shown her the house that she had seen Adam come from? What if they decided to make a trap for him? Maybe had some explosive rigged up? Or thugs waiting for him?

He moved his left arm against his side and felt the comforting feel of the weapon nestled in its holster under his arm within easy reach. He reached the door to the flat and slowly and carefully placed his holdall on the ground out of the way then inserted the pick tool using his left hand in an awkward reverse manner. In his right hand he held the weapon pointed at the door. He gently applied pressure to the pick and felt it beginning to move as he stepped further to the side. The lock clicked open, the sound audible to anyone listening within twenty feet and the door moved half an inch inwards.

His nerves were taut, his eyes and ears straining for any give-away movement or sound. He was motionless. He was used to the pressure of waiting, he had done it many times, and he knew that most people couldn't do the same. They had to move. He waited for another full minute before swiftly pushing the door with his foot at the same time as reaching up and around with his left hand to switch on the light, while his right hand moved in an arc around the room. He instantly switched the light off once again, plunging the room into darkness. If they were wearing night-vision equipment, the light would render the equipment useless for several seconds. If they weren't, then their usual night vision would be ruined for up to several minutes. Either way they would be blind compared to him.

Not relaxing for one moment, Adam peered into the room from floor level, looking long distance to the other side of the room from left to right then bringing his examination forward to right in front of him. Everything was as he had left it, the doors leading from the room at the same angles he had left them. He checked the stairway below and remained still for a further minute. He quickly grabbed the holdall then entered the room, closing the door quietly behind him. He walked slowly about the flat, taking in every one of the security measures he had left to satisfy himself that nobody had been there. He relaxed slightly but knew that, if his position had been compromised, an attack could happen at any time.

He positioned the holdall tight against the door to the flat, ensuring that some of the strap was under the door to prevent it being opened silently or quickly, thus giving his back some cover. He erected the cameras as he had previously and had just resigned himself to a wait when he saw the front porch light of Jackie's house come on. He quickly glanced at his watch, six thirty, front door opening, car headlights coming into the crescent and heading towards his end, slowing. He watched and at the same time gave himself a running commentary: 'Two women on the top step of the house, front door closing, car stopped but headlights still on. Two women running from the house over the grass towards the car.' Adam moved his position. 'One girl into the car, front passenger seat, larger than the other girl, smaller girl walking on, towards the main road where the café is, the same girl as yesterday, Monica …'

Adam was a flurry of activity as he moved the cameras away from the window and rushed toward the door. He opened the door quietly then stepped out on to the landing. A door at the bottom of the house opened, a light was switched on, the ground floor. Adam froze mid-step, heard footsteps, a mumbled word, more steps then a door closing, front door opening then seconds later closing. He silently used the light from the ground floor to guide him quickly down the stairs. He reached the front door. His right hand was down by his side. It held the gun just behind his leg, his finger running by the side of the trigger guard. He opened the door and jumped to one side. Nothing. He moved forward and glanced around the crescent. One man walking down the pavement on the side of Jackie Smith's house, hands thrust deeply into his duffle-coat pockets against the cold wind blowing in off the sea. Adam was down the steps and walking briskly towards where Monica had gone, checking to make sure that nobody else was about as he replaced the gun in its holster.

When he reached the corner with the main road he saw Monica forty-five or so yards in front of him. He slowed and found a bus stop with an intact glass shelter. He stepped into the shelter and continued to watch Monica keep a steady walking pace. Apart from her the pavements were quiet and only two cars passed in the time Adam watched her. As she walked opposite the café, she glanced towards it and slowed for a fraction of a stride before continuing. Adam noticed that and as he started to follow her again he noted that she was approaching the main road as if to cross it, that meant she would look back in his direction to check for vehicles, so he found a doorway in which to stand.

They were still the only people out walking and only the occasional bus or car had passed them. Adam saw her cross the road then turn the corner into a side road. Adam left the doorway and walked quickly, gradually getting more of the side road into view until he was opposite and could see no one on either pavement. The only movement from the street was a plume of exhaust smoke from a car parked in a row of cars against the pavement. Before he had decided to wait and see if the car drove off or if Monica came into view from somewhere, the passenger door of the car opened and Monica stepped on to the pavement. As she opened the door, the interior lights on the vehicle came on before they quickly went off as she closed the door. The car headed northwards away from Adam's position while Monica started to walk back towards the main road and Adam's position, causing him to turn back and head in the direction he had come from. He counted to ten before suddenly turning in to a doorway. He peered around the corner and saw Monica turn right from the small road to continue on the same pavement she had been on before on the main road. As soon as she was settled into her pace, Adam made his mind up and crossed the road to be on the same pavement as she, then jogged to catch her up. She was startled by his suddenly appearing at her side and turned towards him aggressively.

Adam kept a little distance from her then held his arms up in a mock surrender while smiling at her.

'Hi, fancy meeting you at this time of the morning again. Where's Jackie's little girl or is this morning just for grown-ups?'

Monica glared at him and then looked all around her.

'What are you doing?' she hissed at him.

'Just out for a walk and thought I'd walk with you. There are some naughty people about, you know,' he replied lightly.

Monica looked around again. 'You have to go. You'll get me in big, big trouble if we are seen together.'

'What was the meeting in the car about, Monica?' he asked in a serious voice.

'Nothing to do with you. Now go away,' she said, slightly raising her voice.

'I saw you meeting Dutch, saw the other girl go with him, then you walk off. You can talk to me as we walk,' he said, turning to walk in the direction she had been heading.

She followed him, keeping just behind him, unsure of what to do.

'If we are seen, you don't know what they'll do to you,' she said.

Adam stopped and stood to one side, at the same time opening slightly his jacket, which he knew would give a view of his holster and weapon.

'I'm not worried about them and if you talk to me you won't have anything to be scared of either.'

'Big man!' she said before walking on. 'Don't you think they have the same, more, and they will use theirs. Would you use yours?'

Adam fell into stride with Monica. 'Where are we going?'

Monica stopped. 'You can't come with me. I have to see men at the right times in the places I've been told to go. If I am late, they will go and I will be punished when I get back. You don't understand who you are dealing with. I don't know who you are but you will just cause trouble.'

'Why are you seeing the men, at this time of the morning?' he pressed.

'To give them something.'

'What?' he asked quietly.

Monica let out a sigh and then smiled. 'What do you think? Now, go away I've got to go up the next road and he will be watching for me.'

Adam suddenly sprinted away from Monica towards the road that was still over fifty yards away, reducing his speed to an amble as he turned the corner. The road was only a hundred yards long and parked three-quarters of the way up and on the same side as he was was a car with tell-tale exhaust being emitted.

'Bloody amateurs!' he muttered to himself. 'It's a cold morning, so they have to have the heater on.' He walked on the opposite pavement towards the car and looked at the houses on either side of the road. They were all large three-storey terraced houses with small, and in the main unkempt, front gardens where the rubbish and recycling bins were stored. Several houses on his side of the road appeared to be more unkempt than others and he chose one of these, entering the garden through where the front gate ought to have been. Adam skipped up the steps and appeared to press one of the numerous buttons by the door. He then cupped his hands together and blew into them all the while looking over the top of them at the car.

The driver was sitting back in his seat smoking a cigarette. He appeared to be middle-aged and overweight. Adam bent down and sat down on the top step. He was in dark shadow and wearing dark clothes, so he knew that, unless someone peered right at him, he couldn't be seen. He watched Monica walk towards the car, all the while looking all around her. As she approached the car, she stopped and looked around again, her gaze sweeping straight past Adam, then pulled a handkerchief from her pocket and appeared to blow her nose. She walked into the road then opened the front passenger door, the interior light illuminating the inside of the car. The man was facing towards Monica and Adam was able to gain a fleeting look at his face before Monica obstructed his view as she sat in the car, closing the door to switch off the interior light.

Adam could make out the shapes in the car and fifteen seconds later the interior light again came on as Monica stepped into the roadway. She closed the door then retraced her steps towards the main road. The driver in the car had a mobile phone to his ear as he pulled slowly into the road and slid the window down, throwing out his cigarette that landed with sparks on to the road. The car came to a stop in the road and Adam froze wondering why the driver hadn't just driven away. Adam remained where he was, mentally urging the man to finish his call and drive off. Adam saw Monica reaching the corner with the main road and in that instant the car accelerated away up the road.

Adam stayed where he was, scanning the street for anyone else who might also have been witnessing what had happened. The last thing he needed was to stumble into a police surveillance operation when he was carrying his weapon, or someone working for Dutch, who could be checking that the meeting took place exactly as planned. He allowed a full minute during which there wasn't any movement in the street before walking down the steps and heading back towards the main road.

Monica was some fifty yards ahead of him as he reached the corner and he increased his walking speed to catch up with her. More vehicles were now on the road and Adam was aware of more people being about on the streets. He caught up again with Monica.

'Two meetings down. How many more?'

'Two,' she replied without looking at him.

'Or – I hold on to you and call the police, then you'll have no more meetings. That will cause a problem, won't it?'

'Please, just leave me alone. I don't know what you want. I have to do what I am told to do. I want to be left alone and you said you weren't police so how will you explain that,' she indicated his left arm.

Adam didn't reply but continued walking alongside her.

'I'll leave you alone but tell me: are you coming back this way?'

Monica nodded. 'I've two more, along here.' She glanced at her watch. 'Twenty-five minutes and then I'm finished.'

'OK, hope the meetings go well,' he said before stopping and crossing the road towards a side street that led towards the seafront.

For the next twenty-five minutes Adam kept a long way from Monica, making sure that he was out of her sight whenever she crossed the road or turned to look back. He saw her enter another two side roads and was out of his view for about two minutes each time before she came back on the main road.

At last she began retracing her steps. He waited among other people at a bus stop, with two cups of coffee that he had bought from a small takeaway café. A bus arrived and he hung back as the others in the queue boarded. That moment Monica arrived.

He lifted a cup towards her and indicated for her to stand next to him. She instinctively took the coffee and moved to be next to him, all the time looking around her. She was scared. Adam didn't say anything but sipped his strong coffee. Monica took a sip from hers before she looked at him. 'So if you're not the police, are you a rival of Mr Townsend?'

Adam laughed. 'Not in the criminal sense no, but I do wish him all the bad news I can give him.'

Monica was silent for a minute.

'If I tell you things and they find out I spoke with you, they will kill me, but only after they kill my parents and little sister.'

'Talk to me, Monica, here and now, then we'll catch the bus back to make up the time. Then you carry on as usual. I will be around and we will sort out how we can make sure nothing happens to your family before I do anything that could hurt the Townsends. I promise that your family's and your safety will come first.'

Adam still had his eyes closed as he finished recounting the conversation with Monica as Brian made the occasional written note. They were in armchairs in Brian's living room with the fire burning brightly.

'Getting complicated, Adam,' Brian said, quietly aware of the strength of feeling Adam felt over what he had been told. 'We started out with the intention of killing five people, all bad people, in revenge for the savagery they inflicted on Ray and Ann Black. That is a big job in itself and I agree that approaching Monica was a good idea to find out more about Jackie, but now where are we going? OK there is a huge well-organised drugs business, Lenny and Geoff at the top and Jackie involved, so if we stick to our original plan we will destroy the drugs ring as well. This man Dutch, as she calls him – Van Brubeck as we know him – he'll probably step into the vacuum and become the new drugs lord of Brighton. If not him, then someone else will, that's for sure. And what do we do about Monica's family? Suppose you are right and she's telling the truth, sister and parents confined to a small village in Spain who will be killed if Monica doesn't do as she's told. How the hell are we supposed to protect them? We can't just turn up and take them away. I'm sorry, Adam, I'm just trying to explain possible consequences. I do actually agree with your sentiments and am happy to think that we could finish them as a drugs gang. Fine, and maybe Keith Mendip would even help us catch the corrupt policeman, but are we taking on too much – that's the question?'

Adam sat still, his eyes closed as if he were gently sleeping, his chest moving in a steady rhythm.

'Just thinking … every week a delivery worth over half a million pounds to Brighton, cocaine, every week, and it has been going on, according to Monica, for over a year, probably longer. They are organised and have a system that works, but what are the police doing about it?'

'I know, I hear you. Let's give it twenty-four hours to think about what we can reasonably do. In principle, I agree with you but I don't want us to lose track of the ultimate purpose for why we got together.'

Adam agreed and decided that in the morning he would throw himself into four hours of exercise, first a run, then a bike ride and then the internal work. The effort would help him think clearly, and anyway he always felt better when he was in good physical shape.

12

The following day Adam arrived back at the house having spent the morning cycling and running, with sit-ups and press-ups in between. He was soaked not only with sweat but also from the incessant rain that had fallen all morning. As he came out of the shower, Brian called for him to join him in their operations room.

'Worrying development this morning but I think it's worked out OK for us,' said Brian as he pointed to the screen that showed the pictures from their cameras at Townsend's house.'

Adam looked and through the rain he could see a group of six men and a dog walking in a line in front of the Townsend house. Two of the men had metal detectors that they swept from side to side methodically in a manner that both he and Brian recognised from their training. 'Professionals or ex mob,' said Brian. 'They've found two cameras, not ours I hasten to add, and picked up a couple of other things that were too small to see, maybe microphones or relays. They started at eight. No sign of Geoff or Pat, just Dutch with eight men in a van and three cars. Two men went inside with suitcases but I haven't seen them since.'

Inside the house Geoff Townsend and Pat were sitting in their lounge saying nothing, just watching the two men working slowly and carefully around their house. They had started in the kitchen, emptying every cupboard and swiping every area with a small machine, walls, floor and ceiling included. They didn't speak except in a muttered tone and after an hour had given the thumbs-up to indicate that the kitchen was clear of any listening or recording devices. They adopted the same procedure as they cleared the dining room, study, hallway and cloakroom before beginning in the lounge. Both Geoff and Pat were seething with anger, especially when the two cameras had been found outside the house together with two relaying devices but they resisted the opportunity to talk. They wanted to be sure that the house was clean and that the men had gone before they would talk to each other.

'Bri,' said Adam, 'how about this as a plan. Monica said the drugs came in every week but that was the first time that Jackie had gone when Monica thinks they are being delivered, she's usually at home. The next day Monica is given four packages, each roughly the size of a small matchbox, which she delivers to four men in cars as I saw. She says they are samples and that is her involvement. The bulk of the cocaine isn't ever brought to the house, but held somewhere else. The other girl – and that can be Katja or Greta – goes with Dutch and they make five drops, more out of the city. Always done early, the same routine. If we are going to take the fear to Townsend, why don't we intercept Dutch next week? If we got him together with a few of the samples, we could cause Townsend all sorts of problems, especially if after they're satisfied all the s/v stuff at their house has been found.'

Brian was thoughtful. It was just like Adam to want to go on the attack, cause mayhem and see where all the pieces landed. Still, Brian saw merit in the idea and if it were executed the following week, it would give them time to prepare. The plan would also take any suspicion away from the girls working for Jackie, especially Monica. The weather forecast for the forthcoming week was for snow and ice sweeping in from Siberia. Brian agreed that they should look at finding a suitable way of lifting Dutch and taking him to a quiet place where they could talk to him.

Geoff telephoned Lenny that night to inform him that altogether three cameras and relays had been found monitoring the outside of the house but that inside was clean with no devices found. As Lenny had suggested, Geoff had rapidly converted the pool room into a place where four security men could be housed while taking turns to patrol the grounds twenty-four hours a day.

Feeling relieved that at last they could talk freely, Geoff and Pat discussed the arrangements for Kieran's funeral, which, if the coroner agreed to release the body, could go ahead during the first week of January. They knew that it would be a large affair with many people wanting to pay their respects, though not so much to Kieran but to Geoff. Pat wanted it to be a grand affair to show the family's status and planned for a wake in a large hotel in the city, with no one invited to the house. Now the house was a surveillance-free zone, they intended to keep it that way.

The only time they laughed was when Geoff said that in the morning he would hand in the cameras at Brighton Police Station as lost property, telling them that, if the equipment wasn't claimed within the next thirty days, he would like to claim it for himself!

13

It was the 29th December. Brian and Adam had worked hard, with each taking responsibility for separate areas of their plan. Brian had scouted the countryside to the north of Brighton until he found a disused old factory whose roof had partially collapsed and where the nearest building was a quarter of a mile away. The building had a long-deserted look about it. A track with fields on each side didn't show any wear from vehicles or people. It must have been the previous summer that anyone had last used it.

When Brian reached the factory he was careful to avoid any mud and walked around the outside before deciding to gain entry by the rear door. The wood gave way to a slight shoulder pressure, the hasp falling clear from the rotting wooden doorframe. The smell was a strange mix of staleness, musty damp and fresh cold air as he made his way along a passage that had once had glass-fronted offices either side. The glass in the main was now broken and he was careful to avoid the shards that lay on the ground, picking his steps with care. At the end of the passage he walked through an open door into a warehouse area that measured over thirty yards long and about twenty yards wide. The high roof had fallen in at the far end and pieces of wood and metal roof supports swung gently in the breeze. Brian gave a slight shiver. The temperature had fallen to close to freezing point and the forecast was for snow. That, as he had discussed with Adam, could be both to their advantage and disadvantage.

Brian examined the area from where he stood. If Dutch were taken to this place, what would the advantages and disadvantages be? He liked the remoteness. There was little chance of even a farmer coming near. It was a harsh place – cold, damp and entirely without comfort – the type of place where someone held would feel helpless. Good positives, he thought. On the other hand, getting here would leave tracks, car wheels, footsteps – could they be seen? Was there an escape route? How about if the police deployed a helicopter with thermal heat-detection capabilities? Brian had another look and tried to imagine Adam here with Dutch. There were three sets of chains hanging from pulleys near to where he stood – could be useful – an old office chair with a swivel seat, a wooden desk, but nothing else except for the debris that lay on the floor, pieces of glass, some twisted pieces of piping, a few bricks and felt from the roof.

Monica had been back to work with the other girls, although there were few clients. Most of her time she spent child-minding Charlene. Jackie had been out every day, returning early evening berating the new security systems the large stores had in place for the January sales, besides the extra police deployed both in uniform and plain clothes. She had had three girls arrested for shoplifting in one morning and the returns from the other twelve were far below what she had expected. A new team of four Eastern European girls had been sent out to pick pockets and handbags and after a promising start on the first morning they had fallen foul of a plain-clothes police officer who had managed to hold on to one of the girls in the process of stealing from a woman's handbag. In the mêlée that had ensued, the police officer was bitten and scratched and had to be helped by members of the public, which resulted in a large article appearing in the evening newspaper and a mention on the evening local television news. The public had been warned to be on the lookout for the gang and opportunities had dried up for the pickpockets.

Jackie was explaining the problems to Dutch in the living room of her house, while also talking about the success of their weekly cocaine run. Between them it was their responsibility to ensure that the sample packages were delivered to the representatives of the various purchasers and then to fulfil the orders when they came in. There hadn't been any problems at all as far as they were concerned and the tried-and-tested operation was running smoothly with a constant demand for their product. Apart from delivering the samples, Jackie usually kept a distance from the main cache, except for this last week when she had wanted to take a more hands-on approach. Dutch had argued against this, saying that she had an important role with the girls, the prostitutes and shoplifters, who provided the cartel's steady low-risk income, but Jackie had eventually won the day. Every now and then she craved a bit of excitement and, besides, it was good to show the men that she was capable of doing their work if they fell down in their jobs.

In fact, as she admitted to Dutch afterwards, she had been nervous meeting the courier and taking receipt of the box even though she had two very capable men with her. It was at the collection time – the actual moment she touched the box – that she was vulnerable to any police action. She and her two minders couldn't know if the courier had been compromised, the box tampered with by the police with a tracking device inserted, or an undercover cop introduced somewhere along the line.

Having taken possession of the box, Jackie and the two men had delivered it to the warehouse in Newhaven. She had been impressed by their disciplined manner as every man knew exactly their role and carried it out as if their lives depended on it. She had been carrying a handgun for the first time and had been brazen with her two bodyguards, quietly letting them know that she was capable of looking after herself, although she had never fired a weapon before. Her reputation was as a fighter who would punch, slap, kick, bite or scratch an opponent, man or woman ... do whatever she thought was needed to enable her to emerge as the victor. Where the box was taken from the warehouse she didn't know. Only Dutch, she assumed, knew of those arrangements and that was fine with her. She was happy with the arrangements that over the years had paid her so handsomely with so little hassle from the police.

'I fancy doing the delivery again this week,' she said to Dutch. He smiled at her. 'Yes, I expected you to.'

She smiled back at him. 'I need something to liven up my life at the moment.'

Dutch looked at her. There was no doubt she was an attractive woman who could turn on the charm anyway she wanted, but underneath, he knew, she was a hard, cold-hearted bitch. He worked with her and to some extent they were partners in this part of the operation, though he was in overall charge of the distribution and the logistics that it entailed. He had allowed Jackie to get involved the previous week and she had done it perfectly, but he didn't want her to do the run every week. It was too dangerous and a needless exposure to risk. He was on the point of refusing her when she smiled at him again.

'You can have Monica if you want. She's upstairs doing nothing. I know you have a special preference for her and she's had an easy time of late, mainly looking after Charlene.'

Dutch laughed. 'OK, OK, this week but then no – we have to find another to do it. It is too high risk. We can't have you out of the game. You're too valuable.'

Jackie smiled sweetly at him. She knew he couldn't resist an hour of sexual cruelty and, though it would probably mean that the girl couldn't work for a week afterwards, there were other jobs she could find for her, and anyway it was a quiet time for her business.

Adam and Brian were standing in the ruin that had once been a thriving warehouse, looking at the interior. It gave Adam everything he wanted as he visualised how he would tie Van Brubeck to one of the chains that hung down, then use the pulley system to raise his arms above his head, then his body, until he was standing on his toes, and then until his toes cleared the ground. He grabbed hold of the chain and held tightly as Brian pulled the other end through the pulley. Apart from a little noise the pulley worked perfectly, easily taking Adam's weight. He calculated that Van Brubeck might be heavier but, if the pulley did collapse, there was enough material lying around that he could use. He had already bought various pieces of equipment from different shops and in his mind knew what he was going to do, and how. Brian had insisted that he would also be there, to lend a hand if needed, but also to cover Adam's back if required.

'Weather forecast is for snow,' commented Brian.

'Good and bad, but we'll use it in our favour,' said Adam.

Monica lay on her front, naked on the bed, as Katja gently sponged the welts that Van Brubeck had left from the tops of her shoulders to the middle of her thighs.

'He is an animal, that man,' said Katja. 'No, an animal wouldn't do this for fun. What is the matter with a man like him? Why can't he just have sex? Why does he have to do this before he is aroused?'

Monica was gritting her teeth against the pain and crying without any tears. This time he had been worse than the other times, but she had to take what he wanted to give her because – well – what was the alternative?

Jackie entered the room without knocking and saw Katja applying the sponge gently to Monica's thighs. Blood was again beginning to seep from Monica's shoulder wounds, the red of her blood mixing with the red sores that were slowly beginning to swell. Jackie walked to the bed and Katja looked up, fearing that she would be in trouble for helping Monica.

'Leave us, Katja,' said Jackie.

Monica hadn't heard Jackie enter the room and the sound of her voice startled her. She started to painfully move towards sitting up.

Jackie waited until Katja had left the room and closed the door before she spoke.

'Dutch has given you a reminder, and the other girls as well, of what you can expect if you mess with me. You live here in good rooms, centrally heated and furnished, and there's good food. I only expect you to see four clients a day, so if any of you decide to cause any trouble then you know you will be moved to the other house where the clients are a damn site rougher than the gentlemen we have here. You don't have to work for three days, until the swelling goes down, but I expect you to make up your earnings after that. In the meantime you can look after Charlene, get her out of my hair. She's done nothing but be a bloody nuisance since the school broke up. Take her out for the day tomorrow. I don't want to see or hear her, understand?'

Monica looked up and used the back of her hand to wipe her nose. There was no fight in her. The strength she had felt in the past few days over Christmas had just been beaten out of her firstly by the evilness of Dutch then by the coldness of Jackie. She nodded meekly and asked in a whisper, 'I haven't got any money. Where do you want us to go?'

Jackie turned and headed for the door. 'I'll leave money on the hall table. Go wherever you please, but make sure she's out of here before I wake up.'

14

On Wednesday, 30th December Brian drove up the crescent at just after six in the morning, parking exactly where Adam had told him. He waited for thirty seconds then drove off, using the route taken by Dutch before parking in a side street just off the main road on the north side. He walked to the café to find Adam at a table at the back of the café. The owner was surprised to see another customer so early in the morning. She opened at six but didn't usually get customers until twenty past. As Brian sat next to Adam, the owner finished turning on the hot water urn and plugging in the hot food storage display. On her way to them she took down the last chair from the table where it had been lifted the previous evening while she had mopped the floor. She took their orders, two full breakfasts and a large mug of tea each.

'Didn't see you,' said Brian.

'I was between two cars and could see you through your back window. I saw you looking in the wing mirror down the road and then towards the houses.'

'Good. So, the girls reach the car, Monica gets her four packages, puts them in her pockets then walks off while the other girl gets in the car and is driven off to her customers. You plan on muscling in before he can drive off?' said Brian.

'Yes, instead of her, I'll get in the passenger seat, hit him with the cosh and pull him towards the passenger seat while you get in the driver's seat, and push him towards me. I'll get him in the back then you drive off.'

'With the girls screaming?'

'Could be, but what are they going to do? They have drugs on them They don't want any fuss there and then. They will have to go back to the house and tell Jackie. By then, we'll be well away. If they haven't got the drugs, then yes, they may scream, but in any event we will be away. The route means we can drive slowly and we'll be at the warehouse at just about seven when we won't need any headlights. We can park up and get started on him.'

'Where did you leave your car?' asked Brian.

Adam explained that he had parked his car away from the area in a side street where parking restrictions didn't apply.

Brian looked around, sensing that the owner was bringing their mugs, and smiled his thanks as she put them on the table.

'Early birds, aren't you?' she said cheerfully.

'Yes,' replied Adam as cheerfully as she. 'Early birds catch the worms and all that sort of thing. Don't you get many customers in at this time?'

'Nah, a few regulars half past six onwards, then I get busy seven, seven thirty, then it's mad up to seven when I close.'

'Bloody hell, that's a long day,' said Adam.

'Got to save for my retirement,' she said with a laugh as she returned to the kitchen.

Adam and Brian exchanged a look. 'I thought that surveillance meant that you shouldn't draw attention to yourself. Inconspicuous I think was the word, never to be remembered is what it means. So not passing the time of day with everyone,' said Brian from the side of his mouth.

Adam smiled. 'True, but I hope not to return to this fine establishment again and once you've eaten the breakfast, you'll see why.'

Brian chuckled. 'But you've already eaten here and you're back for more, just to see if it is as bad as you remember?'

Adam laughed and heard the owner shuffling towards them.

They had both finished their breakfasts and were finishing their second mugs of tea, watching the café slowly fill up as it passed seven.

'She was right, getting busier,' said Brian.

The door opened again and Adam nearly spilled his drink as a little girl was pushed gently into the café, looking apprehensive as heads turned towards her. Monica entered just behind her and pointed to a table, gently ushering Charlene towards it. Adam stared at her and was aware that Brian had recognised her as well. Monica looked around and saw Adam, before quickly turning her head away. She sat Charlene facing the front window while she went and sat facing the inside of the café where she could see Adam and Brian. She leaned slightly against the wall with her shoulder to lessen the pain as she couldn't straighten her back against the back of her chair. Charlene was obviously in a petulant mood and looking at a small book that Monica gave her from her shoulder bag that she had been carrying. Barely looking at a page, Charlene roughly turned the pages while Monica tried to persuade her to take her time and read the story.

They became the centre of attention as several of the men eating breakfasts made subdued comments about why a young girl should be out so early when it was so cold. One comment was spoken loud enough that Monica heard it and she gave the man a stare that ensured that his next comment was muttered under his breath.

Adam was thinking of the best way to make his approach, mindful that not only would everyone in the café see him but also that Charlene would recognise him from a few days before. In that case, would she mention it when she got home to her mother?

'Let's leave,' said Adam as he got up and walked to the counter to pay.

Brian raised himself and walked slowly to the door, barely glancing towards Monica and Charlene. Adam paid the owner at the counter and thanked her for his breakfast, then turned and looked at Monica to see her looking directly at him, almost willing him to return her look. She held his eyes. Adam looked around the customers and noted that they were all men. He returned to the counter and used a pen to write his mobile number on an order pad that the owner had left there, turned and looked at Monica again. He saw she was watching him and felt her eyes on him as he headed towards the toilets. As he reached the two doors for the respective toilets he hesitated and looked behind him to ensure that she was still watching him – she was – and then went into the ladies' toilet. He left the piece of paper face down in the empty rubbish bin then left and walked from the café to join Brian on the pavement.

They walked off at a slow pace as Adam switched his mobile phone on and explained to Brian what he had done.

Brian returned to his car and drove back to his home in Crawley to monitor the cameras at the Townsend house while Adam returned to his car and sat hoping for a call. It was cold in the car but he reminded himself of the rule about not letting a car engine run so he turned up his jacket collar and wrapped his arms around himself. Anyone who spent time doing surveillance knows that the quiet times are the worst, when the cold and boredom can lead to mistakes that could give away your presence and when your patience is tested to the nth degree. Adam was very self-disciplined and remained as still as he could using his eyes to keep a look out at traffic on the road and the wing mirrors to see people on the pavements approaching from behind. He had a system of working around himself clockwise: from looking in front through the windscreen, right to his wing mirror, behind through the rear-view mirror, left by the passenger wing mirror and then back to the beginning. To keep himself on his toes, he changed the pattern, working first anti-clockwise then missing one part of the sequence on each round before starting all over again. It worked, the system had worked in many countries and in many situations. He had never fallen asleep or been caught unawares and now he was thinking of how to remain professional. Twice he had been under-prepared, but not again, he thought. How long would he remain there would depend on whether he got a call, but he had a lot to occupy his mind. He had seen Monica's face, it was drawn, her eyes looked tired and she seemed smaller than he had seen her before – smaller or more timid? he wondered. What was she doing again with Charlene at this time of the morning? She had said the drugs run was weekly but it hadn't been a week – was she telling the truth? But more worryingly he wondered if he was being set up, if she was luring him into a trap where Townsend or one of his men could grab him. Stupidly he hadn't brought his weapon with him that morning as he didn't see any risk on a dry run, though he could now feel a very empty gap where he wished the weapon in its holster to be.

He checked the car facia clock again and saw that he had guessed wrongly. It was only twenty-nine minutes since he had last looked at it when he had calculated it to be thirty-two minutes. He looked again through the driver's wing mirror to check the pavement behind him – nobody – and continued with the round of mirrors. He slowly lifted his mobile phone from the seat next to him to in front of him where he needed only to move his eyes to see the battery was fully charged, the five bars that showed there was a full signal, and the volume was on high. It was a sign of nerves to recheck something that you know already. He thought of Van Brubeck. From the camera shots at Townsend's house and those times he had seen him in person, he appeared to be six feet tall or thereabouts. He had a large build and probably – from his gait – going to fat; he certainly wasn't a fit individual. Monica hated him. She almost spat when she talked about him, but she was very scared of him, too. Adam speculated that it could be Van Brubeck who had contacts in Spain and throughout the Continent, but then Jackie could have those as well. It could be both, he decided. Time would tell.

He completed another round of his surveillance routine, anti-clockwise this time. There was an old lady approaching slowly from behind on the pavement wheeling an old canvas shopping trolley, shuffling slowly towards him, her head down looking at the pavement, a fawn hat and a long matching coat to keep her warm. Sturdy shoes, brown, colour-coordinated. Adam smiled as he watched her, independent and determined, a threat of snow at anytime, freezing cold yet still out there shopping. Probably passed the same time every week and even more probably with the same groceries. That's how Ray's wife should have been able to live, he reminded himself, not tortured and murdered in her own home. He refocused his mind and looked again through all the mirrors and windows in the routine – check, check, check.

Monica had waited five minutes before entering the toilet and finding the piece of paper, memorizing the number before flushing the paper down the toilet. She had a mobile phone with her but it was the one that Jackie gave her to use to contact her if there were any problems when she was looking after Charlene. Any private calls could be discovered and she knew Jackie well enough to know that any hint she had been in contact with someone outside of their circle would meet with severe punishment, certainly a return to the other house, and probably worse. She shuddered at the thought of that house and what she had done there, the endless procession of men, one after the other, all colours, sizes and smells. She felt ashamed of herself, ashamed at what she had done and how if her parents knew it would break their hearts. She had to be strong for their sakes and that of her little sister.

She held Charlene's hand as they walked to Western Road and then to Churchill Square, the main shopping area of the city, where they could visit shops in the heated mall. Charlene wasn't happy at being taken from shop to shop. Even toyshops didn't hold her attention for long – she wanted to go home and watch the new films she had got for Christmas. She repeatedly asked Monica when they could go home and each time she was told that her mummy had said that she would telephone them to let them know when they could return. Until then they had to try and enjoy themselves. This was, she knew, a lie but at least she could blame Jackie for their predicament and have Charlene angry with her mother rather than with her. As lunchtime neared, Monica took Charlene on a bus ride. It was warm and the motion, she hoped, would send Charlene to sleep but of course that day it didn't happen. Monica saw the bus turn into the Marina at the eastern edge of the city, a place she hadn't visited before. Out of the window she saw a large cinema complex with advertisements for a number of films showing that afternoon and in an instant she grabbed Charlene and jumped from the bus. As the bus drew away, Monica held Charlene's hand and pointed to the advertisements and asked Charlene which film she would like to see. Charlene brightened instantly and looked at each advertisement in turn, asking Monica questions about what the film was about. Eventually Charlene chose one which was due to start in twenty minutes. Relieved that for the next two hours she would be warm and have a contented Charlene by her side, Monica happily bought a bucket of popcorn and a can of fizzy drink for her. Grasping the drink in one hand and the popcorn in the other, Charlene followed Monica into the auditorium, which was only half full. As Monica looked about for seats, Charlene tugged at her arm.

'There's Pip,' she said excitedly. 'Hi, Pip!' she called loudly towards a small girl sitting next to a woman in the central seating area who appeared to be slightly older than Monica. There were empty seats next to Pip and Charlene pulled Monica towards them. Pip's mother turned and smiled. 'Charlene! Hello, dear, come and sit next to Pip.'

Monica was smiling at Pip's mother, who indicated that she should go around and sit next to her, allowing the two girls to talk among themselves while she and Monica made small talk until the lights dimmed. Monica explained that she was Jackie Smith's au pair and had been asked to bring Charlene to a film for the afternoon while Jackie did other things. Pip's mother knew who

Jackie was and her reputation, and guessed that this sweet young woman wasn't a true au pair but nonetheless thought she was pleasant and spoke very good English.

'Oh,' Monica said to Pip's mother, 'I forgot to charge up Jackie's mobile phone and I have to tell her what time we will be back.' She looked worried for a second before seeing Pip's mother reach into her handbag and pass a mobile to her. Monica gratefully accepted it and indicated that she would use it outside.

Monica left the cinema and dialled Adam's number.

Adam was startled by the sudden ringing and quickly checked the number calling but didn't recognise it. He answered.

'Hi.'

Monica spoke slowly while her eyes scanned the area for anyone she might recognise.

'It's Monica. I'm at the cinema complex at the Marina. Come here and I will talk to you.'

Adam agreed straight away and as he closed the call he started the engine.

Monica returned to the cinema and handed the mobile back to Pip's mother. In a whisper she asked if she could leave Charlene while she did some shopping. Pip's mother happily agreed and Monica promised to be back before the film ended, a secret to be shared between the two.

Adam drove steadily, arriving at the Marina barely five minutes later, updating Brian as he drove. Paranoia was setting in as he wondered again if he was being set up. But it was that feeling of paranoia that had kept him safe over the years and he wasn't about to change his attitude now.

He drove past the cinema complex twice, seeing Monica both times, looking small, alone and vulnerable. She stood just outside the doors looking at a brochure as Adam took in the other persons in the area before checking the car-parking areas opposite. The area was safe and he pulled into the parking area opposite the cinema, watching Monica check her watch then look both ways. Her manner was what he expected, timid and nervous, but where was Jackie's daughter? Why was Monica alone? Again, alarm bells sounded and questions rang in his mind.

He got out of his car, stuffed his hands into his pockets and, head lowered, walked directly towards Monica, who saw him and started to walk towards him, meeting him at the edge of the pavement.

'Come on,' he said, turning and guiding her towards his car where he opened the passenger door, allowing him the opportunity to have another look around the area.

Seated in the warm car Monica unbuttoned her coat and told Adam about what the man Dutch had done to her and why she believed she and Charlene had been sent out for the day by Jackie. Adam asked questions that Monica answered quickly and, as far as he could tell, honestly. Monica talked for over ten minutes before he raised the question of her parents and sister.

'Monica, we are looking at your village to see what it's like, but if you tell me now it will save time. For instance, are there any people there who will help us?'

Monica shook her head. 'No, no one will help. They are too frightened. They are good people, they are honest and work hard, but they are scared of what could happen to them.'

'Are your parents fit? Can they walk if necessary? Do they own a car, a reliable one?'

'No, their car is very old. Sometimes it starts, sometimes not, but it doesn't go fast. They can walk, yes. They are fit and healthy and strong.'

'Monica, we have to act now, quickly, and I repeat what I told you before, I promise that, whatever I do, I will think through everything very carefully beforehand to make sure that it cannot be connected back to you. I promise you that.'

Monica looked at him. 'And when you steal the drugs – they're only samples, a small amount – what will you do then? They will search for you. Why are you doing this?'

'I can't tell you the reason. It's better for you not to know, safer for you. You have helped me a lot and you must now forget me. You have to be surprised at whatever happens.' Adam looked Monica directly into her eyes.

Monica shrugged. 'I hope that what you do hurts Dutch.'

Geoff Townsend poured himself another large gin and tonic and a glass of white wine for Pat as they relaxed in their surveillance-free house. They were still laughing about what had happened earlier that day when they had walked into Brighton Police Station.

The counter clerk had recognised them and instantly became nervous. Geoff Townsend had placed a plastic carrier bag on to the counter and slowly lifted each of the cameras and relays, laying them in a line along the counter while maintaining eye contact with the clerk. Several people were in the waiting area watching with some curiosity. The clerk knew that Townsend meant trouble and was wishing that he had taken his tea break earlier. Pat looked at him with a smirk as Geoff finished putting the cameras and relays on the counter.

'My name is Geoff Townsend,' he almost shouted, causing the counter clerk to take a step backwards. 'These are cameras' – he indicated the cameras – 'and these are relays so the pictures can be beamed to somewhere else – expensive pieces of kit. I found them outside my house and can't find an owner's name or address on any of them.' He smiled at the counter clerk. 'So, if nobody claims them I would like to for myself.' He maintained his smile and could hear subdued laughter coming from the waiting area. He turned to his audience. 'That's only my right, isn't it?'

There were nods of agreement as Geoff Townsend turned his attention back to the counter clerk. 'Well, don't you have to write it all down. Do I have to repeat my name for you? And if you don't know my address, I'm sure one of your secret squirrels from the surveillance department will be able to help you.' There was another burst of laughter in the room.

To the relief of the counter clerk he heard the Sergeant arrive at his side. Without saying anything, he retrieved a book from under the counter, opened it and started to fill in the page. Not once did he look at either of the Townsends until he had finished his writing and signed his name in a flourish. He tore a copy of the page off and smiled at Geoff Townsend.

'Mr Townsend and Mrs Townsend, thank you for being honest citizens and handing in found property. Without people like you I don't know what this city would be like.'

He turned and left the area, leaving Geoff and Pat Townsend speechless. There was a small tittering among the people in the waiting room. Geoff Townsend regained his composure quickly and as he and Pat walked out he announced: 'Heard it yourselves, honest citizens, that's us.'

He laughed loudly as he walked away towards their car, which they had left parked on double yellow lines immediately outside the entrance. The journey home had seen them both laughing so much that they had to wipe tears from their eyes. They had triumphed. They had shown the 'filth' to be incompetent.

Monica and Charlene arrived at Jackie Smith's house after six that evening having been given a lift home by Pip's mother in her four-by-four. Charlene was excited but tired and thought Monica the best person ever in the whole world for taking her to the cinema. She and Pip had really enjoyed the film and, though at one stage, Charlene had looked for Monica's reaction to a funny part and noticed that Monica wasn't there she hadn't given it any thought but continued to watch the film. At the house Monica had taken Charlene into the kitchen to prepare a meal for her before giving her a bath and putting her to bed with a story.

An hour later when Charlene was asleep Monica had gone to

the top-floor flat and was preparing for a bath to ease the stinging from the welts on her back when Jackie Smith appeared, as usual without knocking.

'Right, in the morning you and Katja are doing the run as usual. Be ready by half past six.'

Monica was confused. It wasn't Friday, which was when she usually did the deliveries. Jackie saw the confusion and sarcastically said, 'It's New Year's Eve, you thick bitch. Everyone parties New Year's Eve, well they do in this country – don't know about yours – so make yourself ready.'

As soon as she was alone Monica felt a wave of panic. She had several times assured Adam that they made their deliveries every week, every Friday without fail. He had been pleased with the routine and she knew that whatever he was planning would happen next Friday but he would arrive and find nobody there and he would think she had betrayed him. She felt like crying. She couldn't leave the house without an excuse and there wasn't one that she could think of that would be accepted by Jackie. Monica went to the bathroom and ran the water while she got undressed, pausing to examine her wounds and wincing as her blouse snagged in the welts. She gently eased herself into the water, feeling pain as the warm water entered her wounds, and lay back trying to think of how she could contact Adam.

Once dressed in loose clothing she looked out of the bedroom window and saw snow beginning to fall gently, highlighted as it passed through the glow from the streetlights. The weather could make a difference, she thought. If it snowed hard, then maybe the cars wouldn't be able to be driven on the roads and her deliveries would have to be cancelled. She felt her spirits lift until she thought that if the snow was that bad they would probably make her walk closer to where the men lived. The more she thought about it the more she knew in her heart that she would have to make the deliveries.

She prepared for bed and was hanging up her clothes when

she felt a weight in her coat pocket and instantly she knew it was Jackie's mobile phone that she had been given to use to contact her if she had any problems while out with Charlene. She switched it on. Her hands began to tremble as she crossed to her bedroom door and opened it, listening to the sounds in the house, hoping that Jackie wasn't checking up on Katja and Greta. Monica could hear the usual sounds coming from Katja and Greta's bedrooms while they entertained their clients, but there weren't any other sounds. She closed her door and threw a dirty jumper behind the door to prevent it opening and dialled Adam's number. The call was answered on the second ring.

'Because it is New Year's Eve we are making the deliveries tomorrow,' she whispered. 'Tomorrow, you understand?'

Adam had understood and knew that Monica was taking a risk by calling him with that information. 'Understood,' was all he said before closing the connection.

Monica looked at the mobile and saw the 'History' option, which she pressed. She elected to delete all the history of the mobile's usage but found that it was impossible to do so as that particular option wasn't available, and there on the screen was the call she had just made – the date, time and number called.

Adam closed the call and saw Brian watching him. 'Monica. Because tomorrow is New Years' Eve, they're making their deliveries in the morning.' Adam ran a hand through his hair and looked at Brian. 'We're ready though, aren't we, so we can still do it?'

Brian smiled. 'Ready and no problem for tomorrow unless the weather prevents us getting down there and of course,' – a serious look appeared on his face – 'the snow will mean that the tracks to the warehouse will be bleeding obvious.'

Adam was deep in thought. 'We can't approach from another direction, can we? The tracks would be even more obvious, so we'll have to chance it. We'll be there a couple of hours max and in any case we'll be making his death public so if someone does it before us, so what?'

Brian didn't like the sound of that but knew the time frame was being dictated to them and so they had to act tomorrow or leave it for another week.

15

The following day Adam and Brian drove slowly along the main roads towards Brighton. The snow was heavier in the north of the county and gradually became less until they reached the outskirts of the city where the snow lay like a heavy frost. The roads had been fully gritted and were clear. This was good news for Adam and Brian, though they knew that the track which gave access to the warehouse would still have snow on it.

By 6 a.m. Adam and Brian were in their positions opposite Jackie's house: Brian crouched between two cars in front of where they expected Van Brubeck to park, Adam between two cars just behind the expected ambush place. Adam was holding a sand-filled leather cosh in his hand and could feel the reassuring heaviness of his holstered weapon under his left arm. Brian chose to sit on the road surface tucking the tail of his coat under him to prevent his bottom getting cold and to gain a view under the cars, ready to slide underneath one if a pedestrian arrived. Adam was crouching on his hands and knees, using his toes to lever himself from his knees every time he felt the knee joints stiffen in the cold, but he felt comfortable and confident that he could manoeuvre in any direction quickly. The cars had a film of frost with light snow over them that glinted in the streetlights, and both Adam and Brian worried that their cars parked in side streets ten minutes' walk away would look obviously different.

Adam glanced towards Jackie Smith's house and saw a light appear in the hallway. He felt a bolt of excitement course through his body. 'We're on!' he thought.

The outside light came on and immediately the front door

opened and two figures passed through the door. The front door closed and the porch light was extinguished. The two figures looked around the crescent then slowly started to walk towards where Adam was. As he watched the figures, he suddenly noticed them quicken their step and a second later he was aware of headlights approaching his position from behind. He tensed his muscles and moved ever so slightly closer to the car behind and beside him to give himself protection from being seen. The headlights and car engine noise approached then passed him, his area being lit by the red braking lights. Adam waited and watched as the two figures started to run across the grass area towards the road behind him.

The running footsteps approached him, then in a blur the two figures passed, followed three seconds later by the sound of a car door opening. In that split second Adam was on his feet and covering the distance towards the passenger door. He recognised the coat that Monica had been wearing the previous day and brushed past her as he sped along the pavement. The other girl, larger than Monica, was by the open car door and preparing to sit down when Adam squeezed in between her and the seat. His right hand holding the cosh was held high and was the first part of his body to enter the car. Instinctively, he knew where the target area would be and a fleeting look confirmed it before transferring the message through his brain to his arm and hand. A blur of movement and the cosh landed on the forehead of the driver, causing Van Brubeck's head to smack back into the headrest, his arms flailing in front of him.

Adam dropped the cosh, knowing that the blow had been perfect, and with his right hand he grabbed Van Brubeck's jacket, yanking him hard towards him. With his left hand he grabbed the larger girl's arm and holding that tight, partly as leverage, he pulled Van Brubeck towards him. Van Brubeck began to slide over the passenger seat as Adam saw Brian entering the driver's door. A second later Van Brubeck was almost thrown towards

Adam, who stepped back, allowing the Dutchman to fall on to the pavement. He pushed his hand into the girl whose arm he held and pinned her against the car, ignoring Van Brubeck. He rummaged in her coat pockets and pulled out three packets from one and two from the other. Each packet was the size of a standard matchbox, though thinner. He threw the packages into the front floor well of the car and roughly pushed the girl to one side while opening the rear car door.

He picked the dead weight of the Dutchman up and threw him on to the rear seat, not caring that the Dutchman's head hit the door on the way in. Without breaking his movement he grabbed hold of Monica and saw that she was holding the four packages in her hands which he grabbed before throwing them into the car with the others and slamming the door shut. He piled in on top of Van Brubeck and held the corner of the front passenger seat. Brian had waited until Adam's feet were off the pavement then in that instant had released the clutch and the car accelerated forward. Adam managed to remain on top of Van Brubeck as the car took the right-hand corner by the 'bottle neck' then the further right turn southward towards the seafront. Adam was unaware that they had passed Jackie Smith's house at over forty miles an hour but clung on as the car took a hard left-hand turn on to the seafront road, which under pressure of the turn slammed the door closed.

Brian drove carefully then, just over the speed limit, and keeping to the quieter roads. Adam eventually managed to bundle Van Brubeck on to the floor of the car, pressing his body down. The Dutchman stirred and began to try and move but Adam punched Van Brubeck under his chin, jerking his head into the floor. Van Brubeck's eyes drifted up into the lids and Adam knew that he would be unconscious for the best part of an hour, which suited him and Brian.

Monica and Katja stood on the pavement, watching the car take the corner. Both were shivering, in shock at what had happened and the speed in which it had taken place. They couldn't speak as they stood there, then as one they turned and ran back towards Jackie Smith's house, which was in darkness. They rushed up the steps and banged on the front door. They were still using their fists on the door and both beginning to cry when Jackie Smith opened it. She was wearing a jumper and jeans and, fearing that the commotion was the police, had delayed opening the door for thirty seconds. This had been her nightmare ever since she'd been a teenager, albeit a worldly-wise teenager. Then she had been arrested in a dawn raid and had been made to get dressed in front of women police officers knowing that their male colleagues were also watching her through the open door, sniggering. She could still recall the redness and heat of embarrassment in her face.

As she opened the door Monica and Katja fell into the hall past her. Shocked, she looked past them to the deserted square then hastily closed the door. The girls were trembling and crying as they got to their feet. Katja was trying to point back to the square while Monica had her head lowered.

'What's happened?' Jackie shouted at them.

Katja took a deep breath and pointed. 'A man attacked us … He stole the packages.'

'What!'

'… Came from nowhere, stole packages and drove off with Dutch,' said Katja.

'With Dutch!' shouted Smith at Katja, before turning her attention to Monica, pushing her against the wall.

'What's bloody happened, Monica?' she shouted, her face directly in front of Monica's.

Monica was genuinely in shock. While she knew Adam was involved, in the maelstrom of speed and aggression she couldn't really recognise him. Her mind was reeling as she tried to stand upright but another push, harder this time, pinned her against the wall. Somewhere in her mind pain from her back was registering but it was taking second place to the threat from Smith in front of her.

'A man, no I think two men … One stole the packages from us, snatched them … Dutch was in the back of the car. I think another man must have been driving. The man who stole the packages was in the back of the car … It drove off.' This was all she managed to say before breaking into a long cry and putting her hands in front of her face.

Jackie Smith acted quickly. She pushed Katja into the dining room and ordered her to stay in there, then pushed Monica into the kitchen and gave her the same warning. She tried to gather her thoughts together. This was totally unexpected and normally it would have been Dutch to whom she would have turned for advice. She quickly made her mind up and raced upstairs to where Greta was sleepily tying the cord to her dressing gown, having been disturbed by the shouting.

'Get dressed,' she barked at Greta. 'Three minutes downstairs.'

Smith was running down the stairs when Charlene came out of her bedroom.

'Mum?' she started to say before Smith pushed her backwards.

'Stay in your bloody bedroom until I tell you you can come out,' she shouted before slamming the bedroom door closed. She continued downstairs and into the kitchen.

Monica was standing by the sink apparently staring blankly out the window but in fact she was inwardly cursing her stupidity. She had lain awake a lot of the night thinking about what Adam might do and in any of the circumstances the one thing she was going to do herself was to get rid of the mobile phone. In the heat of events, however, she had remembered to get the drugs out of her pocket but had forgotten the mobile phone. It was only now that she realised she still had it and on it was the evidence that would condemn her.

Smith was in turmoil as she listened to Monica's account. Who knew that the girls met Dutch in the mornings? Why didn't

Dutch see whoever was waiting? How did the man or men know to grab the drugs from the girls? What had happened to Dutch? Then slowly she started to think of other questions: was it real or was Dutch involved in a scam? The weekly delivery had been slightly larger than usual but not big enough for Dutch to risk everything. They had a good system that saw everyone receiving a large and reliable income though not so big as to draw the attention of the regional or national police teams. The system had remained unchanged in four years and in that time there had been not the slightest hint of trouble. Suddenly she was struck with a thought: the main cache – only Dutch knew where it was held this week out of his various safe places that he used.

Greta wandered into the kitchen staring at Monica and Smith, wondering what all the fuss was about. She was told by Smith to get to Geoff Townsend's house and tell him that he was needed as soon as possible. Smith was used to dealing with all sorts of problems with staff, and over the years she had seen and heard of most excuses and never believed any hard-luck stories. She didn't believe what Monica was saying now but Katja appeared to be saying the same, so could they both be lying?

Brian kept his speed low, not wanting to risk an accident or drawing attention. He could just make out Adam's body shape in the back of the car as he lay on top of Dutch, who appeared subdued. Brian slowed as he approached the track that led to the warehouse, noting the twigs he and Adam had placed a few yards up the track. They were still as they had left them, unbroken, which meant that no vehicle had been up there since they had left.

As he drove up the track, he tried to keep to the hard ground, avoiding any ground foliage, but when he looked in his mirror he could still make out the tyre tracks in the snow. He parked at the rear of the building and in the half-light looked around and listened before helping Adam lift the unconscious Van Brubeck from the car and into the warehouse. Only the sound of their feet scrubbing on floor debris and their heavy breathing broke the silence, as each man knew instinctively what they had to do. Van Brubeck was held upright by Adam, as Brian tied Van Brubeck's hands together then affixed them to the chain that ran through the pulley. Brian pulled the chain until Van Brubeck was wholly suspended from the chain and his feet were only just touching the floor.

The movement stirred Van Brubeck, whose eyes slowly opened as he tried to understand what was happening to him. As he took in his surroundings, he showed his fear. He had been in places like this a few times, acting on orders from Geoff Townsend, but never had he been the captive. He knew what he had done to men, systematically beating them until he had extracted all he wanted to know before leaving them until a relative or friend had been told of their whereabouts. He understood how it worked and now he looked at the two men who were busying themselves around him and he felt fear. Neither spoke. One was slighter in build and not as tall as the other. 'Little and Large, that's how I'll remember them,' he thought.

The larger man went behind him while the smaller man stood in front of him. He felt his jacket being pulled away from his body and then heard the sound of scissors as the taller man started cutting his jacket. The man worked in a methodical way, cutting straight up the back of the jacket then along each sleeve so that the jacket fell away with the front zip still intact. The jacket was handed to the smaller man who searched the pockets. The mobile phone was found and while Brian opened it and looked through its contents, Van Brubeck felt the scissors work their way up the back of his jumper then again along the arms until that, too, was pulled from him.

'Hey, man, that's not necessary. What do you want?' he said

He didn't get any reply but felt his vest being cut and shortly that joined his jumper on the floor.

'Come on, speak to me,' he said. 'What do you want from me?'

Again he received no reply and he watched as the smaller man laid the items from his jacket pocket on the ground. The small lock knife that he had carried for many years lay looking innocently at him. How he wished he had that and wasn't tied up. He would make both of them pay for this.

Adam used the scissors to cut through Van Brubeck's belt then down the seat of his trousers and each leg. The trousers fell to the ground. He kicked them towards Brian. Van Brubeck had noted how the men didn't speak and how they appeared to move always just out of reach of his legs. He felt his underpants tugged just before the scissors cut them. They fell to the ground and suddenly he felt a surge of rage. To hold him and question him was one thing. He expected to receive pain, but not the humiliation that they were inflicting just for the sake of it.

'This isn't necessary,' he said, trying to put calm into his voice.

The smaller man finished searching the trousers and threw them on top of the jacket before examining the small bunch of keys that he had found. Brian showed them to Adam and kicked the jumper and vest to join the trousers and jacket. Adam walked in front of Van Brubeck.

'The next few minutes will determine three things: firstly if you live, secondly if I kill you quickly, or thirdly if I kill you slowly and as painfully as possible. I have experience of all three and, though I'd prefer the third because you are such scum, I'm prepared for the first or second option. Up to you.' Adam had spoken in a quiet almost conversational tone.

Van Brubeck felt himself shiver. He would have wanted it to be from the cold but in truth it was more from the matter-of-fact tone in which he had been spoken to. He had realised that the two men were good at what they were doing but there was an almost detached way in how they had got him into his present state, hanging naked save his socks and boots. They were professionals, he knew. Even the warehouse looked as if it had been carefully selected. He took in the broken roof, the debris scattered over the floor, and knew that the warehouse was in a remote location. They wouldn't be disturbed and therefore there wasn't any hope of his being rescued. He inwardly knew that he would try and brazen it out with these two, but he had a worry that perhaps he had met his match with them.

Adam continued in his conversational tone. 'A few simple questions from me, a few simple answers from you, and then we can all go on with our lives and put this sordid little event behind us.'

Geoff Townsend had been woken by one of the security men tapping gently on the bedroom door.

'What do you want?' he had shouted.

'Mr Townsend, there's a girl here, says she's Greta from Jackie Smith, wants to speak to you urgently. She arrived by taxi.'

Townsend swore, then quickly got out of bed and put his dressing gown over his pyjamas. Pat, lying next to him, stirred and, though she had heard the security man, kept her eyes closed in the hope of going back to sleep as Townsend walked to the bedroom door.

Downstairs, Townsend opened the door and recognised Greta standing there, huddled in her thin nylon jacket, with the other security man standing next to her.

'She's clean,' the security man said to Townsend, who hadn't thought of whether she might or might not have been. He made a mental note: these two were good. He'd find out more about them and maybe look towards giving them a more active role working for him.

'What do you want?' Townsend said.

Greta was shivering against the cold and knew that what she had to tell him could result in Townsend being sent into one of his notorious rages. 'Jackie asks if you can come to her house as soon as possible please. She has a problem. Monica and Katja were robbed this morning and she can't raise Dutch.'

'What?' was Townsend's response as he started to think quickly before rushing back into the house. He was about to use a clean new throwaway mobile phone when he stopped himself. It could be some sort of action by the police, revenge for their equipment being returned. He quickly got dressed and made so much noise that Pat gave up any hope of sleep and asked him what was the matter. He didn't reply but left the bedroom door open as he ran down the stairs and left the house, grabbing hold of Greta's arm as he went.

He jumped into the driver's side of his black BMW four-by-four vehicle and started the engine as Greta settled into the passenger seat. He gunned the motor, throwing stones as his tyres fought to get a grip on the driveway. The gate was already open and he sped through it, barely seeing the security man standing to one side. He drove quickly, muscling and bullying his way through the early commuter traffic, arriving at the front of Smith's house in less than ten minutes. He jumped out, ignoring Greta, who during the brief journey had sat mutely in her seat, scared both by the driving and the barely suppressed rage that emanated from Townsend. He reached the door and pounded on it with his fist until it was opened a few seconds later by Jackie.

'What's going on?' he raged.

'Here,' she replied, ushering him into the lounge. He followed her in and remained standing as she lit a cigarette then spoke to him.

'This morning Monica and Katja went on their usual delivery run. I saw them out with the usual packages. They say that when Dutch arrived they were suddenly attacked by a man, though there might have been two. They say the man or men grabbed Dutch and threw him into the back of his car, robbed them of their packages then drove off. They think there were two men: one would have been driving, the other with Dutch.'

Townsend didn't speak but stared at her. She was as reliable as anyone, had never let him down once in all the years. He didn't doubt her but this whole thing was wrong. He brushed his hand over his baldpate before throwing both arms into the air and turning towards her.

'How?' he said. 'How did anyone know about the arrangement? How did anyone know?' he repeated. 'It's been running as sweet as anything. We've never had a problem, have we?' He looked at Smith, who took a draw on her cigarette then spoke through the smoke.

'Never! The question, as you say, is how, then who. I've kept the girls separate so, if they're telling lies, we can find out but so far their stories are the same. They're scared and I think in a bit of shock.'

'Come on, Jackie. Let's have a word with them and see if they're telling the truth.' Townsend stepped to one side to allow Smith to pass him.

Monica was sitting at the kitchen table when Jackie followed by Townsend stormed into the room. She stood and in a quiet and frightened voice repeated what she had told Jackie earlier and as best as she could she gave a description of the man who had attacked them – Adam.

Townsend appeared to be satisfied that she was telling the truth but continued asking questions to check her story and make sure that when he spoke to the other girl he would know if she was telling the truth or not.

Van Brubeck was in pain. The tall man had selected a length of rubber-coated wiring from the floor and with a smile had gone behind him. He knew what to expect but was still surprised by the amount of pain it caused when he was struck on a shoulder, then the other, then the top of one leg and the top of the other. It was systematic, a steady rhythm of a blow to one side of his body followed by a similar blow to the other. There was no hurry and apparently no effort by the man with the wiring – just a constant thwack and the conversational, confident tone as he asked questions.

'I tell you: I am just a runner for Mr Townsend. My job is to pick up one of the girls and take her where she tells me. Sure, I know she has drugs but they are only small amounts. I can't tell you anything else.'

He had repeated the speech in various forms for ten minutes. No other question had been asked but the beating continued in its slow and careful way. His back had been struck now down its entire length, as had his legs. The stinging he knew would be the result of welts being made by each blow, but the pain was dulling his feelings everywhere and the whole of his body was beginning to feel as if he'd been run over by a bus. What was worse, he knew that the beating would continue until he changed his story.

Adam had considered his routine systematically: he was going to change his angle so that the next blows crossed the welts and cuts that were already developing. He wasn't going to show any urgency. He knew that in these circumstances the person being interrogated looked for any hope, any sign that the interrogators were under pressure of any sort themselves. He wouldn't give Van Brubeck any such signal and would continue with the laid-back approach as if they had all the time in the world.

Van Brubeck recognised the new pattern and knew that the man wouldn't stop: he was far too professional and practised in inflicting pain. Van Brubeck knew that when the man had finished the pattern he would select a new one, most likely his front, first from one side then the other. It was what he would do if the circumstances were reversed, but now each blow was causing him more pain than he could cope with and as each new strike landed he fought mentally to disregard that one and prepare for the next. He closed his eyes against the pain and made involuntary noises from his throat: screams were developing at the same time that tears were causing his eyes to mist. The man sitting in front of him was now smiling gently and had Van Brubeck's knife in his hand.

'OK!' Van Brubeck shouted. 'Ask me questions, anything.'

Brian looked at the knife as another blow landed on Van Brubeck's leg, then back up at the man who was now close to breaking. He could see that the resistance that was there at the beginning was already being eroded. His strength was being sapped by the relentless pressure, from both the physical and mental assault on him. Brian knew Van Brubeck was watching him to see if he did anything to indicate that the beating would end, that he and the taller man would change their tactics. If they did so, it would be a small, perhaps ever so small, victory for him; it could give him some hope. Brian, though, wasn't going to give him any hope and steadfastly refused to switch his gaze even momentarily towards Adam.

'What can I say?' Van Brubeck screamed.

Brian smiled at him. Victory was in sight. A scream was always the first sign that desperation had crept in.

'Stop and I'll tell you anything.' Van Brubeck shouted, breaking into tears.

Adam looked at Brian and caught the faintest of movement of his head.

'What is the set-up, from beginning to the end?' said Adam evenly.

Van Brubeck felt a small victory. He had made the bastards talk, he had broken their routine. A second later another blow landed and another. He knew, then, that it was he who had broken, that there would be no let up until he told them what they wanted to know. If he did, Townsend might kill him. If he didn't, these two would kill him. It came down to him making the choice.

Another blow. His head was now hurting from the pain inflicted on his body. It was his choice. Another blow. Head pounding. Noise, he could hear noise. It was him, trying to scream, crying … Another blow. Why was his head hurting so much? He hadn't been hit there. Another blow. His right leg collapsed below him and his arms strained against the chain with the sockets of his arms now so painful he couldn't have described it to anyone. The muscles of both his upper and lower arms were screaming at him as was his head, his back and legs. Every part of his body was begging his brain to do something to end the pain before they all broke down.

'Townsend and his brother are the top,' Van Brubeck almost shouted, then in a spurt of words that ran into one another he continued: 'Drugs in through Gatwick, every week … don't know how but I arrange pickup and hold the bulk. Samples run out every week … When the orders come in, I deliver or get someone else to.'

Adam walked to the front of Van Brubeck and used the cable to land a blow at the top of Van Brubeck's right thigh.

'More detail, Dutch. A lot more detail. I'll take a break while you talk, but I'm looking forward to your front being criss-crossed like your back unless you give us everything.'

Townsend walked out of the dining room, leaving Katja in tears. He was satisfied that the story the girls were giving was the same but they hadn't thrown any light on what happened to Dutch.

'Jackie,' he said, watching her light another cigarette, 'do you know where the cache is this week?'

She shook her head from side to side. 'No, I don't know where Dutch keeps it. He's never said and I've never asked.'

Townsend was thoughtful. 'It must be the cache they are after. That's why they took Dutch. I know he uses four places but I don't know which one he used this week. I leave that up to him. I'm going to check the four places that I know. You carry on as usual and keep ringing Dutch. Something may come up. Oh, get hold of Plod, see if he can find out where Dutch's car is … and have you a shooter?'

Smith understood who Plod referred to and the work he had done in the past for them and agreed to ring him straight away. She had anticipated the request for a gun and had already put it under a cushion of the settee in her lounge. She handed it to Townsend, who checked the magazine and breach before putting it into the back of his trouser band. He ran down the steps towards his car, planning the route to cover the four likely places where the cache would be.

Smith closed the front door after Townsend and was heading towards the kitchen to tell Monica that she could go upstairs when Charlene appeared at the top of the stairs.

'Get in your bedroom!' Smith shouted, causing Charlene to burst into tears. She continued into the kitchen, telling Monica to go and look after her daughter. Katja was to go back upstairs to the flat.

'The address, Dutch?' said Brian, quietly holding a pen and notebook. 'What was it again?'

'Billy Down's garage, a mews just off Western Road, by Waterloo Street. I've a safe there at the back of the garage, behind some tyres and old stuff. He doesn't know what's in the safe, just that we keep stuff in there and we go there from time to time. He don't ask any questions. We just give him a drink for his troubles.'

'And you say Jackie Smith has some cocaine at her place. Where does she keep it?'

'In a safe she has behind books in her lounge.' Van Brubeck had decided he might as well answer the questions and then live to fight another day and, boy, was he going to fight another day when he got hold of these two.

'Geoff Townsend, you say, never gets his hands near any drugs?' continued Brian.

'Never.'

'And the money you collect for him, you give it to Pat once a week when she's shopping?'

Van Brubeck was sorry to have included Pat but he had answered without thinking. The relentless systematical application of pain had tipped his thinking towards saying anything to stop the situation getting any worse for him. He could address any problems later, but only if he were alive.

'Yeah, clothes shop in the Lanes, Classic Boutique. I meet her there at ten every Thursday, give her the money, then follow her to her car and she drives off. Used to have Kieran with her most times.'

Adam smiled. 'Not any more she doesn't.'

Van Brubeck looked at the smiling taller man.

Adam looked at Brian. 'Anything else, or are we finished?'

'Finished I think.'

Van Brubeck felt his spirits rise. True he would have a problem explaining to Geoff Townsend why he had talked but seeing the marks he felt Geoff would understand and in time he would be forgiven.

'Just one other thing, the girls who work for Jackie Smith. You keep their families back home under threat, so the girls here have to work as prostitutes, correct?' said Adam.

'Yeah, but they're nothing,' Van Brubeck replied, not caring if he told them about the girls. There was nothing these two could do about that part of the business and in any case he felt his cooperation would mean the end of the beating and pain.

Adam walked behind Van Brubeck and swiftly placed a dirty piece of material across Van Brubeck's mouth, tying the ends together behind Van Brubeck's head.

Van Brubeck was caught by surprise by the move but hoped that it signalled the end of the beating. He hoped that the two would now leave and tell Townsend where he could find Van Brubeck and in a few hours he would have his back treated and he and Geoff Townsend would be after these two.

He watched as Adam kicked all of Van Brubeck's clothes into a pile around his feet before dropping the length of cable he had used on top.

Van Brubeck's spirits rose, so much so that he almost missed what Adam had asked him.

'Monica, sweet little girl, she's been forced into prostitution, hasn't she?'

Van Brubeck was thrown by the question. Why was he worried about her? He nodded.

'And you beat the crap out of her the other day, didn't you?' Adam said.

Van Brubeck felt a sudden wave of fear. His eyes opened wider, then wider still, as he saw Adam walk to a small rucksack that he hadn't noticed before. Monica, he'd kill her the little cow. He watched as Adam pulled a small can of lighter fluid out and walk towards Van Brubeck, all the time looking him directly in his eyes.

'Her back is very sore and she's too frightened of you, Jackie and the gang back home to say anything, but ...' – Adam smiled and removed the top of the can – 'I'm not, and I know she would love to do this herself, but as she can't, I'll do it for her.' Adam poured lighter fluid on to the pile of clothes then, looking Van Brubeck in the eye, he moved the can higher and poured some over his genital region, allowing the fluid to run down Van Brubeck's legs. Adam moved the can under Van Brubeck's face then poured the remainder over his chest and back.

'Not your face, Van Brubeck. I wouldn't want your eyes to be damaged so you can't see the flames.'

Adam nodded to Brian who put Van Brubeck's mobile and penknife into the rucksack and started to walk towards the exit.

Van Brubeck was trying to plead through the dirty material as he saw Adam take a box of matches from his jacket pocket, strike one, then drop it on to the clothing on the floor. The flames crept through the clothing and as Van Brubeck tried to lift his legs from the heat and avoid the fluid on him catching fire, his arms couldn't take the weight. The fluid caught fire on his body and in seconds he could feel the heat creep up him. He was screaming as the flames gently fanned over his chest and back, joining with those from his genitals and legs. He tried to move but couldn't.

Adam smelled Van Brubeck's burning flesh and stood back, looking above at the thin, light-blue smoke that rose towards the broken roof. Satisfied that the smoke wouldn't be seen, he looked again at Van Brubeck, whose body below his shoulders was now all alight, his skin blistering and tearing. Van Brubeck's eyes and mouth were contorted in silent rage, unfocused though powerfully explicit in pain.

Adam turned and walked from the warehouse without a backward glance.

Neither he nor Brian said anything on the drive back to the city centre.

Geoff Townsend almost ran from the house on the housing estate on the outskirts of the city, such had been the smell inside. The single mother who lived there was high on something and sitting on the broken settee in just her underwear, showing her thin and diseased body to him. Her daughter of about a year old was lying on a blanket on the bare floorboards crying. The house smelt of urine, stale smoke and general decay and so strong was it that he felt the back of his throat gag in repulsion. He hadn't needed to talk to her; he knew where he wanted to go. He pulled three floorboards up from the corner of the lounge then used a key to open the safe that was set into the concrete below. The safe was empty. He swore then locked the safe and walked out, not daring to say anything in case the putrid air penetrated his lungs. He knew he would have to throw his clothes away after being subjected to the smell and, in all likelihood, the fleas. He ran back to his car and started the engine. He drove off quickly, watched from behind grubby net curtains by neighbours who wanted to know what was going on but, realising it was Townsend, would be too scared to ask.

Brian parked Van Brubeck's car on the seafront while Adam walked along Waterloo Street and the whole area that the Mews was in, locating the garage and noting possible escape routes. They had both voted to take the drugs as quickly as possible, knowing that their loss would hurt Townsend but, more importantly, it would increase the pressure on him. Brian had speculated that perhaps they could draw him out of his house and make him get his hands dirty.

Townsend drove quickly out of the estate and headed along the A27 road towards the city centre and his second address. This was a shop whose owner he had known for many years. The man had always been reliable and trustworthy, the added bonus being that he, like his home and shop, was immaculate. The shop was located just before the junction with Elm Grove on the Lewes Road and he knew that parking was only possible on double yellow lines but he wasn't in any mood to worry over trivia. He parked immediately outside the shop on the yellow lines, which drew a long blast of the car horn from the car behind him. Townsend got out and went to the driver's door, snarling with rage and swearing at the top of his voice. The woman in the car was terrified and, putting her hands to her face, broke down in tears as Townsend banged his fist first against her door window then the front windscreen. Two women pushing pushchairs stopped to watch the commotion and were about to say something when Townsend swore at them to get out of his way. He crashed through the shop door and walked past the assistant towards the back where the office and storeroom were located. Dave Prentiss had heard the shouting from the street, which normally wouldn't have been sufficiently unusual to have disturbed him but he had recognised the voice, and that was enough. He had just reached his office door when Townsend came around the counter with the assistant hard on his heels.

'Hello, Dave,' Townsend said pleasantly. 'Tell this shit head to get out of my sight before I do her a permanent mischief.'

Townsend carried on into the office while Dave tried to soothe his assistant and tell her to carry on with her work. Townsend shifted the metal filing cabinet with some effort, revealing a safe cemented into the wall behind.

'Nothing in there, Geoff,' said Dave from the doorway. 'Dutch was here last week and took everything. He said he'd be back in another week or so.'

Townsend heard what Dave Prentiss said but still searched his key ring for the safe key. He had to check and make sure for himself. The safe was empty as Dave had said.

Townsend turned and walked out of the shop. The two women with the pushchairs were consoling the woman driver who had dared to use used her horn against him. He shouted at them all and got into his car, started the engine and began to crawl forward in the traffic.

'Garage, then Hove,' Townsend said to himself as he waited for the traffic lights to change. He knew that at this time of the morning the traffic would be heavy but he had made good time. In any case, he knew that Dutch wouldn't say anything, even under duress. Would he?

Adam got back to Van Brubeck's car and sitting in the passenger seat explained the setup to Brian. Adam looked at Van Brubeck's bunch of keys and identified four that would fit safes. The others weren't of the right size or make, so he only had four to check.

'Right, I'm off. See you at the end of the mews in five,' Adam said before he got out of the car. He felt the weapon in its holster and ran through a couple of possible scenarios as he walked towards the mews, paying attention to the small buildings on either side to make sure that Brian wouldn't be obstructed by any sudden movement from anyone.

Townsend tried to bully his way through the traffic, but was thwarted by several drivers who showed that they were prepared to have their old cars scratched as long as he was prepared to have his new expensive car also scratched. Townsend didn't care about the car. He could buy ten of those the next day paying cash, but in all likelihood he would be forced to stop and he didn't want any delay. He made it to the Brighton Pavilion whose gold domes sparkled against the clear dark-blue sky and was waiting for the traffic lights to change so he could reach the next set of lights after which he would have a clear run to the seafront. The traffic would move more freely along the seafront until he reached the road that would take him to the mews.

Adam walked into the garage and saw two mechanics working under an old-looking car that was on a hoisted platform above them. Another mechanic was walking with a clipboard in one hand and a pen in the other as he slowly counted the motor-vehicle parts and accessories that were arranged on a shelf. There was a smell of grease about the place and a radio was playing music. As he had expected, Adam was quickly able to identify the area that he was interested in – Van Brubeck had described the area perfectly. Adam pulled the keys from his pocket and walked up to the man with the clipboard.

'I'm here for Dutch. I need to get in the safe,' Adam said, trying to appear casual and looking towards the pile of tyres.

The clipboard man looked at Adam. 'And who are you? Dutch never said anything about you coming.'

'He got tied up today, so asked me to come instead,' Adam said, unable to stop himself from breaking into a smile at this play on words.

'Nah, mate,' the clipboard man said, 'when Dutch tells me and not before. You could be Old Bill for all I know, so bugger off and get Dutch to call.'

Adam sighed and for an instant he looked at the ground before his left hand with fingers pointed came up with the heel of his hand, connecting with the jaw of the man whose eyes almost popped out of their sockets. His knees folded and Adam grabbed him to lower him gently to the ground. He looked at the two mechanics working at the car and saw that both had their backs to him. He moved quickly to the stack of tyres and began lifting and throwing them away.

The commotion alerted the mechanics, who shouted something at Adam, but he wasn't concerned. What could they do? They were under a car, with equipment in their hands, and would be nervous in any case. Even if they did decide to have a go, he would already have moved the remaining tyres by then and could deal with them. He saw the safe and the make of it, old but reliable, cemented into the wall in a purpose-built fit.

It was then that the first mechanic reached him.

'What the hell is going on?' He had spotted the prone figure of his colleague on the floor.

'Go away,' Adam said simply, as he selected one of the two possible keys.

The mechanic went to push Adam, but Adam was too quick for him. He moved out of the way at the same time as he swivelled on one foot and lashed out with the other, catching the mechanic exactly where he intended – the knee cap. There was a scream as the mechanic fell to the ground, clutching his knee.

Adam calmly put the key into the lock. It didn't turn. As he was taking it out, the other mechanic came forward, holding a large spanner above his head. Adam half turned in a crouch and, putting his whole weight into the punch, buried his fist into the mechanic's stomach. He gave a loud hissing noise through his teeth as he slowly sank to the ground with his arms hugging his stomach. Adam inserted the second key and turned it. He felt the key turn and heard the click: the lock was undone.

Townsend reached the seafront and headed west, weaving in and out of the traffic using his horn aggressively to aid his progress. At the foot of West Street he was about to gun the motor through the traffic lights as they changed from yellow to red but was thwarted by the car driver in front of him changing lanes to gain pole position.

Townsend blasted his car horn and received a single straight finger in response from the driver who was looking through his rear-view mirror. Enraged, Townsend undid his seatbelt and reached behind him for the weapon, but just as he reached for the door handle he saw a police car approaching from the opposite direction. He sat back in his seat and in a matter of seconds was almost grateful for their presence. He would have shot the driver, that was certain, but also as certain was that he would have been identified by any number of car drivers in his vicinity.

Adam opened the safe door and saw a box inside which had rope handles at the end. He pulled it out and found it was lighter than he expected. He held it in his left hand and was planning on how he was going to get past the three bodies sprawled on the ground when he heard a loud voice.

'Put it down,' it shouted aggressively.

Adam looked up. Above the working area of the garage was a small office outside of which now stood another man dressed in blue mechanic overalls. This man, though, was holding a side-by-side shotgun the barrels of which were shorter than the legal length. He held it in both hands, his right at the trigger and the left along the barrel. Adam had always acted on instinct and knew that if you made an unexpected movement it would invariably give you the edge. He didn't hesitate but rolled forward, holding on to the box and at the same time trying to move to his left side. As Adam started to draw his own weapon, he heard the roar of the shotgun. The deafening retort echoed from the walls and ceiling and Adam rolled forward again. He had his gun aimed towards the man above and saw flames from the barrel as at the same time another deafening sound echoed around the garage. Adam was on his feet.

He knew the man was holding a two-shot weapon, but the man had already broken it and was in the process of lifting the weapon to release the spent cartridges when Adam fired. His aim was to the bulk of the man and the bullet hit him in the centre of his chest, knocking him backwards. Adam didn't know or care if the man was dead or would die. He certainly was no longer a threat to him, which was all that concerned him as he sprinted from the garage and down the length of the mews where he saw Brian waiting in Van Brubeck's car at the entrance to the mews. The rear door on the passenger side was open and Adam jumped straight in. The box slammed into his side as he fought to reach over it to close the door. The task was made harder by Brian's acceleration as he turned left towards the seafront, throwing Adam to his right as the car took the corner.

Townsend cleared the lights and knew that the road he wanted was small and liable to be congested, so he decided that he would take a more major road then make two turns to take him into the mews. As he approached the traffic lights where he was to turn right he saw the lights beginning to change from green to yellow. He put his foot hard to the floor and passed the light as it changed to red. He pulled hard on the steering wheel at the same time as taking his foot from the accelerator and managed to hold the turn.

Brian had made two turns then headed towards the seafront where the traffic lights were showing red against him. He slowed in preparation to stop when he saw a large black four-by-four hurtle from the seafront road into his. The vehicle looked to be almost out of control. Brian was thinking of where he could manoeuvre if the driver did lose control and then noticed the traffic light was changing in his favour. He accelerated slightly, preparing to cross the line when the green light showed. He caught a glimpse of the driver of the black vehicle. A fleeting half-second was all that he needed to know it was Geoff Townsend.

Townsend struggled with the steering and was unable to sit properly in his seat as he turned into the road. He fleetingly saw a car being driven towards him then a second later it struck him. It was the same colour and make as Dutch's car. He looked in his interior mirror and saw the car finishing its turn on to the seafront road, heading west towards Hove. Townsend braked hard and looked at how he could turn around, but in the road with cars parked in the area he was in it would have been difficult. He drove on and used a side road to begin to make his manoeuvre. He reversed in and started to pull out when he saw traffic approaching him. He stopped in order to prevent what would have been a sure accident, and knew that in that half-minute he had lost the chance of catching Dutch's car. One thing he had noticed, though, was that the driver appeared to be the only occupant and that he definitely wasn't Dutch.

Townsend drove towards the mews and was about to park when he saw people approaching the garage. His heart sank – he knew that the man driving Dutch's car had been there. He parked the vehicle against a wall and ran to the garage, pushing a couple of bystanders out of the way. Inside, he saw that where the tyres were usually stacked, two mechanics were lying on the ground and another in another part of the garage. People were pointing and following their fingers he saw another blue-clad figure lying on the metal grating on the higher level outside the office, red blood dripping through the grating.

There was a smell of cordite in the air and he noticed the sawn-off shotgun lying on the floor a little distance away. An empty shotgun cartridge lay nearby, but worst of all was that he could see the safe door was open and that the safe was empty. Had it always been empty or had it been emptied in the last few minutes? He had seen enough to know that he had to get to the last address quickly in case the cocaine had been left there. He got into his car and was driving towards the seafront when he heard the wail of a police siren. The police car came into view, its blue lights flashing off the plate glass in the surrounding buildings. He slowed in the traffic and as the police car passed him saw that the officer in the passenger seat turned and looked straight at him. The officer said something to the driver and at the same time appeared to grab his radio. Townsend looked away, cursing and swearing, knowing that his being in the neighbourhood at the time of a shooting incident would mean that the police would suspect his involvement.

Brian had seen Townsend and, after turning towards Hove, had in fact taken turns to take him inland and on the route to drop Adam off so that he could collect his car and then follow him to where he was going to leave Van Brubeck's car.

Half an hour later Brian checked again to make sure that Adam was still following him as he drove Dutch's car into the wood situated on the outskirts of the housing estate behind the Marina. He did a cursory search, but no one was around. He undid the petrol cap and lowered a sock into the tank using a stick. He retrieved it soaking with petrol and repeated the procedure with another sock, then dragged them both over the sides of the car and across the seats. He left both the socks inside the car then threw in a matchbox with a lighted match tucked in. He heard the muffled whoosh sound as the socks ignited as he ran to Adam's car. As Adam started driving back on the road, Brian turned and looking back he could see a pall of black smoke drifting through the tops of the trees followed by a sudden spurt of flame, which indicated to Brian that the petrol tank had caught fire. Although the fire brigade would probably put the fire out before the car was entirely destroyed, any DNA evidence would be thoroughly destroyed and frustrate the police enquiry.

Adam drove Brian to collect his car before they drove by separate routes back to Brian's house in Crawley.

Townsend had been to the Hove address and opened the safe to find it empty, as he had half expected having seen the chaos at the mews garage. Now in a furious temper, he drove on to Jackie Smith's house where he and Jackie sat in the lounge discussing where at this late stage they could find more cocaine in order to supply their customers; it was, after all, one of the biggest nights of the year. Jackie had suggested a man she knew in London and Townsend agreed that she should try to contact him and get enough for their immediate needs. At all costs they had to keep the theft of the cache just between them. They would have to ensure Monica, Katja and Greta kept their mouths closed, too. Any word that they had been ripped off would lower their standing with two possible results: firstly, the customers would think them unreliable and look to source their supply elsewhere and, secondly, sensing that they were incompetent and weak, someone would try to muscle in on their patch. Either was a potential disaster for them.

Adam and Brian were in the operations room, having showered and changed and burnt the clothes they had been wearing in the lounge fire. After the clothes were just ashes logs were added and the residue ashes were raked with the fire tongs to ensure that no threads remained. Just one could be sufficient to identify their clothing. The box Adam had obtained from the mews sat on the table next to Brian's computer, together with the nine packets they had taken from the girls. Adam opened the box using a screwdriver. Inside were four polythene packets, each about eight inches long by two inches deep and three inches wide, containing a white powdery substance, and under them at the bottom of the box was a larger clear polythene bag that contained a mix of roughly chopped leaves that looked like dried herbs or lettuce.

'Skunk,' said Adam. He lifted two blocks of brown substance closely wrapped in some kind of cling-film. 'Cannabis, though what sort I haven't a clue.'

Brian whistled through his front teeth. 'The coke is worth a fortune and I bet the other stuff is worth a few bob as well.'

Adam looked at it all. Everything he hated was there, either in his hands or within touching distance. He had always been strongly against any form of drugs, had despised people who made their living from other people's misery. He had seen people destroyed by their drug habits, and now here he was in possession of an amount that would be enough to send him to prison for many years, even by a lenient judge. Worse, his friends and ex-colleagues would think he had stooped so low as to be a dealer.

After Townsend left Jackie Smith's house, he drove straight home and told Pat what had happened including his being seen near the shooting incident at the mews. Pat told him that the local radio had carried a newsflash that there had been a shooting in the city and that a man had subsequently died. It was now a murder investigation. Townsend was worried at the prospect of the police questioning him, as he knew they surely would, and he telephoned his solicitor to alert him that his services would be needed that day without any doubt.

The solicitor, Edward Jones-Mitchell, had worked all the thirty-five years since he qualified as a solicitor in the city and knew many police officers of all ranks as well as criminals and their families. His contacts within the police were in the main straight down the line, honest officers who were passionate about their task of catching and seeing villains locked up. He was used to talking with officers both formally and informally, at court or at the police station, and worked hard at being seen as an almost independent observer, though his aim, as everyone knew, was to ultimately frustrate them in their pursuit of his clients. He had been successful many times, especially when it concerned Geoff Townsend, a man he'd represented frequently over the years on various charges that he knew Townsend to be guilty of. He wouldn't call Mr Townsend a friend but he liked being paid the retainer every month to be on call. He enjoyed his lifestyle and now at the age of nearly sixty was able to take as much or as little work as he wanted, allowing him time to enjoy his two passions – sailing and playing golf.

Jones-Mitchell's office was based just a hundred yards from the Brighton Pavilion: one of his large office windows looked towards the magnificent building and another towards the sea. The waiting room was cosy and a small office led to where his legal assistant-stroke-secretary worked. His law firm consisted of just the two of them. He had resisted overtures to increase the size of his practice, which would have meant a lot more income for him but also a lot more hassle, and that he did not want. Much of the work that he signed off and for which he charged his rate was in fact completed by Paula who had worked for him for over twenty-five years and was completely trustworthy.

It was Paula who took the call from Geoff Townsend and confirmed that when Edward Jones-Mitchell returned from court he would immediately drive to see Mr Townsend at his home – the usual practice as Townsend, like many criminals, didn't want to be seen going to a law firm; it could damage his reputation.

It was just before lunchtime that Townsend received a call on the mobile phone he kept for only one person, his 'Plod'. Townsend listened without saying anything for over a minute and closed the call still without speaking a word. He looked at the mobile then at Pat.

'Plod, says it was Del at the garage, shot, one round in the middle of his chest, probably died pretty instantly. The boys there say it was one man who went in and knew exactly what he was doing. Said Dutch had sent him. Moved the tyres, opened the safe. Plod says that the three of them attacked him but he was too fast for any of them, dislocated Jimmy's kneecap and he's a hard little so and so. Plod says that they all say the safe was empty, never used. He's getting them to leave out the bit about Dutch sending him obviously and to say the bloke must have known the safe was there but didn't know it wasn't used. Plod will give me a call later with a proper description of the bloke. He said he'll come up late afternoon to interview me about my being seen in the area. Better him than someone else.'

Pat sat down. 'Who is the bastard? I thought they were all hard at the garage. Del was that's for sure.'

'Fired twice with a sawn-off – that was Del,' Townsend said sadly.

'I'll get some flowers for his wife. He still is with Cathy, I take it?'

Townsend laughed as he and Pat knew Del liked to party, especially without his wife, who stayed at home watching the television while he had a few drinks and chanced his arm with a girl. Pat gave a half-laugh but looked at Townsend with a worried look on her face.

'So what's happened to Dutch. You don't think anything bad, do you?'

Townsend stopped laughing and shrugged his shoulders. 'Not looking good, is it?'

Jackie Smith had cancelled work for the three girls while she went to London to see the man she would obtain her supply of cocaine from. By putting herself out and visiting the man in person, she would show him respect and answer any questions that he might have, such as why she didn't have her own stock. She could brazen out any challenge and by the time she arrived home the quantity she ordered would have been delivered to the shop in Lewes Road, which Geoff Townsend had visited that morning. From there she would instruct her local suppliers to visit the shop at intervals, where she would meet them and personally hand out the cocaine. It was something that Dutch always did but in the current circumstances she was more than happy to step up to the breach.

Adam and Brian had left the box and samples in the attic while they thought through their next move. They had heard on the radio of the murder of a mechanic in Brighton that morning and listened to the description of the wanted man, which while the description was not very accurate in that the height, weight, hair and eye colour were all wrong it disturbed them both that Adam was officially 'wanted' by the police.

'So, we have some options,' said Brian. 'Let's work our way through them to see which we think is best.'

It would take them some time, so each settled into their armchairs and Adam closed his eyes to ready himself for the task.

Edward Jones-Mitchell arrived at Townsend's house at lunchtime and explained that he had been in court all morning but had now freed up his afternoon so he had all the time that Mr Townsend wanted.

Geoff Townsend told him openly of the day's events, from the robbery of samples from the girls and the assumed abduction of Dutch, to the raid on the safe at the garage. Townsend knew that he was better telling everything to the solicitor, who could then protect him from the police when they interviewed him.

'Geoff, as far as Dutch and everything connected to him is concerned, I think you shouldn't say anything at all. Let's see how that develops and Jackie should do the same. The girls I am sure you will speak to, so that whole episode is airbrushed. As for Dutch's disappearance, have you spoken to his wife?'

Townsend realised that he hadn't. She was a logical person to speak to.

'I have,' said Pat, who was sitting next to her husband. 'I gave her a ring this morning while you were flying around the place.' She looked at her husband. 'Just a woman-to-woman chat about how she and Dutch were, that sort of thing. She said everything was fine, that he was busy, and that they had had a good Christmas even though he was out a lot. He's not expected back until this evening then they're going to a dinner and dance at the Metropole.'

'She'll be lucky, I reckon,' said Townsend. 'If he was lifted

– and the alternative is that he's behind the rip-off and I don't believe that – then the chances of him being at any party this evening aren't good.'

Mr Jones-Mitchell intervened. 'As for the garage, you have a choice: to say that you don't know anything and were just in the area shopping for something for Pat, or that Del was someone you knew and you were just popping in to see him. As you got there, it was obvious something had happened so you went away. Assuming the police can show that at some time in the past you and Del were friends or, at any rate, associates, I would suggest the latter. A touch of honesty carries a lot of weight in a difficult situation. As for the safe, just deny any knowledge of it. They can't prove anything to the contrary, can they?'

'Nah, Dutch was the only one to go there in the last year or so. I just knew about it and had a spare key.'

'I should get rid of that key, then. We wouldn't want the police to find it, would we?'

Townsend searched his pockets and handed the key to the solicitor, who placed it in his briefcase.

Adam and Brian had finished their planning and also had talked about what they had done that day. As far as Dutch was concerned neither man had any problem with what they had done to him, and that went for the mechanic, too. It was a basic rule in their business that, when you were under attack, you dished out more violence than you were being offered.

'Right, I'll go and make the calls,' said Adam, rising from his chair. It was four o'clock in the afternoon, just in time to cause some confusion and perhaps worry Mr Townsend.

Adam walked for a quarter of an hour until he reached a public telephone box that wasn't damaged or covered by a CCTV camera. He referred to his list that he had written before leaving the house. He made his first call to the *Argus* newspaper, based in Brighton.

'There's a man who works for Geoff Townsend, known as Dutch. He's missing and his car was set on fire near the council tip at Whitehawk this morning.' He replaced the receiver and inserted another twenty-pence piece.

The news desk at the local BBC television station was answered on the first ring.

'Geoff Townsend's right-hand man, Van Brubeck, is missing and so is a load of Townsend's cocaine.'

Again, he replaced the receiver and inserted a further twenty-pence, looking around him to make sure that he was still alone.

The number for the commercial television station was answered by a man who sounded as if he was working reluctantly or under duress when he would rather be getting ready for a party.

'A man has been murdered, in a warehouse near Poynings. It looks like he was tortured before he died.'

He replaced the receiver and left the area, walking past every CCTV camera with a limp, his shoulders hunched and the long coat covering most of his legs. The hat he wore was black, large-brimmed and pulled down over his eyes. If film of him was examined, it was unlikely the police would tie the image with that of the man who had walked down a street in Brighton before or after Kieran Townsend was found dead. He knew the three desks he'd just called all recorded their calls and would have automatic caller identification facilities so it was likely that they would all call the police quickly and they would want to speak with Geoff Townsend. Adam smiled.

The Detective Chief Inspector had asked all the right questions and the Detective Sergeant who accompanied him had recorded every question and answer. There was nothing else to be discussed and Mr Jones-Mitchell was preparing his diversionary tactic for the Sergeant when the Townsend home telephone rang. It was an unusual occurrence as both he and Pat used and relied on the various mobile phones that were in the house. Pat looked quizzically at her husband then walked to the corner of the lounge where she answered the call.

'Hello,' was all she said.

Geoff Townsend watched her and, because he did so, Mr Jones-Mitchell and the two detectives also looked at her, each waiting for her to say something.

They all saw her face suddenly turn red before she shouted, 'Who are you?' and slammed the phone down. She realised that everyone was watching her and had heard her outburst. 'They rang off,' she said, looking directly at Geoff and sending him a subliminal message that he instantly understood. Pat was upset by the call – that much was evident to everyone – but she regained her composure in time not to thoughtlessly repeat what the caller had said. She ignored the looks and instead collected the empty mugs, signalling that as far as she was concerned the interview was finished.

Mr Jones-Mitchell turned to the Detective Sergeant: 'Perhaps I can ask you something regarding another matter while we walk to our cars?'

The Sergeant glanced at his senior officer, who shrugged his shoulders in agreement and pretended to collect his paperwork together. As Mr Jones-Mitchell and the Sergeant left the room, Pat re-entered and, seeing that it was just the three of them, said, 'The call was from someone who said that Van Brubeck' – she looked at her husband – 'has gone missing and so has your cocaine.'

The Detective Chief Inspector looked from Pat to Geoff with shock. 'What?'

Geoff Townsend looked at him. 'That car number I asked you to look for was Dutch's car. Have you traced it?'

'I was just going to tell you: it was found burned out at lunchtime, just in the woods in Whitehawk.'

Geoff Townsend's face showed anger and started to turn red as his rage mounted. 'Someone is messing with me. I saw that car this morning as I was going to the garage. He wasn't driving; it was a smaller man, not Dutch, and I only got a quick look but it wasn't a face I've seen before.'

'Is Dutch missing?' the Detective Chief Inspector asked.

'Yeah,' Geoff Townsend admitted. 'It looks like he was lifted this morning, and before you ask, yeah, all the coke was in the garage safe, with some skunk and stuff. I can't believe he'd rip me off, not Dutch, so I have to think he really has been lifted and made to talk. Can't believe it. Can't believe that he would talk. He knows everything. He's … well, just not that sort. You know Dutch. He's as hard as bloody nails. Christ who would have a go at him?'

Pat said quietly, 'Maybe someone is harder, but whoever is behind all this knew about the girls meeting Dutch?'

Geoff Townsend looked at Pat. As usual she was thinking positively. 'Jackie, Dutch and the girls would have known where they met up, but then there's the nine suppliers who the girls met. Any one of them could, I suppose, have followed them – you know, reverse following.'

The Detective Chief Inspector looked worried. 'Geoff, this is serious. Whoever shot Del was either lucky or very good and, given how he handled the mechanics and had the balls to go there alone in the first place, I think he is a serious player. Descriptions have been given and a drawing will be done and released but from what we've got at present he doesn't look like anyone we know. Also, we don't want a bloody gang war. I know,' – he stopped talking and held up an arm – 'and nor do you, but we can't have one, Geoff.'

'I've lost a week's coke and more and my main man is missing, I know it's bloody serious. I'm down half a mil because of this bloke and I want him, or them, and I don't bloody care who they are or who they are bloody working for or anything else. And I'll tell you something else: if it's a gang and they want a war, they'll bloody get one without any problem.' The venom in Geoff Townsend's voice reeked.

Adam and Brian had a quiet evening talking and drinking cans of beer. Adam had cleaned his weapon and refilled the magazine, as always wearing gloves to avoid leaving fingerprints or sweat on the cartridges from which DNA could be obtained. He knew his DNA was held on file, as was Brian's, because of their previous jobs – for identification purposes should they be killed or held hostage.

They were planning their next move, hoping to put more pressure on Townsend until he made a mistake that they could use to their advantage. Brian told Adam that he still couldn't find Williams, which was very strange. In the past, he had always been able to find anyone he was looking for even if, as in this case, he was hampered by not being able to speak with any relatives, friends or even an ex-wife. There were still other avenues he had open to him and he hoped for a result within the next few days.

Sandra and Raymond Black were enjoying a quiet evening before she returned to her home just before midnight to celebrate the New Year with her husband. Raymond hadn't bothered to stay up to see a New Year in for over thirty years as it was just another day as far as he and Ann had been concerned.

'So, Dad, do you think Adam will go on to kill the others?' Sandra asked.

Raymond held his glass containing a small whisky aloft and smiling said, 'I hope so, love, I hope so.'

Sandra smiled at him. They had spent more time together recently and their old relationship had returned. He had always doted on both his children but there had always been something special about Sandra. In his eyes she really couldn't do much wrong.

'I got an email from Dave yesterday. He said he was well, sends his love, and hopes to see us soon,' she said.

Raymond smiled. 'That'll be nice.'

Jackie Smith had spent the evening in the back office of the shop, waiting for the dealers to arrive. None of them seemed that bothered by the unusual procedure and nobody really doubted the quality of merchandise. She returned to her house satisfied that at least all those they regularly supplied had received their goods and that the price she had agreed to pay for them in London had been reasonable in the circumstances. Their reputation was intact. She poured herself a large vodka then kicked off her shoes and slumped into an armchair. It wasn't the extra work that worried her or the fact that she had to be more hands-on, increasing her risk of being caught, it was the question of what had happened to Dutch that caused her to worry. She had phoned Geoff Townsend and told him that everything had been sorted out at the Brighton end and he had seemed relieved that at least something had gone right that day. He had reassured her that everything would be back to normal in a week or two and that he'd spoken to Lenny, who was sending over someone to take Dutch's place. There would be a complete overhaul of their system, everything would be changed, but when the dust settled they would be running smoothly again with all the profits restored.

Jackie next telephoned Dutch's wife at home and, although she rang three times and allowed the tone to ring out, she received no reply. She was about to order a taxi to take her to Dutch's house to see whether he was there or had left in a hurry when a thought suddenly struck her. She poured herself another vodka and sat back in the armchair and concentrated again on what her two girls had said about being robbed. There was a difference in their stories, she was sure, a small one somewhere but she couldn't place it. She smoked a cigarette but after another drink still hadn't been able to identify what it was that they had said that was different. Frustrated at knowing there was something niggling at the back of her mind she decided to do something positive in the hope that whatever was in the deep recess of her brain might be jogged forward.

She ordered a taxi from her usual company with whom she had an agreement and sat in the back as she was driven through the city along the seafront. She liked the vibrancy of the place, the people, thousands starting their night out, some wearing dinner suits, others in casual clothes, and some dressed in jeans and old clothes. She liked them all – they were customers or at least potential customers for her. The house with the other girls who worked for her would be busy tonight and at least she would make a good income from them to make up for the loss of earnings from the three girls who worked from her house, though they would be told they would have to make up the losses themselves by extra work. Perhaps, she thought, things weren't quite so bad.

As she approached Dutch's house, she saw two marked police cars parked directly outside the house with a number of plain cars in the vicinity that she recognised as being the type used by CID officers. She told the taxi driver to drive past the house slowly so that she could make sure that the police were at that house and not another though she already knew the answer. Her suspicions were confirmed as she gained a clear view through the large window of uniformed officers and plain-clothed men and women clearly visible in the lounge. She ordered the driver to take her back home.

Geoff and Pat Townsend were drinking while watching a television programme with the sound down, each deep in their own thoughts, when Geoff's mobile rang breaking the quietness. He saw the caller was Jackie Smith and answered the call. She explained what she had seen at Dutch's house, and he told her about the call that Pat had taken earlier. They agreed to talk later and in the meantime she would keep calling Dutch's house to try and find out what was happening.

Two minutes later his mobile rang again and, thinking it was Jackie Smith ringing to give him the news, he immediately said, 'Tell me the news then.'

But it was the Detective Chief Inspector. 'Geoff, the call Pat got earlier, it was from a television station. They and another station and the paper all got calls saying basically that Dutch was missing, along with your cocaine, and one call said he had been killed. The caller said Dutch was in a warehouse and gave a rough location near Poynings. The boys in blue have searched and found him and from the first report he appears to have been beaten badly then set on fire. In fact, they say that they can't really be sure it is Dutch. It looks like a dentistry identification will be needed as whoever it is is charred beyond any normal identification.'

Townsend winced, hoping that Dutch had already been dead when he was engulfed by the flames.

'What's happening then? Do you have any clues to follow up?' he asked curtly.

'Too early yet. Forensics will be there all night and probably all day tomorrow. I'm not on the case but I expect it will get linked with Del's murder, so I'll get an idea of where we're going. I'll let you know tomorrow.'

'Yeah, OK, thanks,' he said abruptly and closed the call.

He turned to Pat and dialled Jackie Smith's mobile. He told her the news and arranged to meet her in the morning. When Lenny's man arrived, they needed to sort things out.

16

On New Year's Day Jackie Smith was up early to visit her other house and collect the takings. She returned home to find Charlene in the kitchen eating a bowl of cereal with Monica sitting opposite her at the table. Monica stood up and prepared a coffee for Jackie, who put two slices of bread into the toaster as Charlene started to tell her mother about what she wanted to do that day – to go and watch another film like the last time. She asked if Pip could come over to play in the morning then go with her to watch a film in the afternoon, to which Jackie replied dismissively that it was up to Monica what they did as she was busy.

A thought struck her. 'Just to let you know, Monica, Dutch was murdered. Maybe you and Katja had a lucky escape.'

Monica couldn't hide her surprise and held a hand over her mouth as she gasped, 'Murdered?'

'Seems he was beaten then set on fire, so whoever had a go at you is a nasty piece of work. You said that he didn't rough you, or hit you in any way?' she asked in a conversational tone.

Monica shook her head. 'No,' she said quietly.

Jackie Smith was looking at Monica closely, looking at her eyes and her hands, trying to pick up any message that was being given off involuntarily. She had known the girl for a while and trusted her as much as she trusted anybody who worked for her. She had been a good earner, but a thought suddenly struck her.

'Dutch was rough with you the other day, wasn't he?'

Monica blushed wishing Charlene wasn't listening to these things. She looked at Charlene who was munching on a mouthful of cereal and watching her. Monica looked at Jackie Smith then at

Charlene, hoping that they could have gone to the lounge out of Charlene's hearing. Jackie Smith wasn't in the least concerned.

'Well?' she demanded.

'Yes,' Monica replied.

'So, you're not upset about Dutch being murdered, are you?' Jackie Smith said in an accusing tone.

'I didn't like him but I wouldn't want anyone to die like that.'

'Katja said that he searched her pockets for her samples to find them. He grabbed her ... pushed her.'

Monica didn't answer.

'He pushed her hard, she nearly fell over. He didn't push you though, did he?' she said, her tone becoming firmer.

'No,' was all Monica could think of saying.

'So why didn't you run or shout or something. Why stand there like a stuffed dummy?' Jackie Smith said, moving a pace towards her, warming to the idea that Monica may be about to say something she hadn't mentioned before. Whatever had been niggling her since hearing Monica's and Katja's accounts was now becoming a scream in her mind. She knew she was getting closer to finding what that niggle was. She was on the right track and she was going to pursue it until she knew exactly what had happened.

Monica looked frightened. 'I was scared. It was so fast. Katja and I didn't see him. He just appeared and it all happened so fast,' she stammered.

Smith noted that tears were beginning to form in Monica's eyes. Smith scented blood. She knew she often scared her girls and Monica was a timid girl.

'Katja!' she shouted. 'Katja, get down here now!'

Monica was surprised by the sudden shout from Smith and gasped loudly while Charlene's spoon hit the side of her dish with a loud 'ping'. Smith stared at Monica.

A few seconds later Katja appeared in the kitchen and instantly saw Monica was nearly crying, which made her even more worried than she usually was when summoned like this.

She was frightened and looking at Jackie standing with her arms folded, with a hard stare on her face. Charlene was finishing her cereal as if nothing unusual was happening.

'Right, you two, Katja. You say the bloke pushed you and searched your pockets for the samples. Is that right?'

'Yes,' replied Katja.

'But you, Monica, you weren't pushed, so how did he get your samples?' Smith said, walking up to Monica and staring straight into her eyes.

'He searched me as well,' she said, her voice barely audible to Katja, who was standing no more than six feet away.

'Is that what you saw Katja?' Jackie said, without moving and keeping her glare firmly on Monica.

'It was so fast, Jackie. Honestly, I don't know.'

'Did you see the bloke search Monica, yes or no?' Jackie almost shouted.

'No.'

Monica couldn't hold her tears anymore and had closed her eyes when she felt a slap to the side of her face.

'You bitch!' Jackie screamed, slapping Monica's face again. 'You're a lying bitch. He didn't search you for the samples. You handed them over to him, didn't you? ... *Didn't you?*'

Monica tried to turn away from Smith's blows but walked into the seated Charlene and was trapped. The blows continued to rain down on her face and head in a furious flurry before they suddenly stopped.

In a calm voice Smith said, 'You set Dutch up, didn't you?'

Monica looked at Smith and shook her head. 'No, no,' she said as the tears ran freely down her face.

'You're a lying bitch. I think you had something to do with it,' Smith said in a calm voice that was even more frightening and threatening than her raised one. She jabbed her finger into Monica's face. 'If you did, you will watch what we do to your sister, then to your mother and then your father. You will watch and hear everything then it'll be your turn. Tell me now and I'll not touch your family. Lie and so help me they'll be on the first plane here.'

Monica knew that any threat would be carried out and visions of her sister and parents being hurt made her shudder. She had a choice to make, to tell her about the man, or not tell her, a straightforward choice, but either way she knew that she would be punished severely by Smith and Townsend.

Charlene looked up at Monica with an almost disinterested look as if to see her mother slap another woman and scream at them was all in a normal day's events. She had, of course, seen and heard it before and also been on the receiving end herself, it was just her mother when someone had upset her, she reasoned.

'Charlene, when you and Monica have been out, has she talked to anyone?' asked Jackie, looking sweetly at her daughter.

'Pip's mum at the film. They sat together and I sat next to Pip.'

'Anyone else?'

'Er,' said Charlene, thinking. She was enjoying being the centre of attention in the drama and creased up her face as if concentrating. Suddenly she brightened. 'That man in the café, you spoke to him,' she said, looking at Monica.

'That's right, I did,' said Monica, desperately trying to think of an excuse as to why she should talk to a man in a café. 'The man came over and started to talk. I think he maybe fancied me. He asked some questions about why we were out so early and I told him it was none of his business and to go away. He did. The café owner as well, I spoke to her,' she added as an afterthought and hoped she sounded honest.

'Who was this man?'

'We only spoke for a minute. I didn't ask him his name; he didn't say. He was just a nuisance, and I told him to go away and he did.' Monica tried to make her voice sound strong because she thought Jackie Smith would believe her if she wasn't defensive and timid. She looked Jackie Smith straight in the eye. 'He was just a strange man. It was early and I think he thought I'd be easy to pick up, that sort of thing.'

'At that time of the morning, that's bloody nonsense,' said Smith sharply.

'He didn't sit down or anything, just came up and started talking and I told him to go away, didn't I?' Monica looked at Charlene for support.

'Yes, he just stood there and said something to Monica,' Charlene said to her mother.

'What did he say?'

'Don't know,' Charlene answered slowly.

'You were there. You must have heard something, so what did he say?'

'Can't remember,' Charlene said in a matter-of-fact voice.

'Right,' Smith said, 'I'm not happy, Monica. I don't believe in coincidences and until we get to grips with this you don't leave the house … for anything.'

Charlene looked up at her mother. 'What about meeting Pip and going to see a film?' she whined.

'Shut up!' Smith answered sharply before turning and walking from the kitchen, slamming the door closed behind her just as Charlene burst into tears.

Monica looked at Charlene and felt some sympathy for her – she was only four years old and with a mother like Smith what chance did she stand of growing up to be a nice person? Then she thought about her own situation and what could she do about it. She felt her whole body shake as she remembered that Dutch was dead, murdered. It had to be that man. He didn't look like a violent man like many of the men she met.

Adam had started his cycle ride just after seven o'clock in the morning. There was nothing else on the road and he was able to make good speed as he reached the other side of Crawley and began to head south on the country road towards Haywards Heath. He was beginning to sweat heavily as he reached the town centre and after a tour of the town he headed back. The route was perfect for him and he enjoyed the challenge of each hill he encountered on the return journey until he arrived back at the house. The living-room curtains were still drawn closed, which probably indicated that Brian wasn't yet up, so he left the cycle by the front door and started on his run which took him along pavements and roads to Tilgate Forest on the edge of town, then along paths through the trees before again using the pavements to return to Brian's house. As he arrived he noticed the curtains had been drawn open and his cycle had been moved. He used his key to open the front door then nearly fell over his cycle that was leaning against the wall in the hallway. He walked through the house to the kitchen where he sat on the floor and started his sit-up and push-up routine before his mobile rang. He answered it.

Brian had, in fact, got up just after Adam had left the house and had watched the TV news bulletins on television: Van Brubeck's murder was the second item. The police spokesman gave scant details, just that after an anonymous tip-off officers had found the body of a man in a disused warehouse, that formal identification had not yet been made and that forensic teams had worked through the night at the scene. The road that led to the track to the warehouse was closed to the public and there was an appeal to the public for help to identify anyone who had been seen in the vicinity during the past week. A formal press conference by the senior investigating officer would be held later in the day.

Brian had expected little information to be released at that time and wondered what Townsend would make of the news that his number-one helper was dead and the week's drugs stolen, not to mention Del's demise at the garage. How would he react? What would he do about the situation?

Townsend had dressed and was ready before nine o'clock, waiting for Lenny's man to arrive. He knew of Charlie Tompkins by reputation: his ability to sort out even the trickiest of problems. Charlie was a native of Newcastle and had at an early age followed his father into crime, specialising in violent robberies of jewellery shops. With faces hidden behind novelty masks and using brute force, they stormed into shops wielding long-handled hammers which they threatened the staff with before using them to smash the glass display cabinets. Several times, members of staff had been struck and suffered broken bones. It was known within the criminal fraternity and therefore by the police that the Tompkins were the robbers, but luck had always been on their side, especially during their last robbery. They had been under police surveillance the whole morning but at last, owing to the pressure of costs, it was lifted. Just two hours later a shop had been attacked and an assistant beaten with a hammer, causing life-threatening injuries. The two robbers had made their escape before police could arrive at the scene and, although both father and son were arrested that evening at their home, there had been insufficient evidence to press any charges. The day following his release Charlie Tompkins had left Newcastle for the Costa del Sol in Spain where he obtained work as a bouncer of a nightclub.

At just over six feet tall, Charlie was a fitness fanatic who took pride in his large physique and wore clothes that showed it to its most intimidating effect. He shaved his head but had a small goatee beard that he fondled with his fingers from time to time while his large brown eyes could strike fear into people just by his staring at them. Within a year of his arrival in Spain he had graduated from being a club bouncer to being a minder for a well-known criminal and within another he had been recruited by Lenny as his personal assistant and bodyguard. For the past four years he had been at Lenny's side learning the business and had now become his right-hand man, running things on a day-to-day basis. During the time he had been in Spain he had returned to England only once, to attend the funeral of his father who had been murdered in Newcastle by two unknown gunmen. He had made himself a new life in Spain and enjoyed his work there. He wasn't so keen on returning to England, but he had known and liked Dutch and was only too keen to help exact Townsend's revenge.

Charlie Tompkins had landed at Gatwick Airport on the early-morning flight from Málaga and taken a taxi to Geoff Townsend's house via a short stop at an address in Merstham, Surrey, not far from the airport. At the gate he paid off the taxi before walking towards the two security men standing watching him.

'Lads,' he said, before opening his jacket to show a firearm holstered under his left arm, 'not to worry, Mr Townsend's expecting me.'

The security men had been briefed and given a description of Charlie Tompkins, but they were disturbed by the sight of the weapon. 'Thought I'd be up front with you lads rather than you finding it. I take it you would have searched me ...'

The security guards were caught off guard momentarily but recovered quickly, asking for Charlie Tompkins' passport, which he handed over. One of the security men took the passport and examined it before turning and heading for the house where the front door opened and Geoff Townsend stood there with his hand outstretched for the passport. He looked at it briefly then waved for Charlie Tompkins to be admitted. Once in the lounge, the two men and Pat sat with a coffee each as Geoff brought Charlie up to date with what was happening.

'OK, Geoff, so it boils down to someone knowing about the two girls and also knowing that Dutch was responsible for the bulk goods. You and Mrs Townsend knew the arrangement, Jackie Smith knew, the two girls obviously ... who else?'

'Another girl who's done the run as well with Dutch, possibly Dutch's wife, though I doubt he told her much, if anything. Our buyers, I suppose ...' – he paused and thought for a minute – 'Nah, on second thoughts I can't see that. We've been doing business for years with everyone getting on just fine, so there's no reason for anyone to get greedy. If they did, then everyone would turn on them, so I'd forget them for the time being.'

Tompkins agreed and asked about the cash pick-up arrangements. Again, Townsend explained the details involving his wife visiting a boutique in town, previously with Kieran but latterly with Dutch.

Tompkins was thoughtful. 'So whoever tortured him probably knows about the collecting routine as well ... Let's do the collection tomorrow as usual but only Pat by herself, though I'll be there watching to see if anyone tries anything.' He smiled at both the Townsends. 'But let's keep this strictly to ourselves.'

Townsend wasn't too happy at the prospect of Pat being used as bait but she insisted that she was happy to do it to avenge the murders of Dutch and Del. Eventually she won the argument and they discussed how they would do it in such a way that Tompkins would be able to see and hear everything going on around Pat.

'Right,' concluded Charlie, 'let's crack on with finding out how Dutch got to be lifted. How about I talk to the girls as a starting point?'

Pat offered to drive him and they soon arrived at Jackie Smith's house where after an introduction and brief word Pat drove off. In the lounge Jackie Smith explained what she had learned that morning and of her doubts regarding Monica. It might sound flimsy evidence, she admitted, but she was following her instinct.

That morning Monica had returned to her room and stared at the mobile phone, wondering what she could do with it. No point throwing it out of the window as it would land in the back garden and be easily seen from any number of rooms in the house. She wanted to hide it but couldn't think of anywhere – and anyway what would she say if she were asked for it by Jackie? She finally took the plunge and dialled Adam's number.

Later she heard someone arriving at the front door and then

a man's voice together with Jackie's before they had gone into the lounge and the door was closed. She hadn't recognised the voice. It wasn't Geoff Townsend's but it was English and strongly accented – an accent that she couldn't identify. She checked her watch again.

Adam received the call from Monica as he was changing into clean clothes after his run. He went down to tell Brian and about his plan. Brian had responded with a long whistle and a 'Dangerous game, mate.' But they needed to think on their feet.

Brian drove as they headed in Adam's car to Gatwick Airport. Their plan was, as most good plans are, very simple and straightforward: Adam would head to Spain and try to protect Monica's family while Brian was to go to Brighton and the hospital with Adam's weapon and the spare ammunition in a carrier bag, which Adam had placed in the glove compartment of the car.

Charlie told Jackie to bring down the girl Katja first. In all probability Katya was innocent but making Monica wait would increase her anxiety.

Monica heard Katja being summoned and the lounge door being closed after her, followed almost immediately by the sound of a hard slap and a cry from Katja. Monica felt panicky and helpless. She sat on her bed waiting for what was going to be a very painful time for her, but even worse was the thought of what they would do to her parents and sister. She checked the time again and inwardly knew that there was no hope for her. She thought back to the conversation and what she had been told to do by the man she now knew was called Adam. 'Another three minutes,' she said quietly to herself, noticing that her hands were shaking.

She remembered the mobile phone and what Adam had told her. She undid the back and took out the small SIM card and the battery. She saw her birth-control pills and from the strip tore a small piece of metallic backing from it, then carefully laid it on the battery connections in the phone before replacing the battery. It fitted as she had been told it would. She took the SIM card and laid it with the computer workings side upwards and carefully drew the point of a scissor along the length. She examined the SIM card and could see a faint scratch along its length, barely visible even when examined closely. She was satisfied. She replaced it in the mobile and pushed the 'On' button. She waited but there wasn't any change to the plain black colour of the screen. The phone didn't work and she felt a surge of relief that at least the first part of the plan had been completed successfully.

At that moment she heard the lounge door open and a crying Katja enter the hallway. Panicked by the sound, she quickly put the mobile into her coat pocket and rushed back to her dressing table. She tried to stop herself from crying.

'You've been right about everything so far,' she said out loud, though there wasn't anyone to hear. 'I hope you are right about the rest.'

She hastily unscrewed a plastic top from one of her two bottles of eau de toilette, lifted it to her lips and swallowed the contents in one gulp. She unscrewed the second bottle and tipped some down the front of her and wiped some into her hair before laying it next to the first bottle on the dresser. She started retching as the liquid she had drunk reached her stomach. 'Hold it down!' she could hear his voice quietly saying to her. 'Don't be sick or it will all come out. Keep calm and carry on,' he had told her. She was suddenly startled to hear her name shouted from below and quickly unscrewed the top of the plastic nail-polish remover. She put it to her mouth and tipped half a mouthful into her mouth, swilling it around before spitting it out. She tipped the remaining contents on to the floor under her bed, then lay down on the bed.

Her name was shouted again but she could feel a wave of nausea flood over her and she didn't care. Her stomach felt as if the muscles were rejecting the liquid but she tried to calm herself. She closed her eyes and felt a little dreamy, though her head was beginning to buzz. She heard her name called again, this time by Katja from outside her bedroom door, and then her door being opened. Monica lay as still as she could, even trying to control her breathing.

There was a scream, a piercing scream that was so sudden and unexpected that Monica opened her eyes and nearly started to get up. Katja was standing in the doorway, turning away from Monica and facing towards the stairs. Katya released another scream, followed by footsteps thundering up the stairs towards them. Katja was thrown into the room, landing on the floor just as Monica closed her eyes.

Charlie stormed into the room followed swiftly by Jackie. Katja yelled as Charlie stepped on her as he raced the three steps across the room to Monica.

Monica felt herself being dragged into a sitting position then a stinging slap to her face. She was feeling drowsy and the effect of the slap was to increase the buzzing sound in her head and as well as, oddly, her feelings of sleepiness. She felt her eyes open ever so slightly but couldn't identify the snarling face in front of her. She heard Jackie Smith almost shout: 'Is she dead?'

The man prised open an eyelid then shook his head. 'Nah.'

Jackie Smith looked around and saw the two empty eau de toilette bottles then the empty bottle of nail-polish remover.

'Shit, Charlie,' she said urgently. 'She's drunk the bloody perfume and the nail-polish remover. She's poisoned herself – she'll die!'

Charlie looked at the empty containers and was thinking quickly, trying to go through the consequences of any decision he made.

'Going to have to call an ambulance,' said Jackie.

'Yeah, then she goes to hospital and we lose control of the bitch,' answered Charlie.

'Can't have her die here!' shouted Jackie Smith, 'Oh no, not here.'

'Got a straight choice, haven't we? She dies here or she recovers at the hospital. She dies here and we'll not find out who she's been talking to. If she goes to the hospital, we'll have no control over her – she could walk.'

'No she won't,' said Jackie with assurance. 'She knows what will happen to her family if she does and, anyway, we have a couple of nurses on our books ... even a couple of doctors.' She smiled, remembering two regular customers one of whom had a particular liking for Greta.

Charlie slowly turned from Monica and looked at Jackie. 'You're sure?'

'Yes,' she replied, 'and anything is better than her dying here.'

Katja had started to rise from the floor and was looking at them.

'Go to your room and don't come out!' Smith ordered, prompting Katja to hurriedly get to her feet and run from the room.

'OK,' said Charlie Tompkins, 'you ring. I'll stay in your lounge. I don't want to be seen.'

Jackie ran down stairs and made the emergency call, then stood in the lounge with Charlie waiting for the ambulance.

'I'll go with her,' she decided, 'in case she says something and then I'll find out what the score is at the hospital. I'll let Geoff know from there when I know something.'

'Bitch!' Charlie Tompkins said quietly. 'She's the rotten one but we've got to find out who she's in with.'

Jackie nodded in agreement then saw the blue flashing light as a paramedic unit arrived outside her house.

She opened the front door then led the paramedics, one man and one woman, upstairs, explaining to them that the girl Monica had received some bad news from home and had drunk some cosmetics. When they reached the bedroom she stood to one side, allowing the two paramedics to attend to Monica. The three empty containers were examined and placed in a plastic bag by the male paramedic while the female paramedic made a methodical check of Monica.

Monica kept her eyes closed and her breathing to the lightest rhythm she could. She felt gentle hands systematically touching her, but sleep was pulling her away and she willingly surrendered.

The paramedics held a short quiet conversation between them before the male announced to Smith that they would take Monica to the hospital where she could be more fully assessed and the poison that she had ingested examined to see what, if any, damage had been done to her internal organs. He left the room, returning two minutes later with a chair and a blanket.

Jackie was told that she could accompany them to the hospital, which was to be the Royal Sussex County Hospital in central Brighton, so she went to fetch a coat while Monica was carried downstairs and settled into the ambulance.

Charlie watched the ambulance leave then used his mobile to call Lenny in Spain to tell him of the development.

17

Brian drove steadily to Brighton then followed the signs that took him towards the seafront before heading eastwards to the large hospital. He followed the signs to the multi-storey car park and then headed into the casualty department, walking at a slow pace to give himself time to see everyone in the area and assimilate the general layout. He queued at the desk for the receptionist and casually looked around him. He had covered all the faces within the area and was wondering whether Monica had followed Adam's instructions and, if she had, whether Smith or the man Monica had said was with Smith had called an ambulance. He moved forward in the queue until he was behind the woman talking to the receptionist. It was then that he noticed a white-coated doctor leave a curtained examination area. As the curtain opened, Brian saw the unmistakable Jackie sitting on a chair in the corner flicking through a magazine. The woman in front of him moved away from the window and he followed in her footsteps, sitting in a chair near her but from where he could still see the examination area in which Smith sat.

Brian was a patient man used to staying alert for endless hours while manning observation positions. It was a level of concentration built on self-discipline where his eyes could stay focused on a particular spot or area while his mind busied itself working out the endless permutations of what could arise. It was planning for the unlikely that meant that he was always ready for anything and could respond to any situation without hesitation. His role, he knew, was to cause as many problems for the Townsends and this new man as possible. Distracting them here in Brighton might gain Adam vital moments as he sought to find and protect Monica's family.

After a quarter of an hour Brian had decided on his first stage. He walked back to Adam's car and pulled the carpet away from the floor behind the driver's seat. He picked up two of the four sample packages Adam had obtained from Monica and put them into his jacket pocket before walking at a relaxed pace back to the reception area. The queue at the reception desk appeared to have not moved forward and the chairs were still occupied by the same people waiting to be seen. The curtain to the examination room where Smith sat was at the same angle but he walked briskly past to check that firstly Smith was still there and that the examination trolley was occupied. From the corner of his eye he saw Smith still turning pages of a magazine and a small shape under a blanket lying on the trolley next to Smith.

As Brian returned to his seat, he again checked the location and angles of the CCTV cameras and the position and alertness of the two uniformed security people, a man and a woman. Neither appeared to be very interested in the people inside the waiting area, talking to each other with the occasional smile and from time to time looking outside. The cameras didn't move, which meant that Brian was able to work out a route that he could walk while making only a fleeting appearance on the monitors. It was unlikely that the monitors would be scrutinised as closely at that time of day with so many elderly and young people in the area compared to later in the day and night when the drunk and drug-affected people would arrive.

Smith was bored and checked her watch again to confirm it was close to midday. She'd been there for over two hours. Monica was apparently asleep and was fitted to a breathing tube to supply oxygen while the doctor had taken various readings and a sample of blood and saliva. He had examined the containers the paramedics had recovered from Monica's room and smelt the eau de toilette, which he discounted as being a problem in itself. Although it wasn't a good thing to have drunk, it wouldn't cause any long-term problems. The greater concern was the nail-polish remover: the ingredients used to make it were far more toxic and could damage internal organs, which is why he had asked for a quick turn-round of the samples he had taken. He had smelt her breath and the odour of nail polish remover had been very strong around her mouth, but he was surprised that she didn't appear to be in greater distress with internal pain or burning of her throat area. He had taken an instant dislike to the woman who accompanied Monica. Her coldness regarding Monica's condition struck him as she asked endless questions about when 'her friend' could be released and whether she could speak. He didn't believe the story that she was a friend of Monica's: a friend would have been much more concerned and would hardly be flicking carelessly through the pages of a magazine.

The doctor was busy with another patient when an orderly returned with Monica's results. However, an incoming emergency resulting from a serious road traffic accident prevented him assessing them straight away. In all the haste, he pushed Monica and her condition to the back of his mind.

Brian checked the area again, confident that he had three possible courses of action depending upon what circumstances developed. He allowed his body to relax into what appeared to be a bored slump while he kept an eye for any developments or opportunities.

He watched the workstation area and noted how the doctors and nurses disappeared behind a curtained-off examination cubicle to attend a patient then returned to their station to make notes, telephone calls or talk to another member of staff. There was a constant flow of medical staff – the doctor he had seen leave Monica's examination cubicle, however, was notable by his absence. Brian hadn't seen him since he had attended a patient being wheeled in on a trolley by two paramedics and that was over two hours previously. This was good, he thought. Every minute there wasn't any movement on Monica's case meant that Adam had another minute.

Smith looked at her watch for the umpteenth time and with a loud sigh put the magazine on top of the others she had read or flicked through on to Monica's trolley between the edge and Monica's legs. Smith stood and looked at the sleeping figure of Monica, then walked from the cubicle through the waiting area towards the exit doors. Brian on seeing Smith became instantly mentally alert though his body shape didn't move an inch. Having watched her walk through the sliding doors, he stood up and aimlessly walked towards a picture hanging on a wall. By studying it he was able to stand at an angle that gave him a view outside where Smith had already lit a cigarette and was making her way to a designated smoking area. She was pulling a mobile phone out of her bag as she walked.

Brian turned and without looking around him casually walked into Monica's cubicle. Smith's coat was still slung across the back of the chair she'd been sitting in and he moved towards it. His right hand slipped from his pocket a second later as he turned he appeared to brush the hand against her coat. In the same movement he casually walked out of the cubicle and towards the exit, his head lowered. By glancing to his left at the exit doors he avoided the camera sited high on the right getting even a profile look at his face.

Back in the car park he used a mobile phone to dial the emergency number.

'Police, please.'

When the police operator answered he spoke in a deliberate even tone: 'At the RSCH Jackie Smith is with a patient in A&E. She has coke with her that she is going to plant on the patient, a girl called Monica. Can't say who I am but what I'm saying is true.'

He closed the connection, removed the SIM card and battery, and discarded each into separate rubbish bins at the entrance of the multi-storey car park. He took the concrete steps to the third floor where he'd left Adam's car, then walked to the rear and lifted the boot lid. He used the lid as cover and turned to watch the area below where he saw Smith still talking on her mobile opposite the ambulance arrival area. Smith tossed the cigarette into a metal tray and immediately lit another. Brian waited.

18

Adam had had a smooth flight during which he studied the Spanish–English phrasebook he had bought from the departure lounge at Gatwick. He had arrived at Málaga Airport mid-afternoon and both his passage through the arrivals and collection of the hire car were completed within half an hour. Now he was on the Autovía del Mediterráneo heading generally eastwards towards the large town of Almeria and the town of Nerja where Lenny had his bar and nightclub. He soon passed the city of Málaga to his right with the dark-blue Mediterranean behind the city and a short distance later stopped at a Repsol petrol station. There he bought various items from the shop before heading back on the motorway, which at that time of the day had very light traffic. The weather was bright and sunny with the temperature in the mid-60s Fahrenheit, which was a pleasant temperature.

The map he had purchased was open on the seat to his right and he was able to refer to it as he drove, remembering some of the towns and villages from his previous visit and thus able to work out the route he needed to take. The village he was headed towards was named Cútar and situated in the area known as Axarquía and about half an hour inland from the motorway at the turn off to Vélez-Málaga that was in turn half an hour from the airport. On his previous visit he had driven past the small village, access to which was by two roads that led from the main road that wound around the perimeter on its way further into the hills of Málaga. He recalled the village was built into the side of a hill and consisted of a cluster of white-painted houses each vying for a view down the valley towards the sea. In summer, large bushes of bougainvillea turned the village into a blaze of colour. He had thought of it as a pretty village but hadn't had the time to explore it as he had spent most of his time on the other side of the deep valley, opposite Cútar near the hilltop town of Comares.

Comares was situated on the crown of the large imposing hill. Its array of dazzling white buildings perched on majestic cliffs of rock had stood the test of time. The town, unless swathed in low cloud, was a landmark, clearly visible for many miles even from the motorway, which was some half an hour's drive away. Lenny's house was accessed from the main road that led to that town and Adam was aware that from his house Lenny would have a commanding view of the village of Cútar together with the whole valley that divided Comares and Cútar. The valley flattened out towards the town of Benamargosa then became plain-like towards the motorway and the coastal town of Torre del Mar, which was only two kilometres from Vélez-Málaga.

He saw the turn to Vélez-Málaga and at the roundabout took the turn inland towards the area of Trapiche and the town of Benamargosa where the hilly road to Cútar turned off the main road. It was seven kilometres from Benamargosa to Cútar but if he continued on the main road through Benamargosa for a further three kilometres and took the turn, it was seven kilometres from that point, all uphill, to Comares.

As Adam drove into the town of Benamargosa, he recognised the way of life he had witnessed before: the supermarket closed for the afternoon and the three bars clustered nearby at the road junction where men sat at the tables playing cards or dominoes or just watching the world go by. Usually, he had driven straight on but now he took the left turn that took him on the narrow bridge over the dried riverbed, after which the road meandered uphill. On the left vines, olive trees and walnut trees spread upwards while to his right the view surged across to the landmark hill with Comares perched on top.

When the road temporarily straightened Adam looked across

and could make out Lenny's house, standing alone with the large wall around it. As he approached the village of Cútar he slowed and took the turn following the small road to a car park and what was almost a dead end. As with many of the small villages and towns the narrow streets were only just wide enough for a car to pass along, and then slowly and carefully, which meant that most people parked their vehicles at the edge of a town or village and walked. He parked his car and looked around. There were two streets that led from the car parking area into the built-up area of the village. No one was around.

He consulted the map and found Calle de la Fuente was the right of the two streets and he took that. The sun was warm and reflected from the white walls as he walked steadily, feeling strangely alone – all the doors and windows to the houses were closed. Now and again he heard voices from inside a house and caught the smell of burning wood and cooking. He continued walking past the imposing Casa Consistorial – town hall from whose first-floor balcony the Spanish flag flanked by the Andalusian and European Union flags hung limply. The building looked out of keeping with the character of the village and the small white buildings that appeared to have grown from one another. He noted the steps on his right that led down to a bar with an area outside. During the summer it would have had tables set out but at this time of year it seemed desolate, though he guessed the bar would be open. A further thirty seconds of walking and he saw the road that he wanted branch to the left – Calle de Rodriguez de la Fuente. He folded the map and stuck it in his back trouser pocket and from his jacket he took out the piece of paper where he had noted the phrase Monica had said for him to use to introduce himself.

He stopped and looked at the door to the house: a sturdy wooden door polished over the years, with two tiled steps leading to the door that had clearly been washed clean that morning – traces of soapy water were still on the pavement. He knocked gently on the door and stood back at the bottom of the steps. The door opened a little.

Brian had watched as Smith had smoked her second cigarette and made a further call on her mobile phone and knew that she regretted not wearing her coat. The weather was milder than it had been and for the time it took to smoke one cigarette she would have been fine but the second cigarette had seen her shiver. He saw her throw her second cigarette to the ground then walk away, leaving it to smoulder. She had been away from Monica for twenty-one minutes. Good, he thought, but another five would have been better. He checked the car park around him and was surprised and pleased at how few comings and goings there were. He knew that over fifteen minutes had passed since he had made the call and wondered if the police were going to take any action.

He was just becoming concerned that they were going to ignore his call when he saw an unmarked car drive slowly into the area reserved for ambulances. Several of the bays were free and the car slowly manoeuvred into the furthest one. A man and woman alighted from the car and walked together towards the entrance of the hospital. Brian was thinking of what Smith would have done when she re-entered the hospital, perhaps visited the toilet or got a drink from a vending machine. One or the other would have been good but both would have been a lot better. He wanted to see what was happening but knew that what was done was done. It would either buy Adam time and divert attention from Monica or it would prove to have been a useless waste of time. Again, he waited.

Adam had a smile as the door opened but as the face of a man appeared he felt the smile begin to fade. He had expected the door to be answered by either a man or lady in their fifties or by a girl in her late teens. Monica hadn't mentioned anything about a man in his late twenties. Adam had to think quickly as the man with his body hidden by the partially opened door looked at him with hostility.

'*Hola!*' he said brightly, knowing that the friendly greeting was almost the extent of his Spanish vocabulary. The man didn't reply or move.

Adam sensed that it was probable that the man had a weapon of some description and by having the advantage of height and the protection of the door Adam was at a serious disadvantage. Also counting against him was Adam not knowing if the man was an enemy, a potential enemy, or just a friend of the family.

'Ah,' said Adam, fumbling for the phrasebook and opening it. He appeared to be reading from it then turned a page as he took the first step, then the second and without lifting his head he suddenly sprung forward using his right shoulder to crash against the door. As soon as he hit the door he felt some resistance but he was already swivelling to his left through the gap, using his left hand to reach towards the man. In the same flowing movement his right hand had dropped the book and from a low starting position had come upwards along the front of the man's body. Adam used the heel of his right hand to strike upwards but missed the intended area of the chin and instead caught the nose. There was a crunch sound as the cartilage broke. Adam was now fully inside the room and quickly took in his surroundings. A man, woman and girl were sitting in wooden hard-backed chairs close to a large wooden table. A fire was alight and the overhead light was on. Another light came through a doorway that opened towards the back of the house.

The man who had answered the door was still falling to the floor as Adam closed the door and looked down at him. There was a dull sound of metal hitting a ceramic floor tile and Adam saw a heavy metal adjustable spanner falling from the man's hand. He looked at the three people on the chairs, noted that they were all in the same posture and moved quickly to the room at the back. It was the kitchen – small but neatly laid out and maintained. The door leading outside was closed and no one was in the room.

Adam returned to the three people and saw that each had their arms tied with rope behind the backs of the chairs. He noted for the first time that each had a terrified look in their eyes. Adam looked at the woman. She looked older than the fifty-six years that Monica had described her mother as and he suddenly realised that she was the woman he had seen being driven from Lenny's house in the four-by-four vehicle.

He started to speak then stopped himself, frustrated that he couldn't speak any words that they would understand and he wouldn't be able to understand any words they spoke to him. He fumbled in his pockets and found a piece of paper on which were some scribbled words. Taking a breath he read out the words that Monica had dictated:

'*Nancy quiera cuider de ti, confia en este hombre.*'

There was no sign from any of them that they had understood, so he went to the man and showed him the paper. The man slowly looked from Adam to the paper then moved his head backwards as he adjusted his eyesight to the distance. He didn't say anything as he looked again at Adam, holding the gaze for five seconds before he spoke quietly. Adam didn't know if the man was talking to him or to his wife and daughter. There was no inflection in his voice and all the words appeared to be spoken quickly so that they joined together to form a continuous sound.

The woman's eyes widened as she looked at Adam while the girl smiled at him. Adam sensed that they had understood the message and that they would trust him. He moved behind the man and quickly undid the rope tying his hands. Adam moved on to the woman and girl, repeating the process. The man on the floor by the door began to move and Adam went swiftly over to him, moving the spanner away. Adam methodically searched the man's pockets, finding no other weapons or anything of interest. Adam was aware that the man, woman and girl were standing, rubbing life back into their hands and at the same time hugging one another. Adam hauled the man from the floor on to the chair previously occupied by the girl and used two pieces of the rope to secure his hands separately to the back of the chair. He used the remaining piece to tie one ankle to the chair leg then made a silent request to Monica's father for another. The girl was the first to move, disappearing into the kitchen and returning with another length of rope. Adam secured the other leg then went into the kitchen and returned with a drying cloth that he tied securely around the man's mouth. Adam looked at the man's nose from which blood was beginning to pour and with no warning grabbed it between his thumb and forefinger and gave it a hard tug. There was a grinding noise as the cartilage was forced back into place. The man's head suddenly jerked, reacting to the pain. Adam went to the kitchen and grabbed another cloth, which he used to wipe the man's nose and clear the blood from his nostrils. He wanted the man incapacitated for a while, not to be dead and have the Spanish police hunting for him.

Adam turned to the man and woman, indicated his jacket and pointed towards the front door. Again, the girl was the quickest to respond and with a flurry of movement she appeared with a heavy coat that she threw to her father and another that she handed to her mother. She put on a leather jacket that was not too dissimilar to the one Adam wore. Adam went to the door then saw the phrasebook on the floor, which he retrieved. Adam opened the door and stepped outside. He checked both ways that no one was about, then gestured for them to follow him. He walked to the main street and began to retrace his steps towards the car, aware that three sets of footsteps were following him. The woman's shoes were making a noise that alarmed Adam and he turned to indicate with his forefinger to his lips that they needed to be quiet.

Reaching the end of the street, he stopped while he had a look around the car-parking area, but it appeared to be as quiet as it had been when he had arrived barely six minutes previously. He gestured towards his car and walked quickly towards it, using the fob to unlock the doors. The man sat heavily into the front seat next to Adam while the girl squeezed in behind Adam with her mother behind her husband. Adam started the engine and slowly manoeuvred the car back towards the main road.

Since reading the paper none of them had spoken, but as Adam started driving down the hill back towards Benamargosa there was a conversation between the mother and father. The words were spoken too quickly and Adam couldn't understand a single word, but from the tone he thought the two of them were arguing. The girl reached forwards towards Adam and, saying something, reached towards Adam's jacket pocket. He was taken by surprise, and his initial reaction had been to knock her hand away but he realised it was the pocket that had the phrasebook in it. He gave her the book, which she took and opened, sitting back in her seat. The father and mother became silent as Adam drove steadily, keeping to a safe speed around the bends. Though speed was essential, safety was even more so. The father looked at Adam then at his daughter and became more agitated as he said something to her. She replied with a staccato burst. The father looked at Adam with a worried look on his face then held his hands out in front of him and slowly moved them upwards and downwards. Adam made a swift interpretation and applied the brakes, which brought a smile and nod from the father.

'OK,' said Adam quietly, 'you want me to slow down – why?'

Adam pulled off the road on to an area of rough ground and managed to park behind an olive tree that at least hid part of the car from the road. The young girl had showed him the book and pointed to a phrase: 'Excuse me, but we need help.'

Adam nodded his agreement.

She flipped to another page. 'Please telephone the police,' he read. Startled he looked at her to see her waving her finger from side to side – 'No,' she said.

Adam held up his finger and took out his mobile phone and dialled Brian's mobile. Adam was met with a constant sound which told him that the number called was unavailable. He redialled another mobile that Brian had and heard the ringing tone before it was answered by Brian.

'Bri, what's happening your end? I've got them out but having a problem as they don't speak any English at all.'

Brian was still watching the parking area while listening to Adam and he updated Adam with events at the hospital.

'Bri, do you speak any of the lingo? We're sitting here trying to go through a bloody phrasebook.'

'Sorry, only Arabic and German, mate. What are your plans?'

Adam told Brian that he just wanted to leave them somewhere safe so he could get back to England as soon as possible. It was likely that time could be against them if someone went to the house and found they had gone, in which case there would be repercussions for Monica.

'Bri, can you get her out of there? It would sort out a lot of problems, not the least of which would be that she could talk with her family and bloody well get me out of this mess.'

Brian was thoughtful. 'I'll try but I'm not sure exactly how. Is there a message I can give her to say that her family are safe?'

Adam thought of how he could ask the family for a coded message such as Monica had given him. He gave an exasperated sigh. 'Not in under ten minutes. Bri, Mum is wearing a long blue coat with a pink scarf; Dad has a brown coat and her sister has a brown leather jacket, similar in style to mine. Maybe Monica will recognise the clothes. Try that – otherwise, call me and they can talk.'

'OK, Adam, take care. Speak later,' said Brian before he finished the call.

Brian started walking down the concrete steps and was reaching the last flight when he heard a siren and saw a second later a police patrol car dash into the ambulance bay. He quickened his step slightly and, mindful of the route he had selected to avoid the CCTV system as far as possible, he made his way in through an adjacent door. The two uniformed police officers had hurried into the A&E waiting area and Brian caught sight of them running towards the general area where the examination cubicles were. Brian could hear a woman shouting at full voice, swearing and seemingly fighting as well. He stood among some other people who had also turned their attention to the source of the commotion – Monica's examination cubicle.

Brian felt a surge of happiness as the screaming and swearing persisted followed by a piercing scream from the same woman. He could see the two uniformed officers moving back and forwards in the confined space. A nurse and doctor joined them. Amid the chaos Brian couldn't see exactly what was happening until one uniformed officer backed out of the cubicle carrying Smith's legs by the ankles. Smith's wriggling body gradually came into view followed by the other uniformed officer holding her shoulders, though clearly with some difficulty. The two plain-clothed people then moved in to help and she was carried, still shouting, through the waiting area and outside. Brian moved quickly towards Monica's cubicle, arriving just as the nurse was pulling the curtain closed.

'I can help Monica,' Brian said. 'Just a couple of words.' And without waiting for a response from either the doctor or the nurse he continued: 'Monica, Adam is with your parents and sister. They are safe and away from Cútar.'

Monica had been lying on her side with her eyes closed for the past thirty or so minutes. She had felt drowsy and only half aware that Jackie had been sitting by her bedside until she had heard Jackie's screams and something about some drugs in Jackie's coat pocket. She couldn't fully understand what was happening, it all felt like a dream. Now this new voice was saying that Adam was with her parents and sister and that they were out of their village, Cútar he had called it. Not even Smith would have known the name of the village, she thought. Dutch would have, but he's dead. The voice wasn't rough like Townsends' but softer and more assured, confident like Adam's.

Monica groaned a little and opened her eyes, slowly trying to see the stranger before making any further signs of recovery. She tried to focus on Brian but the doctor moved into her line of vision, took hold of her left wrist with one hand while moving so that his face was directly in front of hers. He peered into her eyes and was smiling.

'How are you?' he said in a soft voice. 'You are in hospital but I'm sure you are fine.'

Monica tried to smile at the doctor and at the same time look past him but her view remained blocked. The nurse left the cubicle and while the doctor took Monica's pulse and used a torch light to shine into her eyes Brian stood at the foot of the bed behind the curtain, hiding him from anyone who might be trying to see into the cubicle. The nurse returned with some papers and a quizzical look on her face as she handed them to the doctor.

'The results are back. I think you need to see them.'

The nurse looked at Brian in a questioning manner as if he was some part of a conspiracy and responsible for what had happened. The doctor read the first page then flipped to the second before looking up.

'No sign of acetone in the blood. In fact, her blood is just about clear and in working order. I don't understand,' he said, looking first at Monica and then at Brian. 'The admission note says that you swallowed nail-polish remover, which should have damaged your internal organs and would certainly show in your blood results.'

Monica said in a quiet voice, 'I didn't swallow any. I just wanted to make it look like I had. My boyfriend told me we were finished and I wanted him to come and see me. I love him and need him.' She looked at Brian for the first time.

Brian felt his face flush but was quick to counter. 'You daft thing! I love you but I thought you didn't want me. That's why I told you that we had better stop seeing each other.'

Brian walked to the bed and took Monica's hand and kissed it.

'I'm not happy about what you did, young lady. You've wasted time and effort, not to mention being part of the biggest shouting match and fight we've seen in A&E for the past year. You can go! You are discharged,' said the doctor, all the while looking at Monica sternly.

Monica looked sheepish as she climbed out of the bed assisted by Brian, who uttered his apologies to the doctor and nurse and led Monica from the cubicle. He guided her along his now well-rehearsed route until they were outside the hospital and walking towards the car park.

Jackie Smith continued to shout and swear even as she was forcibly pushed into the rear of the marked police car. The female Drugs Squad officer piled in after Smith and pushed Smith's head away from her and towards the car window on her side. Smith shouted and kicked her legs backwards at the female officer who managed to squeeze into the back seat behind the driver. As the car started and pulled away from the parking area Smith focused her eyes out of the window to see the profile of Monica walking towards the car park with a man's arm around her shoulder.

'You bitch!' she screamed at full voice as she saw Monica turn the corner and pass from her sight. She only fleetingly caught a part-profile look at the man's face – she didn't recognise him. Smith suddenly became silent as she tried to work out in her mind what had just happened. A sudden surge of rage overcame her as the thought struck her:

'You bitch – there was nothing wrong with you,' she whispered.

'I'm Brian, by the way,' he said. 'Are you OK?'

'I'm OK but worried about my parents and sister. Has Adam really got them safe?'

Brian repeated what Adam had told him. 'He suggested that you ring him. We'll get away from here then you can call him and speak with your parents.'

Brian led Monica to Adam's car, then as he drove out of the car park and used the smaller streets to head north out of Brighton he handed her his mobile phone. He took care to watch the traffic behind him as he slowed at each junction then kept a steady speed along the narrow roads running parallel to the horse-racing course to his right and the main road to Lewes on his left.

Adam had remained in the pull-off while he and Monica's sister exchanged the phrasebook, pointing at passages with additional comments such as '*Si*' and '*No*'. Monica's father was agitated and looking at the road tensing whenever a vehicle passed. The most that Adam had understood was when the father had said, pointing to the road and the town of Benamargosa, '*No, robido.*'

Adam was frustrated and knew that valuable time had been spent on him learning nothing that would help, valuable time that were the opposition alerted could make all the difference to them.

He got his mobile out and was about to call Brian when he received an incoming call from Brian's mobile. He was relieved to hear Monica's voice and that Brian had saved her and they were driving away to safety. Adam said he was pleased then told her to speak with her father. She had one minute maximum to talk to him. She wasn't to tell him anything about her, only that she was safe, but Adam wanted to know what the man was trying to tell him. He handed the mobile to her father. By watching his face Adam could see the delight at hearing his daughter's voice, then he looked at Adam and said something sharp to his daughter. He listened for a few seconds then talked, or rather nearly shouted down the phone. Adam sat and watched the road and the father before twisting in his seat to see the expressions on the faces of Monica's sister and mother. Both were looking very upset especially her mother, who was holding a handkerchief to her nose. The sister twice said something to her father. The first time he waved at her, dismissing whatever she had said, but the second time he stopped his talking for a second before carrying on as if there hadn't been any interruption.

Finally he stopped talking and thrust the mobile at Adam.

'Adam,' Monica said, 'my parents are very scared. They are grateful for you rescuing them but they know there are people who work for Lenny who live in the area. If they are seen, Lenny wouldn't just keep hold of them like they were in their house; he'd kill them and my sister. My father says that at Benamargosa you will have to drive to the main road and turn right by the speed bumps and crossing. Do you know where I mean?'

Adam did. 'Yeah.'

'When you slow down, men in the bars or on the pavement will see them and if one of them works for Lenny they will report it straight away and he will know they have escaped.'

'Right, Monica, tell your father he's to get in the back seat with your mother. They are to lie flat down with their coats on top of them. Your sister is to sit in the front of the car with me. She will sit on the floor and will have my jacket over her. I will drive past the bars and away towards the motorway but they must stay down until I say it is OK for them to sit up. Tell your dad and let's move. We've wasted too much time already.'

He thrust the mobile at Monica's father and made a 360-degree check around them before getting out and making the rearranged seating arrangements. Satisfied, he drove on down the hill.

During the journey out of the city Monica had been subdued but when they began driving on the dual carriageway she began to speak. 'Did you put the packets of coke in Jackie's coat?'

'Yes' was all he said.

Monica laughed lightly. 'I was lying on my side so my face was away from her and when she came back in I could smell the cigarette smoke on her. I knew someone had quickly been in while she was out. I heard a faint footstep.'

Brian nearly groaned aloud and hoped that she wouldn't repeat that to Adam, who would have fun teasing Brian on how to walk quietly on the soles and sides of his feet.

Monica continued: 'Then there was a man's voice, said he was police, drugs squad and wanted to search her. Believed she might have drugs. Jackie has a foul and very quick temper. She hates the police anyway so she started shouting at him. Then a woman's voice told her to shut up and that got her really angry. I almost could have laughed. The woman talked to Jackie trying to get her to be quiet. She was for a few seconds, but then the man said something like 'What are these?' and Jackie went mad. She said someone had planted them on her, in her coat I think they were, and then I tried to just stay still, really still. Someone fell on top of me. They were banging into me and I heard the man tell Jackie she was being arrested. It went on for a long time, fighting and shouting, and then she was taken away. I heard the man say 'Two packets. I'm surprised at her' then something like he thought that she didn't touch the drugs herself.' Monica laughed. 'Thank you, Brian.'

Adam drove steadily over the river bridge looking towards the junction where the bars met and where the two speed-calming humps had been built in the road. A car had stopped in front of him and the driver was talking to a man who was standing in the middle of the road.

'Damn!' he muttered to himself as he quickly checked again to ensure that Monica's parents were covered and lying down on the back seat. Monica's sister was curled into the passenger foot well and Adam knew that she would be on the side of the man in the road when he passed the car. He leaned forward a fraction and, as he went past, gave a friendly wave towards the man in the road, who in the event barely gave Adam or his car a glance before continuing his conversation. Adam continued through the junction and headed towards the motorway, checking off the towns in his mind that he should avoid due to the presence of English people, and trying to think of a safe location for the family. Time was all important, as he wanted to get back to England that evening, though the security of Monica's family had to take precedence, he knew.

The drive to the Police Central Custody Suite at Hollingbury took just over ten minutes during which barely any words were spoken in the car. Smith was lost in her own thoughts while the police officers were just grateful that the fighting and shouting had subsided.

'Charlie,' Geoff Townsend almost shouted down his mobile phone, 'Jackie's been arrested. Get in the lounge and listen carefully.'

Charlie Tompkins finished emptying the safe and was in the process of closing it when he heard a squeal of car tyres braking outside the house. He looked quickly through the edge of the net curtains and saw an elderly man clearly with nerves on edge sitting in the driver's seat strumming his hands on the steering wheel. This was not a usual role for a solicitor. Charlie ran from the lounge and down the steps to the car, closing the door with a slam. Instantly the car lurched forward and headed towards the seafront. Charlie looked at the man who was perspiring and in an obvious state of fear.

'Relax, just drive normally,' Charlie said as the car skidded to a halt with the main seafront road.

Ten minutes later Charlie was in the sitting room of Geoff Townsend's house with the contents of Jackie Smith's safe spread over the coffee table. Among several piles of cash were papers and letters, several small jewellery boxes and a large box that Geoff Townsend had quickly opened, revealing small polythene bags each containing about a teaspoon of white powder.

'What's going on?' said Pat quietly, looking anxiously towards her husband.

Charlie sat down heavily in an armchair and gave a sigh.

'Someone is having a go, that's what's going on, and they were using Monica to get the inside track,' he said quietly. 'Someone has either got some balls or they've a death wish, but they'll wish they'd never been born when we get hold of them,' he continued.

'Right,' said Geoff Townsend, 'let's see what's happened today. Monica knew the game was up so she took an overdose to get herself into hospital. A clever overdose – not enough to do any damage but enough to convince the ambulance people she was ill. Then she makes a fantastic recovery and Jackie gets fitted up at the same time ...' His thoughts were interrupted by his mobile phone ringing.

He answered the phone but didn't say anything; it was obviously not good news he was hearing. Several times he appeared to take deep breaths as his face became redder and redder.

'Right, now I'll give you our bloody news,' he said in a raised voice, before appearing to calm down as he explained the day's events. As he finished talking he looked at the ceiling and nodded his head several times, obviously agreeing with what the caller was saying.

'OK,' he said as he closed the call and turned to Pat and Charlie Tompkins. 'Monica's parents and sister have been sprung,' he said evenly, 'released, whatever ...' He waved his hand around him. 'They've bloody well gone. Apparently a bloke just knocked on the door, smashed the guard in the face, released them all, tied the guard up, then buggered off. Oh, he reset the guard's nose before he left. For Christ's sake, just what *is* going on?'

He slumped on to the sofa and looked at Charlie. 'Lenny's not happy,' he said quietly. He looked at the antique china clock above the fireplace, 'So Mister Solicitor will be with Jackie and we'll get the full story of what happened at the hospital, and Lenny's already on the case for Monica's family. I'll get Plod up here and have a chat with him. It's about time he earned his bloody corn and, Charlie, I'll get a couple of the lads to collect you and take you on a visiting mission. Perhaps you could spread the word that we're not ready for a takeover. This business is solid and ready for anybody who thinks otherwise.'

Adam checked the sign and changed lanes to take the next turn from the motorway, towards El Alhambra. The drive to Granada had taken over two hours and after the conversation between Monica and her father via his mobile phone the mood in the car had relaxed. Adam hadn't been able to understand what they had been talking about but from the tone of the father's voice he had guessed that Monica had told him to trust Adam and that all would be well, or he hoped that had been the case. He had also spoken to Monica and explained his plan which was to find a small hotel or somewhere for the family to stay, he would be able to pay by his credit card and for him to give them all the cash he had on him and that he could withdraw from the ATM. After that they would have to just sit tight to await word from Monica when it was safe for them to move. He would be back in England either later that day or in the morning.

Geoff Townsend listened while the Solicitor Edward Jones-Mitchell finished explaining what Jackie Smith had told him of the events at the hospital. Sitting uncomfortably in another chair was the Detective Chief Inspector who was very aware that his visit to Townsend would whatever excuse he gave to his senior officers be, regarded as unauthorised. An unauthorised visit to Townsend would raise too many questions in other officer's minds for him to answer so he wanted to get out of the house as soon as possible. In fact Mr Jones-Mitchell had been equally worried by the presence of the Detective Chief Inspector during the discussion, but both knew that after taking Geoff Townsend's money for years this was the pay back. Edward Jones-Mitchell had the excuse to leave in order to return to Jackie Smith's side to ensure that she was granted bail while the contents of the two bags found in her coat pocket were forensically examined. After the solicitor left the DCI tried to sound upbeat.

'I'll get the hospital CCTV looked at straight away, they were walking towards the car park so I hope we'll find their car as well, in which case I'll try and get their route and see where the car is. The Spain angle, it's a long shot but I'll see what planes landed there today, in Málaga initially, and try for the passenger lists. Assuming it was not a local who rescued Monica's parents, that's an area that you'll have to look at through Lenny's contacts, we may get lucky but we don't know what we're looking for.'

Geoff Townsend nodded his agreement but was thinking of who would have the balls or be so stupid to take on his firm. Nobody, not even the really big boys from London and the big northern cities, would try and take over his empire in Brighton. His little patch worked well for everyone. It was a smooth operation, without complications, and gave everyone a slice of the cake. And that cake was big enough for everyone.

Brian had cursed as he toured the streets trying to find a parking space that, due to road works in the town centre, had caused shoppers and commuters to park their cars in the side streets and parking areas of residents in the housing estate where he lived. Monica had been quiet on the last part of the journey, staring out of the window and wondering what lay in store for her and her family, though confident that Adam and now Brian would know what to do. After ten minutes of searching Brian found a parking space in a road about a quarter of a mile from his house. As he locked the car, he felt rain starting to fall and putting his arm around Monica he guided her towards his house.

It was after eleven that night that Geoff Townsend heard the first bit of good news that day. The DCI rang to say that the man and

Monica had left the car park and that the car had been tracked by the police automatic number plate recognition system to Crawley town centre where it had passed a particular camera three times. The downside was that the car was not registered to anyone and the previous keeper had been able to only give a brief description of the man who had purchased it from her and that description wasn't the same as the man at the hospital. He planned to have the areas surrounding the town centre swept street by street until the car was located. Two constables would then watch the car for when the driver returned, and then he would be arrested for the murder of Del at the garage. Geoff Townsend was pleased that the DCI was earning his money and acknowledged the good work that he had done, but insisted that his own watch for the driver once the car had been located. They would carry out their own style of arrest after which there would be a questioning period followed by a punishment that would save the country the need of a costly trial.

The DCI tried to argue against Townsend's proposal, but eventually caved in. What choice did he have, really? The DCI knew he would have to prepare false evidence to enable the search for the car to take place and that the false evidence would have to be such that, having found the car, the local officers would leave it *in situ*. Not an easy thing to do, and for an hour he had thought about how he could achieve it without too many ramifications for himself. In the end, deciding against some long, involved plot, he instead wrote an email request to the Crawley police night-turn supervisor just asking for the car to be found: no surveillance was to be kept on it as he would supply a fully qualified team who were ready and on standby. He didn't give any indication of the offence the car was wanted in connection with, but left the local officers to their own suspicions.

19

Brian had cooked a small dinner for himself and Monica before changing the bedding on Adam's bed and throwing his belongings into the third bedroom that he used as a storage room. A cot bed was made ready for Adam's return sometime the next day while Monica took over Adam's bed. Brian had decided against showing Monica the operations room in the attic until he had discussed their future plans with Adam and whether Monica would be part of those.

Adam had asked Monica to think of somewhere where her parents would be happy to stay, where they would be unknown and where Adam would feel happy about their security. Various suggestions had been made and it was after a conversation between Monica and her father that she had told Adam of a place where the family had stayed on a holiday some years ago. Monica couldn't remember the address or name but gave the directions to Adam as best as she could recall. The three-way conversation with Adam and Monica's father passing the mobile phone between them would have been humorous in other circumstances but Adam was aware of the time slipping on.

Following the rather hazy directions, Adam drove towards the Sierra Nevada region: given the family's lack of suitable clothing and the heavy snow on the mountains Adam was wondering if perhaps the place they had chosen was a poor idea. The father gestured to the right and Adam swung the wheel. The headlights picked out a sign by the side of a small road: Monachil. Snow was banked up at the sides of the road and for a moment he hesitated until Monica's father waved his arm for Adam to drive on. Adam took a deep breath then drove carefully, shortly passing a sign indicating that they were entering a national park. Monica's father was smiling at Adam, perhaps for the first time, then leaned forward to see better through the windscreen. Another minute later and he excitedly pointed towards a sign on the right: '*Atención bandas sonoras*'.

'Speed bumps … out here!' muttered Adam to himself.

Monica's father then broke into rapid-fire Spanish and pointed to a building that had come into view: '*Si, Restaurante Ruta del Purche.*' He smiled and spoke to his wife and daughter. Adam called Brian and explained where he was and what the situation was. Monica took over from Brian and explained to Adam that there were small chalets available to rent and her parents and sister would be happy there. They could get a lift to the town the following day to buy some clothes and provisions after which they would stay in the chalet, only going out for walks during the daytime. Their needs would be basic but they would be happier there than in a hotel where they would be scared to venture out of their room.

Adam gave Monica's father all his cash and accompanied him to the reception where after the registration process Adam used his credit card to pay for two weeks' stay for the family. Together they went to Chalet 1 and climbed the wooden steps to the door, which Monica's father unlocked. He turned on the light to reveal a large comfortable room furnished with sofas, chairs and a dining table. A small kitchenette was at the back of the room next to a door that appeared to be the bathroom. Another door led to a bedroom. Adam walked around the main room and then the bathroom and bedroom, checking the windows and shutters, before returning to find the family huddled together.

Monica's father broke away and clasped Adam's hand. '*Gracias*' he said more than once before saying something else the only word of which Adam understood was *amigo*.

Monica's mother and sister each hugged Adam. '*Gracias*,' they said in turn.

He gave them his mobile phone and showed Monica's sister the number she could call Monica on. Adam left them standing in the doorway as he turned his car around and gave a cheery toot of the horn. He looked at the clock on the facia and groaned: it was already far too late to get a flight that evening. There would be another three hours' drive to the airport where he would have to wait for the first check-in desks to open the following morning. He felt tired as he drove, straining his eyes as he passed along the narrow snow-packed roads, all the while trying to put together the whole picture of where he and Brian were.

He felt strangely elated: he was more like his old self, invigorated and motivated, pinning his wits and skills against the enemy, knowing that the slightest mistake could cost him his life.

20

The weather was cold with heavy rain falling from dark-grey mountainous clouds as Adam's plane touched down at Gatwick Airport. He had spent the whole flight with his head turned towards the window, planning the next steps and retracing the events that had led him to where he was now. Brian was a major factor in his success so far and he knew his friend would be needed even more in the future if his goal was to be achieved. He gave scant thought to his personal safety, having complete confidence in both his own and Brian's ability to overcome any problems that the likes of Townsend could present. Ann's death couldn't be changed: her pain and suffering that she had endured couldn't be undone and nothing could really ease the heavy heart that Raymond Black suffered each and every day. He just knew that he and Brian were doing the right thing: in his mind it was a simple question of justice. Destroying a drugs baron's empire in the process was an extra bonus.

'Just trust me,' said Brian, taking a large mouthful of his bacon sandwich before washing it down with hot sugared tea. 'I'll pick him up and we'll be straight back. I'll probably be an hour or two at the most.' He smiled reassuringly.

'And I am to just wait here?' said Monica, taking a small nibble from her bacon sandwich.

'Yeah,' said Brian, pushing the remaining sandwich into his mouth and wiping his mouth with a paper serviette.

He stood up and walked to the hallway, where he pulled on his waxed jacket – it would provide ample protection against the cold and the rain. He turned and gave Monica a cheery smile and wave as he headed for the front door.

Outside, Brian walked along the path to the pavement, turned up the collar of his coat and looked up at the leaden-grey sky from which rain was falling so hard that it was bouncing a foot off the ground. Water gushed along the street gutter as he pushed his hands deeper into his jacket pocket, and kept his head down, all the while managing to keep an eye out all about him as he made his way towards the car he'd parked a quarter of a mile away.

The DCI had slept well until just after four o'clock when he had been awakened by the duty sergeant supervising the night turn at Crawley with news that the car had been located. The sergeant gave the address and after receiving a 'well done' from the DCI had dismissed the whole enquiry as just another job completed. The DCI had telephoned Geoff Townsend and supplied him the details, then returned to sleep without thinking any more of the consequences of his actions. Geoff Townsend had called Charlie Tompkins and passed on the details, which meant that by half past four Adam's car was already being watched by Charlie Tompkins and a man named Jack in a car parked fifty yards away, as well as by a team in a Transit van just ten yards away. The driver's seat in the Transit was occupied by Chas with Derek in the passenger seat while in the back were Pete and Dom. Pete and Dom were sitting on chairs, which enabled them to stretch their muscles to prevent stiffening of the joints. Each of the latter wore a woollen balaclava and carried a baseball bat. They were focused and alert, poised for action whenever the order came from Charlie. For three hours they remained in position, twice slowly standing and readying their hands on the door opening mechanism, only to be told that the person had continued on past the car. They all waited as the rain thundered against the roof of the car and van.

At seven thirty Charlie Tompkins looked again in his rear-view mirror and used the rear screen wiper to clear the water from the window.

Brian was twenty yards from the back of Charlie Tompkins' car and registered the movement but continued walking on the pavement that would take him past the passenger side of the car. He intended to walk until he was opposite Adam's car then cross the road in front of the car and walk back to the driver's door doing very basic anti-surveillance as he went. For Brian, this was all second nature, something he had done ever since he had first worked in civvies in hostile territory, alone and frightened on the street, imagining bad people at every turn.

He passed the car whose rear window wiper had swished once. Man in the passenger seat, large build by the size of the bulk. Two men in a car – why? Why there? Watching, waiting? What for? In his mind a bell sounded and his body was on full alert. He walked on at the same pace, suddenly stopped, then looked in both directions. He started to cross the road. White Transit van – a usual and common vehicle. A car parked between that and Adam's car, a gap between the back of the van and the front of the parked car. Double yellow lines painted on the roadway. The alarm bell sounded again – why park there? Space around the corner. When was it parked there? Couldn't say: the road was so wet underneath the van. Besides everywhere else was wet with the rain. What was wrong? He looked into the passenger mirror of the van. Movement, someone shifted in his seat, which meant that there was someone in front of Adam's car in the Transit and two men behind Adam's car. Adam's car was in the middle. Others were, too, but he wasn't interested in them. Brian took another look as he reached halfway across the road. Nothing else drew his attention.

He had two choices: to reach the pavement then turn to his left and continue along that pavement in the original direction or go to the car and test his instincts. As he reached the pavement his mind was made up.

In the back of the Transit Pete and Dom were now standing, their masks lowered over their faces, a baseball bat held in one hand and the other touching the door opening mechanism. Brian turned left, keeping the same pace and posture. He chanced a glance at the side mirror of the driver's door: a person was sitting in the driver's seat. He continued to walk past the van, using his self-discipline to stop himself from giving any sort of backward glance. He continued until he reached the town hall, where there was a taxi rank, twice crossing the road to check behind him. He walked to the leading taxi and sat in the front next to the driver.

He knew he had just taken a chance: an experienced surveillance team would have recognised that walking so far in such atrocious weather to get a taxi was suspicious – why wouldn't he have just called for one to pick him up from his home address? But, a good surveillance team wouldn't be watching Adam's car like they were, these were amateurs, maybe keen amateurs, but nevertheless amateurs. Not so amateurish, though, if they were Townsend's men and had found Adam's car. That wasn't amateurish at all; in fact, that was a really frightening thought.

Adam exited the Arrivals area at the North Terminal at Gatwick and saw Brian standing fifteen yards away with both his hands in his pockets and the collar of his jacket turned up looking bored and disinterested. Adam knew the score and slowed his walk, falling behind Brian as he started to walk towards the transit train that ran between the North and South Terminals. They waited on the platform for a minute before the transit arrived then each boarded separate coaches but within sight of each other.

Adam knew that Brian was on the alert and that something was wrong. Brian was giving signs that, in the old parlance, something was 'up'. Adam looked at the other travellers in his coach and saw no one who looked to be anything other than what they appeared to be. He changed his position when the transit lurched a little on a bend in the tracks and looked at

Brian and the passengers in his coach. Nothing alerted him and he chanced a look at Brian, who removed both hands from his pockets and turned down the collar of his jacket. They exited the coach and met up, shaking hands as if it wasn't a pre-arranged meeting.

Brian quickly told Adam about the car and Ford Transit and his concerns. They decided to take separate taxis and meet back at Brian's house, arriving from different directions to allow each to make their own assessment of the neighbouring streets. They would avoid the street that Brian's car was parked in.

Monica was pleased to see first Brian arrive followed a few minutes later by Adam and quickly made sandwiches for them to eat and mugs of tea to drink. Adam told both Monica and Brian exactly what had happened in Spain and how her family was safe for the next two weeks during which time a longer-term arrangement could be considered if necessary. He asked Monica how her parents knew about the chalet and expressed his concerns that the family would be ill-prepared for their stay there. Monica had responded by saying that her father had been born on a small farm in the area and knew the hills and valleys like the back of his hand. She was sure he could, if necessary, find someone with whom they could stay. The fact they were both from that area wasn't known to people in Cútar so to look for them there would be a very lucky long shot. Monica also told Adam and Brian that she and her sister had had few holidays when they were children due to the cost but she remembered visiting the area and felt her parents and sister would be safe there.

'One thing I don't understand,' said Adam 'why were your parents and sister held in their house and tied up? Why wasn't your mother working for Lenny? Why wasn't your father at work, why were they all being held at your house?'

'I asked my father that and he said he didn't know the reason but that morning three men had arrived before my sister went to school and tied them up and said they had to stay there all day. He didn't know why.'

'Maybe it was a reaction to you going to hospital?' suggested Brian.

Maybe a result of Dutch going missing or the drugs going missing …' mused Adam. 'Whatever, it was a real stroke of good fortune.'

There was a general catch-up on recent events. Brian and Adam told Monica about the possible surveillance of Adam's car and both men expressed their thoughts. If Brian was right and Adam's car *was* under surveillance, then there were some serious questions to be addressed.

'First,' started Brian, 'how did the car end up getting connected to the whole affair?'

'It has to be the hospital,' suggested Adam. 'When you were leaving, was Monica sitting in the front seat?'

Brian was quick to answer. 'Yes, she was.'

'So perhaps you were being watched? Perhaps someone just happened to spot her.'

'No, I don't buy that. Even if there was someone, would they really have had the presence of mind to note the car registration? No, I don't buy that.' Brian shook his head.

'OK, so CCTV has to be the alternative. Thing is, has Townsend got the influence to get hold of that kind of thing?'

Brian jumped straight back with his answer: 'And more importantly, does he also have the influence to trace the car as well? We weren't followed – of that I'm one hundred per cent … absolutely one hundred per cent. So someone must have organized a search to find the car. Come on, he couldn't do that …' Brian realized he was answering his own questions.

Adam looked at Brian with a worried frown. 'So, that means the police?'

Brian nodded. 'Who else? The car was found overnight, from mid-afternoon yesterday until this morning. They located it in a residential street of a town thirty-odd miles from Brighton and they still had time to organize at least four men to watch it. But I would be amazed if they were the police. They were just too amateurish …'

'So, what are we going to do?' interrupted Monica.

Both men looked at her with the same word on their lips. '*We?*'

Monica looked from Adam to Brian then back at Adam. 'We, I am involved and I want to hurt them more than you, so yes, we – I can help.'

Adam shifted in his seat, showing Brian that Adam was uncomfortable about Monica's suggestion.

'Monica,' said Adam, 'Jackie Smith is a bitch and to work for her must be hell, but, er, maybe it would help Bri and me a bit to understand how you got to be working for her in the first place.'

Brian shared Adam's discomfort – it was a question he had thought about asking himself. He saw Monica shift in her seat as she took a breath and sat upright, her hands firmly clasped together.

Her gaze switched from Adam to Brian repeatedly as she spoke, her voice even and without emotion.

'I lived with my family, my sister and parents and fell in love with a boy from the village – Paco, that's his name. He came from a family who were, shall we say, not thought of too well. His father didn't like work and his mother told stories about other people. They weren't really liked but I fell in love with Paco, not them. There are few jobs in the village and Paco, a year older than me, found work doing odd jobs. He is much cleverer than people think and he went to Nerja to work as a waiter. I didn't see much of him for the summer as I was working with my mother cleaning the houses that are rented to holidaymakers. At the end of the summer Paco was working at a nightclub in the town and he told me he was doing well, not just waiting or working at the bar but doing other jobs for the boss. He said he could get me a job there also, so I agreed and we lived in a small flat in Nerja during the winter. I was working as a waitress and also at the bar. The boss tried to get me to work with the special clients, as he called them. They were older men and they only wanted a girl for the night and I wasn't going to be a prostitute. I wasn't like that – and I loved Paco and wanted to be faithful to him. I had been with men before Paco, but now I was not going to go with other men.'

Monica twisted her fingers and looked at both men, who were sitting back in their seats, watching her face, her eyes and her hands – looking for evidence that she was either telling the truth or telling lies. Neither man moved.

Monica took a breath then continued: 'It was this that made us argue, at first a little but then more and more. Paco wanted me to see these special clients. He said I would get a lot of money. But I didn't want to – I was happy. The flat was small and not very nice, but we were together and I thought that, maybe after a year or two, we could have saved some money to move to a better flat. Then, one night at work he wanted me to see a client, an important man. He told me that I had to do it or we were finished. We argued, we shouted at each other. We were in the kitchen of the bar shouting and I shouted "no" then walked into the restaurant to serve at the bar. I didn't see Paco again.

'Later, when all the staff got together at the end of work the boss and his manager took me into the office. They showed me a desk drawer that was open, the lock was on the floor, they said that money and other things had been in the drawer. I know "other things" meant drugs. I knew that Paco was selling some to people in the club. I said that I didn't know anything about it. I didn't know things or money were kept in the drawer, I didn't go in the office. They didn't believe me. You see, Paco had gone. Of course, it was him who took the money and drugs before he went but the boss thought we had pretended to have the argument and I was planning to meet Paco later. I swore that I didn't know anything. The boss hit me, many times. I was made to stay in the office.'

Brian and Adam could see that Monica's eyes were moist and noticed that she was now squeezing her fingers tighter together, fighting to hold off the tears. They did not comfort her. They knew they had to learn the truth to be able to trust her with their futures. Neither man moved or said anything.

'They said that I had to pay back Paco's debt, every euro's worth and all the interest that was due. To do that I had to see any client they wanted me to, to become a prostitute for them. I didn't want to. I hit the boss, smacked him in his face. Another girl who worked for him was there and she turned around. I remember it all in slow motion. She turned her back and then I felt pain to my head, then I was on the ground and the boss was kicking me. The kicks didn't hurt at the time. I remember thinking "Why don't the kicks hurt?" I think now the punch or what he did to my head must have made my brain not work because I didn't feel any pain. I was made to stay in a room near the club; the girl stayed with me. The next night I was in the room when the boss and a man came in. The door was locked from the outside. I was told to do what ever the man wanted. He was fat and smelt a lot. I refused. The boss and the man left. I thought that maybe I had won. Maybe the boss would let me work again as a waitress.

'The next day he came with the girl and two men. They dragged me from the room and into his car and drove me to his house. I knew where he lived was opposite my village, a big house. He made me stay in the car with the two men and the girl. He went into the house and came out with my mother. He stood with her and she was crying. She wouldn't look at me. The boss came to me and said that they had beaten my father a little, and my mother would be his cook and cleaner until I had paid the debt I owed. If I didn't do what he wanted, he would make my sister work for him. I was nearly twenty and she was just fourteen. He said it was a family debt. I argued. I said it was Paco and his family that should pay the debt not me and my family, but he laughed. He said Paco's family were not worth anything. I had no choice.'

226

Monica looked at the ceiling and bit her bottom lip before continuing. 'I worked at his club for some months then he told me I was going to work in England where I could earn more money – the debt could be repaid more quickly. I agreed. It is the same really, going with a man in Spain or with a man in England, but if I was to get more money then it would finish quicker and my family would be free from him. I worked hard but the interest kept increasing. Last year I was allowed to speak with my parents on the telephone twice, once in the summer and once at Navidad, that's Christmas in Spain. It was hopeless: my mother was made to live in the boss's house so I would not cause any problems – she was a hostage. My father was made to work in his gardens, to gather the oranges, lemons and olives but without being paid. My sister has not been touched – yet – but for how long? I know how wicked this boss is. He would make her work in his club, too, if I didn't do well in England.'

There was silence in the room. Monica's body gave small shudders as the tears at last fell on to her hands that were tightly entwined on her lap. Brian and Adam exchanged a glance and each knew that what they had been told was the truth. The silence lasted another minute before Adam spoke gently.

'Monica, we're both very sorry to hear what has happened to you and your family. We cannot begin to put it right but we can make sure that these men pay for what they have done and make certain that they won't ever again ruin anybody's lives.'

Brian stood. 'Right, so here's my plan: we can, one, see if they are cops at your car – I think we'll find they're not. Then, two, we can either beat the crap out of them now or beat the crap out of them in the future. I have some trackers, so we could get one on the car and another on the van and see where they go.'

Adam smiled at Brian's straightforward planning. So much for subtlety, he thought. Brian was supposed to be the thinker and Adam the one who winged it in any situation.

'Is there any point,' he said out loud, 'in finding out where they go really, if they're not the police. If they are the baddies, why don't we take the message to them? Monica, would you be a love and make the coffees while Bri and I have a chat. It's best if you don't get involved with this, but don't worry I think you will get your chance. In fact I *know* you will.'

He smiled at her and saw a faint smile on her face as she wiped the tears from her face and walked into the kitchen.

Adam and Brian discussed what they were going to do and by the time Monica had brought in the coffees they had made their decision. Brian went upstairs for five minutes before entering the lounge with an ice pick, a ball hammer and two penknives with four-inch blades.

Adam was about to reach for the ice pick when Brian held up his prosthetic hand and smiled: 'Owner's benefit – I get that.' He laughed.

Adam and Brian put their jackets on, then left the house leaving Monica in the lounge. As they reached the pavement, the rain increased and with it the wind, which forced most people to lower their heads. This could be an advantage to both men if it meant potential witnesses had their eyes to the ground. As agreed, they split up and took different directions to the road where Adam's car was parked and when there, they would use their mobiles to confirm that each was ready for their coordinated approach.

As Adam slid his mobile away he again glanced around the corner and measured the distance between him and the Transit van parked facing him. It was about fifty yards away. The rain was being carried on the wind and would be behind him as he walked towards the van – a plus, as it would also be driving into the windscreen of both the van and Brian's target, the car containing the two men, obscuring their vision. Daylight had faded and streetlights struggled to penetrate the driving rain. The two street lights that were relevant to Adam and Brian were situated close together on opposite sides of the road, which for Adam meant that he was walking towards the light situated behind the Transit, and for Brian that the light was in front of the car.

Adam chanced another glance along the road and he made out the faint outline of a solitary figure passing under a streetlight on the opposite pavement, fifty yards from the target car. Adam knew that Brian was moving steadily and he turned the corner. He walked at a pace that he knew Brian would be keeping. They knew by instinct what the other would be doing and thinking. Adam kept his head lowered but in his mind was counting off the distance. His hands were deep into his pockets. His left held the open penknife, the other the ball-head hammer whose shaft rested inside the jacket sleeve alongside his wrist. That way the hammer could quickly and smoothly be brought from the pocket without catching any material. Little details he knew, made the difference between winning and losing.

Brian was watching Adam and inwardly feeling a touch more nervous than he had expected. This would be the first time that his prosthetic hand would be tested under such exacting conditions and failure could have serious consequences for both of them. Adam hadn't mentioned the hand at all – there had been no question as to whether Brian would be able to cope.

Twenty yards to go …

In the car Charlie Tompkins was still in the driver's seat with Dom alongside him. Tompkins' concentration had been maintained the whole day during which he had twice reminded the others for the need to be alert, but in the last fifteen minutes he had felt the cold and damp reaching into his body and thoughts of starting the engine and allowing the heater to work for a few minutes had been considered, then abandoned. He was low in the seat and felt cramped, the collar of his jacket rising to his ears. His eyes remained fixed on Adam's car in a bored manner, his earlier alertness diminished by tiredness and cold.

In the Transit van cab Chas was still in the driving seat but like Tompkins he had lost concentration. Pete sitting in the passenger seat next to him was asleep, leaning against his door window. Chas closed his eyes for the umpteenth time, his head resting against the headrest. In the back of the van Derek and Jack had both settled into their seats with their eyes closed. There was a gentle rhythmic sound of breathing from one of them. The back of the van was in total darkness and the only time the two men had moved, apart from when Derek had used the plastic bottle to relieve himself, was when they had settled into their seats some three hours previously,

Adam was five yards from the front of the van. Brian a similar distance from the back of the car. Both men made a quick look around them to confirm what their eyes, ears and senses had told them, that nobody else was on the street. They were now two yards before each would reach their starting positions and neither had been seen by the men in the car or van. If someone had been watching, what they would have seen next they would have described as a routine that could have come from a ballet.

At the same time both men went into a crouch and their hands came free from their jackets. One hand went directly towards a tyre, a blur of movement as the body weight was transferred and shifted so that the other hand which had risen into the air now came down with speed and force. The sounds of two windscreens being broken at the same time wouldn't have sounded as loud as a witness might have expected, but while trying to understand what they had seen the witness would have missed the next movement that took Brian's ice pick through the side front window. The point of the pick smashed into, but failed to penetrate, the skull of the man. Adam's hammer had penetrated the driver's door window and followed through to the man's jaw. The two men unaffected by the attack would in that instant have had the same expressions on their faces, mouth and eyes wide open as they looked at the person sitting next to them with blood rushing from their wounds. Their brains would be trying to gather pace from a standing start trying to assimilate the facts as their eyes were relaying messages and in that time their eyes hadn't followed the men moving in front of their vehicles to the other doors …

Again, with almost perfect synchronisation the glass in each door was shattered and the man's face inside received a blow from either Brian's ice pick held side on to avoid the spike or straight edge or Adam's hammer. Brian reached inside the car and started to search the unconscious Tompkins' pockets. Adam was about to do the same when he heard a muffled shout from the back of the van and a sudden movement. Brian had warned Adam that the position of the van could indicate people in the back waiting to pounce so Adam was more than prepared as the two back doors opened. He stood on the pavement and saw the man nearest him jump to the ground. His action told Adam within a fraction of a second that the man had landed poorly – his joints would have been stiff from inaction. Adam dropped the penknife as his hand balled into a fist and continued until it met with the man's jaw. There was a crunching sound and Adam knew that the man's jaw was shattered, while he would only have sore knuckles the next day. The man furthest from Adam had landed on the road but hadn't seen Adam, as for some reason his brain had told him to look at the car he was supposed to be attacking rather than where the sounds had been coming from. Adam brought the hammer down on the back of the man's head with a solid 'clod'. The man fell forward on to his knees then collapsed on to the road with his head making a heavy crunching sound as it struck the road surface.

Adam looked around to ensure that nobody was present then methodically searched the four men. He removed every item that he could from their pockets stuffing them into his own without examining them first. He looked into the back of the Transit van: a baseball bat lay on the floor next to a chair, – the first man in his panic hadn't even remembered to take his weapon with him.

'Idiot!' Adam said as he hauled the two men into the back of the van and closed the doors.

He picked up his penknife and quickly ran around the vehicle using the knife to slit each tyre. The action was more than was necessary to prevent the van from being moved, but it was designed to send a message and he knew that the message he and Brian were sending would be received.

Brian had also searched his two men in the car and slit the tyres before walking to Adam's car with a big grin across his face. Adam grinned back then went to his car and dropped into a press-up position using his hands and feet to support his body. He examined the underside of his car and was joined by Brian doing the same from the roadside. Brian went to the back of the vehicle and repeated the procedure as Adam went to the front to examine under the engine. Both men stood and Adam took the key from his jean back pocket, kept separate from any other item. He and Brian jumped into the car but kept their doors open until Adam had the engine started. He drove quickly away from the scene to the top of the road close to where Brian's house was and slowed to allow Brian to leave. Brian was finishing emptying his pockets of all the items he had taken from the two men in the car except for the mobile phone he had taken from the car driver, leaving everything on the floor where he sat. The ice pick and penknife were under the wallets, mobile phones, cash, tissues, keys and other assorted items.

Adam drove on, avoiding the town centre, and headed for the route he had ridden on his bike, to Haywards Heath. He knew that the police had various cameras on the route but he chanced that there wouldn't be so many officers on duty in Haywards Heath as in Crawley. He found a parking space in the large car park behind the Marks & Spencer store and parked. The light was poor but sufficient for him to search through his pockets and sort out the proceeds he had taken from the four men. He took the batteries out of the mobile phones and examined each of their wallets, discarding other items into a pile. He twice looked around to see if anyone was paying him any attention, but each time all he could see was an expanse of empty car park being washed by the rain with a few cars at the far end closest to the shop entrance. He checked the interior light was switched off, then opened his door, gathered all the items he was discarding together, and dumped them into a rubbish bin, knowing that there would be a good chance of the items being found by the rubbish collector the next day. By then it wouldn't matter. He drove back to Crawley and parked the car in another area of the estate in among a row of cars. He noted the other cars and how they were parked. Having been caught once, he wasn't going to take the chance again. He walked back to Brian's house.

Monica had made a meal from an assortment of ingredients she had found in the fridge, freezer and storage cupboards, and the three sat around the table discussing what they had achieved that afternoon and early evening and what they could do next to pile pressure on Townsend and Smith. They had agreed that Lenny Townsend would be in Spain coordinating the search for Monica's family, so at that time they would concentrate on Geoff Townsend and Smith. The possessions taken from the six men didn't give any clue as to who the men were, or who they were working for until Brian scrolled through Charlie Tompkins' mobile and saw the names of Geoff and Lenny among the addresses.

Geoff Townsend was at home, venting his frustration and anger at anyone and everyone who came within his view, except Pat who knew when to say something and when to keep her opinions to herself. He had last spoken to Charlie Tompkins just after four o'clock that afternoon, over two hours ago, and was impatient for events to happen. Again he rung Charlie's mobile, more in frustration rather than in hope that anything had happened. He listened at the ring tone as it went through to the answering machine. His heartbeat went that bit more quickly. Something must have happened, he thought.

'Charlie, ring me back,' he said before disconnecting the call.

In Crawley, Brian watched the screen and saw that a voice message had been received. He nodded to Adam that he was going to retrieve it. Monica was almost laughing as she heard Townsend's voice.

'Let me speak to him!' she urged.

Brian smiled. 'A good call. Confuse him, won't it? And Monica, I think you have a few things that you would like to say to him, haven't you?'

Adam agreed but insisted the call should not be made from the house, as he was sure the police were involved in finding his car and, if so, they would be able to locate the address where the mobile was used as well. The three put on jackets and walked towards the town centre, knowing that there would be places where Monica could make the call out of view of any cameras and from where they could quickly move to avoid the call being traced to their location. They kept to side and residential streets until they arrived close to the town's further-education college. A bus stop offered them shelter from the wind and rain.

Monica held the mobile to her ear and listened as it rang.

'Charlie!' Townsend said.

'I'm not Charlie. I'm Monica,' she said brightly. She could hear the intake of breath from Townsend and imagined the look of shock on his face. 'Do you remember me? I used to work for Jackie Smith, but I don't anymore – I resigned. Did you want to speak to Charlie?' She looked at Adam and Brian with a large smile and missed the first few words shouted by Townsend. She only heard '…kill you' at the end.

'Oh I'm sorry. Charlie is unavailable at the moment, Mr Townsend. Are there any instructions I can pass on to him?'

Townsend's mind couldn't handle the caller being Monica in the first place, but her asking for instructions to be passed through her to Charlie broke all his thinking patterns and he was stuck for an immediate answer.

Monica continued: 'He and the other men would appreciate some grapes and perhaps a bunch of flowers delivered to them in hospital – *if* you could find it in your heart,' she said, before breaking into laughter.

Adam took the mobile from her. 'Townsend, you scum. We're coming for you, your brother and Smith.' He closed the call but felt disappointed at what he had said in the heat of the moment. It wasn't what he wanted to say.

Brian disconnected the battery and SIM card before they walked back to his house.

Townsend had shouted and sworn for over a minute non-stop after the call, not caring that the two security guards standing in the porch to the front door could hear his every word. He redialled, this time the DCI. He tried to be calm as he listened to the DCI clicking his keyboard as he accessed the main incident database.

'Found it. Hang on while I get the incident on the screen. Bloody hell. A car with two men and a Transit with four men .... Every tyre slashed ... Six men treated at the scene by paramedics. All have serious injuries but none appears to be life-threatening –broken jaw, bad cut to the head, fractured cheekbone ...'

'I don't want a bloody list of their injuries. I don't give a monkeys about them! Just what bloody happened?' Townsend shouted.

The DCI continued to scroll down the report. 'Called to the scene by a passer-by, old man, blah-blah, taken to East Surrey Hospital at Redhill. No identification on any man. Bobby at the hospital says that two men who could talk refused to speak to him, told to go and, yeah well, himself. No immediate reports from the scene of any witnesses ... CID putting together a team at Crawley. Forensics at the scene .... will be there overnight. Question over whether it is a gang-war type of crime.'

'War! You bloody better believe it. This *is* bloody war and there won't be any prisoners. Now you earn all that dosh you've had over the years and I'll throw in a bonus of fifty thou. You get on the bloody case. Do whatever is needed. I want to know who's behind all this and I want to sort it out myself. Bloody understand?'

The DCI held the phone away from his ear as the intensity increased then muttered, 'I'll do all I can. Don't worry – I'll get up there myself and see what I can do.'

Townsend closed the call then threw his mobile across the lounge as Pat sat on the settee sipping a gin and tonic. He turned towards her and she held up a hand.

'Don't have a go at me. Just sit down and think – be rational. I only heard one side of the conversations but this is a time for thinking. Take our time then we'll get the bastards. Geoff, have a clear head and let's think.'

Townsend stood for a second longer before sitting down heavily on a settee. He put his arm along the back of the settee and stretched his legs in front of himself. 'OK, let's think. You and me – we're a good bloody team. Let's just calm down, think about everything and then kill the bastards.'

Pat smiled. That was her Geoff, that was the man she loved, the man she adored – strong and fearless. Even when things looked hopeless, he came up with the idea to save the situation. This time she'd be there – she wanted to be.

Adam, Brian and Monica talked for the next hour during which time they each suggested various scenarios that would injure Townsend and Smith. Adam's and Brian's ideas moved increasingly towards killing both Townsend and Smith, and as the seriousness of their potential actions was discussed they watched Monica to gauge her reaction.

Eventually Adam sat back in his chair and looking directly at Monica. 'Monica, this afternoon we hurt six of Townsend's men, *hurt* them, some more than others but we only hurt them. You know as well as us that if Townsend got hold of either Brian or me that we would be killed, murdered. You know that Dutch was murdered. You know that Kieran was murdered but do you know who murdered them?'

Monica looked at both men for a full minute without saying anything. She nodded. 'You.'

Adam looked at Monica. 'Monica, we were in the special forces. It has been our job to rid the world of … of' – he looked at Brian for the word, but received none – 'the people who corrupt our society, who kill innocents and by their greed inflict hurt and pain on weak and defenceless people. That was our job – we were paid to do it. Townsend and his gang have caused so much hurt. They have killed ordinary honest people – decent people – they corrupt everything and we've had enough. You are free to walk away from us. You can go, live wherever you like, do what you like, and honestly we'd be happier that way.' He looked at Brian, looking for confirmation.

'Monica,' Brian said, 'that's true, If you do go away, you can be sure that we are going to finish Townsend, Smith, his brother, the lot, finish things once and for all.'

Adam looked Monica directly in her eyes. 'I killed Kieran, I murdered Dutch and I shot the man in the garage. I intend to kill the rest of them. I'm not proud of what I'm saying but it's the truth. I will kill them or maybe they will kill me.'

Monica sat rock still. She stared at Adam and thought about what he had said, of what he had done in the past and of what he was going to do. She felt herself almost rise from her seat. She smiled at Adam then at Brian.

'The first time you spoke in the café I thought you were a nice man, a good man, but I couldn't talk to you. I didn't know you and I couldn't trust you. Now, I know you, maybe not everything but enough, and you, Brian,' she added, looking at Brian, 'I understand what you are saying and I know that really I can not help much, but I want to. They have hurt my parents and sister.' She stared defiantly at Adam then Brian. 'They destroyed our family and they have destroyed others, *destroyed*, not just hurt a little. I want to help you destroy them. I want be a part of it. Please, I cannot just go and read in the newspapers about what you have done.'

Brian looked at Adam then said to Monica: 'Look, if this goes wrong, if we cock it up, then there's a good chance we will end up dead, not hurt or in prison, but dead. Our lives finished. Neither of us has family to speak of and we're probably all we've got – sad I know – but he's the bloke I love and would do anything for and I bloody well hope he feels the same about me,' – he smiled at Adam – 'but it's our choice, always has been. We live, we die, our choice, but you, you have a family, a future – why don't you go and have a life? Just walk away, join your family.'

Monica looked at Brian. Her face was set. 'This is my fight. I've been screwed by hundreds of men – smelly, fat, dirty men. I've spent hours, days, weeks lying under their fat bellies looking at their fat ugly faces while they thrust their dirty cocks in me, and you think I want to walk away? I want to see their faces. I want to hear them cry. I want to hear them beg and then, only then would I pull the trigger. And I will smile. I will do anything to rid them, to see them go to hell.'

Brian smiled. 'That's an in then I take it.' He laughed.

But Adam remained deadly serious, his face unsmiling. 'OK, Monica, but you must agree to do what you are told. Any time you want to walk away, you can. You do not have to stay, honestly. Do we have a deal?'

Monica rose to her feet and went to Adam, leant down and kissed his cheeks then did the same to Brian.

Charlie Tompkins finished dressing into his blood-stained clothes and walked unsteadily out of the toilet situated at the end of the ward. A nurse approached him with a smile.

'And where do you think you are going?'

'I'm discharging myself,' he said through barely parted teeth.

21

'The weather forecast is for heavy rain,' Adam said to Brian, 'and high winds later tonight, isn't it?'

'Yes,' replied Brian.

'Then how about we take the fight directly to Townsend,' said Adam with a smile, 'and I mean *directly* to him?'

Brian and Monica were sitting, watching Adam as he paced the room as he sketched out his plan.

'Sounds really good,' said Brian. 'We can refine a point or two on our way but I'm all for it.'

'What can I do?' asked Monica. 'I want to be a part of this, not just a coffee maker and cook.'

'Monica, you have two jobs to do while Brian and I are in Brighton and I have a feeling you will enjoy doing both of them,' replied Adam.

Twenty minutes later Adam and Brian left the house wearing warm and waterproof clothing and their old and trusted boots. They walked apart as they made their way towards where Adam's car was parked and slowed as they approached it. There was nothing to give cause for any alarm but they still automatically went into their routine of inspecting under the car. They were looking for UCIEDs, or Under Car Improvised Explosive Devices, but also for any leakage from the hydraulics or any device that could track the car's movements. Satisfied that the car was clean, Adam drove them towards Brighton, noting that the car had over half a tank of petrol.

Monica sat at the back of the bus on the upper level as the vehicle made its slow journey between Crawley and Redhill in the neighbouring county of Surrey. It was mid-evening and there were few passengers so she was able to relax.

Her first call was to Jackie Smith, the next to Lenny Townsend in Spain and the last to Geoff Townsend in Brighton. In each of the calls she made sure that her voice sounded confident and bright and even managed to laugh when Jackie and Lenny had made their predictable threats against her and her family. She changed buses in Redhill then used another of the mobiles that Adam and Brian had given her and repeated the calls. Adam had said that by repeating the calls from different mobile phones would affect the Townsends' and Smith's confidence still more and could lead to them making a rash decision. She had four mobile phones and was to make the three calls once every hour until eleven o'clock that night when she was to return to Brian's house with the mobile phone's batteries and SIM cards removed. Brian had left a new mobile phone in the house for her use when she was in the house but on no account was she to use it to ring anyone other than Brian or Adam.

Geoff Townsend answered his mobile after checking the caller's ID, which was withheld.

'Yeah?'

'Hello, Geoff,' Monica said, laughing. 'Are you having a lovely evening? Stay in tonight. It's very windy and raining. I wouldn't want you to catch a chill.' She finished the call before he could start his foul reply and left him looking at the machine.

Pat was sitting watching Geoff and knew that for the first time in many years Geoff was struggling to keep in control of the situation. The six men being put into hospital had shocked Geoff. All six were known to him and each had a pedigree of being handy at times of crisis. He had tried to analyse the situation from all angles, even that the car had been driven around Crawley to draw attention to it so that it would be found easily. He didn't consider it was just a case of Brian's difficulty in finding a parking spot.

'It was a trap,' he had said to Pat. 'It was a trap and we walked straight into it.'

Convinced of this he had told Lenny about the theory but his brother was sceptical and dismissed it quickly, which led to him and Geoff arguing for several minutes.

When the call was finished Pat was quick to admonish her husband. 'I reckon that you and Lenny falling out is just what they want. Divide you two and it will make things easier for them.'

'To do what?' Geoff had shouted at Pat, but instantly regretted his show of temper. 'Sorry,' he murmured.

'See what they are doing?' she said evenly. 'You falling out with Lenny and then having a go at me. They're playing a game with all of us. Fixing up Jackie was part of it. They'll be planning something else now. Geoff, what you've got to do is go on the front foot, get everyone out on the streets tomorrow in Brighton. Someone will have heard something. They can't be trying a takeover of some sort without someone hearing something. A new face in town or an old one, anything, but you need to show who the boss of this city is. You've got to show your strength and be ruthless. Show them, Geoff.'

Adam and Brian had driven to Haywards Heath before heading west and then south to approach the Townsend house from the north. They parked away from the road and hidden from view. Against a backdrop of howling winds, they went through a whispered final check-through of their plans and synchronised their watches. Adam set off on foot towards the trees and at the edge of the wood knelt down. He knew the time was now after three o' clock and that he had twenty to twenty-five minutes of hard crawling before him if he was to be in position on time. He leaned forward on to his hands and knees and lowered his back before setting off at a steady pace. The extra padding he had wound around his knees would certainly help but even so he knew that his knees would be painful in the morning, though any thoughts on that subject were firmly pushed to one side as he fully concentrated on what he was doing and the area surrounding him. In that weather most people would have risked walking carefully, perhaps bent at the waist, but Adam wouldn't take the chance.

Brian drove to his selected spot and mentally ran through exactly what he would do, how he would need to change his weight position, which leg he would use as his lead leg, how he would move around the car … every detail was planned in his mind. He checked his watch. It had been twenty-eight minutes since Adam had started off through the woods. Two minutes to go.

Adam was now leopard-crawling the final two yards to the gate of Townsend's house and peered around the corner towards the house. A security guard was standing in the porch way of the front door, sheltering from the wind and rain. The other security guard was six feet in front of Adam, wearing a long black plastic cape which the rain hit with a constant patter. He had his back to Adam, allowing the wind and rain to hit his back rather than face the gate and have the wind and rain in his face. Adam moved his arm slowly – ten seconds to go. He moved into a crouch and then, making sure he was behind the pillar, stood up. He moved his muscles and was pleased that they all appeared to be flexible and not seized or stiff from all the crawling.

Car headlights briefly lit the front of the house before they were turned off. With just its sidelights showing a car approached the gate. The man in the porch ran towards the gate while the man near the gate had turned and was watching as the car came to a halt. The driver's window was lowered. The guard who had been in the porch shone his torch at the car and saw one occupant in the driving seat. He kept the beam on the driver while the other security guard unlocked the gate and walked towards the driver's door window. Adam moved quickly and delivered a chop to the back of the security guard's neck at the same time Adam's other hand grabbed the guard's clothing and held the body upright.

The other security guard continued to shine his torch directly into the face of the car driver, watching the driver's every move. It was because his attention was so focused on what he was seeing in his torch beam that he didn't realise the figure outside the beam of the torch wasn't his colleague, but Adam. Adam used three strides to reach the guard who became aware of his presence only a second before he received a solid palm punch to his nose. The blow was delivered quickly and with enough force to instantly break the guard's nose without forcing the broken cartilage into the head, where death would be the likely result. His death was not planned or wanted – his incapacity was. He fell to the ground as Adam grabbed him and pulled him next to the first security guard. Adam rummaged through their pockets, taking their mobile phones then moved the guards out of the way.

Brian saw Adam run towards the house pulling items from his pocket, and he slowly moved the car forward, listening to the tyres crunching over the stones. He waited until he was ten feet from the house before he gunned the engine and the car lurched forward kicking stones into the air behind it. Brian braced himself for the impact as he drove the car into the porch. Metal screeched against the bricks and the car lurched violently as the front wheels hit first the step then crashed through the front door of the house. Brian had been anticipating the impact but even so he was thrust forward and his hands hit the windscreen. He quickly undid his seat belt and managed to climb on to his seat, which allowed him to lean forward through the open side window. He landed on his hands and felt the pain as the joint of the prosthetic limb was jolted against his arm but ignoring the pain he scrambled to his feet and to the back of the car. He ran towards the back garden running his hand against the side of the house to guide him until he broke clear on the grass and pool area.

Adam had moved as soon as the car came to a stop and

pushed a length of rag down the open petrol tank tube before pulling it out and stuffing the dry end into the tank. He could smell the petrol on the rag and knew that he would have petrol on his gloves. He struck a match and pushed it towards the rag. Instantly his gloves were alight but he ignored the flames and dropped the rag on to the car before ducking as he ran towards where Brian was at the back of the house. It was just as he turned the corner that he heard the whoosh sound as the petrol in the car tank caught. That sound was instantly followed by a further and more violent sound, which he knew meant that the tank had dropped from the car and flames would now be spreading along the length of the car towards the house. Brian meanwhile found the rockery and quickly grabbed a large rock. He ran towards the kitchen window and threw the rock at the window, shattering it.

Adam heard Brian's rock break the window and knew that Brian would already have a second rock in his hands, ready to throw through another window. He jogged steadily towards the perimeter fence and heard another window smash. Adam reached the fence and waited for Brian to catch him up, watching the outline approach him. Then Brian stepped into Adam's cupped hands and reached up for the top of the wire, which he grabbed and threw one leg over. He lay on top of the wire and held his good arm down along the fence. A second later he heard Adam expel air from his lungs and then his arm was caught by Adam's hands. Brian pulled and Adam grabbed the top of the fence. Brian jumped down and Adam landed next to him. They exchanged a quick glance then headed off towards the woods at a gentle run.

Townsend had been awake in his bed listening to the rhythmic breathing of Pat when he had been aware of a car beam briefly shining on the house but didn't take any notice of it. His thoughts were directed towards the problems he had and of the orders he had given to over twenty people who would be on the streets of Brighton at first light. Others had been instructed to go to

Crawley and find out anyway they could who owned the car and who had attacked his men.

He was thinking of other calls he would have to make in the morning when he suddenly heard car tyres kicking up stones in the drive below. Startled, he sat up, trying to make sense of why a car would be in his drive at that time of the morning before he felt the house shudder as Brian crashed the car into the porch.

'What!' was all he could shout before he heard another movement. He jumped from the bed and pulled the curtain in time to hear the sound of petrol igniting and a few moments later a whoosh as the petrol tank caught fire. The whole front of the house was illuminated. He was unaware of Pat waking or that his body had started shaking. He continued to look out the window, mesmerised by the sound and sight of flames below him.

Suddenly he pulled his brain together and ran to the bedside table to grab his mobile before running down the stairs towards the hallway. There he completed dialling the emergency number as, to his horror, he saw flames from a car engulfing the front door that was held upright by only the top hinge. He stopped the call and ran into the kitchen just as the window was shattered and glass flew across the room towards him. He backed away confused: the fire behind him and a window being broken in front of him. There was another crashing of glass from his right and he ran to the lounge to see that the largest window had been broken. Glass had fallen from the frame and lay shattered into thousands of pieces on the carpet. He ran back into the kitchen and grabbed the fire extinguisher from the wall before running to the front door and using the extinguisher against the flames.

Smoke from burning tyres came into the hallway, but he crouched down and continued to dampen the flames until the extinguisher had given out the final drops of foam. It appeared that the flames had been put out but the smoke continued to pour into the house. Townsend shouted for the security guards, then ran back to his bedroom, where he grabbed the shotgun he kept behind Pat's dresses. He always had two rounds loaded and, checking that they were in place, he ran out of the bedroom, still not seeing Pat as she finished dressing, or listening to her frightened questions. He ran out the kitchen door then around the house towards the front gate where he saw a figure staggering. He ran to the security guard who was rubbing the back of his neck and obviously slowly recovering from an injury. The other guard lay unconscious on the ground.

Townsend stood and screamed obscenities at the rain and wind. He was still wearing just his underpants. The door to the pool room suddenly flew open and two figures in the process of pulling coats on ran into the garden. Obviously they had been asleep and undressed when the commotion had started. The two guards took in the scene and each ran off to check whether the attackers had already left the garden.

Adam and Brian made good progress, not worrying whether they were seen or not at that point but trying to put distance between them and the chaos they had left at Townsend's house. They ran for a time as they made their way north parallel to the main A23 road, then east using the South Downs Way to Ditchling Beacon. From there they chose a path that led them down the side of the hill, sometimes under the cover of bushes and trees but at other times exposed on grass. They knew where the road was but avoided it until they reached the bottom of the hill where they took to the road and headed north through the village of Ditchling.

At that hour the road was virtually deserted and they could jump into trees or bushes at the first sign of any vehicle's headlights. Half an hour later they passed the Ditchling Common country park on their right and became aware that more traffic was beginning to use the road. They had initially planned to go to Haywards Heath railway station but realised that their wet and bedraggled state would be noticed by workers and early-morning commuters. After a quick stop and reference to the map they headed for Wivelsfield station instead. They agreed to separate so that only one of them would be seen at a time, which would hopefully draw less attention.

Townsend sat in his lounge drinking coffee from a mug and watching rain being blown in through the shattered window. He was dressed in his full outdoor clothing as was Pat who paced the living room listening to her husband rousing people from their beds and ordering them to scour the streets and countryside to find the bastards who had disturbed his sleep. He didn't explain to anyone exactly what had happened, merely that someone had attacked his two security guards, one of whom Pat had driven to hospital, the other being merely bruised. No mention had been made of the car jammed in his front door or the broken windows, the combination of which had turned their house into a wind tunnel.

Pat had asked Townsend about the windows. 'Why break the windows when they've tried to burn the house down?'

'Because they bloody well could,' he had replied. 'Look at us now, sitting here with a bloody gale rushing through the house and rain pouring in with a car stuck in the front door. I don't know if they were trying to burn the house down or not, probably not, but they wanted to upset us – not kill us. That is their mistake because when I get hold of them I will kill them as slowly and painfully as possible.'

Pat had agreed. She wanted to be there to watch them scream for all the damage they had caused to her lovely home.

Townsend's call to Lenny in Spain had been over twenty minutes in length as Lenny first tried to calm his younger brother before analysing exactly what had happened to them in the past few weeks, trying to make sense of who could be so stupid as to take on the Townsend family. He was upset that Charlie had been injured but not as upset as he was about the fact that two men had somehow beaten up six of their men, with none of them seemingly able to offer any resistance. Lenny told his brother that he would fly to the UK that day and use his influence to put a stop to all of this 'nonsense', as he put it.

Geoff Townsend's call to DCI was short and to the point. He was told to get to the Townsend house within thirty minutes for a chat. Townsend's tone was unanswerable. 'Plod' arrived exactly twenty-eight minutes later.

'Geoff, what the …' was all he could say as he looked at the car in Townsend's doorway. Black scorch marks stretched up the side of the house and into the hallway where black soot and smoke damage showed on the ceilings and walls throughout the entire downstairs. The DCI walked slowly through the hallway, noticing the sweet smell of petrol and seeing the blackness of the walls and ceilings up the stairs. He walked past the kitchen, avoiding the glass swept into a pile by the sink and the gaping hole where the window had been smashed. Finally, he walked into the lounge, nodded towards Pat, then walked to the smashed window. Townsend had been following the DCI, not saying anything but allowing the police Officer to assess the scene as a professional.

The DCI looked at the Townsends. 'I don't know what to say. I'll get the forensics up here straight away and put a callout for anyone suspicious to be stop-searched. we'll get the CCTV footage from …'

'No!' interrupted Geoff Townsend. 'No forensics, no stop and search, but yes to the cameras, every bloody one in the county if you have to. And if you haven't got the people to look at them then I'll supply them. No publicity at all, none, do you understand?'

The DCI was taken aback but saw that Townsend had a good point, though how he was to get the house back in order without attracting any comment was beyond him.

'It's difficult to carry out all the enquiries without having a crime to attach them to,' observed the DCI.

'Believe me, that can be arranged. How about corruption of a senior detective for starters, a bloke who's had thousands from me and others over the years, had free holidays, nights out, lives in a big house and wife dresses all smart, all paid for by me and my friends?' Townsend stared at the DCI, who felt a wave of contempt rush towards him and knew that the threat would be carried out. In his heart, he had long feared the moment when a senior police officer would knock on his door in the early hours and announce his arrest on a charge of corruption. He had always recognised that the good days would have to be paid for some day.

Geoff Townsend's mobile rang, breaking the silence in the room. He answered it.

'Geoff, have you seen my car?' asked Monica sweetly. 'Only someone's taken it and I think I'll have to report the theft to the police.'

Townsend's face was red as he inhaled air and then broke into a tirade of abuse at the mobile as it flew off into a corner of the room. He turned on the DCI. 'Find out where that call came from … and I mean the exact place. I want the answer – NOW!'

Adam and Brian caught the train but were at opposite ends as they mingled with the commuters, their wet and muddy clothes attracting disapproving looks. They both alighted at the Three Bridges station in Crawley and on leaving the station saw Monica waiting on the forecourt by the passenger drop-off zone. Adam and Monica were to walk one route to Brian's house while Brian was to take the more direct route. Adam and Monica walked towards the town centre with the workers arriving from the railway station but stopped as soon as they were away from the crowds. Monica pulled a mobile from her pocket and called Townsend. As she finished the call and removed the SIM card and battery, she and Adam burst out laughing. They would be at Brian's house within a few minutes, where there was the promise of a full breakfast.

22

By midday the car had been removed from the Townsend house, the windows had been replaced and cleaners had been brought in from Jackie Smith's house, the girls being given alternative work for the day. Townsend had paid everyone extra as a reward for keeping their mouths closed about what they saw and did and backed the sweetness with the threat that he would break every bone in their body should they talk to anyone.

Lenny arrived and surveyed the damage before briefing his brother about the measures he had taken. Despite all these 'distractions', as he called them, they had to keep up the show of everything running as normal. True, the usual warehouse collection would have to be scrapped in favour of a more direct route that carried far greater risks but the business had to continue, no matter what. The weekly collection would be made by Jackie and Charlie Tompkins, something of a gamble given their importance to the whole organisation, but at least both could be relied upon. Lenny was taking the reins and some sort of order could and would be restored, he insisted.

Geoff and Lenny Townsend were standing near the point in the perimeter fence where hours before Adam and Brian had left the grounds and Lenny saw the footsteps in the muddy edge of grass. The sight of the footsteps were sufficient to almost start Geoff Townsend into another rage when his mobile rang. He felt nervous about answering it until he saw the caller was his DCI.

Geoff closed the call without saying anything but to Lenny he said, 'The calls we've been getting are all from the Crawley and Redhill areas, the last one was from near the town centre.

Plod says that the bitch was travelling about and that the phones were always switched off except for when a call was made. They can't trace the locations of the phones until they are switched on and even then there is a delay unless he can tie them into a murder enquiry, which he can't do at the moment. He'll find a way, though.'

'Well, that's one thing we know,' his brother said. 'They're in the Crawley area so that's where we'll put some people. I know a couple of lads there who know what's happening in the town, so we'll flood the place and flush them out.'

Adam and Brian sat back in their chairs and watched Monica as she made mugs of tea for them all. They had spent the past hour discussing what they would do next.

'Adam, the idea was to kill them for a reason, to revenge Ray's wife, and now we're going off at a tangent and I'm worried that we're losing the focus. I know I've still to find the last person involved so I will concentrate on that but I seriously think we should now be planning on how we are going to kill the Townsends and Smith. We've disrupted their organization and if we carry on like this we'll stand a greater chance of them getting more security, so making our task harder. They may even go to ground.'

'I know … I know,' Adam conceded. 'And there's a chance that they will find us, too.'

'Yes, a possibility, probably a fair one. It's certain that they have police resources so we're up against them as well.'

Monica placed the mugs on the table before taking a seat. Adam looked at her. 'And we must think about your family. They've got to be safe. Have you had any thoughts about what's best for them?'

Monica looked nervous. 'They can't go back home now but if Lenny is killed then they could. People know them and I will explain to some influential people what happened and I know they will be safe. But until Lenny is killed his presence will always be felt and people are too scared to fight against him. He has a reputation and, as we know, it's well deserved.'

Brian looked serious. 'Adam, another reason to push on with our original goal and to forget about wrecking their organization for fun is because at the end of the day that is all it is – fun. Be honest, as soon as they are killed someone will step into their role and the racket will continue anyway. One thing, we can take Smith out but we don't want to harm the girls. How many are there and have they all been forced into that life, like you were?'

Monica thought. 'About twelve girls work from the other house and another twenty or so from their own places, flats or houses in Brighton. The girls who work from their places, they're happy, they will continue to work somehow. The girls in the house, I would guess about half and half – some are being forced but not all of them.'

Adam was shocked at the casual manner Monica described the Smith setup. 'The police must know about the house, surely?'

'Yes, they know but I think perhaps they're rewarded for not doing anything.'

'Right,' said Adam, 'why don't Monica and I go to Spain and sort out Monica's family at the same time as we plan something for Lenny. Then, Bri, you can find the last one, Williams, and perhaps think about how we get Jackie Smith and Geoff Townsend.'

Brian agreed. 'One issue: Monica, have you got your passport?' he suddenly asked.

Adam was startled by the question – it was something he hadn't thought of.

'I don't have a passport. Jackie has it – it was taken from me – so I suppose she has it or maybe Lenny has, I don't know.'

Adam felt deflated.

'And I don't have any clothes,' she added, looking at her jeans and top.

'And I don't have a car now,' Adam pointed out, 'so, why don't you both go and get some clothes for Monica while I go and buy a car?'

'And Monica's passport?'

'We'll have to think about that,' said Adam. 'That's a real problem. We can't exactly apply for one, can we? I mean not in time.'

Brian thought for a moment. 'I could forge a passport but it wouldn't be anywhere near a standard that would pass examination, even by a trainee border official.'

'In Spain we have identity cards and we use those to travel as well,' said Monica. 'We use them instead of passports really.'

Brian and Adam stared at each other. 'Of course,' exclaimed Brian, 'on the Continent people use their ID cards, but…' – he hesitated – 'I can't do one of those either to the standard needed, enough to show the police maybe, but not a border official.'

'I've got mine. It's in my room, that and a photograph I hid from them. I taped them to a drawer,' Monica said.

'OK,' said Adam, 'we'll have to think about how we're going to get it, so in the meantime, we'll need a change of plan.'

By mid-afternoon the weather had cleared and the temperature had dropped, with the likelihood of a frost that night, but the Townsends weren't concerned about the weather. There had been no progress from all the people who were searching for the two men and Monica, no leads or even descriptions in either Brighton or Crawley. The one positive piece of news that they had received was that there wasn't any talk on the streets of anyone trying to take over the family's business. While that was good, it didn't lighten the mood of the Townsends who were at a loss to understand who and why they were being targeted. Geoff Townsend was constantly on his mobile phone demanding updates from everyone, issuing threats and promises of reward. Several people had been taken to addresses where they had been questioned under violence but nothing had been learned. The Townsends knew that the word was definitely out when the DCI rang Geoff Townsend telling them that several informants had come forward with reports that the Townsends were 'very unhappy' and that trouble was afoot. The DCI asked Townsend to ease off in case the issue became one that he couldn't keep the lid on, but Townsend's response was sharp and direct: there wouldn't be any easing off until he had the two men and Monica. No discussion about it.

Brian was sitting on a bench in Queens Square in the shopping area of Crawley casually looking about him as people went about their business. It was colder and he had his hands deep into his jacket pocket and was wearing a flat cap to prevent his head becoming cold. A group of three teenage boys were moving around the square, occasionally stopping in a huddle, after which one would leave the group before returning a few minutes later. One of the group was constantly taking calls on his mobile, his eyes always on the move scanning people walking in the square. Brian smiled to himself: what was the point of what he and Adam were doing when three youths were actively taking orders and delivering drugs in the middle of the afternoon in a town like Crawley.

He looked back to the precinct where Monica was in a shoe shop. She would then visit the clothes shop next door, then walk to the square where Brian was waiting. His attention was distracted by a youth walking directly through the square with a vicious-looking dog straining at its lead. The youth, who was about eighteen years of age, over six foot tall and strongly built continued to walk in a straight line that would take him into a group of three women, the youngest of whom looked to be over seventy years of age. Two elderly men of a similar age were walking towards the women.

He muttered an oath under his breath. Golden rule when working on the street was to do nothing, absolutely nothing, to draw attention to yourself. Always stay in the background. He watched. He saw Monica walking out of the shoe shop then enter the clothes shop. The youth hadn't changed his route and his body had become more erect, a sure sign that he was preparing for confrontation. Brian watched the old people. They were talking and smiling and hadn't seen the youth now twenty yards away. Brian stood and walked directly towards the old people, calculating that he would reach them a stride before the youth would. He lengthened his stride to arrive a step earlier. Two steps bought him an extra second.

Charlie Tompkins had been swallowing paracetamol tablets all day in an effort to stem the pain from his face. He had seen in window reflections that he was badly bruised and knew from his poor vision that the area around his right eye was still swollen and that his face would be remembered by anyone who saw him. He realised people would be scared of him; his size alone usually had that effect. He stared at anyone daring to make eye contact and saw them quickly avert their gaze and move away. By comparison, Jackie Smith at his side looked almost demure and ladylike unless anyone looked closely at her eyes and the firmly set jaw. Still, she looked angry and there was a fierceness about her that suggested that she and Charlie Tompkins were looking for any excuse, however small, to attack someone. They walked across Queens Square with the intention of using the route as a short cut back to her car, which she had parked under the nearby shopping mall. They had not had a good day, having spoken to many people who under normal circumstances they wouldn't have passed the time of day with. They were looking forward to making their way back to Brighton.

The youth was now four strides away from the old people and out of the corner of his eye he became aware of a person walking from the side towards him. He looked and saw Brian staring at him without any fear. He instinctively sneered a confident challenge and prepared himself for the confrontation that was about to happen. He didn't care about anything at that point. He wanted a fight and he knew he was going to have one with this man who was staring at him. The old people had just noticed the youth with the dog and in shock two of the ladies had brought their hands to their faces. The dog snarled at them as if ordering them out of its way. Without any interruption in his stride Brian kicked the dog in its ribs, causing the animal to leave the ground. There was a yelp, and in the same movement Brian turned so his back was towards the youth but his right leg was bent upwards. The youth took one further step forward and with his momentum he could do nothing to prevent Brian's booted foot from crashing into the kneecap. There was a sound of tearing muscle and bone followed by a howl from the youth as he fell to the ground. Brian knew he had dislodged the patella, a painful injury that would need an operation followed by weeks of physiotherapy before the youth would walk again. The dog was trying to stand against a low wall to a flowerbed and whimpering. Brian quickly looked towards the old people then walked towards the shop that Monica was in.

Jackie Smith had vaguely been aware of the youth walking ahead with the dog and also of a man walking towards the youth, but her mind was elsewhere. It was only when she saw the man kick the dog that her mind raced back to real time and place, to where she was. She saw the man turn his back and the youth fall to the ground. The man walked off. Nothing unusual about the man, average height and average build, a jacket and flat cap, a type you could see anywhere in any street. Not her problem. Maybe he's drunk or off his mind.

Charlie had also witnessed the man kick the dog and seen the movement of the man as he with the greatest of efficiency dispatched the youth into a heap on the ground. He couldn't help but give him his due.

'He's a good fighter,' he mumbled to Jackie under his breath.

The pair instinctively turned to follow the man with their

gaze. He was walking at a steady pace, his back to them and thirty yards away, when out of a shop doorway in front of him Monica appeared. Jackie Smith and Charlie Tompkins both stopped still and watched as Monica walked towards the man smiling. She took his arm and he took the carrier bags she was carrying and both turned to walk towards Smith and Tompkins, who instinctively lowered his head to one side. Smith just stood still, watching Monica smiling and looking at Brian as she said something to him, which made him laugh.

Brian was still laughing as he looked towards where the old people were and the youth on the floor. Two other people had now joined the group – a man and a woman. Despite all his years of training, he felt a look of amazement cross his face, though the first thing he did was point to the side at a shop window displaying women's underwear and then veer Monica towards it. He moved Monica a little further towards the shop while looking in the glass reflecting the scene behind him. Smith was talking to Tompkins and they were looking towards him. Every sense he had was screaming at him that they had been seen and every second would now count. His mind was calculating the possibilities. Without Monica his escape would be easy. He could simply outrun them but with Monica he doubted they could. He saw Smith turn her back to him to face Tompkins. She was using her mobile phone.

Brian took hold of Monica's arm and pointed at the window. 'Look into the shop and don't move your head a fraction. Just stay calm. We have a problem.' Lead them into it gently, he remembered being taught many years ago. 'Smith and a man are about thirty or so yards away and have seen us.' He felt Monica's body stiffen. He retained his grip on her arm. Smith was still talking on the mobile. He felt his heart sink as in the reflection he saw two police officers had appeared, one bent down to the youth on the floor, the other was speaking to the old people. The man with Smith had a damaged face, so he must have been one of those in the car or van. Undoubtedly he would want his revenge Brian thought.

'Monica, go into the shop, tell the assistant that you are being followed by your ex, who will be violent if he catches you, and go out the back way. Throw your jacket away and put on something you have just bought, then walk – don't run – to the pub in the centre of the High Street. Get a drink and sit somewhere out of sight of the doors. Stay in there. If anyone finds you, shout to the staff to help you, call the police … anything, but do not leave that place. I will see you or get Adam to meet you there. Now get going.'

Monica didn't look back but walked into the shop. Brian turned slowly, trying to look bored and looked at his wristwatch, though he didn't notice the time. He ambled to the front of the shop then leaned against the glass, casually looking up and down the precinct. Smith was finishing her call and talking to the man.

'Now, or are we waiting for reinforcements?' said Brian to himself. One of the old ladies pointed towards Brian and the police officer turned to follow her finger.

'Oh bloody hell, lady,' he muttered to himself. He looked over his shoulder into the shop to be met by two assistants standing in the middle of the shop glaring at him. He gave them a half-wave, relieved that their presence meant that Monica had been believed.

'A choice, Brian old lad: the police or Smith, not too tricky a decision.'

He slowly walked towards the shops Monica had been in. Another three steps, four, five … The exit from the precinct was twenty yards or so away and that would be where the reinforcements would be arriving from, if they knew what they were doing, he thought.

'Oi!' Brian heard. 'You, come here.'

Brian turned and saw the police officer standing next to the old lady and waving Brian to him. Smith and the man were within feet of the police officer. Brian for a split second appeared to be doing as requested but then turned and reached a full sprint within four strides. He used his arms to pump and barely slowed as he reached the corner and turned into a short alley with brick walls to either side extending to the height of the first floor of the shops, a minimum of twenty feet. He ran and at the end of the alley found himself with choices, one of which would take him towards the High Street. He took the other option and relaxed his pace a fraction, enabling him to conserve some energy but also to assimilate his surroundings. He knew he needed to avoid roads if possible at this stage. If forced to use one, then a one-way road would be preferable to a two-way. He knew that the CCTV cameras would all be searching for him and police cars would be directed towards him. If it came to it, he would allow them to catch him rather than Smith and the man with her.

He continued to run, glad that the light was fading quickly and that the streetlights were on – a little something in his favour. He saw a blue light strobe at the end of a short street he was in, though it was difficult to tell exactly where the car was. He knew he would be at the corner quickly and that if he turned to his left there was a short stretch of one-way road. From there he could use an alley to access a housing estate. He reached the corner and slowed to a walk, spotting the police car in traffic heading towards where he had been. He turned left, away from the police car. He walked the short distance, taking off both his cap and jacket, which he instead carried under his arm. He saw the alley and knew that with gardens to houses each side he had already doubled his options. He walked briskly into a road lined with semi-detached houses, each of which had a front garden separated from the pavement by a low brick wall. Some gardens were tended carefully with flowerbeds and mown grass while others were overgrown with shrubs, long grass and children's toys. It was these he noted.

Smith continued to talk into her mobile phone.

'The bitch went into a shop and when we went in there after

her the two assistants attacked Charlie. They thought he was her ex and had beaten her. He had to sort them out but by the time we were out the back she had gone. Not sure where the man's gone, but we've got over twenty men in the area and more arriving. We've put the word out there's ten thou for whoever gets him. A complication is that the police are also looking for him. He beat some kid up and nearly killed his bloody dog.'

Geoff Townsend couldn't believe what he had heard. 'Find him, Jackie, and her. I want them both by this evening. If the police get him, then we'll deal with that, but I want them. Do you understand, Jackie?'

Jackie had known Townsend for years and had experienced his temper and violence but she was still stunned by the threat implied in his voice. She said that she would do anything and everything to find them then shut down the call. She walked over to the police officer, who was recording the details of the old folk and noted that two paramedics had arrived to attend to the youth. People were gathering around trying to find out what had occurred and comments were being made that she presumed were about the dog – 'He'll have to be put down,' 'Shame, isn't it?' and 'Bloody brute – good riddance!' – but which could equally apply to the youth, she thought. She saw Tompkins approaching.

'OK,' he said through gritted teeth, 'we know where he was headed and I've spoken to Rajah and he's putting his boys around the area. Thirty he'll have. Another ten or fifteen will be here in ten minutes, then we'll search the whole area, street by street.'

Geoff Townsend was talking to the DCI, who was simultaneously reading from the computer screen. He detailed the offence and the response from the police: they were monitoring every CCTV camera and had followed the suspect into a housing area that eight officers were now beginning to search. A police dog was being brought from Gatwick and would be working to track the suspect within twenty minutes.

'The boys are doing a good job, Geoff,' he said. 'Every resource is being used. Don't worry, I'm sure they'll get him.'

'And then I want him understood?' Townsend replied coldly.

Adam had bought a grey Vauxhall Astra hatchback. The car was in good condition and had only thirty-nine thousand miles on the clock. As the weather was cold, he was pleased that he had been able to wear gloves while collecting the cash at the bank and handing it over to the seller. He had filled the car with petrol and was driving towards Brian's house, noting the many police cars that appeared to be in Crawley, some with their blue lights flashing and weaving their way in and out of the traffic. He turned his mobile phone on and saw that he hadn't missed any calls or messages. He drove past Brian's house looking for somewhere to park and was disappointed that the curtains were still drawn back and no lights were shining, Brian and Monica were still shopping, he thought.

Brian saw a car approaching a hundred yards away – 'Too slowly,' he said as he saw the next garden was overgrown. In a split second he had jumped over the wall and crouched behind a shrub. He peered through the naked branches as the car approached, three men all looking out of the windows, looking for him. He watched as the car continued past him and noted that it wasn't a new car and that it wasn't the police. He remained where he was while he tried to think of exactly where he was and the route he would have to take to get back to his house. It would mean crossing the town centre again – not a good move – so the alternative would be to go the long way – around the town itself. That would mean more time out in the open, which was not good either but preferable. He pulled his mobile phone from his pocket and put his jacket back on, feeling the sweat on his back as it pushed against his skin. He put his hand over the screen to shield the light and dialled Adam, who answered on the second ring tone.

He explained what had happened and what his instructions to Monica had been and where she was, he hoped. He could take care of himself but needed Adam to look after Monica. Adam agreed and they briefly talked about a contingency plan should Brian be captured by either the police or Smith. Adam was confident in Brian's ability to stay out of harm and after putting Monica safely in the house he would be out to meet Brian.

Smith and Tompkins stood next to Rajah on the corner of a street just one hundred yards from the street Brian was in. They were satisfied that the streets were being swamped with Rajah's people but impatient for a sighting.

Brian knew he had to move, as anyone coming from the house would instantly see him, as would anyone walking along the pavement looking into the garden. He re-joined the pavement and started walking. At the end of that road he saw another that ran left to right and knew that left would take him towards the town. He turned right. This road had more traffic, and he was aware that more cars would be passing him, but he would have to take his chance. After a minute he was aware of a car behind him. It had slowed, maybe turning into a driveway. He looked over his shoulder: the car was stopped and two figures were exiting the car. Another car was approaching and slowing. Brian looked around him – houses, semi-detached as far as he could see. Two figures exited the car in front of him, followed by a third. The driver remained in the car. He noticed that two of the men were holding long items in their hands – staves or baseball bats? Brian looked behind at the two men, now on the same pavement as he: one had something long in his hand; the car was following slowly. Another car was approaching from in front of him, slowing. He stood still as no bluff would work. He looked to his left where the houses were closer. There were extensions and garages. He looked over the road: houses with garages but one had a side gate. He ran. He judged that he could make the gate before everyone, but what would happen after that was anybody's guess.

He hurdled the wall and reached the wooden gate at full speed crashing into it as his hands reached the top. He pulled himself up and over, landing on his feet. Rubbish bins were lined against a fence but the path led along the house to a rear garden. He grabbed the bins and pulled them behind him as he ran. He heard the clattering of bodies against the gate and the sound of one person landing on his feet with a heavy thump, followed by another. The garden was small: a patch of well-tended grass with plants around the edge and a small pond of some kind directly in front of him. He noted that the two side fences were six feet tall while the fence on the other side of the pool was four feet. He jumped over the pool landing on earth that slid under his weight but the momentum kept him going as he jumped the fence catching his foot on the top. He landed in a heap in a flowerbed on the other side and turned to his right, a six-foot fence that he attacked, reaching the top with his hands, twisting his body and propelling his legs over to land on his feet. He heard someone fall into the pond behind him then a crashing against the fence. He had made time – at least three seconds.

He ran and vaulted the next fence, knowing that he would be in view of the chasers but that they were slower than he. The advantage lay with him but he couldn't waste time on the fences. He vaulted the next fence into a garden that appeared to be strewn with children's toys. He fell over a ball and lay on the ground feeling the pain gradually work its way from his ankle towards his chest. His heart was beating even faster as he stood and put pressure on the ankle, which collapsed under minimal pressure. The pain went through his body as he heard another fence being scaled behind him. He searched the garden but in the limited reflected light from streetlights on the other side of the house he could see only that there wasn't a fence at the other side of this garden. He dived back to the fence he had climbed to get in the garden and pulled as many toys as he could with him. He lay against the fence and was still arranging a plastic train on him when there was a bang against the fence followed by a face appearing.

There was a grunting noise of exertion followed by two feet landing a foot from his head. The figure was looking at the open area in front and ran quickly for it. He wasn't carrying anything in his hands, which explained why he was so close behind Brian. Those with one hand carrying something would be slower. He chanced an arm to pull a child's plastic chair towards him and lay it on his legs. His shape was now distorted – good. Another crash above him, and heavy breathing, as another figure landed next to him and made his way after the first man. The second man was shouting for the others behind to get to the road.

Brian lay still, his ears straining for sounds of any threat. He heard it, a faint sound, a footstep approaching the fence, two footsteps, either one person or two. He knew that he was holding his breath. These were the clever ones who knew something about searching for a person. Send in the dogs to either catch the person or flush them out. Failing that, allow silence for the person to think they are safe enough to leave their hiding place. Brian remained motionless. There were now two people. He heard a whisper. No movement – they were cagey ones, these. His ankle hurt and was at an angle where stiffness would penetrate. Things weren't helped by the wet grass he was lying on.

Brian opened his mouth to breathe through – quieter than the nose. A slight shift of a finger to gain a more comfortable hold on the train wheels. It was a risk to make any move but it worked – a good move. More whispering. Brian looked in the direction that the two running men had gone. What was there? A low wire as a fence where a wooden fence was in other gardens … no side gate … concrete outside the back door which was double-glazed – that would reduce noise from the garden – double-glazed windows, too. A large wheelie bin and other toys were on the concrete path which went down the side of the house out of Brian's vision. Downstairs window curtains closed nearest him. The window next to the door, probably the kitchen window, in darkness. A scuffling noise above him and a leg appeared and lowered to the ground silently, a foot from his head. The left foot, thank goodness for that, thought Brian. More noise and the right leg came over. The man turned, standing directly above Brian. Now he didn't breathe at all but had one eye slightly open to watch what the man did.

Another leg appeared above Brian, directly above his groin area. Wherever it came down it would be on Brian. The light went on in the kitchen. The foot hovered six inches above Brian's groin and an inch above part of the plastic train. The sound of a key being turned and the kitchen door flew open, casting a bright rectangular light across the lawn diagonally, but missing Brian who remained in shadow.

A woman appeared carrying a sack of rubbish in one hand and a lighted cigarette in the other. She went to the bin, opened the lid with the hand holding the cigarette and deposited the sack that by the sound went to the bottom of the bin. The fact registered with Brian: another possible hiding place even if it was just about the worst one imaginable. The woman turned back towards the kitchen door. The man standing next to Brian had crouched a little but had eyes only for the woman. The other's leg was still over the fence but Brian assumed he had bent himself under the level of the fence to prevent his outline being seen. The woman took a long pull of the cigarette and flicked it into the air before starting to turn back to the door. She suddenly stopped.

'What the bleedin' 'ell are you doin' 'ere?' she shouted.

Brian was taken by surprise but remained motionless. The crouching man also.

'Getting the police, you pervert,' she screamed at the crouching man, who realised that he had been seen.

Brian heard the leg above him being withdrawn but it was

seen by the woman, who shouted, '*Two* bleedin' pervs! Get out my garden.'

Somewhere in the house behind her a dog barked. The man who had been crouching started walking towards the side of the house. 'Not a perv – looking for someone, that's all,' he said in an aggressive tone.

The woman took a step back towards the kitchen door, ready to flee if the man turned on her.

'Don't care what you are doin'! Get out of 'ere. I'm callin' the police, right now, and your mate, he can get out an' all. Couple of pervs – should be locked up.'

The dog was obviously in the kitchen, its way into the garden blocked by the woman, who now had hold of the door handle and was holding the door ajar. Brian waited for the inevitable landing of the other man on him and decided that he would take him as soon as his foot touched him. A huge element of surprise would mean he would overcome that man quickly. It was the other man beyond the kitchen door that concerned him. There wouldn't be any element of surprise with him, and there was a distance between them that was too far for him even if both his ankles were warm and without injury.

Brian heard a noise from above as the leg dropped down on to the grass where the first man's foot had, then the second foot – he had used exactly the same method of crossing the fence as the first man and at the same spot. The feet walked away from him. The woman watched his every step. 'Bleedin' perv!' she shouted at the top of her voice. A door opened somewhere that Brian couldn't see. The woman shouted again: 'Got two pervs in me garden, bastards.'

Brian could hear a man's voice. It was from the garden next door where minutes before the two men hunting him had been standing.

The second man quickened his step and was from Brian's view following the path at the side of the house.

'Want a hand, love? I'll bloody well sort them. Got my Jamie here. We'll sort them good and proper,' the neighbour called.

'Nah, thanks, Billy, they're going, but if they come back I'll call you and Jamie and let you teach them a bleedin' lesson.'

'Yeah fine, Doris, just call – we'll be ready,' he said.

Brian watched Doris enter her house and heard the lock click followed a second later by the light in the window next to the door being turned off.

He let his breath out but his brain was working quickly. The men had gone so that threat had receded for a while but the dog would come into the garden during the evening for its toilet and would easily find Brian and the woman could come out for another cigarette. The garden behind appeared to offer the best alternative, at least in the short term. He slowly moved each toy from his body, laying them next to him, then with the slowest of deliberate movements he gradually raised himself into a sitting position. He used a straightened arm and craned his neck with his head tilted sideways. He raised himself so an eye could see into Billy's garden. It was all quiet but he remained in the position, muscles aching while the blood raced around his body. He dissected the whole area, eyes and ears coordinated, checking every window that he could see, curtains, doors, shadowed areas, from left to right, right to left, distance to near and near to distance.

Satisfied that it was safe to do so, in one movement he used his strong ankle to provide the motion he needed to vault the fence using his arms to break his fall on to a flowerbed. He lay motionless but noted the damaged flowers and scoured the garden before he saw the shrub he wanted, against the wall and under the window – a shrub with leaves. He used his hands and knees to crawl into the shrub, rearranged the foliage and settled for the wait. He looked at the grass he had crossed and could make out the indentations he had just made but there were others also from the other men who had been chasing him. He hoped Billy wouldn't be able to read single footprints going in one direction while the others were all facing the other.

Adam walked into the bar and had to make a concerted search before he recognised Monica sitting to the side of a group of men and women who were having some sort of office party. She was sitting so that only her profile could be viewed and that had been disguised by her wearing a woollen hat pulled down over her ears. Adam made no sign of recognising her but went to the bar and ordered himself a pint of bitter, which he sipped while examining the faces in the bar. Everybody appeared to be engrossed in one way or another, talking and laughing. He turned to face the tables, allowing Monica to see him, and raised a hand and walked towards her. He sat next to her and, after noting a brief look of disappointment pass over the face of one of the men nearby who had been admiring Monica, moved closer to enable him to talk quietly. He told her what Brian had told him and how they were going to leave the bar and the direction they would walk in. He would have his arm around her shoulder, holding her close to him, and she would walk with her head slightly lowered as if she was shy or embarrassed. After finishing their drinks they left the bar and a hundred yards later were in Adam's new car, heading for Brian's house avoiding the rest of the town centre, the railway level crossing and the area where Brian was. They arrived at Brian's house without incident and without switching any lights on Monica followed Adam into the lounge.

'I can't stay, Monica. I've got to help Brian. You've got to stay put,' he said firmly.

'I'm not staying here – we agreed,' she countered just as resolutely.

'Monica, this is really dangerous. It looks as if Townsend has called in favours to get as many people out there as possible – plus Smith's here – it really is too dangerous ....' But Monica's stance and look told him that he was wasting his time arguing. 'Right, stay here for a minute while I get something, then we'll go and get Brian,' he said, heading for the stairs. Monica remained where she was while she heard unusual noises from upstairs, but a minute later Adam reappeared.

'Come on,' he said and led her back to his car.

Monica examined the map Adam gave her and while he drove he pointed out different places and the area that Brian believed he was in. Adam checked his watch. It was just before seven o'clock and Brian would call at seven minutes after seven, as they had arranged. Adam noted the number of police cars and drove slowly, keeping up with traffic as it moved through the town centre and then to the area of West Green.

'Somewhere in this area,' he said as he noted some stationary cars with men huddled inside. Several men appeared to be searching front gardens, looking into bushes and occasionally shining a torch into the darker recesses. Adam saw that at each junction there was a car with men in and at least one man standing by the car. He again made sure that Monica had her woollen hat pulled right down to her eyes and that her ears were covered. She was leaning back in her seat so that even her profile was obscured by the door pillar, but Adam regretted her being with him. He pulled his mobile phone from his pocket and placed it on his lap seconds before he felt it vibrate. He pulled into a car parking space and answered the call.

'Are you out?' Brian whispered.

'With Monica,' Adam replied, 'West Green area. Any idea where you are?'

'Back garden but I think I may be able to get into the front. Got a bad ankle. Running is out of the question. A quick hobble is the best I'll be able to do. Give me ten and I'll get back to you.' Brian finished the call.

Adam looked at Monica as he pulled out into the traffic and completed his drive through the area. He had seen what he could and needed to avoid the watchers seeing him too frequently, as attention would be drawn to him and his car. They had stopped just away from the area when Brian called again.

'In front garden, low brick wall, fifty yards from end of road to my left, three houses. Large tree immediately opposite and a streetlight next to it. Layby for cars thirty yards to my right, my side. Junction to left, car, dark, parked under streetlight, two men on pavement by it. Police car just in my view, near that car. Nothing else.'

Adam gave Brian a description of his car and said that he would start the search immediately. He looked at the map to confirm his starting location and put Brian's description into his mind to visualise his position, repeating the distances and landmarks verbatim.

Rajah was sitting in the back of the car that Charlie Tompkins was driving. Jackie Smith was in the passenger seat.

'Got over forty people out there now. We must get him,' Rajah observed.

Jackie had been quiet as she traced the route that they knew Brian had taken. There was the point where he had been last seen, running around the corner of a house, then nothing.

Rajah continued: 'Me and Sami were following all quiet like and the woman came out of that house and called us pervs.' He sounded offended by the allegation and even more aggrieved when there was no reply from either of his companions. He sat back in his seat muttering. 'Must have gone on from there. Maybe crossed the road and then, if he went through the gardens, he could have got to the green and the trees.'

Jackie Smith was becoming angry with Rajah and his idiotic excuses, but knew that he and his men were the only hope they had of catching the man so she said nothing. She was almost continually on her mobile phone to Geoff Townsend, who told her that he was sending another twelve men from Brighton to help in the search. This was not what she wanted at all, to be in

Crawley when it was cold, but the thought of getting hold of either of the men or especially Monica kept her focused.

Adam was methodically driving down each road but in a way that he hoped would not attract attention. He covered each junction carefully and at last located the one close to where he suspected Brian was hiding. There was a huddle of men on the street corner. He saw the layby further on and he pulled into it. He handed Monica his mobile while he got out of the car and walked directly into a front garden where a light shone in the window. He made as if he was ringing the bell and huddled against the cold while looking back to the road. Apart from the men at the end of the road it appeared to be quiet but he knew that if he stopped to pick Brian up he would be seen. In any case, in all probability from their position the men would see Brian getting into the car. Adam appeared to ring the bell again, then waited a minute before appearing to be frustrated, peering in at the window, then walking back to his car.

'He saw us and is ready. The line's open,' Monica said.

Adam raised his voice so that it would reach the mobile that Monica held. 'Doing a U in the layby, stop in road and away. We'll be seen, so take it from there.'

He swung the car into a U-turn and started to retrace the route towards the men at the junction. He hoped that they wouldn't be too interested in him. He had acted normally and those seconds could make the difference. He pulled into the kerb, leaned over and opened the rear door before returning his attention to the junction. He heard the rustle and groan as Brian threw himself on to the back seat and Adam started to drive.

The men at the junction must have been watching intently, as they reacted quickly, one running into the road waving a baseball bat while the others got into their car. Adam sped up and was preparing to take the left turn at the junction, ignoring the man in the road, when he was aware of another car lurching forward.

Adam pushed his foot to the floor: there was a thud noise and a cry from a man could be heard above the roar of the engine as Adam completed the turn just in front of the second car.

Adam focused on his driving, looking ahead to gauge when and if he had to brake as he tried to elude his pursuers. He knew the routes to be avoided: the railway level crossing, the major one-way system in the town centre and all bus routes, all of which could spell disaster. His speed touched seventy miles an hour, which he reduced to fifty for another turn, then straightaway he piled on the speed again. He didn't check his rear-view mirror, a distraction that could slow him or make him not see something ahead. It was Brian's job to watch behind. Adam swung right on to a main road, grateful that a cyclist or pedestrian wasn't in the road, then took an immediate left into another side road.

'Sixty yards and not in control – pushing himself,' said Brian in an even voice.

Monica was holding on to the door handle and seat as she was thrown about at each turn, unable to predict which turn Adam would take next. Brian sitting in the back anticipated Adam's turns and was prepared for them as he maintained his watch out of the back window.

A police car with flashing blue lights appeared behind Adam but was immediately overtaken by the pursuers, which Brian thought could be interesting though it complicated the situation.

Rajah took the call but had difficulty in hearing what was being said as the caller was too excited to speak clearly – that coupled with the roaring of the car engine. Rajah heard enough, though, to direct Charlie Tompkins towards the Manor Royal industrial estate. There was a possibility that it was there that their targets were heading and that they could reach the area before them. Tompkins drove through two sets of red traffic lights and reached over seventy miles an hour in a restricted thirty road as he followed Rajah's directions.

Adam knew the industrial estate was less that three minutes' drive away and offered many possibilities to hide. Or they could pass straight through and head either towards Gatwick Airport or Redhill. He kept to a zigzag route but generally in the direction of the industrial estate.

'Hundred and twenty police car trying to get ahead. Going to end in tears,' said Brian calmly.

Adam's attention wasn't diverted for a moment but he was pleased that the gap between him and the pursuers was increasing. He turned right and immediately left, just managing to avoid the kerb on the wrong side of the road. Second gear was screaming as he changed into third for full power and braked violently as he took an immediate left turn.

'Crash,' said Brian in a calm voice. 'I would guess the police car will have to stop even if it wasn't directly involved.'

Adam slowed a little and concentrated on the road in front which was straight and led to the industrial estate, giving him a feeling of hope. He drove past an entrance to a small factory and immediately a car pulled on to the road behind him.

'Company,' said Brian.

Adam didn't look in his mirror but changed gear and studied the road ahead, accelerating hard.

'Eighty yards, fast car, big engine,' reported Brian.

Adam turned right at some traffic lights that were mercifully green, then sped towards Reigate which adjoins Redhill, his speed approaching eighty-five miles an hour as he saw turnings to Gatwick Airport signposted to his left. He approached a further set of traffic lights at which cars were stationary, blocking both lanes in his direction. He changed gear and moved out, passing the stationary cars and straight towards cars heading in the opposite direction, to Gatwick Airport, then at the last minute returned to his correct side of the road, gunning the engine again. He negotiated a further three hazards at speeds that were over twice the permitted limit before heading on to the road that would take them directly into Reigate and its one-way system, something he had wanted to avoid if possible.

'Sixty yards. Beating you on the open road,' said Brian.

Charlie Tompkins was a good driver and highly trained in aggressive driving techniques. At the wheel of a 3.5-litre Jaguar he felt confident that he would catch any other driver. He knew the man he was pursuing was good but he was better, and his confidence was growing as the gap shortened. Even with a swollen eye he was fast. Jackie Smith was holding on to her seat and using her arm to brace herself against the car dashboard while Rajah was flung about the back seat of the car, loving the excitement.

Adam knew what he was going to do. It was a high-risk manoeuvre but he'd done it before twice and both times it had worked 'reasonably well with room for improvement', as Brian had commented at the time. Adam was now looking for the right place, his mind focused.

'Forty yards,' reported Brian.

Adam saw the spot three hundred yards ahead. 'Spinning,' he said.

Brian gripped the back of Monica's seat against the g-force that he knew he was about to be put under.

Adam briefly touched the brakes hard, causing the car to almost sit on its front wheels, then grabbed the handbrake hard and turned the steering wheel. Even though he was expecting the manoeuvre, Brian was thrown against his side door, but his eyes remained focused out the rear window before he had to adjust his head and eyes to face forwards: their car was now facing the pursuing vehicle.

Tompkins hadn't anticipated any braking manoeuvre. The junction ahead was over two hundred yards away and suddenly seeing the brake lights for no reason he had automatically applied his, only for longer than Adam did. In the time that Tompkins was transferring his foot and deciding on what gear he ought to be engaging, Adam had swung the car around to now face Tompkins, who as an automatic response had braked to turn around himself.

Monica hadn't understood anything about what had been happening other than thinking that they were going to crash and that at that speed they would be killed. Brian understood exactly what was happening. Tompkins had slowed, preparing to perform his own U-turn when Adam suddenly braked hard. Brian could see Adam's arm pointing out the window but among the cacophony of noises he didn't hear the sounds he knew Adam would be making. Brian struggled to move to the opposite side of the car, ready to exit, but Adam already had his car door open and a foot on the ground.

Jackie Smith was trying to regain her position in her seat when she saw a splurge of red flying through the air towards her. Her brain couldn't work out what it was but it did register Tompkins' head being flung back into the headrest. A man was moving towards the back of the car but her eyes were a second behind the movement. Rajah was grinning from ear to ear with the excitement, unaware of what had happened to Tompkins, of the man standing behind the car, or of the two bullets that shortly after hit the back of his head, killing him instantly. Jackie Smith was looking about her when her side door window smashed, throwing glass all over her. She screamed and looked towards the glass in time to see a hand enter through the shattered hole and suddenly her car door was flung open. A gun was pointing at her head.

Monica had been slow to react but had now gathered enough of her senses to get out of the car. She ran around the front of the Jaguar, looking in to see Jackie staring at the gun held by Adam a foot in front of her eyes. He was talking to her, in a calm voice, but it wasn't until Monica got in next to Adam that she could hear what he was saying.

'You were vicious – an old lady! No mercy, no compassion, and you enjoyed hurting her, you enjoyed it all, hearing her scream, her terror, but you carried on. She wouldn't tell you something, would she? She was brave, worth thousands of your type, a decent person who had guts.'

'Adam,' shouted Monica, 'give me the gun. I want to kill her.'

Smith looked at Monica with terror in her eyes and her mouth moved as if she was trying to say something. Monica moved towards Adam, keeping her eyes on Smith, showing her that she was no longer fearful of her.

But there were two gentle sounds that sounded almost as one and two red holes appeared in Smith's forehead.

'Back in the car!' ordered Adam, almost treating Monica as if she were a naughty girl for intervening.

Adam drove quickly. He would have to keep his concentration until they were safe and then he would have to destroy the car and any evidence that could link them to the events. He knew that what he had just done would be headline news in the newspapers and on television, and that the police would quickly link it to the deaths of Dutch and Kieran Townsend. A major investigation would be under way, now involving two police forces, and Monica had witnessed the killings. He had a lot to think about.

23

Geoff and Lenny Townsend were agitated that they hadn't heard from Jackie Smith and their calls to her went unanswered and were directed through to her voicemail. Townsend didn't like not knowing what was happening and somewhere he had a feeling that all was not going as well as he had hoped. His worst fears were realised when he answered his mobile and received a call from the DCI. Townsend listened as the DCI read from the incident log created in Crawley that there had been three deaths by shooting in Surrey just over the border from Sussex. The bodies hadn't been examined and information was scarce but the coincidence would be great if it didn't involve the events in Crawley. Townsend was shocked by what he was told. Even though the facts were sketchy, it was obvious that all his and others' efforts had resulted in failure. He finished the call subdued.

He turned and related the facts as he had been told to his brother and Pat. His mobile rang again and he took a further call from the DCI. The news left him much happier as he interpreted what he was told, though the DCI pointed out that there was no evidence to support any speculation, nor would there be for some hours. Nevertheless when Geoff Townsend finished the call he beamed at Lenny. 'Looks like two men and a female in the car.'

Lenny smiled. 'That maybe explains why Jackie hasn't been in touch, got the three of them and having to get away, I imagine it's a little hot up there at the moment.'

Pat exhaled and stood up. 'A drink is called for.'

It was just after one o'clock when Adam returned to the house to find Brian and Monica sitting in the lounge. They stood up on hearing him arrive.

'How did it go?' asked Brian, who had a polythene bag of ice tied by a towel around his swollen ankle.

'Yes, all burnt and hopefully when it's found everything will be destroyed. We should be safe from that angle,' said Adam, 'but there are problems with yesterday afternoon. Your faces will have been seen. Somewhere there will be full mug shots of you both, in a shop, somewhere in the street, but there will be film and in a month's time, two months' time, they will be published. Maybe tomorrow even …' Adam added as an afterthought.

'I know. Hopefully they'll only get partial views, but you're right, that could be a problem in the future,' said Brian.

'Ankle?' asked Adam.

'Not sure. I hope it's a sprain. I will know in the morning,' Brian answered in a matter-of-fact way.

Monica was staring at Adam with her arms crossed against her chest. Adam knew that she wasn't happy and he knew the reason.

'Monica, I know you're upset and I know the reason why. Let me tell you something that I know a lot about and you know nothing about. When you kill someone you cross a line, a threshold, there is no going back. No shrink or specialist can undo what you've done; no one can help you. In the middle of the night or at a party having fun that moment when you killed someone will come back, everyday for some people, once a week, a month, but it comes back, for ever, for real. You will never be the same person again. Something inside you changes because it has to, otherwise you'd stand a good chance of going mad. You played your part, you helped and because of that you exacted some revenge. I can't pretend to understand how you felt about Smith – being taken from your family and made to do what you were forced to do – I can't begin to understand, but believe me when I say that at least I hope you can feel that you did your bit in ridding the world of her.'

Adam didn't wait to see any reaction or any response but turned on his heels and headed for the stairs. 'See you in the morning.'

Brian looked at Monica and nodded. 'He's right. Well done today. Goodnight, Monica.'

24

The Townsend house had lights on in many of the rooms for much of the night, though the earlier feeling of joy that the two men and one woman were dead had lessened as there was still no word from Jackie Smith, despite all the messages left on her voicemail. By morning the anxiety had increased and, though tired, both men refused to sleep but instead followed the news programmes. The news overnight hadn't moved far forward, with the same reports being issued plus the same camera shots of a car all alone in a street a hundred yards away surrounded by tape and police vehicles. There was speculation that the murders may have been linked to an incident in Crawley the previous afternoon and in the meantime the bodies still had to be identified and post-mortems conducted. A police statement would be issued later in the day.

Adam and Brian had risen just after six and they were watching the same news broadcasts as the Townsends. They had debriefed each other as they would after any operation so each knew fully what had happened before they speculated on their chances of being identified by the police. They resolved that they would have to attack the Townsends sooner rather than later but their immediate concern was to cover their tracks and ensure the safety of Monica and her family. Once the identities of the murdered three were established, the Townsends would move heaven and earth to exact revenge.

When Monica arrived downstairs she was still in a pair of Brian's pyjamas and dressing gown. Her mood was low as she joined the men, sipping a cup of coffee. Little was spoken about the previous day but Adam discussed about getting her ID card. Now Smith was dead, it might be fairly easy to recover.

'Katja could get it,' Monica suggested. 'I trust her.'

Adam liked the suggestion but as Brian was quick to point out it was likely that Smith's house was now being forensically searched by police looking for evidence of how and why she had died, so it would be difficult to take anything from the house.

The DCI arrived at Geoff Townsend's house just after eleven that morning with a grim face, fearful of Townsend's reaction once he had told him the news.

'So, I'm afraid that's it, Geoff. Sorry to bring you such bad news,' he finished.

Both Geoff and Lenny were stunned by what they had been told. The DCI told them that he was still involved in the Brighton murder enquiries but now he would also be liaising with the Surrey enquiry into Smith's and the other two men's murders. He told the Townsend brothers that his ability to pass on any information would now be restricted, though he vowed to do his best for them. He was shown towards the door of the house where Geoff handed him an envelope that had been sitting on the sideboard.

'A present in appreciation of what you've done and for your help in the future – twenty K.'

Back in the lounge he looked at Lenny, who suddenly looked old and tired.

'Geoff, we've got a choice here, and to be honest I'm not sure what I want. Everything tells me to get after the bastards, reorganise the team, bring in new people and get cracking again, but there is just a feeling … well let's be honest, I've got ten mill or so and I love living like I do, so do I need all this?'

Geoff Townsend tried to control his anger but his voice still had an edge to it. 'No decision for me to make. No one does what these bastards have done to me and gets away with it – *no one*. I intend to find out who they are, then find them and then by the slowest and most painful way I can I'm going to kill them. Not only that, I'm going to film it as a warning to anyone who fancies their chances with me. Walk away?' He raised his voice. 'Lenny, you do what you want but that's not on the table as far as I'm concerned, no way.' His eyes were now wild and there was spittle on his chin. 'Who thinks they can take us, *me*, on? Tell me, who thinks they are big enough or hard enough – come on tell me!'

Lenny let out a sigh. He was used to seeing his brother rant and rage and a large part of him agreed with every word, but he just didn't have the motivation for all of this. Everything in Spain was rosy, his house was perfect – every visitor said that – the nightclub and restaurant were legal – for the most part – and gave him a wage to live on, and he had ten million pounds invested. Life indeed was sweet.

At length he said, 'Yeah, you're probably right, just me getting old and soft. Let's talk about what we're going to do.'

Monica had made a call to Jackie's house and spoke to Katja, who told her that after being questioned by the police she was going to have to leave the square and was in the process of packing her own small suitcase. The police were everywhere, she said, and Charlene had been told about her mummy dying. She had cried a little but was now being looked after by a policewoman who was going to take her away to be cared for by specially trained foster parents. Nonetheless she would check in Monica's room for the ID card if she could.

Adam and Brian had travelled on separate trains to Brighton and from different railway stations, Brian going to Gatwick while Adam travelled from Three Bridges. Monica took the train after Adam and by early afternoon they had each done what they agreed that morning. The weather had cleared into a bright sunny day, though a cold easterly wind took away any heat the sun might have given. Adam wore a long overcoat that he had bought that morning along with a suit, a new shirt and a pair of black shoes. He had visited a hair stylist and had his hair professionally cut and restyled, though it was hidden under a new blue hat. He also wore a new scarf knotted at the neck and pulled up to his mouth. He looked a different man.

Now he waited in a shelter on the seafront watching the seagulls dive into the sea before majestically landing on the pebbled beach with their catch. Some people were braving the wind to walk on the pier and he paid them little attention. He was more interested in the people walking along the promenade behind him. He saw Brian approaching and knew that he was in pain from his ankle. Brian had also bought himself a new set of clothes and, like Adam, looked every bit the successful professional man. Brian sat at the other end of the shelter and immediately unfurled *The Times* newspaper, reading with his body half turned away from Adam. Both men were silent while a young couple walked by, relieved that they hadn't decided to shelter from the biting wind alongside them.

'Managed three thousand pounds and can get another three tomorrow, so will that be enough?' Brian said, without moving his face from his newspaper.

Adam casually looked around and seeing nobody within earshot replied, 'Fine, leave the three there. I've got two spare now. I'll need to get a car tomorrow and I'll get another two out. Should be enough between us.'

Brian took an envelope from his pocket, placed it on the seat, then walked away as Adam moved to sit in his position, pocketing the envelope. Brian crossed the road and stood outside the entrance to a large hotel. The time was five minutes before three. Adam recognised Monica from her style of walk as she approached the hotel and noted that she had bought new clothes and carried a new shoulder bag. She was walking purposefully and passed Brian with barely a second glance as she continued towards the roundabout outside the pier entrance. Monica could see Katja standing with a small red suitcase at her feet, alone by the side of a closed kiosk that advertised 'The Best Hamburgers along the South Coast'.

Adam and Brian had told Monica exactly what to do, what to look out for and action to take if things went wrong. Adam began strolling along the promenade parallel to Monica, hoping to be just thirty yards away when Monica met Katja; Brian would be on the other side of the road. No transport was arranged: if this was a trap set by Townsend, Adam and Brian were armed and would take whatever action they needed to. If it was a trap set by the police, then Monica would be allowed to be arrested and she would have to lie her way out of the situation. Monica had been happy with that possibility and vowed that their secret would be safe with her. In any case, she doubted that the police would be able to gather sufficient evidence against her, though Adam and Brian secretly now thought otherwise.

Monica crossed the road and walked directly to Katja, who didn't recognise her until she was almost upon her. They greeted each other like long-lost friends with a long hug then talked for five minutes. Adam walked past to check the eastern side of the pier while Brian held his position on the north side of the road. Adam walked for a hundred yards before retracing his steps when he saw Brian swap the newspaper from one hand to the other, the 'all clear' signal. He approached the women and was formally introduced to Katja, who when he shook her hand palmed the envelope with Brian's cash into hers. A minute later, Adam walked away westwards towards the shelter he had been in previously, noting that Brian had changed his position slightly to gain a better view of the women and still remain inconspicuous. Monica walked away from Katja with a wave and followed in Adam's footsteps, as Brian monitored whether anyone was paying them any attention. No one was.

Monica had only briefly inspected her identity card and the photograph that Katja had retrieved. The photograph was an old one taken at her sister's eleventh birthday party when her parents, sister and her were all laughing at the photographer and holding on to each other's shoulders. It was her all-time favourite photograph. She had looked at it daily in the beginning of her time in Brighton but had grown ashamed of how her life had changed and how her family had been affected by her actions. In the end she had refused to look at it, but now she could feel it in her coat pocket and she couldn't wait to hold it in her hands and look at the smiling faces again.

That evening after watching the early-evening news Adam, Brian and Monica began to plan what to do next. They didn't share any misgivings that they might have held or fear that, due to the publicity and the resulting police activity, the risk of them being captured had increased significantly.

The same news programme had been watched in the Townsend house, though they knew more than the reporter after receiving a further call from the DCI. He had confirmed the identities as being Jackie Smith, a man named Rajah from Crawley who was known to the police in connection with drug trafficking in the area, and a third person, a known criminal named as Charles Tompkins, a native of Newcastle with previous convictions for violence and theft. He also confirmed that the Surrey police triple-murder enquiry was being coordinated with those already under way in Sussex of Del, a mechanic, Dutch and Kieran Townsend. He further said that there was a suspicion that Geoff Townsend was involved in some sort of gang war and that a full surveillance operation was to be mounted on him using all the skills at their disposal. The DCI recommended that Geoff and Pat either stock up and stay in the house or take a holiday.

'Told you, Geoff,' said Lenny, 'they'll be all over you and me like flies around fresh dog shit. They're not going to give up. They can't with all the publicity. I'm going back to Spain first thing in the morning. Best thing you can do is what we talked about, get the trusted five in here, tell them to carry on and then you join me. If they get it sorted, good, but if they don't, then you're out of the way – give it up.' Lenny looked at Pat for support but she remained impassive.

'Lenny,' replied Geoff, tiring of his brother's defeatist attitude, 'I said I'm not giving up, I told you why and I'm sticking to it. I don't give a rat's about the police; they can do what they like but they'll never get enough on me. As for the two blokes and Monica, as we said, she's just a tart and they're only two blokes. They got lucky, that's all. We've a good business going on here and I'm not letting it go – that's final.' He stared defiantly at Lenny who knew that argument was pointless. Pat remained silent, keeping any thoughts she might have to herself.

25

The following morning Geoff Townsend drew back the bedroom curtains and almost choked, causing Pat to sit upright in the bed. Before she could ask if he was all right, Geoff exploded with rage: 'Bastards, bastards!'

Pat jumped out of bed and ran to her husband, who was in the throes of opening the window and starting to shout and scream obscenities. She looked at the object of his abuse and saw a police car parked outside the gate with two uniformed police officers standing alongside. A further marked police car was parked at the main road and three more officers were walking from the road parallel to his house but towards the rear of it.

'We're bloody well surrounded,' he shouted at Pat.

Brian had elected to buy the car this time, saying that Adam's track record wasn't good at looking after his. This was the only bright spot in their morning. He was to use two of the three thousand pounds that he would withdraw from the bank for the car. Adam also withdrew money from his bank before he took Monica to Gatwick Airport where he bought her a ticket for that afternoon's flight to Málaga. From there she could catch a train to Granada, where she would catch a bus to Monachil and then a taxi up into the hills and her family's chalet. Monica was unhappy about leaving Adam and Brian to continue their campaign without her, but the two men insisted that her family's safety was the most important issue for her at that moment. The open-return ticket Adam gave her for her flight she intended to use the following week after she had done all she could for her

287

parents and sister. While Adam and Monica went to the airport, Brian travelled by bus to East Grinstead where he bought a car from an elderly gentleman who appeared to be genuinely sorry at seeing his twelve-year-old Volvo being driven off his driveway.

When Adam returned to the house Brian was washing his hands free of dirt.

'From the Volvo,' he explained. 'One careful owner, so you'd better not drive it!' He laughed. 'I've sorted out the lights and put a switch for the brake lights and a UV film inside the headlight covers. Also the old sign on the bumpers in case you have to follow me in the dark.' He chuckled.

Adam was laughing, too, remembering how during a nocturnal pursuit of a terror suspect Brian had once driven his car using only his night sights with Adam following in another car without any lights and also using night-vision equipment. At ten yards the specially adapted rear lights of Brian's car were just visible, but Adam had driven too close, lost perspective and driven into the back of Brian's car.

'If you'd been driving quicker, it wouldn't have happened,' laughed Adam.

They went outside and checked the car to make sure that everything was in working order. Then they returned to the operations room in the loft. Brian switched on his computer and after a short time he called Adam over to look at the screen. There were several car registration numbers listed and then Brian typed in the registration of his car.

'So, we can use black tape to change the letter "C" into an "O", the "I" into an "F",' He scrolled further down the screen. 'If you remember the other registrations, you can just chop and change ours to one of those. They're all Volvo estates but the owners live all over the country.' He counted. 'Eight possibles for you to remember.'

Adam looked carefully at the highlighted registrations and committed them to memory.

The television reporter that evening was standing in the road where earlier that day the car that contained the bodies of Smith, Tompkins and Rajah had been removed by a police low transporter vehicle. The car was covered by a tarpaulin sheet and followed by a police car, which was using a blue flashing light that contrasted with the orange light of the transporter. Watching from his home, Townsend was trying to control his fury and was managing until the picture suddenly switched to one showing the front of his house as the reporter said that the deaths were being linked to a large drug-trafficking gang based in Brighton.

'Bastards!' he screamed at the screen. Pat was listening as the reporter told viewers the identities of those murdered. There was a particularly long account of Jackie Smith's criminal history and how she was alleged to have been involved in the organization of prostitution and as well as with alleged Brighton 'crime lord' Geoff Townsend.

Brian had driven past the Townsend house three times that evening with Adam in the front passenger seat commentating on what he could see. The fact that reporters were apparently camped outside the house wasn't necessarily a concern, and the fact that the police were there could also, maybe, be turned to their advantage, though neither had any idea how that might happen. Back in Brian's house they watched the same news programme as the Townsends but instead of flying into a rage they smiled and laughed.

'Wait!' said Brian. 'Security guards – is that a possible way in. Who are they? They're not very bloody good, I bet.' He smiled and was soon lost in his thoughts.

26

Adam didn't sleep well, unable to think of a scenario that would enable him to break through the ring of police and reporters outside Geoff Townsend's house, and at five o'clock he gave up altogether on the idea of sleep. Sitting in the lounge in an armchair he had his eyes closed as he turned over another idea looking at it from different angles. His mind kept coming back to the number of 'ifs' in the whole scenario. There were too many, he conceded, but then what was the alternative?

Brian had slept soundly as always, able to compartmentalise his thoughts and put them away until he awoke with a fresh mind. He sat listening to Adam's thoughts and the one scenario that contained so many 'ifs'.

'Audacious, can't see it working but definitely worth a phone call to see if the first leg is achievable and then – who knows?'

Adam picked up his mobile and scrolled through the contacts list and found the one he wanted. It was eight o'clock – early but he wanted to get on.

'Morning, I hope it's not too early,' Adam said.

'Jesus, I know who you are from the caller ID. You've been a busy boy, haven't you?' the voice at the other end said.

'I'm not ringing for you to hear my confession. I have an idea that I would like to put to you – I need your help.'

'Not sure if I want to get involved with you. Just talking with you could get me twenty years.'

Adam could understand the man's reluctance and knew that there was some truth in his comment but he needed his help, so he persisted. 'Can we meet, same place at midday. If I can explain to you what is really happening, you may be willing to help. It doesn't involve you in any danger.' Adam almost winced at the lie, which he knew would be exposed as soon as he detailed what help he needed.

There was a sigh from the other end and silence for over ten seconds before there was a resigned 'OK, midday' and the line was closed.

Adam was early for the meeting, having driven Brian's car at a steady speed and, although he felt he wouldn't be betrayed, he still wanted to make sure for himself. Being an hour early wouldn't do any harm anyway. He was in the same chair he had occupied previously when he saw Keith Mendip enter at exactly midday. Adam indicated the coffee already on the table in front of the vacant chair and Keith sat down.

'Thanks for coming,' said Adam, 'I appreciate your time and I am probably not the person you most wanted to hear from this morning.'

Keith tasted his coffee. 'Look, let's be straight with each other. You wanted background information on Townsend and his family, friends and business. I gave it to you but didn't think you'd do what you've done. I take it you are responsible for the garage shooting as well as the deaths of Kieran and Dutch, besides the three the other day?' Mendip opened his jacket and held his arms out: 'I'm not wired, honestly. I can't condone what you've done but I certainly wouldn't grass you for it. In truth perhaps, a bit of me does condone your actions.'

Adam knew he had to believe Mendip wasn't wired. He needed his help and had to show trust in him, otherwise any request for help wouldn't be given. 'I trust you, Keith. Will you listen to why I need your help before you tell me to get lost?'

Mendip looked around before picking his coffee up and leant over the table towards Adam. 'All ears.'

Adam gave a brief account of what had happened so far, then got the nub of the matter. 'So, to get to Geoff Townsend I have to find a way inside the house. The police are bound to be surrounding it now and if he leaves the house he'll have the force following him. His business will fold, I think. Sure it can carry on for a few weeks, but without Dutch, Jackie Smith or him on their cases someone will break ranks and try it on. The Townsend empire is finished. That's good but I want him so I have to get in the house.' Adam explained his plan.

'So, you said on the phone,' countered Mendip, 'that what you wanted from me wouldn't put me in danger, but I would be directly in the firing line, wouldn't I? Either it goes wrong in which case Townsend will be after me or you succeed in which case the police will be all over me, like a rash as they say. Either way I've a real problem.'

'Yeah,' said Adam. 'Sorry, I just couldn't think of any other way. I knew it was far-fetched and probably not going to work but it was worth a try.'

Mendip thought. 'If I had a phone that was non-traceable to me, if the call wasn't recorded, if I could get away with it ... All the same I don't think he'd fall for it – we're not best friends or had you forgotten?'

'The whole thing involves "ifs". Let's say we can set up the call, get the non-traceable phone, etcetera, and he agrees, then I still have to get in the house, do what I need to do and get out without any photos of me being taken by those reporters, or the police stopping me, or any manner of things. All "ifs" but this morning I had other "ifs": if you'd meet me, if you'd listen to me, if you'd make the call ... There is probably a long list of "ifs" but I believe in starting at the beginning and working my way through as far as possible.'

Adam looked at Mendip and was relieved when Mendip gave a slight smile and said 'OK.'

The men talked about the call and agreed that they could drive in convoy to a layby Mendip knew away from the motorway where it would be quiet.

Fifteen minutes later they were sitting in Mendip's car with Adam dialling Townsend's number into a new and non-attributable mobile. The layby was bordered by a wood to their left and a narrow country road to their right. They had lowered their windows and only the sounds of birds could be heard. They wound their windows up when Mendip pushed the call button.

'Yeah, who's this?' answered Townsend tersely.

'A voice from the past: Keith Mendip, your least favourite newspaper reporter.'

'What do you bloody want?' Townsend asked aggressively.

'Not what you might think. We've never got along but what I wrote was always true, honest and fair. I believe reporting should be about facts, not hysterical speculation. It should be fair and balanced and when I saw last night on TV that the reporter was bringing Kieran into it, I thought it was unfair – especially on Pat who's had such a rough time.'

Townsend had been inclined to end the call at first mention of Keith Mendip's name but was now listening.

Mendip continued: 'I just rang to say that what is being reported on the television and in the papers isn't fair. We both know you're not an angel but they are speculating that you have killed people for fun and, although you're a bastard, they are going too far.'

'So what are you going to do about it?' Townsend almost wanted to shout at Mendip in frustration. 'Why are you ringing? Surely you're not going to write a story about what a decent man I am, how I do so much for charity?'

Mendip raised his eyebrows towards Adam, who could hear both sides of the conversation such was the volume of Townsend's voice.

'I don't write anymore and even if I did I couldn't turn around after those stories I did about you, though the idea itself is interesting,' said Mendip, slowing his speech as if he was taken by surprise by Townsend's suggestion. 'There are people who would take a slant in the story, to tell your side. I don't know,' – he paused to think – 'if you're serious I could make a call?'

Townsend was trying to think about what he had said, what Mendip had said and what the implications were for him. He was tired after so little sleep for nights that he really couldn't think straight. The idea, though, sounded good to him: what if the story came out and painted him, well not as an angel, as Mendip had said, but as a man whose reputation had been exaggerated. He was convincing himself that perhaps he could be painted in a better light, if his side of the story was told. 'Who're you thinking off?' he replied at last.

Mendip took a sideways look at Adam. 'There's a man who's been doing interviews with villains around the country, non-attributable type of stuff, but I was told he was taking a sympathetic view. I can't remember his name. I only talked to him on the phone once, told him I wasn't interested. It was about you. He wanted to know about you because he was going to approach you but I told him to get lost. What *was* his name?' he asked himself, pausing. 'No, can't think of it but, ah yes, he was put in touch with me by a reporter' – he paused – 'yes, Julie, maybe she'd have his details. You can ask her, you know her I would think.'

Townsend knew of the crime reporter Julie and didn't like her reporting, she'd been harsh on the family when Kieran was murdered and he didn't want to talk to her. 'What about you ask her and then you tell me and I'll think about it?'

Mendip hesitated before he replied, 'Yeah, I'm not a big fan of her myself, she took my job then asked me for a favour, cheeky mare.' He paused again then sighed in what he hoped was a resigned manner, 'OK, I'll do it but no promises.'

'Yeah, OK, thanks for that. I fancy putting my side of the story out there.' He laughed and Mendip could hear Townsend still laughing as the call was finished.

Townsend repeated the conversation to Pat, who regarded the whole idea as some sort of wind-up and told Geoff he ought to be careful. She didn't trust Mendip as far as she could throw him, and she wouldn't be even able to pick him up. Townsend told Pat that it could really work in his favour, a reporter giving his side of the story. He'd be able to say that he knew Jackie Smith only a little and barely knew the man everyone called 'Dutch'. He could say that he didn't deal in drugs and thought them a curse on society. He was laughing at the possibilities and dismissed Pat's warnings. This was some relief and of course he'd be careful.

Mendip called Julie who at that time was outside Townsend's house together with another fifty or so reporters from local and national papers and television stations. A German television crew were trying to find out as much background information as possible on the so-called 'crime lord' – a term that caused much amusement among the police officers posted to keep all the reporters on the ground outside of the Townsend land. She walked away from the other reporters to talk to Mendip, who gave her no reason for making the request. All the same she read the number she had stored on her mobile for Charlie Wright.

Mendip thanked her then closed the call.

'I'll ring him this evening and pass on your number to him. Let's see if he calls you,' said Mendip.

'Another "if" but it's worth a chance,' replied Adam, who thanked Mendip for his help and promised that he wouldn't tell anyone of his involvement.

After Townsend had been rung that evening by Mendip with the number for Charlie Wright, Pat had again cautioned him against the whole idea, which resulted in him and her having an argument. This he finished by telling her that he knew best how to manipulate people. He would be in charge from start to finish and it would be on his terms. He would make sure that the reporter wrote only what he was told to write. Cash and promises as to the future would work, he had told her. Pat persisted but knew that in the end her husband would do whatever he wanted irrespective of other people's views.

Adam was sitting next to Brian watching him using different search methods to identify the current whereabouts of Williams but still without any success. There had been no admissions to a hospital as either an in- or outpatient, he wasn't registered with a doctor, didn't own a car and there was no recent history of any credit checks being made on him. Adam speculated that he might have changed his name, perhaps as part of a witness protection programme in which case they wouldn't be able to trace it. The bank account he had and from which he made the regular cash withdrawals also suggested that he hadn't obtained a new identity, although there was a slim chance that he had hidden it from the authorities. He was proving to be elusive and Brian didn't like that.

Adam's mobile rang. 'Hello.'

'Is that Charlie Wright?' he heard.

'Yeah, who's asking?'

'Geoff Townsend. I heard that you're a reporter who likes to interview people.'

Adam smiled. 'Yeah, some people, not film stars, though. Are you the Geoff Townsend currently in the news?'

'That's me. I'm getting a lot of bad press at the moment and would like to put my side of the story, to … well … even it up a bit,' Townsend said having a sip from his glass. It was his fifth drink that evening which wasn't enough to make him drunk but sufficient to relax him.

'That's interesting. But how do I know you are Geoff Townsend? This could be a wind-up. How did you get my number and how do you know I'll be interested in doing something? After all, it could backfire and ruin me.'

Townsend told Adam about the call he'd received from Mendip that morning and the further call he'd received recently.

'Why don't you come and we'll talk about it, Charlie. Let's examine each other's credentials and see if we can do some business. It could be a good earner.'

Adam was silent for a few seconds as if he was considering Townsend's words.

'A good earner?'

'Look, Charlie, let's meet and see how it goes and then we can talk about rewards. What do you think?'

Adam and Townsend continued to discuss the offer with Adam appearing sceptical and not too keen on the idea while not pouring cold water on it entirely. Adam's previous experience of dealing with hostage negotiations gave him an edge in letting Townsend take the initiative so that after a further five minutes Townsend was almost ordering and at the same time begging Charlie to conduct the interview. When the call ended it was agreed that Charlie would ring Townsend in the morning with an answer, having had time to think through the implications of the interview for both of them and whether by doing it his reputation would be tarnished or improved. Townsend had liked the answer that Adam gave him and the self-interest that he showed.

'Another "if" out of the way,' said Adam to Brian.

Brian agreed. It was an outrageous idea that Adam had had and though it was just possible it would work, there were still problems how to get in and out of the house not being the least of them.

27

The following morning after a sound night's sleep Townsend felt much better and confident to the extent that he waved at the reporters as he drew back his bedroom curtains. He then made mugs of tea and coffee that he carried out to them on a tray.

'No comment,' he said, smiling at everyone, knowing that his picture would be in every newspaper the following day, 'except to say how I hope the weather stays dry for you today. The lads' – Townsend indicated two security guards – 'will collect the mugs when you've finished with them, and please don't nick any. I know how many there are.' He laughed at his own humour and saw several reporters smile while they thanked him for his thoughtfulness.

Adam called just after ten by which time Pat had given up trying to make Geoff see her side of the argument. Unknown to Geoff, she'd spoken with Lenny in Spain and told him about Geoff's plans but he had just laughed and said that his little brother knew what he was doing.

The conversation between Townsend and Adam was friendly and, after further persuasion from Townsend, Adam had agreed to do the interview, that very evening at the Townsends' house. Adam could just drive straight in at eight o'clock. His security men would be expecting him and they would make sure that photographers wouldn't see him as he went into and out of the house.

That afternoon Townsend was lying on the settee watching news programmes on television when his mobile rang. It was the DCI. A minute later Townsend was on his feet and yelling at the top of his voice for Pat. When she walked towards him he exploded.

'What are the hell you doing, you stupid bloody woman,' he screamed at her.

Taken aback by his sudden mood change, Pat recoiled and before she could answer he continued his tirade: 'You contacted bloody Plod and asked him to run a check on this reporter, didn't you? … You don't understand, do you? Sometimes a decision has to be made, a risk taken, but when I know the risk I can deal with it, make plans and they don't involve telling Plod beforehand.' His face was red with anger as he jabbed a finger in her face. 'Now don't interfere – bugger off for a few days if you want. You're becoming a liability. Oh, by the way, Plod, for what it's worth, says he's checked with a reporter, who backs up what Mendip said about this Wright man. He makes a speciality of doing stories on so-called villains, putting their point of view.'

Pat was shaken by his outburst and worse was that she knew she had gone behind his back and asked for help from Plod, of all people. It was a risk she had taken and it had backfired.

'OK, Geoff, I'll go and visit my sister. I don't want us to fall apart and perhaps a bit of breathing space for a night would be best, but just for the night.' She smiled at him then walked up to him and put her arms around his neck. She kissed him gently on his lips. 'I love you and of course I worry after what's been happening recently. I don't like seeing you upset, so you do what you have to do and I'll see you in the morning.' She smiled and gave him another kiss. 'Oh, and I know you'll behave tonight. I don't think you could smuggle a tart in here without it being in all the papers in the morning.'

They both laughed and went up to the bedroom where he watched her pack some things.

Adam was feeling nervous as he finished applying the black tape to change the registration number then tied a black plastic bin liner over both the front and rear plates. He took the tax disc down from the front windscreen and finished decorating Brian's car with a 'BABY ON BOARD' sign, sunscreens for the rear door windows and use of a jelly that, spread thinly on various parts of the bodywork, and in the distorted light that he expected, would appear as dents and scratches. He stood back and slowly walked around the car: the transformation was complete – it looked like a family car. He cleaned everything away, sat in the driving seat, then checked his watch. Six minutes before eight: the drive, he knew, was three minutes fifteen seconds long, allowing for a ten-second holdup.

As Adam drove off the main road he noted that two reporters took a momentary interest in him as he pulled slowly forward towards the gate to Townsend's premises. Before driving alongside the reporters, he pulled down his balaclava with his gloved hands and, as the gate opened, drove in and parked up at the front door parallel to the house. He quickly exited from the car and as the front door opened he squeezed through the gap.

'Stay there!' barked Townsend.

Adam looked at Townsend, who was standing barely six feet away holding a foot-long carving knife in front of him. Adam stopped, looked at the knife, then up at Townsend. In the background towards the kitchen stood two burly security guards each holding metal collapsible batons of the type favoured by police.

'Strip!' ordered Townsend.

Adam smiled a little and slowly placed a notebook he had been carrying on the carpet. He unzipped his jacket, held it at arm's length, then dropped it. He slowly removed all his clothes including his shoes until he was standing there in just his boxer shorts. He held his hands at his side and smiled at Townsend.

'And those!' Townsend indicated the shorts and with a resigned sigh Adam duly lowered his shorts.

Townsend ordered Adam to one side while he examined each

piece of clothing, throwing them to Adam as each item passed muster. Dressed, Adam looked at his notebook. 'Want to check that?' he smiled amiably.

Townsend returned the smile then put the knife on to the bottom stair and offered his hand to shake Adam's. They shook hands with no animosity as if the procedure was an everyday occurrence.

In the lounge Adam started by asking Townsend the sort of questions he thought a reporter would have asked and challenged some of the answers given, asking for an explanation or further answer to clear up any ambiguity. He made notes in the notebook, having told Townsend that he didn't have anything electrical on him as some of the people he interviewed were unhappy with any type of electrical appliance. Townsend had laughed at that and warmed towards Charlie immediately, saying that he was surprised that he didn't have the latest iPhone. Adam had replied that he did have such a device but, because it had so many gadgets, including a camera and voice-activated recorder, had left it in the car, assuming that Townsend wouldn't have trusted him with it. Townsend had agreed and said that the reason for the strip search was to not only ensure Adam didn't have any weapons but also any secret recording or photographic devices. Adam's response was that he had had a lot of experience of talking with people who were suspicious of reporters and knew that to carry any item that could be interpreted as a threat would destroy the confidence that he had to have between himself and his interviewee.

Adam covered Townsend's childhood and the start of his life in crime in his teens before two prison terms had taken him into adulthood. Adam was probing in some areas but less so in others, allowing Townsend to boast of his skills in being able to make money in a legitimate way. Townsend readily admitted to knowing criminals throughout the country, and indeed many of his friends and associates were involved in crime, but as for his own involvement he would only say with a smile 'Fifth Amendment.'

Townsend told Adam of how devastated he and his wife had been at the loss of their son, who had been a loving boy, always prepared to help others. Townsend continued to extoll both his own and his family's virtues while Adam made copious notes in a mass of pencil strokes that he hoped looked like shorthand. He had declined any refreshment and tried to play the part of a relaxed friendly reporter, someone who would be able to submit a story that would elicit sympathy from readers. From time to time a sound from hallway or kitchen confirmed that the two security guards were in the vicinity, far enough to not hear all the conversations but close enough to intervene if Adam tried to assault Townsend.

Adam assured Townsend that he would be able to have the interview in at least three national papers that he knew of and expected it to be syndicated to foreign papers and magazines as well. Townsend had been slightly disappointed that Charlie didn't ask for a photograph to go with the story but he knew that his picture would be in the newspapers the following day in any case.

After two hours Adam started to bring the interview to a close and asked to use the toilet, which made Townsend smile but refuse. 'You understand, Charlie, I wouldn't let you out of my sight while you're in my house. No insult intended.'

In the hallway Townsend walked to the bottom step of the stairs. 'Get your iPhone and take a picture of me sitting down with a drink all relaxed,' he said with a smile. The security guards stood behind Townsend, their metal batons in their belt but close enough to be in their hands and ready for use in two seconds.

Adam pointed at his balaclava that he had thrown on the floor when he entered the house.

'I have to wear that if I'm going out. I don't want *my* photo taken by anybody.'

Townsend agreed and Adam put the balaclava over his head then exited the house amid a frantic burst of lights flashing from cameras. He kept his head lowered as he ducked into the driving seat and as lights continued to be aimed at him. Two powerful searchlights were switched on from the top of vans and the driveway was illuminated as if it were daytime. He reached under the driving seat and instantly found the butt of the Sig, which he pushed into the waistband of his trousers. He opened the glove compartment and took out an old mobile that he hoped would temporarily draw the attention of Townsend and the two security guards while he reached for the Sig.

He ducked out of the car and ran back inside the house where the two security guards were standing in front of Townsend, their batons extended and drawn. The security guard to Adam's left had his baton raised above his head while the other held his low. The second it took for Adam's brain to read the situation also recorded that the two knew what they were doing: one would hit high, the other low, simultaneously. Townsend had hold of the kitchen knife.

Adam held out his left hand, showing the mobile phone high above his head,

'What's up?' he asked with a genuine degree of nervousness in his voice.

'No offence meant, Charlie. We're going to search you again,' said Townsend as the security guard holding the low positioned baton stepped forward towards him.

Adam had the closed front door a foot behind him, leaving him no room to retreat, a security guard each side and Townsend over six feet in front. The security guard reached up and took the mobile phone from Adam and handed it to Townsend who looked at it quickly and recognised it as being an old model and a quick check of its back showed no camera lens. His senses were immediately alerted and, as he looked towards Adam with the intention of saying something, Adam leapt forward, veering towards the high-baton-holding guard to get under his downward swing. He pushed into him, making the guard stumble half a pace back. A sudden bolt of pain went through Adam's body as the low-holding guard's swing brought his baton into Adam's thigh. His leg suddenly didn't have any strength and a second later he received a blow to his left shoulder that made Adam twist on to his left leg. He pushed with his left arm while struggling to get his right arm inside his jacket when another blow struck his right arm.

Adam felt the pain race down his arm to the tips of his fingers just as his hand found the butt of the weapon. A further blow to his already numb shoulder made his legs begin to buckle under him. He held the butt tightly, focusing all his physical and mental strength as he attempted to suppress the pain and continue with his mission. More blows landed. He saw boots, black and shiny, closing in, then Townsend's shoes getting closer. He dropped to the floor as a blow scraped the top of his head, which – had it connected as intended – would have split his head in two. He twisted his body so that he lay on his back and lifted his legs with a kicking motion. His hand came free from his jacket at the same time as a boot stamped on his chest causing him to close his eyes instantly and arch his neck forward. He fired the Sig and heard the sound that he had known for so many years.

His eyes were open again in an instant after the stamp and he fired upwards. There was a commotion … Boots moved away … He tried to slow everything down. Slow and methodical, as his training had taught him. He rolled over a complete turn while he looked around him at floor level then upwards. The guards had moved back a foot and were moving back again. Townsend stood there with the knife in his hand, bending down towards him. Adam pulled the trigger twice and saw Townsend's face change at the same time. He knew that both rounds had found their target.

Adam pulled his arm in front of his face as Townsend started to fall, still holding the knife in his hand, the knife pointing towards Adam's stomach. Adam rolled a half-turn and fired twice almost instantaneously as Townsend continued falling. The knife was still in his hand but the hand was losing its grip on the handle.

Townsend fell in slow motion, slowly towards Adam. Adam knew that Townsend wasn't the problem and as the dead weight of Townsend landed on him his focus was on the guards. They were both now eight feet away and were dropping their batons while trying to raise their hands in the air above their heads. Adam hesitated while his brain read the situation, looking up at the two men then hearing the thuds as the batons landed on the carpet. The two men were scared, no longer the bullies full of strength. The twin sights of the gun and their master lying sprawled across Adam's body were enough to make them submit. Adam tried to move, but Townsend's weight and the dumb pain he felt all over his body meant that he couldn't. He pointed the suppressed weapon at the guards.

'Down on your fronts, hands behind your heads, cross your ankles.'

They moved almost in unison in their scramble to get to the ground and follow the instructions. Adam released the weapon to free his hand to push Townsend from his trunk and down his legs until he could get free and begin to sit up. Having used the banister to heave himself to his feet, he collected the Sig and put it into the waistband of his trousers while trying to get his brain working again. Townsend was dead: he'd felt his weight and knew there wasn't any life left. His problem now was to get out of the house. He tried a step on to his injured leg and thought it would buckle, so he tried again, this time slowly transferring the weight until he was able to stand on it. He could only stagger rather than walk and his shoulder wouldn't allow real strength into his arm as he barged from the hallway towards the kitchen. He found towels and drying cloths then returned to the hallway where the two guards hadn't moved an inch. Issuing a string of threats, he tied each of them securely, then rifled through their pockets to find their wallets.

'I'll have these. If either of you even try to describe me to the police, I swear I will find you and kill you both. I don't care if only one of you speaks, you will both die –understood?' Both men nodded their heads and then turned them away from him as if already saying, 'Didn't see the man.'

Adam stood for two minutes looking at the hallway and thinking of the forensic examination that would take place when the alarm was raised. Too late to dwell on that he decided: his objective now was to get away. He had two plans in mind that he and Brian thought might work but with his injuries he knew that the speed he would need to drive to escape any pursuers would be beyond him. He needed to think carefully. For the time being he knew he would be safe where he was and he would use that time as best he could. He rang Brian's mobile and waited, two rings then stop, call again for two rings and stop, call again and on the third ring answer.

'Trouble?' Brian said quietly.

Brian was sitting at his table by the window and watched the pub forecourt as cars arrived and their occupants made their way into the bar. The bar was filling up and the noise increasing as more and more drink was consumed. Brian was only just nursing his second pint of bitter. He had answered the call from Adam: their fears had been realised and now their backstop plan had to be used. Over the weeks they had constantly asked the question 'What if' and looked for the answer. The plan tonight had been straightforward – Adam was to go in, shoot Townsend, come out again and drive home – but nothing ever goes to plan as simply as that, they knew – hence their contingency plan. Had Adam been fully fit they thought his driving ability and knowledge of both Brighton and Crawley and the countryside between would have enabled him to throw any chasers from his tail. Now, his physical injuries precluded any fast driving, so those skills were not going to be tested. Now Brian needed a car.

Brian examined the drivers and knew that a man was trying

so hard to win a kiss from his female companion that his mind was anywhere but on his coat at his side on the bench seat. She, though, would be more aware of Brian walking close to her man. A maybe there. The other driver who interested him was a man playing darts among a crowd of men and women – all young, early twenties. His jacket was on the back of a chair, his car keys in the right pocket. Possible but not too easy – Brian had the length of the bar to walk before he would be outside. He looked at the first man again, forties, drinking shorts, whisky. The woman was now talking to him. Brian looked around the bar. These two were in a quieter area where people were talking earnestly to one another.

The woman stood and the man also stood to allow her out of the seat they were sharing. She started to walk to the toilets. The man took a gulp of his drink, draining the whisky almost in one go, and followed in the same direction. Brian was on his feet in a moment, draining his glass and putting it in his coat pocket. Walking purposefully but not too fast, he took a slight deviation to grab the man's coat. Bingo – inside the left pocket were the car keys. The coat was replaced and Brian continued without a backward glance. He walked directly to the car, a white BMW, using the fob to unlock the car as he approached it. He was in the seat with the engine started before he looked back to see if anyone was paying him any attention. They weren't. He drove out on to the main road and called Adam.

Adam was still standing in the hallway, his nerves taut but feeling the pain that was beginning to settle on him in many areas. He answered his mobile. 'OK' was all he said. He lowered his balaclava and opened the front door, causing a blinding flash of light to hit him. The intensity of light affected his vision as he struggled to adjust his eyesight and move towards the Volvo. He sat in the driver's seat, started the engine and slowly drove towards the gate. Two guards opened the gate, the same guards who had admitted him. He drove through. The lights were fiercer now that

307

the photographers were closer and the searchlights lit the inside of the car. He drove steadily through the crowd and on to the main road where he turned towards the city centre. He kept at the legal speed limit and saw a line of cars forming behind him with at least two motorcycles among the cars. God knew why but the paparazzi were following him!

He drove along the route that he knew would take him to the seafront, where his intention was to drive westwards along the promenade, conscious that at anytime he could be stopped by a police officer who would demand that the coverings on the number plates be removed, his balaclava taken off and that he show proof of his identity. He could feel the tension within his body and was aware that he could not allow his driving to reflect it. The drivers behind would detect any change before Adam knew he had done anything.

He drove through the streets towards the seafront, past St Peter's Church, then followed the one-way system directly south through traffic lights, past the Brighton Pavilion with its domes now illuminated by lights hidden in the grounds, and on to the seafront. At the roundabout in front of the Palace Pier where Monica had met Katja, he turned right and westwards towards Hove taking the opportunity to see in his rear-view mirror the line of cars behind him, following his exact route at the same speed. The two motorcycles were still in the convoy that extended back into the distance. He continued to drive at the same steady speed, making sure that the drivers following would relax and wait for the unexpected to happen at which point they would individually race to get alongside him or pounce when he stopped. He had a clear road in front and the temptation to accelerate suddenly was huge, but he knew that it was through the disciplined manner of his driving that he was most likely to achieve his aim.

He continued along the seafront then headed northwards, a route that was not a natural one but which could be explained by wanting to avoid all the stop–start of driving through the city centre, at least that was what he hoped the followers would think. The cars and motorbikes weren't pushing close to him; they were waiting until either he reached his destination, at which time they would all close up and disgorge their photographer passengers, or he tried to outmanoeuvre or outrun them, in which case they were in a position to quickly follow his every move. He checked his mirror again, indicated to take a left turn and braked a little, then carried on and repeated the move at the next junction. He hoped that the followers would believe he wasn't used to the area and was looking for an address. He continued his slow progress along the street, craning his head as if were reading the street signs. He called Brian on the mobile.

'You there?'

'Ready,' was the reply.

As he approached Hove Railway Station, he slowed again, then indicated that he was pulling in towards the taxis whose drivers were standing on the pavement talking. Adam got out of the car and risked raising his balaclava as the followers were waiting for him to resume his journey. He left the car door open, the car engine running and lights on, then sauntered towards the taxis. Every second now counted. He appeared to be making directly towards the taxi drivers, waving a hand in their direction hoping to convince the paparazzi that he was going to ask for directions. He made sure his back was to the followers all the time – there must be no turning around to see if anyone was following him, no signs of nervousness. Suddenly and without any warning, Adam broke into a sprint, turning towards the footbridge that spanned the tracks at the station. Taking the steps three at a time, he dismissed any pain that surged through his body from his leg and back, used his hand to grip the rail to give extra leverage, then at the top of the steps turned the corner and ran over the top of the tracks.

Adam half jumped and half ran down the steps on the other side of the footbridge and saw a white car at the bottom, side on and directly in his line. The rear door was open and without any pause he threw himself on to the back seat just as the car accelerated away, causing Adam to crash against the back of the seat and his head to strike the other door. The door at his feet was still open but with a thud it closed with the movement of the car. Adam was thrown about the seat as he tried to gain a sitting position behind the vacant front passenger seat.

'Thanks, mate,' he gasped. 'That was close.'

Brian stopped at a junction and turned left, filtering into the traffic and was soon just a car among many others.

'Going to have to dump this soon. I'm not sure when the owner is going to find it missing,' Brian said. 'I'm not worried about your friends. They'll have to drive miles to get to where I picked you up but the police may be looking for this.'

Adam knew that Brian was right on both points. The police would be searching for the stolen car in which they were now driving and the cars and motor bikes following him had no way of crossing the railway tracks unless they drove east or west some miles in either direction. It was just a question of getting home after dumping it and they resigned themselves to another long walk. The reporters would be touring the streets looking for Adam and very shortly so, too, would be the police. It was imperative that they go some way towards Crawley before they decided where they would abandon the car leaving the keys in the ignition. It was more than likely that the car would be stolen and so any forensic examination would be contaminated.

The security guards inside the house knew that Adam had driven away because of the sound of all the other vehicles starting their engines and shouts for reporters or photographers to get in their cars. They had waited for a couple of minutes before managing to loosen each other's binds and shout for help, which was soon answered by another guard. The police officer with responsibility for keeping the remaining reporters at bay outside the Townsend premises was summoned into the house where he saw Townsend on the floor in a pool of blood. The guards had examined Townsend for signs of life, as did the police officer, who radioed in to report the attack. It was during this time that he forgot his responsibility towards the reporters and with the last guard joining the three inside the house the reporters instantly knew a story was unfolding and without hesitation they too went to the house. Two photographers arrived at the open front door and after the briefest of looks they began taking photographs. Then another photographer arrived, followed by a reporter, and pushing began, causing the first photographers to be pushed into the hallway. The guards and police officer tried to use their arms to push the photographers back, but others had already arrived outside the door and, sensing that a big story was either unfolding or available, they pushed forward. A mêlée ensued during which time, or so the forensic officer estimated later, at least a dozen pairs of feet had been through the crime scene making his analysis much more difficult and his findings less certain.

28

The television news was dominated by the events that had occurred in the Brighton and Surrey areas, amid speculation as to who was behind the murders. Names of known major criminals were whispered – everyone seemed to have an opinion. This was also the case in the Major Incident Room where additional staff had been summoned to supplement those already working to capacity. Police officers were called in from their rest days, annual leave was cancelled and even those who had reported sick with minor ailments were encouraged to help out. The Home Secretary even sent an aide to Brighton to hear a full report of what had happened from the Chief Constable, what resources they were using and when the Home Secretary could expect arrests to be made. The Chief Constable in turn demanded the same answers from the Senior Investigating Officer, who amid the chaos and innumerable meetings that he was forced to attend felt the whole enquiry was in danger of spiralling out of control. Uniformed officers were seen out on the streets in numbers never seen before and local criminals wisely decided to suspend their activities for the time being.

Raymond Black shuffled down the road, determined to buy the day's newspapers so that he could actually read in print what he had already watched on television and listened to on the radio. Geoff Townsend was dead. Jackie Smith and Kieran Townsend were dead. He knew, he just knew, that his friendly gardener was responsible and how he wished he could speak to him, to thank him, but the address and mobile number he had were both useless, so Sandra had said after she'd tried to find Adam. He wasn't frightened but knew that the two remaining attackers would be thinking of why their friends had been murdered and by whom. They might guess, they might return for him, they might want their revenge, but he knew without doubt that Adam would get them as well. He shuffled on towards the shop but his heart was lighter and he felt younger and fitter than his posture showed. After Smith's murder, he had spoken to a neighbour, who had stopped him in the street to query whether this wasn't the woman who'd been charged with Ann's murder, but he pretended to not know the name. He had feigned surprise and indifference at the event, though he had read every newspaper and watched every news broadcast. A mumble of words, a shrug of his shoulders, and he had walked on.

In his stone cottage in the hills of Pembrokeshire, Keith Mendip watched the television news and smiled. He wasn't frightened of anyone discovering his association with the man he knew as Charlie Wright; actually he was proud of his limited involvement in ridding the world of Kieran and Geoff Townsend and Jackie Smith. He was thinking back to his time on the newspaper and the articles he had written about the cancer of crime in his home city, and those responsible, not only those committing the crime but those who didn't do enough to fight the criminals.

His thoughts were interrupted by his mobile phone ringing. He smiled, hoping and half expecting the caller to be Charlie Wright but his caller ID showed it to be Julie from the newspaper. He hesitated while he tried to gather his thoughts and watched the screen as the voicemail switched on. He waited until the screen changed to show that Julie had finished her message then he listened to the message.

Her voice sounded bright and cheerful. 'Hi Keith, how's it going in the back of beyond?' There was a slight intake of breath and Mendip knew the real reason for her call was about to start.

'Have you been following the news? Kieran, then Dutch, Smith and now Geoff Townsend have been killed. Can we talk? I think we could put something special together with your knowledge of all their history and my more up-to-date information. Give me a call as soon as you get this. As you can imagine, it's a madhouse here.'

Mendip ended the call and gently put the mobile on the seat next to him. His mood had been broken and suddenly he felt anger and resentment. It should have been him penning the article that would be the front-page story. Against advice from criminals, police officers, other journalists and various people, he had stood firm and tried to stand up the Townsends. He had written the truth and what had happened to him? He had become and outcast and now his replacement needed his help. 'Write the articles your bloody self!' he said aloud. Then a thought occurred to him: why not write a novel about the events, change some names and events … Maybe, just maybe, he thought.

Monica had flown to Málaga before catching the train to Granada and a bus to Monachil where she had taken a taxi to the Restaurante del Purche and after the taxi had driven away she had crossed to the chalets. She was nervous, almost scared, as she walked up the wooden steps and knocked on the door. She heard a movement from inside but the door wasn't opened. Becoming anxious, she knocked again and suddenly heard a noise from behind her. She swivelled around, nearly falling from the step. The light was poor and deep shadows were cast by the only lamppost some twenty yards away in the roadway. A man walked from the shadow with his arms outstretched in front of him.

'Moni?' he said in a voice that was quiet and nearly breaking.

'Papa?' asked Monica, watching as her father stepped into the light.

'*Si, mi Moni!*'

Monica felt tears well into her eyes, something she had

promised herself not to do. She stepped down to the ground and held her arms wide for her father to walk into. He too had tears in his eyes as he gripped her tightly in his arms.

'Mama!' he called. '*Moni es aqui.*'

The door opened and Monica could just see around her father's shoulders her mother silhouetted in the doorway.

'Mama!' cried Monica as her mother ran down the steps to embrace Monica.

Monica's sister arrived at the doorway and jumped to the ground to join her parents and Monica in the family hug.

They went inside the chalet and even as Monica was trying to remove her coat she was still being hugged by her mother and father. The four sat at the dining table holding hands and each of them unashamedly crying as they each expressed their relief that the family were together again.

It was in the early hours of the following morning that the questions turned to the man Adam and his rescue of Monica's parents and sister. Monica told them of how she had met him and how Adam had robbed Dutch of the drug samples, then of how she had faked the overdose to escape Smith's clutches and the role that Brian had played. She continued to tell them how her two friends were determined to exact revenge on the gang for their savage behaviour towards an old man and woman, Mr and Mrs Black. She didn't mention that anybody had been killed and tried to play down the importance of what had happened in Sussex and Surrey.

It was her father who pointed to the television set in the corner of the room and which Monica hadn't noticed previously. He told her that the news programmes were full of the murders in Brighton and the names were ones that they recognised – Townsend, Dutch, Tompkins and Smith. Initially, when the name Townsend was mentioned Monica believed her father was referring to Kieran and was genuinely shocked when her father insisted that it was the father, Geoff, Lenny's brother, who had been murdered, and in his own home.

'Do you know who has done these murders?' he asked.

There was silence in the room as Monica felt the three pairs of eyes looking at her. She lowered her head.

'Was it the man who saved us?' asked her father in a gentle tone.

Monica looked at her father and felt tears begin to at first well in her eyes then fall down her cheeks.

He stood and walked behind her and leaned down to hold his daughter's shoulders firmly in his hands, kissing the top of her head.

'Never say anything about that man, never, never, never …' he said quietly. He looked at his wife and other daughter and saw both nodding their heads in understanding and agreement. 'That man and his friend have saved our lives and have saved our futures. We owe them everything, but we must forget them, we will say nothing of what has happened to us … never.'

29

Adam had showered and joined Brian who was in the lounge watching the news on the television. Neither spoke as they watched and listened to the various scenes on the screen.

'OK, turn it off, Bri,' said Adam. 'We've seen enough, and funnily enough it doesn't make me feel too proud. In fact, I was in bed thinking about how we got started on this – well, how I got started then got you involved.'

'You're thinking that's enough?' asked Brian quietly.

Adam stood and walked towards the net-curtained front window. 'How long do you think it will be before armed cops will come running up the path, maybe stuns already through the windows, nearby houses evacuated quietly during the night. Cops with their adrenaline running at full speed, armour and masks making them sweat, been waiting in the back of a van for hours, all cramped, muscles couldn't wait to get moving, now in full flow towards the front door. What will we do, Bri?' said Adam, turning towards Brian, who returned the look but knew that Adam was going to continue.

'We're not going to fight back. No way could I hurt a policeman, but do we just lie on the carpet and listen to their orders? If we move first, they may suspect a trick, shoot first and say sorry afterwards. Result? We're dead. Obey every order given to us, and the result? We'll be in prison for the rest of our lives. We won't get parole or any sort of early release; we'll be just left to rot and vegetate.'

'Regrets?' asked Brian.

'Nah, I wasn't going anywhere and didn't have a clue what I

was going to do for the rest of my life, so no – at least I can look back and say we did something, right or wrong, good or bad, but at least we did something.'

'Guess so,' agreed Brian. 'What we need to do though is think very carefully about Lenny, after what has happened with Smith and Geoff – hardly low profile, were they? I honestly don't know how the cops are getting along. The news is pretty much going overboard with all the speculation and they're not saying much, just a bland appeal for witnesses. Thinking about it, Ray Black and Sandra would know it was you; Keith Mendip; maybe that girl reporter you met will put two and two together; and, of course, Monica. That's four, maybe five, who could put your name forward and over time they'll get a CCTV picture of you, put that on the telly and some old mates will not only recognise your face but also your skills. Let's be honest, I'd be surprised if the cops aren't already searching through the old files at Hereford.'

'So you're expecting the police to arrive any minute?'

'No, but they *could* do. It's the skills you've used that could undo everything,' said Brian.

Lenny Townsend arrived at his brother's house late in the afternoon to find the house surrounded by police officers and forensic teams working their way through each room. He saw Pat talking to a plain-clothes police officer by the front door and he joined them. He and Pat embraced as cameras clicked amid shouts of 'Look this way, Pat' and 'What have you to say, Pat?'

Lenny let Pat go and walked straight towards the group of reporters, not caring that his photograph was being taken every fraction of a second.

'You bastards!' Lenny shouted at the top of his voice. 'You pieces of shit! Why don't you all just piss off?' He moved towards the low metal barrier designed to mark the dividing line the reporters weren't allowed to cross and then pushed it violently towards the reporters, causing those nearest to him to retreat.

'Go on, piss off the lot of you,' he shouted as he again pushed the barrier.

'You're a piece of shit, Lenny, like your brother and nephew. Reckon you're next,' came a shout from somewhere behind the reporters he'd been attacking.

Lenny stopped and as he lost control spit shot from his mouth. 'Who said that, who said that? I'll kill you – you worthless scum.'

Lenny waded into the reporters throwing punches each side as he went. Amid the confusion cameras clicked, people fell backwards and there were shouts of pain as several of his blows found the faces of reporters. He continued to wade his way forward, kicking at figures who had slipped or been pushed to the ground, continuing to snarl with rage. Suddenly a police officer was facing him, young and smaller in build and stature than he. The officer held an arm forward towards Lenny's chest.

'No more,' he said in an almost conversational tone that Lenny couldn't hear among all the shouting and writhing bodies. Lenny saw the pose and something in him acknowledged the officer's authority, whether it was the smallness of the young man, his guts in moving forwards or the tone of his voice – something triggered reason in him. He stopped just short of the officer's outstretched hand, looked directly at the officer, then turned and walked back towards Pat. He walked past her and to his car before starting the engine and gunning the motor to make as much noise as possible and drove away.

The whole event was captured by television camera crews and would be the lead story on the next news bulletins. Photographs would appear in newspapers from Brighton to Boston to Brisbane and Bangkok. The story of the murders in England was becoming global.

That evening Monica and her family watched the news, the lead item of which was the on-going murders in Brighton, England. The latest murder, that of Geoff Townsend, was being told in a tone that almost suggested admiration for the killer, his nerve, his sheer audacity. To murder a gangster in his own house, with two security guards in the house at the time and with over a hundred cameras outside the front door was beyond most people's understanding. A grainy picture of a man wearing a jacket, jeans and a balaclava covering his face was shown. Monica watched the picture on the screen and knew it was Adam. She felt her lip tremble and tears begin to form again when her father reached over and took her hand, giving it a firm but loving squeeze. Monica's mother reached for the television controls, but Monica said, '*No mama,*' and the controls were replaced on the table. 'I can't *not* watch him.'

At the same time Lenny was sitting in a large armchair facing a forty-six-inch television screen and watching the same footage, only with an English voice describing the events. Sitting in an equally large armchair at an angle to Lenny sat Pat also watching the screen. She gulped at her drink then held her empty glass in the air where it was swiftly taken by the uniformed butler assigned to Lenny's hotel room. Lenny watched the butler replenish Pat's drink then dismissed the butler before turning to Pat.

'Stay here tonight or for as long as you want. I'm going back in the morning.'

Pat looked over her glass at Lenny then at the screen. 'Don't tell me you're packing it in?'

'I said to Geoff that we'd made enough. If some shit wants it, then so what? Let's be honest, we came from nothing, we've got a pile, so why don't we enjoy it? He wouldn't have it of course, not Geoff, got to win, got to beat the bastards who were challenging him, got to be top dog … but you know, Pat, being a dead top dog is not what I want. My life is in Spain, legit, well almost …' He smiled, though he noticed Pat didn't return the smile. 'It's comfortable and almost problem free. You know what?' he looked at her before continuing. 'Monica's family were released probably by one of the blokes who've killed everyone here – an embarrassment for me, of course, but what am I going to do about it? I'll tell you, sod all, that's what I'm going to do, because who cares really? Come on, I can get on with my life without having some nutter coming after me. I suppose you think I'm soft?'

Pat didn't comment but took a large mouthful of her drink.

'OK, but we did it, Pat, you, Geoff and me, we did it, from nothing to this.' He waved his arm around the hotel suite. 'The best dear old Brighton has to offer, a three-bedroom suite, plus the rooms either side, of course – for security. Well, I've got to take the threat seriously now. It seems as if they've been targeting us all along. Maybe if I just disappear they'll forget about me.'

Pat finally spoke. 'You gutless bastard, Lenny. Geoff's not even in his grave and you're bailing out. Are you even going to come to his funeral?'

'Pat, my love, gutless bastard, am I? Well, these days, yes, I suppose I am. The funeral? Don't think he'd bother with mine, do you? You're welcome to all his money. You're a rich widow, but I'd be very careful – move out of the area. It could be you or me they're after next because somehow I think they're not finished.'

Pat drained her glass and rose from the chair. 'What you say is all common sense. We've had a good run and now it's over. So now you're backing out. I can't run the shop like Geoff; he put real fear into people. I couldn't do that and to be honest I don't think I could trust anyone either – not now.' She placed her glass on the table and gathered her handbag. 'Bye, Lenny. Be lucky.' She walked from the room and Lenny leant back in his chair and sighed.

30

'I'm going to Spain,' announced Adam.

Brian continued scrolling down the computer screen. 'He's got to be here somewhere. Nobody can disappear and not leave a trace – I'll find him. Give me twenty-four hours,' replied Brian without looking up.

Adam twisted in the canvas chair and looked around their operations room, noting that the shelves still had plenty of equipment on them. He was still concerned about finding the last man – he wanted to have the option of killing him before Lenny. But he knew that Brian would eventually locate him, no matter what steps he had taken to drop under the radar.

'Got to get away from here as well,' Adam continued. 'I feel that I can't leave the house without everyone looking at me.'

Brian looked up. 'Have you seen the pictures of me in Crawley before Smith saw Monica? It wasn't your face looking from the telly, was it?'

Adam knew what Brian said was true. He could recognise him but he doubted anybody else would. The majority of his face was hidden and what could be seen was grainy and of poor quality. Still, he had to acknowledge that, if it had been him, he wouldn't have been easily consoled either.

'Let's be honest, you don't see or really speak to your neighbours, so I don't think anyone will put your name forward. I know it's a worry, though, so if I go at least only one person will be here if the police say they're looking for two men. Perhaps that will throw someone off the scent.'

Brian sighed and looked at Adam. 'You go and get Lenny, by

which time I'll have the last one ready and then we shut up the whole business and forget it, have a holiday.'

Adam smiled slowly at Brian and agreed that that is what they would do, though both men knew that any time in the future their actions could come back to haunt them.

'Just one thing Bri,' said Adam waving an arm around the space, 'you got all the equipment so I guess someone in the mob knows and maybe they'll be putting two and two together, maybe that's where we'll get the chop from, maybe they'll be the ones to tell the Police?'

'Nah, no worries on that front, it's all covered and with this,' he held his prosthetic in the air, 'I'd be a bloody miracle man if I could do what you've been up to. I've thought about it and wondered if I should have a chat to see if anyone is talking about what's happening but decided against it, don't want to remind people I'm still alive. Go, get going, take two mobiles,' he indicated two in their boxes on the shelf and I'll use a new one. Anything else you'll have to get over there and I could make a call but it would involve another person having some knowledge, a risk I'd rather not take.'

Adam looked at Brian, 'You know Bri as well as me, that if anyone thinks you may be connected then as we've been so close for years, they'll know I'm the other one.'

Brian smiled at Adam, 'Get going.'

Adam agreed and said that he would source anything he needed when he was there and had formed some sort of a plan.

He had packed a holdall with only a few items of casual clothing choosing to buy anything else he would need while in Spain and that decision he had been grateful for when his holdall was rummaged by the Security team at Gatwick Airport as he made his way towards Departures. He had spent his time on the plane persuading himself that he had been the one in ten or whatever number they were working to for a search and had not been targeted by the officials, anything other than a random stop meant that the authorities were seriously on to him. Adam hired a mid-range car at Málaga Airport and drove steadily towards Granada using the motorway, allowing other vehicles to overtake him. His first priority was to see Monica and ensure that her family was safe before turning his attention to Lenny. As he drove, he speculated how the family would now view him and what Monica would have told them about him, all of which could determine how much cooperation he would get. He was particularly interested in whether Monica's mother and father would give him useful information about the layout of Lenny's house and gardens.

At Málaga he had appeared to be casual in his approach to the car hire company, one he hadn't used before and then refused the offer of a free upgrade to a better vehicle, all the while he was suspicious of being under surveillance. A good team would have gambled on him using the same hire company but also chosen another couple before placing a tracker device to some cars one of which they hoped or be directed towards hiring. Adam's thinking was sharp and his anti surveillance techniques put into practice the moment he drove from the airport. He had taken several wrong turnings as he got 'lost' in the traffic then driven at the steady pace to see if he was being followed, pulling in for a coffee at one service then buying fuel at another, all the time checking the make and colours of cars in his vicinity. As he approached Granada city, he noted the road that he would be taking towards the Sierra Nevada but first drove through the city using the same route three times, to make sure that he wasn't under surveillance. Finally, satisfied, he headed out of Granada and immediately the road began its climb towards the town of Sierra Nevada tucked into the snow-capped mountains ahead. Shortly, the road and margins showed signs of snow having been cleared, though there were only pockets of snow in the countryside and in the wooded areas. The sun reflected from the snow ahead so strongly that he had to put on his sunglasses.

He found the road he was looking for and turned right into a narrow road made narrower by the snow that was now thicker and which had been ploughed from the road to its sides. He drove on, the trees on his left casting a deep shadow on to the road surface where patches of ice hadn't seen the sun and wouldn't melt until spring arrived. He was just wondering if he could get through to the restaurant when suddenly the road twisted around a corner and he was out in the brilliant and warm sun again. The road was clear of all ice and snow as the countryside opened out into open moorland. After no more than five minutes he saw the restaurant on the right side of the road. Parking spaces were available and on the left side of the road he saw the 'Camping' sign with a vending machine by the entrance.

He drove through the gate and parked. In front of him were the chalet buildings built at angles with trees in between and paths that led behind the buildings. He estimated there were about six to ten chalets but no vehicles were parked. He stood by his car and examined the ground, seeing only a few tyre tracks, which pleased him. It was unlikely there were many guests – the fewer the better, he thought. The sun was warm and the sky a perfect blue as he walked towards the chalet with a large number 1 on the door.

As he approached the bottom of the steps, the door quickly opened and Monica almost tripped as she ran down the steps towards him. She had a huge smile and as she reached him she threw her arms around his neck. He responded by putting his arms around her waist and they hugged each other. Adam had his eyes closed when he heard a further noise and he looked up to see a girl who was a younger version of Monica standing in the doorway smiling. Her eyes passed over Adam to a point behind him which alerted his sense of danger. He released Monica and spun around quickly at the same time trying to take a step forward and see what or more likely who her eyes had been watching. Adam saw Monica's father standing near a tree with a scythe in his hand held down by his side. He was smiling and stepped forward to shake Adam's hand. Monica's mother appeared, giving him a broad smile and hugging him. She said something in Spanish that he didn't understand but which made the family laugh.

They all went indoors for a while before Monica's mother announced that a picnic she had been preparing was ready for them to eat. Adam walked with the family to a picnic table a hundred yards or so from the chalet and a hundred yards from the road and from where the views extended over the moorland for over fifty miles. Monica explained that where they were was the high point of the road and that the town of Monachil was down a long and steep hill which was used as a training route for cycling teams. Adam looked down the hill but couldn't see the town but recognised the main road far below that he had driven along on his way into Granada. They sat and ate the bread, sausages and cheese accompanied by red and white wine. Monica translated the conversation, which because it was three-way all the time was somewhat stilted. Adam was able to learn how the family were getting on. Everyday, for exercise, they went out for a walk trying to do a figure-of-eight route so that after the first circle Monica's mother could return to the chalet to prepare the lunch while Monica her sister and father completed the second circle. Monica explained that her father had obtained several weapons that he had secretly hidden around the chalet both inside and out. Adam mentioned the scythe and thought it was a strange job to be doing in winter. They all laughed at that. Eventually the conversation turned to how Monica was and how the family watched the news every day to see what was happening in England, hoping that it didn't contain anything regarding the capture of the men responsible for the killing of Townsend and his gang.

Adam told them all he wouldn't speak of what he had done, to do so would put them in a difficult position of having to lie for him.

Monica said that her father was very quiet and withdrawn

for periods, he didn't smile as much as he had in the past and it concerned her. The looks he gave her were so sad she said. Her sister had told her that she wasn't allowed boyfriends or to be out at night and that her father wanted to be at her side all the time he could. He was frightened that having lost a daughter to the gang that they may come for his other, but he would die rather than allow that to happen.

That afternoon when Monica's parents had returned to the chalet and Monica's sister had gone to the restaurant to see a girl who lived there, Monica told Adam that she and her parents had talked about what they could do to help. They hoped Lenny Townsend would die a painful death, so total was their hatred for the man. Her parents would offer any help they could if it would mean they could return to their home. Moreover, they believed that only a handful of men would offer any help to Lenny; everyone else would support the family. Without Monica's sister being present it was easier for Adam to talk to her parents and glean from each as much as he could regarding Lenny Townsend's movements, his security and the general layout of his home. Adam didn't say why he wanted the information nor what his intention was. He was aware that neither Monica's mother nor her father asked the question either – it was obvious.

Brian was still tapping the computer keyboards in the evening when he suddenly felt a surge of satisfaction as there on the screen was the man he'd been trying so hard to find. He was still using his real name but with a new nickname. He had been recruited by a reverend of a local church in Brighton and was working in a refuge for the homeless. The charity that organised this was small and didn't pay Gregory Williams any wages or even his expenses, which explained the regular cash withdrawals and the absence of a record anywhere of his receiving any income.

Satisfied with his work, Brian closed the computer down and looked around his operations room and the equipment on the shelves. None of it would be traceable to its source, but if it was found many questions would be asked and the police would have enough to keep him in custody while they spent months investigating. He gauged the quantity and weight and thought how he'd dispose of it all.

During his time talking to Monica and her parents Adam didn't make any written notes but instead constructed pictures in his head of the layout of Lenny's house and gardens and the security detail he employed. Adam had at first thought Lenny was secure in his own world until Monica's mother said that part of his routine was to visit his club every Friday evening. This he did without fail whatever the weather. Monica had interrupted and said something that reduced her father to tears. She stood up and walked over to him and put her arms around his shoulders. In between his sobs Adam could hear him quietly saying something, but he couldn't understand a word and both Monica and her mother didn't respond to what he said.

Adam was thinking. Tonight was Tuesday, which gave him two clear days to think of something. He would have preferred to have waited a further week and use the time to see if Lenny Townsend had changed his routine due to the events in England but he knew that he would have to act this coming Friday – a short time. Adam had a worry at the back of his mind that some sort of surveillance or trap would be set for him by the police who by now would have guessed that Lenny Townsend was a potential target. It would be essential that he took his time in the planning and executed the kill in as quiet and unobtrusive manner as possible.

Brian had used Adam's cycle to ride to Tilgate Woods on the outskirt of Crawley near the M23 motorway and used the noise from the motorway to disguise his digging among the trees. It had taken him twenty minutes to dig the hole, then empty the contents of the small rucksack into it. Each item had been wrapped carefully to prevent moisture from the ground penetrating the workings and ruining the equipment. Finally he had carefully refilled the hole and covered it so that it remained in keeping with the surrounding ground cover. Satisfied that it wouldn't be discovered, he identified two similar places, which would be suitable for the rest of his stock to be hidden before riding home with an empty rucksack. He planned to do a trip a day, each time during the early evening and it looked as if for once the rain would continue which would help him.

During the day he planned to clean the house systematically. Every surface would be wiped with a bleach-soaked cloth; every inch of carpet vacuumed, left to right then up and down and then right to left; everything that could be washed would be put in the washing machine or dishwasher or by hand. It would be hard work to complete the job but he knew that the rest of his and Adam's lives could be determined by how well he did it. He started in the bedroom that Monica had occupied, stripping it clean of every item before he vacuumed the carpet and washed down the walls, door and inside the clothing cupboard. The bed was wiped down and the mattress vacuumed twice and all bed linen washed in a hot wash with double the amount of recommended washing liquid. The windows were cleaned and even the outside ledges wiped down. He'd do the lounge and kitchen next, then the bathroom before the hall stairs and landing, and then finally the remaining two bedrooms. Every cupboard, every surface, every item… Meticulousness and discipline were needed and Brian had plenty of both, but he hoped that the police didn't come knocking on his door before he had finished, if ever.

31

Brian's concerns about the police identifying him were at that time groundless, as line after line of enquiry met a dead end. All the work with criminals and informants produced a lot of rumour and speculation that after many hours of investigation always proved to be without any foundation, a fiction of somebody's imagination. Even some of the Security Service had been diverted away from watching potential terrorists to watching criminals, which didn't sit well with the staff. The overall effect of all these efforts was to reduce the amount of petty crime that otherwise would have been taking place.

Another effect was the public outcry about the wave of criminality that was overtaking the country and the role of vigilantism in stopping that wave. The public was polarized over the matter. One newspaper even conducted a survey among their readers to gauge what the public 'really thinks of these murders'. and whether vigilantism could ever be justified. On a television programme a well-known newspaper columnist suggested that the murders were of a benefit to society as a whole and he hoped the murderer or murderers wouldn't be caught. Everyone seemed to be following the progress of the investigation and everyone had an opinion. As such, the affair was now of concern at the highest level of government.

A team of over thirty people were examining around the clock as much CCTV footage as they could manage before their eyes were strained but all they were producing were grainy pictures of people 'who the Police wish to identify, asking that they come forward to be eliminated from the enquiries.' Footage of film was shown on television that led to a large number of calls being received by the Police, each of which had to be followed up until the person suspected had been identified and eliminated from the enquiry. Relatives, ex-lovers and despised work mates were all confronted by Police Officers turning up demanding to know their whereabouts at a given time and day.

In Spain the news coverage was still high on the news programmes on Tuesday and Wednesday but by Thursday morning Adam was pleased to see that it had been dropped, overtaken by the on-going Euro crisis and the meeting of European leaders the following week in Paris. He had agreed with Monica and her family that they would stay at the chalet for the next week while he went to Nerja in an effort to meet with Lenny Townsend. Still nobody had used a word to indicate what they all knew, that Adam intended to kill, murder or otherwise hurt permanently, Lenny Townsend.

Brian was finishing his cleaning of the hallway at ten o'clock at night on Thursday, satisfied that with all the equipment safely buried and with the most likely areas and items of the house to be linked forensically with Monica now thoroughly cleaned he was on course to finish his cleaning the next day. The house would, of course he knew, if examined by forensic officers be 'too clean', they would know that a thorough clean had taken place from which they could suggest that incriminating evidence had been deliberately destroyed. Okay he had thought, suggest all you like but that isn't the same as finding a hair, a fingerprint, some DNA that would link Monica with being at the house, suggestion is not evidence so he would finish the job including washing down Adam's cycle to remove most of the traces of mud and wood litter which may indicate where the cycle had been. And the garden, back and front, he'd sweep the paths, make sure that the areas under windows is clean, empty the rubbish bins and wash the bins themselves. He had to think of everything, his and Adam's futures were at stake.

On Thursday morning Adam walked through the street market in Torre del Mar hearing but not understanding the stallholders' cries for him to inspect their wares. Behind one of the stalls he noticed a bookshop and went in to buy some local maps, one of which even showed individual houses in red. He quickly identified Lenny Townsend's house – the detail of the map was much better than anything he had previously used before on his visits to the area.

Adam walked lazily towards the seafront using the stalls and shop windows to vary his pace and route while having the opportunity to see people both in front and behind him. He was as sure as he could be that he wasn't being followed. The small hotel he had found in the town centre had been quiet and little notice was taken of him by the staff. In the past he could feel the hairs on his neck tingling when something was wrong or there was a threat, but at the moment he felt secure and alone as he sat at a seafront café, ordering a coffee and opening his maps. He planned on buying more clothing later that morning before heading towards Lenny Townsend's house in the evening for a last inspection after which he would finalise his plan.

He was weighing up two options. The first would involve visiting the house during the night. Monica's parents had helped him identify weaknesses in the security: a guard prone to falling asleep on the job, a window that didn't lock properly … and these enabled him to hatch a simple plan that played to Adam's strengths. The second option he didn't like so much but acknowledged that it had to be considered – this one took place at Townsend's nightclub in Nerja. Adam had been to the bar beneath the club during the day and had drank a beer, which gave him the opportunity to look around the building noting the fire escape doors and positions of the windows. The bar itself was in a side street off the plaza which during the day was always busy with tourists and locals alike. There were tables with chairs outside the bar and a daily menu was advertised. The whole of the area was pedestrianised with a warren of narrow streets that led in a myriad of directions from the plaza. No vehicles were allowed and he surmised that to get to his club Townsend would have to walk through the narrow streets, perhaps with one or possibly two minders. The location itself appealed to him more than the house option, but to get away from the area was more problematical, especially if the police were alerted quickly.

He was confident that either option would allow him the opportunity of killing Townsend. He made a call to Brian to say that he would execute one of his options on Friday night and that he hoped to be back in England on Saturday. Brian told Adam that he had finally located the last member of the gang and that he was currently engaged in a clean-up campaign in his home. The thought of the macho Brian arm deep in soapsuds made Adam smile.

32

Adam spent almost the entirety of Thursday night on a recce of Townsend's house. He quickly found the route that took him from where he left his car hidden among some olive trees some distance from the house to the wall where Monica's father had said a branch from a tree inside Townsend's garden hung over the wall, obscuring that part of the wall from the camera situated at the corner of the property. Monica's father had been told twice by Lenny Townsend to cut it, but he had been busy doing other jobs and hadn't yet managed to get round to it. Now the branch was starting to come into leaf and was thicker than before, a potentially large bonus for Adam.

The sky was very dark with little moonlight and it was cold, with frost predicted a few miles away in the higher hills. Adam took his time, knowing that a trial run was just that, a trial to test what he had been told. At the wall Adam noted that the face of the wall had been rendered with cement that had been painted white in keeping with other houses in the area. He had hoped for the rendering to be rough, which would have helped him climb it, but instead it was smooth. He scoured the ground using his fingers for over twenty minutes before he found a three-feet-long piece of discarded metal tubing. In the dark he tested its strength and, satisfied that its two-inch diameter was sufficient for his foot to rest on, he wrapped his T-shirt around the tube and filled the tube with loose soil. If the tube fell, he knew it would make a softer sound, one that would be heard by a dog but not by a human over twenty yards away, especially with a wall in between. He propped the tube against the wall, then slowly placed his right foot on the top end of the tube and levered himself upwards. His hands stretched against the wall until he was satisfied his balance was secure on just his right leg before moving his hands to the top of the wall, which was just above his head. He felt for glass embedded in the top, or wire or anything else that could cause him a problem, but it was clear. He used his arms to pull himself up and swing his legs on to the wall, enabling him to lie flat along the top. He heard two dogs arrive on the other side of the wall as he started levering himself upwards. The resulting barks broke the silence of the countryside and immediately other dogs in the vicinity howled their response. By the time he had pulled himself to the top of the wall and laid still for ten minutes, the dogs in Lenny's property had lost interest in him and with a last gruff had wandered back into the garden. Adam had seen one guard move in the area of the main gate but it was only to throw his cigarette butt into a flowerbed.

Adam soon identified the window described by Monica's mother and ran through in his mind how he would cross the ground to get to it and how he would enter the room. The rest of the plan appeared to be straightforward, although he'd have to make it up as he went – confronting Townsend, telling him the reason he was to die, and then breaking Townsend's neck – the method of despatch he'd chosen, deadly and silent. A backup plan was available using the ten-inch-bladed knife that he would carry.

Satisfied with his reconnaissance, Adam lowered himself back to the ground, recovered his T-shirt and left the pipe on the ground before making his way back to his car. He reached his hotel just after five o'clock that morning, intending to sleep for much of the day to prepare himself for the night.

Lenny Townsend was in a foul mood after a telephone call to Pat. She was now insisting that she would carry on Geoff's business alone but needed some advice and help from Lenny to enable her to do it. Lenny tried to argue her out of it: any attempt by Pat to resurrect Geoff's business, he feared, would end in failure and probably her death. He had ended the call with a curse and told her he would call her the next day with as much information he could give her – after which he didn't want to hear anything about her activities. She would be alone on this one.

His plan for the day was the same as most Fridays: the morning spent in his home gym – cycling, running on the treadmill, a weights session; the afternoon spent sleeping before he got dressed and visited his club in the evening. He liked his routine but in his current mood after the conversation with Pat he felt less inclined to make the effort to go out. He didn't need to go to the club; it was well run by staff he trusted and though he enjoyed picking up a new girl from the club for the night he could arrange that just as easily by making a call.

Adam was dressed and finalizing his plan. Option one, it was to be. He would arrive at Lenny Townsend's house early evening and watch Townsend leave for his club, aiming to stay on the wall for several hours to ensure the whereabouts of the guards and that no surprises were in store for him. He would leave his car where he had the previous night; then, after killing Townsend, he would take a different route back towards the coast, followed by a five-hour drive north to Madrid where he would catch a flight to Dublin, Ireland. From there he intended to take a sea ferry to Hollyhead in Wales, arriving, he hoped, at some point on Saturday while the police were trying to get their enquiry started in Spain. He had no doubt that they would connect Lenny Townsend's death with those in Sussex and Surrey and of course their first line of enquiry would be the airlines. The fact that he had arrived at Málaga and left from Madrid would undoubtedly cause his name to be flagged up, so he had asked Brian to concoct a story that, if necessary, he could use if questioned in the future.

At midday he checked out of his hotel and drove into the hills above the village of Cútar, where he could park the car in a quiet spot and walk to where he could see the Townsend house in the far distance over the valley. He used a new pair of binoculars to check the property every fifteen minutes but otherwise just viewed the general area. The house looked empty and indeed the whole countryside appeared to have been deserted such was the quietness. He watched as the sun headed west casting shadows across the countryside and noted the smoke starting from chimneys as householders lit fires in preparation for the chilly evening ahead. After six o'clock lights started to appear in some houses as darkness began to descend and just as he was starting to be concerned about Townsend's house he saw a light appear in an upstairs room.

Adam looked through the binoculars and confirmed that it was Lenny Townsend's bedroom where the light had been switched on. Within minutes other lights had been switched on throughout the house and even in the garden two spotlights illuminated the pool and a display of large ceramic pots. Adam looked at the shadow the strong lights gave and smiled as he saw his entry spot was made darker by the shadows. He returned to his car then drove to the olive grove he had used the previous night, locking the car and leaving the key resting in the bark of an old gnarled olive tree. He checked his pockets for their contents to ensure no sound would be made by loose coins or anything falling from them. He carried a towel that he had bought to wrap around the pole, as he suspected that his exit from Townsend's house would need to be quick and the unwrapping of his T-shirt would take too long. He carefully and slowly made his way to the side of the wall where he found the metal pipe where he had left it. The night was quiet and chilly with again the promise of frost higher in the hills and mountains. A soft breeze blew that Adam calculated would carry his scent away from the wall into the countryside rather than into the garden.

He repeated the same procedure with the wall and with the same result: the two dogs approached and began to bark.

He heard a security guard shout something in Spanish, which he imagined would be for the dogs to be quiet. He also heard a man's voice shout in English from inside the house about shutting the dogs up. Adam lay still on the wall and watched the dogs retreat under their master's instructions, though every now and again they looked back towards the wall and gave a slight gruff.

Adam saw more men moving by the side of the house and heard a car engine start. He checked his watch – half past nine. From his position he could see through the foliage and branches that the vehicle was a large four-by four that had its engine idling and headlights shining, with, Adam assumed, one man in the vehicle's driver's seat. Another man moved near the house, before the front door opened casting extra light down the steps and along the ground towards the vehicle. A man appeared in the doorway and even from his position Adam recognised Lenny Townsend striding towards the vehicle. He was wearing a long overcoat that in the light appeared to be a blue or black. Adam heard two doors closing, then the vehicle moved away towards the gate, which opened as the vehicle approached and swung closed as the red backlights of the vehicle bounced down the track towards the main road.

Adam was tempted to lower himself from the wall – his muscles were beginning to protest about being used in such an uncomfortable manner – but he decided against any movement. It was better to let the two guards and the dogs settle into their routine. He had time to again run through his plan, trying to foresee problems that could occur before he was caught off his guard. He noted that in the guard's room where the CCTV screens were the shutter was raised and the window open. Adam wondered briefly why, when the weather was chilly, the guard would have the window open.

In his mind he was in the house when a sudden vibration in his leg nearly caused him to move so quickly that he could have

338

fallen from the wall. It took him a second to identify the vibration as being his mobile telephone. He adjusted his position to free his hand and pull the mobile from his pocket. The handset was covered in black tape so no light showed. He couldn't see the caller but expected it to be Brian. He pressed the handset tightly against his ear.

'Got a problem. Monica's dad's gone AWOL. Probably three, maybe four, hours ago. Maybe joining you or going to another party. Nobody knows,' said Brian.

Adam silently cursed then tapped the mike area twice with his finger to acknowledge he had received and understood Brian's message. He waited for five seconds but as Brian didn't speak again he closed the call down, his mind racing as to what the news could mean to him and his plans. He blamed himself. He should have realised how upset her father was about how Monica had been abused – being a proud man he would want to exact retribution himself, not leave it to another. What would he do? From the chalet he could have walked or hitched a lift to Granada, but then what? Perhaps there was a bus, a coach connection, but to where? Adam discounted the possibility of him stealing a car or forcing someone to drive him someplace – Monica's father just wasn't like that.

So if he did get here, where would he go? Would he join him? Or would he …? Then it dawned on Adam. Of course, he wouldn't come here – he wanted to take his revenge all by himself. That was his code, the honourable thing to do; he wouldn't let another man – especially someone who had nothing to do with his family – take revenge for him. Adam now knew that speed was all-important but he still had to be careful as he lowered himself to the ground. His legs took a couple of seconds to lose their stiffness. He moved the pipe back to where he had found it, unwrapped the towel, then moved away from the wall and back towards his car with more haste than he knew to be safe. On the way he called Brian and told him that he would have to go to the club in Nerja. All his planning had gone out of the window – this would really be a test of his skills.

Lenny Townsend got out of his car in the large and mostly vacant car park that stood on the edge of the warren of streets that surrounded the plaza. The night was cool but warmer in Nerja than it had been at the house up in the hills and after a sleep he felt happier about being at the club, his earlier feelings of discontent now brushed aside. He waited until he had a man either side of him then strode towards the small alley that would lead them from the car park into the narrow streets that led to the Balcòn de Europe, the plaza and his club. The day visitors to the town were now nowhere to be seen and everybody else seemed to be indoors: at this time of year it might be warm during the day but in the cool evenings the diners at the restaurants preferred to eat inside. The smell of wood fires drifted gently in the still air with no other sounds other than that of six feet treading on gravel. The entrance to the alley was narrower than the three men abreast could take, so Townsend's man to his right took an extra step forward. The one light at the end of the alley barely showed the painted wall to their left but in any case all the men had seen it before and now paid no attention to the painted sea and birds that adorned it.

At the alley's end the first man turned quickly to his right into the narrow pedestrianised street while looking to his left without breaking his pace. Townsend and the other man didn't even look to their left but joined the first man who stepped back to form a single line of three again. Nobody was in the street as they took the next turn to the left and continued towards the Balcòn. As they entered the plaza they could see people along the Balcòn and others standing and sitting in small groups: the bars here had some customers sitting outside at tables under the gas-fired patio heaters. Townsend and his men paid no attention but continued towards the small side street in which Townsend's bar and club was situated.

They were passing a small group of people when suddenly a figure jumped out, lunging towards Townsend. Taken by surprise, Townsend immediately stopped while his guards moved forwards. The figure's eyes were blazing but he didn't utter a word as he pushed the guard on the right back into Townsend, who stumbled back three steps. The guard who had been on Townsend's left drew a short metal bar from his pocket and landed it with a dull thud on the figure's head. The figure appeared to slow but then, emitting a loud guttural sound, lunged forward again, his hands straining forwards towards Townsend's neck. The man with the bar raised his arm again to deliver a harder blow as the figure's hands reached and closed on Townsend's neck. Townsend was so surprised by the force and power of the figure that he could now feel panic starting to envelop him. The bar descended again and this time caught the back of the figure's neck and head together. The man fell to one side, his hands drifting away from Townsend's neck as his body slumped to the ground.

Townsend stared at the now prone figure who had blood coming from the back of his head and from somewhere at the front of his face, which was pushed into the ground. The man with the bar knelt on the figure's back and looked around for any further threats.

The whole incident had lasted no more than seven seconds and nobody in the plaza had witnessed the entire event. Townsend stood and shrugged off the attentions of a bystander who came to ask if he was OK. One of the guards turned over the fallen man and the three men instantly recognised Monica's father.

'Pepi!' Townsend exclaimed, feeling a surge of hatred. 'Pick him up!' he ordered sharply and watched as Monica's father was lifted up by his two men and half carried and half dragged towards the bar.

Reaching Nerja, Adam parked away from Lenny's four-by-four and in such a position that his route across the car park would take him close to the vehicle, enabling him to look at any occupants. There weren't any, and a look around the car park showed that nobody else was around either. Adam knelt quickly and within three seconds there was the hiss sound of air escaping from the tyre. He checked that he was still alone then drew the knife from under his jacket and reached under the vehicle until he found the thin metal brake hydraulic pipe. He used the knife in a sawing motion and heard the metal scrape into metal as the knife cut through the pipe. He stood and replaced the knife, noting the fluid now on the ground around the tyre. At least, if his exit was to be a quick one, Townsend's vehicle wouldn't be chasing him.

Townsend stood in the centre of his office looking at the unconscious figure of Monica's father who had been tied with rope to a hard-backed chair, his head slumped forward and resting on his chest. The office wasn't luxurious but comfortable. There was a large desk, a winged high-back leather chair behind it, and a settee along one wall. The floor was tiled with a large rug in the centre and there were gold-framed pictures on the walls. The two windows were closed, as were the shutters. The two men who had accompanied him from the house stood behind and at either side of Monica's father.

'Pepi!' said Townsend. 'Time to wake up, Pepi. We need to talk.' He threw a glass of water and then another until Pepi's head started to move.

Adam had walked quickly along the same route Townsend had taken and entered the plaza, noting the various groups of people. There wasn't any sign of Monica's father and all appeared to be as he expected it to be at that time on a Friday evening. He ambled through the plaza and towards the church at the far end, which took him past the narrow street where Townsend's bar was. He kept his hands in his pockets and appeared to be looking down at the ground as he moved slowly. He knew the route he was taking and where the CCTV cameras were situated as he continued to the church and leant against its walls. The view he had was of the whole plaza: every street and alley exiting from and into the square could be seen from his position. What his plan was he hadn't yet worked out, having hoped to find Monica's father first and persuade him to leave the business of revenge to Adam. There wasn't any sign of Monica's father, though. He waited ten minutes before deciding to cross the plaza. If Monica's father hadn't appeared in another twenty minutes, he would have to assume he hadn't made it there – yet.

Pepi's face jerked to one side as it was struck. A further slap followed that made his head turn in the other direction. He was aware that blood, his own, was all over his face. His eyes were burning as the blood ran into them, while his nostrils and mouth were filled with blood, making him gasp. He could taste the blood in his mouth and also feel the loose pieces of teeth swimming about in it. His right hand hurt, too, when a piece of wood held by Townsend crashed down on to his knuckles. He screamed in pain and saw Townsend laughing at him.

'It is a club, stupid – there's soundproofing everywhere, so there's no point screaming, Pepi.'

Townsend knelt down so that he could see into Pepi's face and decided that this was a turn of events that he had not thought possible. He had someone he could bargain with for more information. Suddenly he felt reinvigorated by this stroke of good luck.

'We're going back to the house. Take him,' he said to the two men, who moved forward in unison to untie the rope then lifted Pepi to his feet.

Adam was sitting on a stone seat in the plaza next to some shrubs that partly hid him from view. He was half slouching in his seat, wondering where Monica's father was and what his plans could be, when he felt his mobile vibrate gently against his leg. He accepted the call and held the machine closely to his ear.

'Not heard anything?' Brian said. 'Anything I can do?'

'No sighting. Having to make it up as I go.'

'Yeah, you're good at that,' said Brian. 'I'm mobile. Ring if I can do anything from here.'

Townsend looked at Pepi, whose face had been wiped clear of blood only for more to gently seep from his nose and mouth. His hands were firmly tied behind his back under his jacket which had been zipped up and a cap found to cover his head. Unsteadily, he moved forward, feeling strong hands grip his arms as he was led downstairs and through the bar. Aware that heads were turned to watch him, he didn't look up but concentrated on taking the next step. He could have just refused to move, used his dead weight to slump to the ground or suddenly jerk up to lessen a grip, perhaps to barge into a table, but he didn't. He wouldn't have been able to explain why, but he knew it was time to go with Townsend. He had thought of Adam, wondered where he was and whether he would be able to help. He'd half hoped he'd be in the plaza when he had attacked Townsend, but nobody had intervened.

Townsend led the way, walking more slowly than usual to allow his men to keep Pepi moving at a steady pace as they reached the plaza. He looked around the area – everything seemed much as it had earlier – they continued across the plaza, heading towards the narrow streets that would take them back to his vehicle.

Adam saw the men exit the area, first Townsend, then three men, the middle one much shorter and stockier in build than those either side of him – Monica's father! Adam moved himself a fraction at a time, deeper back into the shadow of the shrubs. Adam watched the men cross the plaza and waited until they had turned the corner before standing, casually looking around the area and slowly walking after them. He knew he couldn't use the same route as they and frantically tried to bring back into his mind the map of the area he had studied previously. He took another narrow street that didn't have any restaurants or bars that he hoped ran parallel to their route. He knew the area quite well but in the labyrinth of streets he also knew some were peculiar and didn't take the direction they started in, instead going at an angle that could take him well away from the car park.

Once away from the plaza he broke into a steady jog. By now, he thought, he must have already passed Townsend's position if they had continued at the same speed, and if the route he'd chosen was the correct one. He ran more quickly until he suddenly skidded to a halt as he recognised the name of a restaurant whose back, he knew, overlooked the car park. He walked into the restaurant and ignoring the waiter who approached him continued through the table area towards the toilets where he saw the door that led to the rear garden. The door was unlocked. He jogged through the garden towards the wooden gate. It was open. He peered through the doorway into the car park and saw that the alley where Townsend would emerge from was some fifty yards away. Adam looked to his left – nothing was moving – but to his right he saw a car reversing into a space close to Townsend's alley.

Instantly Adam knew that that the reversing car presented him with his opportunity. Its presence would attract Townsend's attention and those who were holding Monica's father, maybe for only a second or two, but that would be enough. He sprinted across the gravel to Townsend's vehicle and slid underneath, scraping his back on the bottom of the engine block as he manoeuvred himself under the centre of the vehicle. He noticed the liquid from the pipe he had cut earlier and saw that it had run along the ground to the side of the vehicle furthest away from which Townsend would approach.

A man and woman had got out of the newly parked car. They embraced and then, holding hands, walked towards the alley. Adam watched them closely as, just at that moment, the couple stopped and moved to one side. Townsend came into Adam's view followed by the three men. Townsend strode towards the vehicle and Adam heard the click of the doors being opened remotely. Flashing lights reflected on to the ground. He moved slightly towards the other side of the vehicle. He saw Townsend's feet move towards the rear door. The other three pairs of feet approached the same area.

Fleetingly he regretted cutting the pipe and letting the air from the tyre. Ideally he would have allowed them to return to Townsend's house and then taken them at his own pace. He saw Monica's father's shoes had blood on them and more blood dripped on to the ground near where he was standing.

One pair of shoes ran around the back of the vehicle past the deflated tyre but in his haste the man didn't spot the tyre. The man stood inches from Adam's head then Adam heard the man opening the car door and climb inside. As soon as Adam was sure the man was in the vehicle he rolled out as fast as he could towards Townsend's feet, colliding into his shins. The surprise and sudden jolt to Townsend forced him off balance and he fell to the ground, by which time Adam had leapt to his feet and used the heel of his hand to strike the other guard's chin. The man had been pushing Monica's father into the vehicle but now fell away. Adam gave him a chop to the back of his neck, sending him to the ground either unconscious or possibly dead – Adam didn't care. It was one of his favourite strikes that over the years he had frequently used though with mixed results.

Adam grabbed Monica's father by the collar of his jacket and yanked it as hard as he could towards him, causing Monica's father to fly backwards to the ground. Before he had landed Adam had already thrown himself into the vehicle's rear seat where the other guard was leaning forward still trying to reach where Monica's father had been a second previously. The guard was staring ahead directly at Adam with a look of total amazement on his face and didn't see the solid closed fist punch Adam threw that landed squarely between his eyes. His head rocked backwards then stared at the roof lining before slowly sliding from the seat and backwards out of the car on to the ground. Adam knew the man was unconscious and even when he came around he would be unable to see, such was the damage to his eyes.

Adam saw Monica's father on the ground trying to stand up and, near him, Townsend, who had just finished getting to his feet. Townsend was looking around trying to understand this sudden turn of events. Adam instantly reached out and grabbed hold of Townsend's coat, pulling him towards him. He half turned him then slammed his back into the vehicle, repeating the procedure a further three times until Townsend's body had no fight. Adam threw him on to the ground and ignoring Monica's father he moved around the four-by-four, heaving Townsend's two unconscious men into the back of the vehicle. He grabbed hold of Townsend and turned him on to his front.

Ten minutes later Townsend was sitting in the front passenger seat of his vehicle watched by Adam. His arms were tied with the same bindings that had secured Monica's father and his coat fastened over in a similar style to how they had tied Monica's father. His seat belt was secured in place, his mouth was stuffed with a handkerchief and his eyes stared back at Adam and Monica's father, who stood next to Adam. Townsend was scared. He had soiled his trousers and now felt his body tremble.

'Lenny Townsend, you are going to die in a minute,' said Adam in a calm voice, 'and so too will your men in the back. I am going to set fire to this vehicle and you will burn to death in two or three minutes. It will be painful, very painful, and hopefully slow so you get the full benefit of the pain.'

Townsend tried to scream through the handkerchief, his eyes wild and his head shaking from side to side. Monica's father stood there smiling. Though he did not understand a word of what Adam had said, he saw the effect the words had on Townsend and he loved that sight.

Adam continued: 'And why are you going to die, Lenny? Because you, with your brother Geoff, Jackie Smith, Kieran and Williams, tortured an old couple some years ago – that's why. This is revenge for their torture and her murder. I want you to think back to that night. Remember their faces, their pleas, their blood, their absolute terror… Remember your laughter at others' pain. Remember the vile threats that were made to the old lady. Do you remember all this, Lenny?'

Lenny had stopped moving and trying to scream. His eyes showed that he did remember and also that he had no hope of any mercy from the man in front of him.

Adam drove steadily up the hilly streets away from the town, aware that an orange ball of flame was lighting up the night sky behind him. Neither he nor Monica's father had spoken a word or even shared a look after Adam had lit the trail of petrol to the vehicle and now Monica's father was looking straight ahead.

The silence continued for the next hour until Adam pulled off the road and made a brief call to Brian to say that he had finished the business and was now taking the old man home to his family.

33

Adam paid off the taxi driver and looked at Brian's house. Even the front garden looked tidy with the concrete path swept and the grass cut. As he approached the front door it was opened by Brian, who extended his hand for it to be shaken. The men sat in the lounge each nursing a can of beer while Adam told Brian what had happened in Nerja and how Monica's family had reacted when her father was returned to them. It was obvious from his facial and hand injuries that he had been involved in a fight and Monica's mother fussed over him as the returning hero. Adam didn't tell Monica what had happened but asked her to remain at the chalet for a few days more before they returned to their home in Cútar. This she agreed to do, even if it meant locking her father in the bedroom. When Adam had left them to drive to Madrid, Monica's mother had tears in her eyes and spoke softly to Adam, but Monica didn't translate the words.

'So, just one to go,' said Brian quietly, 'unless you think enough is enough.'

Adam took a long pull on his beer. 'Can't do that, Bri. I've started so I'll finish it but, after all your efforts,' – he waved his hand around the spotless room that still smelt unpleasantly of bleach – 'it would be better if I did it alone and away from you. I couldn't have done this much without you but we both know there is a good chance, better than fifty per cent, that I'm going to get caught. My luck has to run out.' He sighed, 'I've thought about it. I'll move out tonight, then you won't have much cleaning to do again.' He smiled at Brian. 'I'll head down to Brighton then probably back to Spain for a while. I'll

349

certainly see the summer out down there. One last holiday!'

Brian was about to protest but Adam finished his beer, crumpled the can in his hand and stood up.

The DCI heard the news about Lenny's murder and instantly knew that a suspicion he had harboured since Geoff Townsend's death was right. Lenny had been part of Geoff's world, so his death meant that all this was more than about someone wanting to take over Townsend's patch; it was more personal than that. The only thing that tied Lenny Townsend into the recent deaths was an incident that had occurred about three or four years ago at an old couple's bungalow outside Crawley; there couldn't be any other explanation. This was all about revenge, not greed. One by one, all those who had been charged and then acquitted had been brutally murdered. There was just one remaining – Williams – though he was unable to find his current whereabouts. Perhaps he was already dead? He considered revealing his thoughts at the daily briefing but thought that he'd be better seeing the old man – Raymond Black was his name – first to try and gauge from a casual conversation whether he knew anything about the murders that had set the country talking.

Adam awoke to the sound of rain being driven on to his bedroom window. He had slept well and was ready for the day ahead, after which he hoped he could finally walk away from all that he had started.

He dressed and by ten o'clock was in Brighton city centre with the intention of buying clothes. But three times during the morning he took a detour to pass the church whose name and address Brian had given him and he hadn't yet made any purchases. The church wasn't very large but looked solid and reliable, a safe haven from life's storms, he thought. Situated near houses and flats, a stone's throw from the shops and a couple of hundred yards from the luxury flats on Hove seafront, the church appeared to be well attended and from the posters displayed was involved with many local community activities. Adam stopped at the notice board and pretended to be writing details from a poster displayed there, using the time to take a closer look at the front of the church and the small grass area to the right side that led around the back.

Adam put away the paper and casually passed through the black wrought-iron gate to the grassed area. He followed the concrete path to the back of the church and saw that the path ended at the door to a small building that Adam guessed was probably the original vicarage. The area in front of the house was bare dirt where the grass had worn away and this extended along the front to the edge where there was a small door that looked modern and out of keeping with the character of the building. Adam continued to the main front door and saw that it was locked before walking to the new-looking door, which was ajar. He raised his hand towards the door and, without actually touching the door, he appeared to knock on it. He stood back and turned around to casually look over the area. He saw that four houses on the road had windows overlooking the spot where he stood and while gazing about him he inspected each of the windows.

Adam knew that by now the police might have worked out the link between all the murders and have realised that only one of the people arrested for the Black incident was still alive. If that were the case, Adam would have expected the police to either have full surveillance on the survivor in the hope of using him as bait to catch the killer, or to have spirited the potential target away to a place of safety. He considered the chances of anybody having worked out the true aim of the killings were to be about fifty-fifty, but any chance wasn't good from his point of view and he did not wish to fail at the final hurdle. He had thought of Raymond Black several times during the day and wondered what he had made of the murders. Whether he was pleased or perhaps unhappy, he guessed he'd never know.

Adam heard a noise from within the building followed by a grunting sound made by a man just behind the door, which was then opened inwards slowly. Taken aback by this sudden development Adam turned his attention to the man who now appeared in the doorway and what he was carrying. The man was about fifty years old and, had he not been bending under the weight of a pile of broken furniture, would have stood at over six feet. His wiry frame was strong and the rolled-up sleeves of his shirt showed a faded tattoo of a blue seagull, the symbol of the local football club. The man was struggling a little and Adam stepped forward to assist.

'Thanks!' gasped the man as Adam took about half the wood and looked questioningly at the man as to what he should now do with it.

'Here,' said the man as he brushed past Adam and turned the corner of the building towards the back of the house where Adam could see a small pile of rubbish was stacked against the trunks of pine trees that bordered the property. Adam followed and dumped his pile of wood on top of the man's.

The man straightened and looked at Adam through eyes that were older than his years. The man hadn't shaved. His grey beard was untrimmed and the long grey eyebrows formed a roof to his eyes that now looked at Adam more closely. The eyes took in Adam's build, clothes and stance. The man's mouth had thin lips that pressed together before opening as he said, 'Best go inside.'

Adam followed the man into the house, closing the door behind him, then down a small flight of concrete steps that led into a large room with beds ready made along the length of the two walls to Adam's left and right. A large table was at the far end of the room with wooden chairs arranged around. The room was cold and Adam almost shivered. He looked at the man in his rolled-up shirtsleeves but he didn't seem at all aware of the cold.

'Let's sit down,' he said, watching Adam. 'I've been expecting you.'

Adam was thrown by the words and manner of the man.

The man turned and walked slowly towards the table then pulled back a chair and sat down. He pulled a small metal tin with a cigarette lighter on top towards him.

'Can a condemned man have a last smoke?' he asked with a faint smile.

Adam's eyes swivelled around, noting a door behind the table, several small windows high in the walls and the door behind him – the only ways in and out of the room. He knew that it was he who was at a large disadvantage. He didn't have any element of surprise and instantly he knew that his alternatives were based on fight or flight, to fight with no hope of winning or flight with maybe a chance of getting away.

Sensing Adam's predicament, the man gently and deliberately opened his tin and took out a packet of cigarette papers maintaining his eye contact with Adam all the while. He pulled a sheaf of paper and then dipped his fingers into tobacco and laid it on the paper before rolling it between his fingers.

Adam walked to the table and pulled a chair out on the same side as the man and sat down. Both men stared into the other's eyes while a flame shot from the lighter and the man raised it to his cigarette. Blue smoke passed in front of his face but his eyes didn't flinch.

'You know who I am?' Adam asked.

'Not your name but what you've done and why you're here, yes, I know.'

'You could have shouted, could have run – why sit here?'

The man shrugged and gave a small smile from the side of his mouth, then diverted his eyes to roll some ash from his cigarette on to the lid of his tobacco tin. 'You are avenging what we did, yes, what *we* did to Mr and Mrs Black three, nearly four, years ago.' He shrugged his shoulders. 'I don't blame you, I honestly don't.'

'So you know I'm going to kill you?'

'Yep!' replied the man. 'When Geoff was killed I had a feeling that I would be next but then Lenny got it, so now it had to be my turn. It's almost funny – sad but almost funny.'

Adam looked at the man. 'What's almost funny?'

'When Kieran was murdered in the street and the two lads with him weren't I thought, well, it's wrong to kill but at least it was Kieran. Let's face it he was going to be as bad or maybe worse than his dad so, sad, but there we are. Dutch, a bastard, shouldn't swear, but he was nasty, cruel, so when he died, again hardly the worst thing to happen, was it? Del the garage man, shame but he'd done his share of work for Geoff in the past, not a nice man.'

Adam smiled, recalling the moment the man had appeared with a sawn-off shotgun on the landing.

'It was obvious that whoever it was knew what they were doing but for all the world it looked like a takeover by another gang.' He shrugged again. 'It happens.' He again rolled the ash from his cigarette.

Adam listened to the words being spoken but also watched Williams' body shape to anticipate any sudden movement. It was all classic stuff – the speaking in slow, soft tones, the lack of threat or menace, and then, when the listener was absorbed by the words, to suddenly strike. The element of surprise – always a winner.

Williams continued talking. 'Geoff ... well, how you got away with that? In the old days I would have taken my hat off to you and by all accounts the way Jackie was murdered was very professional. How's it to be for me?'

Adam kept his gaze. He had wondered the same question himself and still hadn't reached a decision.

'You know,' the man continued, 'everyone you've killed has been a nasty person and, had they had the opportunity, they would have done the same to you. You know your job, so I suppose congratulations are in order.' The man stubbed out the remainder of his cigarette then pointed at the tobacco. 'Mind?' he asked. 'Time for one more?'

Adam gave a slight movement of his head but his mind was racing. Was this a trap? Was the room bugged for sound to record some sort of confession from him? Were the police now armed and surrounding the building? Was the man in front of him who appeared so relaxed, so resigned, about to produce a weapon? And what was the man saying? Was he almost condoning the murders?

'You think this is my job?' Adam said as the man rolled a second cigarette.

The man looked up. 'Isn't it? I thought you were a professional. You must be from what I've read.'

It was Adam's turn to smile. 'An enthusiastic amateur.'

The man looked at the ground. 'Why are you doing it? As I said before, part of me says well done to you, but my new side says: it's wrong to kill, not even an eye for an eye.'

Adam remembered Raymond Black watching the news programme and the joy on Kieran Townsend's horrible face. He recalled the newspaper articles and of Keith Mendip's pure hatred of Townsend and all those involved.

'Mr and Mrs Black, why them?' Adam asked, suddenly curious.

The man gave a loud sigh. 'In those days I was part of Geoff's team, not in a big way, but in truth I'd been a villain all my life one way and another. I'd never heard of Mr and Mrs Black, didn't know anything about the drugs, just did odd jobs for Geoff or Lenny. Suddenly Lenny called and they wanted me to join them in questioning someone who'd ripped them off. I was short, so for a hundred quid,' – he stopped talking and shook his head from side to side – 'a hundred bloody quid, I said OK. So on the way up there no one spoke about what we were going to do. Lenny just said for me to be there, numbers I suppose. Jackie and Kieran were there, I mean, Kieran was an idiot, going to be nasty, but I didn't think he could do anything very bad then, and Jackie …' – he looked up at the ceiling and took and long pull on his cigarette – 'well, what a mare she is, sorry was, a vicious cow of the first order. I didn't know it then. I knew she and Geoff had been together and that she had a reputation for being a hard one with her girls, but Christ, sorry, she showed herself that night.'

'What happened?' asked Adam, interested in what the man had to say but at the same time not wanting to hear the details.

'We got to the house, a bungalow actually. Geoff went straight in, shouting, using his bat against the old man, Mr Black. I didn't know they were old. Nobody said they were pensioners, real ones, not just retired either – they were proper old. Mrs Black, she was old, like my grandma was you know, like most of them get, small and quite thin but mentally strong. She was up and had a go at Geoff, and Jackie grabbed her, threw her into a chair and started to smack her. I couldn't believe it. I couldn't believe that these two old folk had been running the drugs for Geoff and Lenny and had then ripped them off.'

Adam felt his jaw drop as he sat forward. 'What?' he exclaimed.

'That was what I thought. Surely not. But quickly it became obvious that Mrs Black did know something, but Mr Black … well he was as shocked as I was. She told Geoff that she'd hidden the drugs and was going to flush them down the toilet as soon as they'd gone.'

Adam tried to clear his head.

'That night when I got home my missus was her usual self and I could only think of Mrs Black and I just looked and listened as my missus went on about how I should be closer to Lenny and Geoff, make more money. I was sick, really sick. When we were all nicked for it, I just didn't care. By then I'd left home and was spending the days walking along the seafront. I even went to Beachy Head …'

Adam knew the high cliff outside of Eastbourne further along the coast from Brighton. It was beautiful and featured in many pictures of the cliffs along the south coast, but it was also a notorious place for suicides.

'Thought about it, sat there and thought about my life, the times I'd spent in cells, police and prison, all that sort of thing, a wasted life. But Mrs Black – that was so much worse than what I'd ever done myself – she was decent, you know, a mum, a decent lady.'

'Go on with what you were saying. What happened?'

Williams gave a sigh, then was silent for over a minute.

'Geoff used the bat on Mr Black while Lenny and Kieran held Mrs Black in her chair.' Williams took a long draw on his cigarette. 'Jackie was sort of going between them both, just mad, threatening one then the other, slapping their faces. Geoff was shouting at Mrs Black, demanding to know where the drugs were and when she refused to say he used his bat on her husband.' Again Williams took a draw on the cigarette before looking to the ceiling and blowing the smoke upwards. He remained looking at the ceiling and was silent again for a time, as if reliving the events. 'Mrs Black just refused to say where she'd put the drugs. She'd found them in the garage then hidden them, or that's what she said. Just refused to say. She could see her husband being hurt but she wouldn't say. I think that's when they started to use the bats on her.'

Williams moved his head to look at the floor, leaning forward with his elbows resting on his knees, the smoke from his cigarette drifting up into his face. Adam sat still, not daring to move in case he interrupted Williams' train of thought. He allowed the silence to continue for over a minute before he asked, 'What were you doing? You said you think that was when they started to use their bats on her?'

Williams continued to look at the floor. 'I actually felt sickened by what they were doing to her and said I'd search for the drugs. I went, made a lot of noise banging and crashing stuff in the kitchen, threw a couple of things on the floor, that sort of thing but didn't really search. Any excuse to get away.' He paused and shook his head. 'That's not right. I was sickened but I was there. I knew what we were there for. I'm not making excuses for my being there, but I couldn't just stand there and watch them.'

Adam listened and continued to probe Williams for the next twenty minutes learning as much detail as he could, not only about the events that evening but also about who was involved in the drugs supply.

Adam gently pulled the front door closed and looked at the windows of the houses opposite, almost expecting for a horde of police officers to descend on him. He stood still by the door for half a minute, feeling that he didn't care if the police did suddenly appear. He felt spent, exhausted. He examined the knuckles of his hand and saw blood gently seeping from three of them. He walked slowly back to the pavement, unsure of what he was going to do next or where he was going to go.

34

Adam checked his watch and saw that he was on time – a quarter to six on Tuesday afternoon. He turned into the driveway and saw the BMW car parked on the driveway then continued to the front door where he knocked hard with his fist. He heard two voices then the door was opened by Sandra dressed in her uniform with a shocked look on her face.

Adam pushed past her and strode into the lounge where he knew Ray would be sitting in his armchair. The room hadn't changed. The same furniture was all in the same place as were the newspapers, though there was a new pile of newspapers under the table. He looked at Ray and heard Sandra close the front door then enter the lounge.

'How are you Ray?' Adam asked.

Ray gave a broad smile and was about to stand when he saw from Adam's face that all wasn't well. 'Adam, it's great to see you.'

'Oh Adam, we've been wanting to thank you for what you …' Sandra began.

She was interrupted by Adam who turned towards her and pointed at the other armchair. 'Sit'.

Sandra complied and looked at her father.

'So why were you attacked, Ray?'

Ray knew from Adam's face and stance that the question wasn't asked lightly, and he knew that Adam knew the answer. He slumped back in his chair but didn't say anything.

'Sandra, tell me why your mother was tortured and killed.'

Sandra stared defiantly back at Adam. 'Because she had found some drugs and refused to hand them back.'

Adam stared at her and knew she was frightened by his manner. He pointed at her. 'You were getting the drugs in at the airport, weren't you?'

Sandra looked at Adam, scared to take her eyes from him, fearing that in that instant he would harm her, as he had those who had harmed her mother.

'Did you know?' shouted Adam and pointing at Raymond.

'No,' Raymond replied. 'I didn't know.' His voice was quiet. 'Not when they arrived, I had no idea.' He looked at Sandra. 'Her mother found them in the chest in the garage, the metal trunk. Ann knew they were drugs. She'd said to me before that she didn't know how Sandra and David had so much money.'

Adam stared hard at him. 'So Ray, tell me,' he said with a real menace in his tone.

'She was frightened, not of bloody Townsend and his cohorts, but of what would happen to Sandra and David. You see, she'd worked it out. She'd seen things, I suppose, and she put two and two together. I just thought Sandra and David were earning a lot of money. It wouldn't have ever entered my head that they were … were dealing drugs. Ann was a practical woman and nobody's fool. She somehow worked it out that every week Sandra came here she went to the garage for something, borrow a tool, put one back, whatever …' He looked at Sandra and continued. 'Then the next day David always arrived and he'd have some excuse for going to the garage, too. I just didn't think, you don't, do you?'

Adam stared hard at him. 'So?'

Raymond continued: 'Ann said she knew something was wrong and found the drugs. She hid them somewhere, but she didn't say a thing to me. I think she knew that I'd, well, I don't know what she thought I'd do, but she didn't let on to me. That was on Tuesday night, after Sandra had been. That's what she said when … when, she was being punched by that bloody woman Smith. It was the first I'd heard anything about drugs when they arrived. It was a complete shock when Townsend asked about

360

them. I started saying we didn't know anything, that they were at the wrong house. They kept on hitting her, and then she said she'd found them but wouldn't say where she'd put them. They hit me with a baseball bat to make her talk. She didn't care what they did to her, you see; she only said something when they were hitting me. They didn't have to touch her at all; they only did that because they liked it, especially that Kieran and Smith woman. Ann was trying to protect Sandra and David.' Suddenly he leant forward, tears streaming from his eyes.

Adam stared at Raymond and allowed the silence to grow.

'When I knew Ann had died ... was dead,' Raymond said between his tears, 'the police wanted to know why we had been picked on. I was in hospital. I couldn't tell them – how could I? Ann had died ... no, been murdered only because she refused to say where the drugs were. If I had told the police that, then Sandra and David would have been arrested, wouldn't they? I just couldn't do that.'

'We are talking about David the *photographer*, are we?' asked Adam sarcastically.

Raymond gently moved his head up and down to agree.

'Whose idea was it to put the photographs together?' Adam asked. 'So you could pretend that was your son?'

Raymond looked towards Sandra, who said, 'Mine, to explain why he isn't here.'

Adam turned to Sandra, 'And?'

Sandra had tears in her eyes. 'On Tuesdays I collected a package from the airport and put it in my old trunk in the garage, as Dad says. Dave came on Wednesday and took it somewhere, I don't know where or who was involved. Dave used to leave five hundred pounds in the chest for me. One Wednesday he phoned me asking where the package was. I said in the trunk as always and he said it was gone. He was panicking and saying that I'd ripped him off and he wanted it back. I swore that I had put it there.' She wiped her eyes with her hands. 'He said that they'd kill him, they'd say he ripped them off.' Sandra paused then looked at her father. 'Dad, Mum found them and then hid them, but Dave told whoever he should have handed them to, obviously the Townsends, that they'd been stolen from the trunk. They were going to question him, you know what that means – questions followed by a bullet. He rang me, then he ran. They thought by hurting you and Mum they'd get the drugs back.'

Adam stood there. 'And you, Sandra, why didn't they ask you, you know, question you? Why didn't you run, Sandra, or weren't you afraid of a bullet? Come on, Sandra, tell me and your dad why you weren't questioned. Come on!' By now he was shouting.

Sandra looked at Adam. 'You,' she said, pointing at him, 'have secrets, and so do I.'

Adam stared at her, barely able to control the anger he felt. He held her eyes until she looked away.

'Ray, what about Williams? What did he do?'

Ray looked up at Adam and was quiet. Adam could see that Ray was thinking back to the evening.

'Not much. He didn't hit Ann or me. He just stood over there.' Ray used his head to indicate the doorway. 'I think he went off to look for the drugs.'

'Where's David now, Ray?'

Ray shrugged. 'No idea.'

Adam suddenly looked at Sandra. 'Yes, we have secrets, you and me. Are you threatening me? Are you going to betray me, after all that I've done. Are you saying you will go to the police?' said Adam incredulously.

'Sandra?' said Raymond.

'Yes I am. Now get out,' Sandra said, suddenly rising from her chair and pointing towards the front door.

Adam stared at Sandra then at Ray. He was speechless but there was pure anger in his eyes. He was trying hard to contain himself.

'You!' he said, pointing at Sandra. 'You and your brother, you, were the reason your mum was murdered. You and your brother. How can you live knowing that it was your actions that caused all of this agony? Where is your brother?'

She returned his stare but said nothing.

Adam turned his glare towards Ray. 'You knew! You let me go and murder all those people when you knew it was your children who started it all … It was them. Without their actions Townsend and the rest of that scum couldn't have run the drugs. It was your children that got the drugs to Brighton, your children who are responsible for the misery caused by the drugs. Townsend's power base was based on the financial returns your bloody children helped them make!' His voice had become louder and higher as he spoke. Ray Black and Sandra both sat still and neither spoke as Adam looked from one to the other.

'Where is David now and what is he doing?' he asked in a quieter voice.

Sandra and Ray both looked silently and blankly at Adam, who suddenly turned on his heels and left the bungalow leaving the front door open.

The DCI stood next to the hospital bed looking down at Williams lying on his back with the sheet pulled over his chest. An oxygen tube hung from his nostrils but otherwise he was free from wires or tubes. His face made it difficult for the DCI to recognise Williams. It was one large bruise, from ear to ear, and from above the eyes to his chin, a black–and–blue collage with splashes of red to the sides of his mouth. The DCI gave a quiet whistle.

'The docs say you've been punched in the face and looking at you I'd say they are rather sharp in their diagnosis. I would have brought some grapes but as you don't have any other injuries I would say there is more to your assault so I will withhold my sympathy until I know the full story. They say you were punched twice, left cheek and right cheek, your nose not touched. Who did it?'

The DCI thought he would be lucky if Williams even tried to speak so he offered a small notebook and pencil towards Williams. Williams moved his eyes to see the book then closed his eyes and gave a sigh.

'You have been very hard to find, Williams. If you hadn't been beaten up, we'd still be looking for you. You and I both know what this is about, don't we? The question is though why you have been allowed to live. Everyone else involved with the Black murder is dead – why aren't you?' the DCI asked almost conversationally.

Williams' mouth moved as if trying to smile but his eyes remained closed. The DCI waited a full minute without any response from Williams, then turned and walked towards the door of the private room. He looked at the uniformed police officer sitting in a chair and shrugged his shoulders.